A single stroke can ch

Xander Fairchild can't stand people in general and frat boys in particular, so when he's forced to spend his summer working on his senior project with Skylar Stone, a silver-tongued Delta Sig with a trust fund who wants to make Xander over into a shiny new image, Xander is determined to resist. He came to idyllic, Japanese culture-soaked Benten College to hide and make manga, not to be transformed into a corporate clone in the eleventh hour.

Skylar's life has been laid out for him since before he was born, but all it takes is one look at Xander's artwork, and the veneer around him begins to crack. Xander himself does plenty of damage too. There's something about the antisocial artist's refusal to yield that forces Skylar to acknowledge how much his own orchestrated future is killing him slowly…as is the truth about his gray-spectrum sexuality, which he hasn't dared to speak aloud, even to himself.

Through a summer of art and friendship, Xander and Skylar learn more about each other, themselves, and their feelings for one another. But as their senior year begins, they must decide if they will part ways and return to the dull futures they had planned, or if they will take a risk and leap into a brightly colored future—together.

This book is a work of fiction. The names, characters, places, and incidents are products of the writer's imagination or have been used fictitiously and are not to be construed as real. Any resemblance to persons, living or dead, actual events, locale, or organizations is entirely coincidental.

Heidi Cullinan, POB 425, Ames, Iowa 50010

Print ISBN: 978-1-945116-10-0
Edited by Christa Soule and Sasha Knight
Cover Art by Natsuko
Cover Design by Kanaxa
Proofing by Lillie's Literary Services
Formatting by BB eBooks

First publication 2017
www.heidicullinan.com

Antisocial

HEIDI CULLINAN

For Sayo Yamamoto and Mitsurō Kubo

Thank you for removing my impediments and restoring my happiness.

山本沙代先生、久保ミツロウ先生へ
困難に立ち向かう勇気を与え、私を幸福に導いてくれたお二人に、感謝の気持ちを込めて。

Art enables us to find ourselves and
lose ourselves at the same time.
—Thomas Merton

ACKNOWLEDGMENTS

This book took me several years to complete and wouldn't be possible without the help of many, many people carrying me.

Thank you, Anna Cullinan, for your in-house artist advice and for putting up with all of Mom's asinine questions. Thank you, Dan Cullinan, for being an unparalleled assistant and guy Friday, man-about-house, and above all, my perfect husband and partner. Thank you, Damon Suede, for beta reading, for letting me call you when you're spent and busy, for being a font of knowledge, and of course, thank you for all the blood. Thank you, Sara, for reading, for advising, for listening, for cheering me on, and for being a cherished and wonderful friend. You aren't a starfish, but I think you might, in fact, be a demigod, because you have talents and powers that forever leave me in awe. Thank you, Christa and Sasha, my two amazing editors who helped me make this book better, and Lillie, my beloved proofer who made sure all one hundred twenty thousand words were in order. Thanks to Paul for making the book look great inside, and Nathalie and Natsuko for the breathtaking outside. Thanks to September Scanlations translation help so we could get to that gorgeous cover. Thank you, Iggy Toma, for giving the seven gods (and Fudō Myōō) their voices. And thank you to Tenjin-sama for accepting my offerings these months and listening to my prayers as I found my way through this book.

Most importantly, thank you to my patrons. Without you this book would not be possible. Thank you for the financial support, the emotional support, the community, the spiritual center you provide to me and to everyone in our hub. You are *my* gods, the precious gift I cannot believe I deserve and yet there you are, every day. Thank you from the bottom of my heart and soul. It is a joy to create books for you, with you. Thank you, all of you, especially Pamela Bartual, Rosie M., Marie, Sarah Plunkett, Tiffany Miller, Erin Sharpe, Chris Klaene, Sandy C., Sarah M., Deandre Ellerbe, Deanna Ferguson, Michele C., Kaija Kovanen, Jennifer Harvey, Katie M Pizzolato, Ninna, Karin Wollina, and Maija.

Now let's go make more art.

Chapter One

THE PAINTING, THREE by four feet and propped on an easel in the center of the room, arrested Skylar Stone, emptying every thought from his head, save one. This piece of art was the most incredible thing he'd ever seen.

He paced a semicircle around the canvas, unconsciously hooking his index finger into his collar to loosen his tie, as if looking at this painting required more room to breathe. It assaulted his senses and made him too dizzy to think. How did it possess so many colors and yet seem kind of purply blue? There was gold in there, somehow, and red, and...God, *everything*. What was the figure in the foreground? A man? A dog? A boulder? Somehow it was all three. A hulking mass of darkness looking out at...stars. Or perhaps it was someone lying on a blanket. Or it was a gargoyle looking over a city. A city on fire.

Or maybe it was a city being formed?

It looked like a child had painted it. Or a grand master. It took Skylar's breath away.

"I *said*, can I help you?"

Blinking, Skylar turned toward the speaker, a

mousy, scrawny, hunched male student with a permanent glower stitched on his face. He wore a dark-blue apron stained with paint, several brushes sticking out of the right-side pocket. The plaid shirt the apron protected was frayed at the collar and cuffs, and it fit the man so poorly it looked like he'd dressed in his father's closet. His jeans were equally worn, and his tennis shoes sported soles flopping open at the toes.

The man glared at Skylar with dark-brown eyes peering from a shag of slightly curly, too-long bangs as he waited for Skylar's reply.

Skylar cleared his throat and struggled to find his usual confidence, feeling clearer with the artwork out of a direct line of sight. "Sorry. That painting is so gorgeous it knocked me off my game a little." Digging his smile out of his stupor, he crawled back into what his fraternity brothers called Silver Stone Mode and stuck out his hand. "Skylar Stone. I'm the risk manager for Delta Eta Sigma. I'm looking for Mr. Xander Fairchild. Can you tell me where I might find him?"

The mousy guy didn't accept the handshake, and if anything, his scowl deepened. "What do you mean, the painting is gorgeous?"

Skylar turned back to it, rubbing the smooth line of his chin with his thumb and forefinger. "I mean that the painting is gorgeous. I feel like I could look at it for hours."

"The paint is too thick, and the brushstrokes are a mess."

"That's kind of what I like, though. The thickness.

The roughness. It feels almost 3-D. I don't know anything about art, so I wouldn't know a brushstroke if you hit me with it, but I love this painting. Do you know who did it?"

Scowling Guy snorted. "Me."

"Wow. Really? That's fantastic. I can see someday I'll be forking over an arm and a leg for the right to hang your work in my living room."

The artist hunched his shoulders and glared harder. "What do you want?"

Right, no more compliments. Skylar got down to business. "Like I said, I'm here to see Mr. Fairchild. Do you know where I can find him?"

"You already did. Now tell me what you want, so I can tell you no and get back to work."

"You mean—you're Xander Fairchild?"

"Yes. And you're one of the frat boys who spray-painted penises all over my mural."

Here, finally, Skylar found his groove. "No. I'm one of the officers of the fraternity where three members are on probation for vandalizing your work. I'm here to apologize on behalf of Delta Eta Sigma and see what we can do to make amends for our brothers' inappropriate behavior."

"There's not much you can do. It can't be replaced. I'd have to repaint the whole thing, and it'll never be the same as the first time. It'll always be a copy, which means it's going to suck. I told the dean to take it down and forget it. I'll do another mural somewhere with less chance of roving drunken monkeys. Or I won't do it at all. I have my portfolio and BFA project to think about."

That news disillusioned Skylar on multiple levels. He'd assumed he could sentence the freshmen to eons of community service *beginning* with cleaning, but hearing the mural was ruined meant things were more serious than he'd been led to believe. Also, he'd *liked* that artwork. It was on the wall of Gama Auditorium, which meant he passed it every time he walked into school, and he walked almost every day. It made sense, he supposed, that he'd liked the mural so well, since it was by the same artist as the painting in front of him. He liked the painting so much better, though. The mural had been stylized, designed to represent Benten College more than being art. It depressed Sky to think it would be removed, not repaired.

He realized he was woolgathering, not focusing on his mission, and he cleared his throat. "I'm sorry to hear the mural is ruined. That will change our punishment of the offenders, though I can't imagine that's much recompense for having your work destroyed. At the very least, I'd like to apologize on behalf of Delta Eta Sigma. As someone who enjoyed your mural, I will miss seeing it every day."

Xander turned away and wrestled the lid off a paint can. "Whatever."

Normally Skylar would enjoy the challenge of someone so difficult to smooth over, but he wasn't on his game today. "Are you sure the mural can't be saved? Because believe me, these two have *days* of community service ahead of them. If that can't be done, maybe there's some particularly grueling work they can do here in the studios?"

"You think I want them in here? Anyway, why are you asking me? I did the mural as a sophomore special project. I don't have any authority over what happens to it. That said, if you try to stick me in a room full of frat boys grousing about their punishment—"

Skylar held up a hand. "Hey—first of all, I'm asking you because you're the artist. Yes, we're in discussion with the head of the art department, and the Interfraternity Council, as well as campus security, but your thoughts on this situation are also important. Second of all, no one will be sticking you with anything. These two are facing all manner of charges and suspensions, and at this point they're doing nothing but groveling. We take this seriously. That's why I'm here, asking how Delta Eta Sigma can make it up to you."

Xander had the lid off the paint can and waved it angrily at Skylar. "Nothing. Thanks for the effort. Talk to the building secretary about donating money for paint or something, but don't let your goons clean any of my brushes. Meanwhile, I need to get back to work." After dunking a fat, wide brush in the can, he wiped it on the rim and aimed it at the canvas.

Skylar frowned at him. "What are you doing?" When he realized the brush was about to slide across the top of that night sky, he didn't think, only knocked it out of Xander's hand, sending it clattering to the floor.

"*Christ!*" Xander faced down Skylar with his fists

clenched. "What the hell is your problem?"

Skylar felt queasy and slightly shaky. "You were going to paint over it."

"Yes. It's a piece of shit, and I need the canvas."

Piece of shit? "It's stunning. If you don't like it, sell it and *buy* a new canvas."

Xander's nostrils flared. "Like I said, you can leave now."

Skylar should have. He'd done what he'd come to do—he hadn't succeeded, but if he wanted to achieve his goal, he'd need to leave, regroup, and try again another day. But he couldn't leave and let the painting be ruined, so instead of walking out the door, he reached for his wallet. "How much do you want for it?"

This only enraged Xander further. "I said, get out."

Skylar thumbed through his bills. "I only have forty-five on me, but I'll go to the nearest ATM and get the rest of whatever price you name. I want to buy the painting, Mr. Fairchild."

"I'm not letting you take this back to your stupid frat house so you and your *brothers* can use it for a dartboard."

Skylar lowered his wallet and swallowed the impulse to give in to temper. "I have no such intent. I would never use a piece of art so callously. I gather you don't have a high opinion of Greek life, which I'm sorry to hear." Gears turned, and Silver Stone Mode ground back to life. "You don't seem to have much regard for your own skill, either, if you're so unwilling to sell your work. As far as I'm concerned, you belong in a gallery."

Xander blinked at Skylar. For a moment he looked vulnerable, almost eager, his veneer cracking at last. Just as quickly, however, his owlish demeanor was back. He set his jaw as he picked the brush up from the floor. "This is *my* painting. I can destroy it if I want to. I can paint over it, use it as a coffee table, chuck it against the wall. It's not going to hang in a gallery. The closest thing to that I'll be seeing anytime soon is my senior art show, and there's no way in hell I'm letting *that* get laughed down."

"What's to laugh at? I love the painting. The idea of a room full of your work sounds perfect."

"Oh yeah? Tell me why you like my work, then."

Skylar turned to the painting. The power of it hit him every time he looked at it, and he felt self-conscious attempting to articulate why when Xander was so derisive. He considered giving up and leaving. He'd delivered the apology and started trying to engender goodwill. The rest of his work would be done with research and carefully orchestrated gestures. But he really did hate the idea of this painting being covered up.

"I don't know. It gets me, right in the gut. It's so many things at once. It makes me feel aching and lonely but not desolate. This guy who has lost everything and retreated from the world, maybe even hates it, still has hope he can find his niche." He sighed and gestured with his hand. "I don't know anything about brushstrokes or forms or whatever. All I know is I'd hand over a lot of money to take this home with me. I wouldn't use it as a dartboard. I'd hang it in my room, and I'd stare at it while I lie in bed." He rolled his eyes at himself. "Now you'll tell me how off my interpretation was. But it's why I love it."

Xander looked pale, almost trembling, like someone had slapped him in the face. He stared at Skylar with that same vulnerable, aching expression. Then he turned away. "Take it."

Skylar frowned. "Take what?"

Xander made shooing motions at him. "The painting. Take it. Take it and go."

The painting? Skylar pulled out his money again. "Here, let me pay—"

"*Just take it.*" Xander put down the paintbrush, hauled the painting off the easel, and thrust it at Skylar. "It's yours. Go away."

Skylar struggled to accept the painting without dropping his wallet. "I really would pay for it. I *want* to pay for it." He *needed* to.

"We don't always get what we want. You have the painting, and you've apologized for the frat. I accept. There, see? Everyone's happy. Go have a kegger or something."

Xander didn't look happy. He looked upset. Skylar was too. It bothered him to pay nothing for the painting. He didn't like that Xander was so dismissive of Delta Sig, as if they were some reboot of *Animal House.* Though he supposed with the mural incident they looked like it, dammit. Skylar wanted to tell Xander about the two friends who had founded Delta Eta Sigma while caring for the sick, about Delta Sig's connection to the Boys & Girls Clubs of America and how much service they did a year. He wanted to talk about how his housemates truly were his brothers, how the social network the Greek life provided was as fundamental if not more so than his own family upbringing.

He would have, but Xander took off his apron and disappeared out of the studio and down a hallway. The door closed behind him with a quiet *snick*.

Skylar stared at the place where he'd disappeared, letting the quiet ring in his ears. Pulling his business card out of his wallet, he spied a backpack at the foot of the easel and slipped the card into an open flap. Then he tucked his wallet into his pocket, the painting carefully under his arm, and wove his way out of the building and down the hill toward Delta Sig.

THE LAST GODDAMNED thing Xander Fairchild needed was a frat boy interrupting his studio time.

His day had been packed tight as it was, and Pretty Boy's interruption had basically shot everything all to hell. Xander's plan had been to paint over the shit painting, letting it dry while he finished the last panels due for *Lucky 7*. The chore of recycling the canvas so he could paint tomorrow should have taken him a quick ten minutes, and inking only another forty, leaving him time to get the pages across campus to the magazine offices in Tori Hall on his way home. Instead, he had to stretch a new canvas over a frame, and he was priming it and grumbling under his breath when Sara came looking for him.

"I'm so sorry." He put down the brush and wiped his hands on his apron. "I haven't even started. Something came up, and I'm completely behind."

She waved a hand at him, indicating he should stay where he was. "You have the panels drawn, right? I can do the inking, if you don't mind."

Xander did mind, in fact, but he didn't want to sound like a controlling ass. "I have to tweak a few things. Sorry." He washed his hands briskly in the sink. "It won't take me long. I swear."

"No worries. Oh—and Jacob wanted me to tell you, he's not sure when, but he wants to get the guys together to move the last of the boxes to storage until they give us our new space assignment for the fall. He says make sure you either answer your phone, check your messages, or read your email this time."

Xander's cheeks burned, but he nodded, keeping his gaze on his hands as he washed them. "Got it."

She hiked herself onto a stool at the table where Xander had his manga materials spread out, her actions indicating she intended to watch him finish. He suppressed a sigh, knowing damn well he couldn't ask her to leave on several counts. One, he was the one late with his work. Two—he glanced over his shoulder at Sara's leg braces. He was an asshole, but he wasn't *that* much of an asshole, to send her away after coming all the way over from the *Lucky 7* offices. If it had been Cory, Jacob, or Zelda, he might have.

Which, he suspected, was possibly why they'd sent her. Damn it all.

He dried his hands and took up a stool across from her, opening his folio and his ink supplies. "I'm sorry you had to come all this way to find me."

She shrugged. "I texted you as a formality, but then I started walking."

Pausing with his Zebra G nib in hand, Xander winced. He hadn't even brought his cell phone today. "I'm sorry."

"It's all right. Nice day out." She rested her chin against her wrist, which was also in a brace. "Do you have a lot of screentone to add?"

"A bit, but it doesn't take me long." Less time if he wasn't watched, but there wasn't much helping that now.

Damn that frat boy anyway. Xander would already be on his way home, if not for him.

Xander tried to focus on inking the characters in front of him, but all he could see was the way what's-his-name had stared at his shitty painting.

And called it gorgeous.

"Seriously, I can help, if you want."

Xander snapped out of his stupor and glowered at the paper, hunching deeper over it. "No. I'm fine. Thanks."

He worked diligently after that, giving life to the manga. *Lucky 7* had existed as a student magazine since the college was founded in 1899, and *The Adventures of Hotay & Moo* had been a serialized story since day one, but the format had morphed along with the magazine. The name *Lucky* 7 was of course a riff on the Japanese seven gods of fortune, though *The Adventures of Hotay & Moo* were almost entirely based on one of the seven gods, Hotei, and Fudō Myōō, who was a god and one of the five wisdom kings but not one of the gods of fortune.

In the 1940s the short stories had become comics, and in the 1990s a resurgence in the college's Japanese cultural roots had inspired the editorial board to turn the comic into a manga, going so far as to flip the printing order so that the magazine opened to what westerners would consider the back.

Xander was the manga artist for the magazine and had been since his sophomore year, having apprenticed to the senior *mangaka* his freshman year and been a coartist that first year. Sara had been, theoretically, his apprentice this year, but he had been a shitty mentor. Which he felt bad about, but not bad enough to change his ways.

The characters were a true pleasure to work with, and drawing them had taught Xander more than his actual coursework. They'd done nothing but thrive in the hands of devoted artists over the decades. Xander understood the honor given to him, to have the torch of creating them passed to him, and he did his best to take it seriously.

It helped that at this point the two leads basically wrote themselves. Hotay was jolly and eternally optimistic, always leading the duo into the sun—in one story arc, this was literal—and Moo was sour and pessimistic, skeptical of everyone and everything they encountered, ready to do battle. Hotay could get himself out of a scrape if need be, but if a flaming sword were needed, that was when Moo came into play. There had definitely been artists who favored more battle-themed arcs, but under Xander's charge, the storylines tended toward Hotay and Moo having adventures together, encountering problems, and above all arguing.

Well, Moo argued, and Hotay cheered him up and coaxed him into drinking sake and forgetting his problems. Sometimes *The Adventures of Hotay & Moo* was guilty of not having enough plot in its storylines. Which was probably why the readership was dying off.

When Xander finished adding the screentones and everything had set, he handed Sara the folio. "Sorry again that you had to come get it."

"No worries. But maybe this summer, since we're both staying in town, I can teach you how to use the digital drawing software, and all of this can go faster."

That, right there, was why Xander had been a shitty mentor. "I have to get home. See you later."

He left before she could start yet another campaign to convince him to convert the manga.

The walk between the art building and Xander's apartment was just over a mile and a half, and with shortcuts and a pass through the local hospital's campus, Xander had the trek between home and studio down to twenty-eight minutes. The day Pretty Boy confiscated his painting, however, the walk took Xander almost an hour.

This was because he went the long way, winding his way through the state park so he could lose himself in the trees and spend some time staring out across the bluff at the top of the ridge. He could have shaved off ten minutes if he'd used the regular path, but he didn't want to run into people walking their dogs, so he took the hiking paths instead. He stood at the bluff for a good twenty minutes, replaying the exchange in the studio over and over again before stalking the rest of the way home, determined to not think anymore.

He worried he'd run into his landlady, but she wasn't home, thankfully. It was common for her to hear him arrive and come out to greet him, roping him into unwanted conversation, but today the gods looked fondly on him and allowed him to stop at his mailbox in peace before hiking up the side stairs to his attic apartment. After letting himself inside and tossing the mail on the kitchen counter, he shut the blinds tight and collapsed in a flop on the couch, staring up at the ceiling.

A soft *thunk* on his legs preceded a plaintive meow and a second, heavier thud against his chest. Xander lifted his head to see both his cats peering intently at him.

With a sigh, Xander ruffled their fur. "Yes. I'll feed you. Let me wallow here a minute."

Hokusai, the leg-thumper, mewed again, but Hiromu focused on purring like a jet engine and rubbing her head along Xander's jaw. Xander continued to pet them as he addressed the ceiling.

"It was a fluke that he saw exactly what I'd meant to paint. Probably he has some ninja people-reading skill and figured it out from my face." When Hiromu head-butted his chin, Xander sighed and dipped his head to nuzzle back. "I shouldn't have given it to him. Better to have it painted over than have it go with *them*."

The cats, comprehending their human wouldn't be leaping up to feed them, settled into their perches on his thighs and chest to wait.

Xander stroked Hiromu idly, her long, fluffy coat silky beneath his fingers. Despite his vow in the park, he played the exchange with the frat boy over again, trying to show himself where it had been a trap, but mostly, to his shame, the memory of that smile and those twinkling eyes made Xander's heart flutter. He'd already forgotten the guy's name, but it would be a week before he'd stop fantasizing about Mr. Fancy-Talk pressing Xander gently into the wall, nuzzling his nose down Xander's cheek. If only he'd had a little bit of beard, he'd have been perfect.

Groaning, Xander pushed the cats off his body and shuffled to the kitchen, where he drizzled kibble into their bowls. While they ate, he examined his mail. He had all his bills on autopay, so most of it was garbage, but there was one fat full-size envelope tucked inside the local advertising circulars, and when he saw the icon in the return address, his belly did an uncomfortable backflip.

Benten College Department of Art & Art History.

When Xander pried the envelope open, it was exactly what he'd expected it to be: the paperwork for his Bachelor of Fine Arts Exhibition.

He grimaced as he flipped through the pages of the application. If only it were as simple as showing up with a rack of paintings, but no. In addition to requiring their students submit material matching the standards the art department felt represented Benten and the department's vision for postgraduate work, they insisted their BFA students understand the full weight of what they'd be expected to do if they intended to live off their art.

He must *package* himself and his work. He must *advertise* his work. He must put forth—he glanced at the official wording—*significant good-faith effort* to promote his exhibition to the public in the spring or fall of his senior year. When each student's show landed in the calendar was determined by lottery, and lucky Xander was one of the early birds. The application was due May 20, which was just around the corner. This was the third notice, reminding him he still hadn't filled it out.

The only reason Xander hadn't was because of the damn promotion bullshit.

It didn't come out and *say* he'd be judged on attendance, but Xander knew he would be. And he knew however great he might make his paintings, in this aspect, he would fail. No one would come to his show. His advisor, the handful of undergrads filling their exhibition credits. Possibly his aunt, but he doubted it, since she lived too far away. No one else in the entire state of New York or anywhere in the northeastern region of the United States would give a damn. Xander didn't have friends. He barely had *acquaintances.* The only people he knew at Benten were the art majors and the staff of the *Lucky 7,* and they all basically tolerated him.

Well, except for Zelda, but they more tortured him than anything.

Xander's lack of people to drag to his show didn't upset him half as much as the lengths he was supposed to take to advertise, whether or not anyone would come. *Social media.* The department expected him to promote his work on no less than three social networks. They had a handy little bullet list of different types and what each was good for, which probably most students rolled their eyes at because it was so obvious—except Xander wouldn't understand any of them even with a full-on manual. The hell he was *tweeting.* He'd never get a single follower, so what was the point? He refused to even think the word Facebook. As for the rest, he didn't know much about them, and he didn't want to learn.

Except he had to learn. Three of them. And make a *significant good-faith effort.*

Shoving the application to the back of the table, Xander rose to make a pot of coffee. While it brewed, he thumbed through his records, rerouting his brain from anger and fear over the art show and his encounter with the frat boy and nudging it to make a vinyl selection instead.

He was going to paint.

He didn't have a studio in his apartment, but his living space essentially *was* his studio. He kept the paint and supplies away from the cats, but his easel and canvases took up most of his living room. His apartment had plumbing problems and got too cold in the winter and didn't have AC, but it had high ceilings, great natural light, and a more aesthetically pleasing floor plan than the boxy apartments most students lived in. And because it was so simply arranged, getting ready to work was a matter of opening a cupboard, pouring turpentine, donning an apron, and squirting some color onto a palette. The first song wasn't finished before Xander stood at his easel, staring at the blank space while he mixed paint together. He didn't think about what he would paint, he just let the canvas tell him what was there.

Probably he shouldn't have been surprised he painted the frat boy. Smiling, suited, hard and angular yet beautiful as he beamed knowingly out of the painting. Hands in his pockets, a casual stance. Above him Xander painted pretty swirls that almost sparkled. In fact, as that thought occurred to him, he retreated to the kitchen to pick up some glitter and added it to the paint. After he flipped the record over, Xander painted a shadowy shape behind his subject. Crouching. Reaching. Ugly where the frat boy shone. He added Gamblin Cold Wax Medium to those darker browns and blues, just a hint to turn the paint flat. He used thicker paint there, letting it sit in fat, awkward globs.

He'd forgotten the coffee, but he drank it cold as he switched albums. He rinsed his brushes and splashed pastels in a halo around the two figures. When the record turned off, he kept painting as the echo of the music pulsed inside his head and the paint laced the canvas. After he finished, he poured himself a fresh cup of coffee and sipped it as he sat in the kitchen and stared at what he'd done.

It wasn't awful. He wasn't sure it was great, though a stupid part of him was trying to argue this should go into his BFA show. He shut that down, but after a half hour and quarter cup of coffee which once again had gone cold, he had to admit it was better than average, especially for basically fucking around.

But the muses weren't done with him. Somehow painting the man wasn't enough. Still drunk on creating, Xander stumbled to his desk, turned on his light, and pulled out his markers. *Just a quick sketch*, he told himself. A little something different. Less abstract. Something to capture that other side. That…that smile…

When he looked up, it was pitch dark, except for his desk light. He'd drawn more than one sketch. It was a full panel, with shading. He'd gotten out his ink and nibs and done the thing up properly. It was some kind of weird cross between *Hotay & Moo* and something new and strange, and it was…a mess. He left it unfinished, frustrated because it hadn't satisfied him the way he wanted, but it had been a heady rush of creation, and now the beast was spent.

Rising, dizzy and cranky, he glanced at the time and realized he hadn't eaten for about twelve hours. After a poke in his fridge turned up nothing, he put water on and pulled out a packet of ramen. While it cooked, he fished his art history homework out of his backpack.

A business card fell out and drifted gently to the floor.

It was cream with gray stripes, and they were glossed, so when Xander tipped the paper toward the light, the stripes shimmered. SKYLAR STONE, the card read in classy, conservative DeSoto font in small caps. An email and phone number were listed below, and when Xander flipped the card over the stripes were repeated, but in a small square below a list of titles. *Risk Manager, Delta Eta Sigma. Executive Vice President of American Marketing Association, Benten College Chapter. Vice President of Public Relations for Students in Advertising.*

Skylar. That was the guy from the studio. The one who had taken Xander's painting. The frat boy. How had his card gotten into Xander's bag?

Pursing his lips, Xander tossed it at the mini trash can beside the table, put his ramen in a bowl, and did his homework. When that was done, he heated up the last of his coffee in the microwave and poured over the BFA paperwork again.

Halfway through, he set aside the coffee and got out a beer.

Skylar Stone's business card burned in his head like a mocking brand as Xander took in the full depth of what he was expected to do in addition to painting a show's worth of material. Probably this kind of marketing crap had been Frat Boy's freshman first semester. Probably he could do it in his sleep.

Well, Xander couldn't do it sober with a gun to his head. His advisor would be no help. He could maybe ask Sara. Though she'd want to talk about making *Hotay & Moo* digital while they were at it. No thanks.

There was always Zelda, of course. But asking Zelda to help him with a social media campaign was like asking a nuclear weapon to help you clear out a brush pile. Another hard pass. Ditto Jacob and Cory. They'd just complain because they were overworked as it was, and why couldn't he figure his shit out like everyone else?

Well, that was officially everyone he knew, except for his landlady, who had more trouble accessing the internet than he did.

Xander washed out the coffeepot, his mug, beer bottle, and his bowl, and fed the cats their evening treat of wet food. On his way to the bathroom he passed the garbage can and saw Skylar Stone's business card gleaming on the carpet beside it.

You could ask him. That could be his payment for the painting.

Hope flared, tangled with yearning. Across the room the frat boy painting beamed at Xander, bright and shining Technicolor.

On the desk, the four panels lay in silent black and white, harking to a past Xander didn't let himself forget.

Unfinished, reminding him of his shortcomings and the roadblocks to his future.

Nostrils flaring, jaw set, Xander picked up the card, ripped it into tiny pieces, and flushed it down the toilet.

Chapter Two

WHILE THE REST of his fraternity enjoyed a beautiful May afternoon in a nearby park, Skylar sat at his desk in his room at Delta Eta Sigma, staring out the window at the gleaming white brick and glass of Gama Auditorium, trying to figure out what he should submit for his senior project.

He wanted it to shine in a *particular* way, and he hadn't sorted out how to make that happen yet. His senior project was a practicum, essentially: take what we've taught you all these years and show you know how to apply it. It didn't *have* to be something actually implemented, but it certainly looked better on a resume if that's what happened. He needed to find someone—an individual, an entity, or a business—to let him play guinea pig with their brand. To showcase and market them.

The choice he made would define him. Hardcore business? That was what his father would expect, and that would fit with the place in the law firm waiting for him. Except…going that route felt like a trap. It was the obvious choice, which made it wrong as far as Skylar was concerned. His instinct was to find a mom and pop store on Main Street and give *them* a corporate polish. That still didn't feel quite right, but it felt closer to the mark than anything else he'd come up with so far.

This project was his last chance to showcase himself as the package of Skylar Stone. After this, he'd be lost to the dull halls of law school, fighting the urge to be turned into a drone. This was where he staked his claim on his individuality, his artistry. To show he wasn't going to be just *any* corporate lawyer. He'd be Skylar Stone.

Whoever that was.

Of course, the *other* project he had to focus on this summer was his LSAT study. He was slated to take the test in September and had a tutor he was supposed to check in with regularly. As of yet he hadn't been able to get the practice score he'd need for Yale Law, which was more than something of a problem.

He tried to find a perfect project so he could send in the form, get that ball rolling, and get back to his LSAT prep. But all he could do was stare at the ruined mural and think about Xander Fairchild and his angry scowl and how he'd refused to let Skylar pay for the painting.

He managed to get in a good hour of studying, but when he glanced up and saw it was almost two, he closed his book and picked up his phone. His father's secretary answered on the third ring.

"Good afternoon, Skylar. How's your studying going?"

"Very well, thank you for asking, Ellen." Skylar drummed his fingers on his desk, smiling as he thought of the woman on the other end of the line. "How are the girls?"

"They're doing fine, thank *you* for asking."

"Are Chris and Marie stressing about their finals?"

Ellen chuckled. "They *are*, but they loved the survival package you sent them. You're ever the thoughtful one, Skylar."

He smiled, feeling warm and soothed under her praise, as he always did. "Well, you're the one who raised me.

"I should think some of the credit goes to your nannies."

"Yes, but *you're* their mother."

She laughed again, the rich, low envelope of sound that always made Skylar wish she'd been *his* mother, and not simply the woman who had organized most of his life. She hadn't always been his father's executive assistant—in fact, for much of Skylar's youth she was a low-ranking secretary who got stuck managing the care of the Stone child. Sometimes she hired nannies and babysitters. Sometimes she did the work herself. When her own children were old enough, though, she installed them in the positions of caring for Skylar. Meanwhile, Ellen continued to climb her way up the ranks of the office pool, until her patience, curried favors, and wit landed her a job at the right hand of Leighton Stone himself.

Skylar loved Ellen. He loved her family too—her children Sandy, Rosie, and Erin had been his nannies, but so had her sisters Tiffany and Sarah. Ellen's youngest children, Chris and Marie, were Skylar's age, and they had been his playmates. He'd considered them sisters when he was young, and he'd been upset when he couldn't go home with them or that they couldn't stay longer to play with him.

In so many ways, Ellen's family had raised Skylar. Yet he was also aware they were not his family, that he did not belong with them. Of course, he was equally conscious of how little his actual family wanted anything to do with him, and so Skylar kept trying to find ways to attract their attention and show them he could in fact be a Stone after all.

Which was what he was doing right now, in fact.

"Ellen," he began, "I wondered if you happened to know when might be a good time to reach my father." His cheeks heated. "I've…been having trouble reaching him." *Again.*

There was a beat, slightly uncomfortable, before she said, "He's not in at the moment, unfortunately. But let me check his schedule and when might be a good time to try again."

Skylar pushed his smile wider, so his disappointment didn't telegraph through. "I have some information for him he might find illuminating. Maybe…tell him that."

Ellen's voice took on a whip-like quality that said, *Don't you worry, hon, shit is about to happen.* "I'll see to it your father has some time in his schedule to make a phone call as soon as possible. All right?"

Skylar's smile eased into something no longer

forced. "All right. Thanks, Ellen."

"Of course, sweetie. Take care of yourself. Good luck studying for that test."

Skylar hung up and stared out the window. Ellen's voice rang in his ear, lifting his spirit, but it faded all too quickly. He wondered how long it would take his father to call.

Beside him on the desk, his phone beeped. Glancing down, he saw a bubble preview notification, and he couldn't help it, he hoped it might be from his father. But it was only Carolyn from Tau Alpha Kappa.

Could use your company tonight.

Ah. Raising his eyebrows, Skylar opened his phone and checked his calendar. Technically he was free, outside of wanting to get his project turned in. With a sigh, he decided to hear her out. *I might be free. What are you thinking?*

My family's having a fundraiser for the new senate candidate, and I was hoping you'd be my date.

Skylar's heart skipped a beat. *Senate fundraiser.* Oh, Carolyn knew how to sway him. *I can give you a few hours. Shall I pick you up at six?*

Great. Thank you so much. You're the best, Sky.

Skylar turned his phone over and tried to focus once more on his application. He got nowhere fast, however, so he gave up and went downstairs.

Despite most of the brothers having gone to the park to play Frisbee, the main living room still hummed with activity. Many of the guys were getting ready to move out for the summer, and some had already left for internships and opportunities abroad. Skylar felt a pang thinking of how the house would be empty soon, because he would miss the commotion when his brothers were absent.

Thankfully, they weren't *all* leaving. Jeff Turner, better known as Unc, was one of the Delta Eta Sigma members who was staying. Unc could be an acquired taste, but Skylar didn't mind him. Unc sat with headphones on, curled up in a corner of the sofa, decked in his usual well-worn sweats and sporting messy hair—the top section bleached blond over his dark-brown undercut that matched his close-cut beard.

He was nibbling absently on the end of a highlighter while he stared intently at the pages of his econ textbook, but when he saw Skylar, he grinned and waved him over.

"Hey, you." Unc pulled the band to his Beats back with a lusty sigh and shut the textbook. "I hate econ. Like, I *hate* econ."

"You're nearly through it." Skylar plunked down beside him. "Let me know if you need to borrow my notes. I think they're still in my closet."

"I will take those notes, gladly." Unc tipped his head back and shut his eyes, sighing again, even more dramatically than the first time, but he also opened one eye and focused it on Skylar. "So. Did Donovan break it to you about the Delta Sig Executive Council yet?"

Skylar sat up straight. "No, he didn't. What happened?"

Unc sat up too, grimacing. "We're getting fined for

the vandalism. The council is pissed."

Skylar had been afraid of this. "We need a meeting. You or Donovan need to call one. I wish you'd have said something to me sooner. We need to be out kissing administrative and art department ass. Right now."

"*You* need to kiss their ass."

Skylar considered pointing out he was a *risk management officer* and that his term was up in a matter of days, but despite his insistence he wasn't running for office his senior year, everyone assumed he was president-elect. He was always in charge, even when he wasn't.

Unc held up a hand. "I know, I know. I should handle this. Hear me out, though." He leaned forward on his elbows, his silver hoop earring swaying gently. "I seriously thought about going over and talking to the Interfraternity Council and the whole deal. But you know how I get. I thought about taking Donovan with me, in case I put people off. Except." He raised his eyebrows and gave Skylar a knowing look, inviting him to finish the thought.

Skylar sighed. "Except I know how he gets too. Goddamn it, Unc. I'm serious, I'm not running."

"I know, and I don't think you should. I'm not either. I'm going to be on the Interfraternity Council, and that's enough."

Skylar's heart sank. "Jesus, if *you* don't run, and *I* don't run—"

"Then someone else will have to run."

Skylar looked around the room. "What kind of

leadership will we have, then?"

"I don't know. But here's the deal, Sky. Both of us have law school to prep for. I've got more prep to do than you, since I'm pretty much a fuckup. Someone else can fill the gap."

No one else was going to fill the gap, though. Not anyone who wasn't going to fulfill every stereotype Xander had just lobbed at Skylar. "You're not a fuckup."

Unc snorted and waggled his eyebrows. "Come on now. You know better than that." He put an arm around Skylar. "Stop worrying. Here's what I've cooked up. You go smooth things over with the IF, and tonight I take us out. Anywhere you want to go. All the booze is on me."

Skylar pinched the bridge of his nose. "You *know* I don't drink."

"You do, sometimes. The way you've been grinding your nose against those books, I figure you're overdue." He leaned in closer, pitching his voice low. "I'll get us dates too. For decoration or function."

Skylar untangled himself from Unc and stood, pursing his lips against the warning signs of a headache. "Forward me the email from the council. I'll take care of it."

"I'll tell Donovan. You just let me know when we're going out—"

"I have to study." He remembered he'd agreed to meet Carolyn. "And I have somewhere to go at six. But if you're here when I get back, I'll have a beer with you."

"How about when you get back you have a beer

with me *and a couple of girls*?" When Skylar only arched an eyebrow, Unc threw up his hands. "Dude, this is why you get those migraines."

"This is why your dad tells you to apply yourself."

"I do apply myself. Just not to the things he wants me to." Unc splayed his arms over the back of the couch and grinned at Skylar. "Thanks, man. I owe you big. Don't you worry. I'll make sure I pay you back."

Skylar was, to be honest, more worried about the payback than the favor.

He didn't have time to dwell on that, however, so he focused instead on hunting down the phone number of the president of the Delta Sig Executive Council and apologizing, promising he'd take care of this right away and report back as soon as he had news. He sent out an email to the chapter loop. Then he took a shower, shaved, put on his suit and tie, and began the trek to the student union.

He didn't have an appointment, but he understood the Director of Fraternity and Sorority Life well enough to know how to handle her. Though it wasn't even remotely on his way, he stopped by the Java House and picked up a blueberries-and-cream latte and the biggest chocolate muffin in the display. He stopped at a flower cart and picked up a bouquet. Once he wound his way down the hill to the student union, he stopped in the men's room to tidy his hair, and apply his secret weapon: a spritz of L'Homme Libre cologne.

When he breezed into Leslie's office, she was on the phone, but she brightened and waved him over, making a silent fuss of *oh, you shouldn't have* as she accepted the muffin, coffee, and flowers without missing a beat of her conversation. Shortly she ended the call, but before she could speak, Skylar held up his hands. "I'm not going to bother you—I'll send an email to make an appointment, but I couldn't wait that long to apologize for the headache we're giving you, especially this close to commencement."

She all but melted. "Oh, Skylar—don't worry for a minute about it. Here, sit down—I've got some time. Let's discuss everything now."

Since he'd known this was exactly what she'd say, Skylar sat and dove headlong into his fraternity's fracas. "Let me make it simple. We're obviously expelling the members." He hadn't cleared that with the board, but if they were going to turf everything to him like this, they could live with his fiat. "We'll pay for whatever damages need paying for. My concern is the reputation of Delta Eta Sigma and the Greek community. As much as you're comfortable with, I want us involved personally in cleanup, and I'd like to do something for the art department if we can." He recalled his conversation with Xander Fairchild. "I understand there's not much we can do to save the mural, and it might not be our place to do any painting or cleaning. But we're largely business majors, and we all have arms and legs. We can help them administratively. In *any* capacity."

Leslie looked thoughtful as she sipped her coffee. "That's good. Really good. It's true, the liberal arts aren't as represented overall in fraternity and sorority life, where most of you major in business."

Skylar nodded, processing this as quickly as he could through his knowledge of Benten history and its current demographics. "Which is such a tragedy, if you think of it. Since the college was founded primarily as a haven for artists, it's a shame to see us so divided."

"You know, you're right. This effort could be bridge-building. I'll call the department head and ask what they need."

The idea formed in the air between them, so crystalline and perfect Skylar wished he could close his eyes and breathe it in for a few moments. "Tell me what you think of this, Leslie. I'm working on my proposal for my senior project right now. I've been unable to land on anything I like, and I think it's because I was waiting for this opportunity. What if my senior project was to help the art department? They have exhibits and such. They could use public relations or marketing or all kinds of things that fall into the purview of my project. What if that was part of our offer?"

Leslie beamed like a sun. "That is *brilliant*. Only you would think of such a thing, Sky. And nobody could do anything quite as amazing as you would. I'm calling over there *right now*. In fact, I'll *go* over."

"Perfect. I'll walk you, as it's on my way. Unless you'd like me to come along? Do you think that would be appropriate?"

"I think it's the best idea I've heard all day. Let's go." Leslie rose, then stopped and winked. "But let me put these beautiful flowers in some water first."

"Absolutely," Skylar replied, winking back.

XANDER CUT HIS hand on the way into the art building, which felt like an ominous sign.

He was trying to duck around a group of freshmen he knew were going to ask him for advice on their projects, and when he misjudged the width of a doorway, he reached out to brace himself against a piece of metal sculpture and earned himself a gash along his palm. It wasn't deep, and thankfully it wasn't on his left hand, but it required him to stop at the office and get a bandage and a lecture from the secretary about tetanus shots, and in the end he got jumped by the freshmen anyway. He stood in the corner of the office, cradling his throbbing hand, explaining the best way to arrange still-life composition and lighting, wondering the whole time why they wanted to talk to him when all he was doing was telegraphing how much he didn't want to engage with anyone.

They talked so damn much he was late for his appointment with his advisor, so when he arrived at Peterson's door, he felt more awkward and unsettled than usual.

"Come in," Dr. Peterson called when Xander knocked. Xander opened the door enough to tentatively lean into the room, and Peterson gave Xander the first smile he remembered seeing on his advisor's face. "Fairchild, what excellent timing." He gestured to the part of the room blocked by the door. "I have someone I want you to meet."

Xander pushed the door open wide enough to step inside. He cast a glance in the direction Peterson indicated and flinched in a brief shock of unease when he recognized Skylar Stone. Suit, smile, and all.

"We've met before, in fact." Skylar strode forward, smile widening, and held out his hand. "Good to see you again, Xander."

Xander extended his hand toward Skylar, realized this hand had a big goobery bandage on it, and withdrew it. He tried to extend his left hand instead, but that made his backpack slide down his arm, so in the end he tucked both hands against his body and glared at Skylar before glancing dubiously at his advisor. "What's going on?"

"What's going on is I was about to return your BFA exhibit paperwork to have you redo your marketing plan, but before I could do that, this charming young man arrived." Peterson clapped a hand on Skylar's shoulder. "His fraternity is making the art department part of their service work this coming year, but *he* is making us his senior project. He's helping any art student needing assistance with promotion for their work, but he needs one student to serve as a centerpiece. The department looked over all the BFA exhibit applications, and we've decided that student is *you*."

Xander took a step backward. "*What?* No. *No*."

Peterson's smile faded to the glower he usually reserved for Xander. "Don't be an idiot. You need his help. Your proposal was a disaster."

Skylar's megawatt smile mellowed to *comforting*. "I promise I'm advisory only. I won't get in the way of your work. I'll simply help you draft a marketing plan."

This was a nightmare. Xander wanted to object, heartily, but he didn't know how. It didn't seem to matter, though, because Peterson and Skylar carried on as if Xander wasn't even there.

"I've given you all the paperwork you need, but let us know if you need anything further." Peterson indicated Skylar with a nod.

Megawatt returned. "I'm sure we'll be able to manage." He aimed his smile-beam at Xander. "Would you like to set up a time to discuss?"

"Discuss now." Peterson patted his abdomen. "I'm nipping out for lunch. Feel free to use my office."

This wasn't a nightmare, Xander decided. It was a circle of hell.

He tried to slump into the chair by the wall, but as soon as Peterson left, Skylar pulled the professor's comfortable desk chair around the corner and urged Xander into it. "We'll cover the basics for now and meet up again as soon as I've gone more thoroughly over the application and you've had more time to decide what you want from me." He frowned at Xander's injured hand. "Are you all right? Will you be able to paint?"

"It's fine. It's my right hand, anyway, so it doesn't matter. I'm left-handed." Xander hunched hesitantly in Peterson's chair. "Whatever will get the department off my back. They're the ones who care about how the show is promoted, not me."

"But you're a studio arts major, yes? And I understand you're applying for your MFA as well?" Skylar perched at the edge of the plastic seat Xander had intended to take, looking like a magazine ad for *business professional.* He fucking smelled like a magazine too. "You'll have no end of shows to learn how to advertise for. What I'm proposing for you isn't simply a quick plan for this exhibit. I want to design a marketing portfolio for your brand. I want to give you a toolkit you can use this year and for years to come, one you can customize over and over again."

It was a dazzling, too-good-to-be-true proposition, which made it highly suspect in Xander's book. "Why are you doing this? I get they picked me because I'm a hot mess, but why are *you* here?"

He expected more marketing snow job, but Skylar surprised him by dimming the megawatt and morphing into something much less packaged. "Because the incident with the mural has done damage to the college, to the art department, to you, and it's tainted Delta Sig's reputation. I'm not having my fraternity sullied like that. We're a service organization. We're leaders. We're not drunken fools who vandalize. I can say that all day long, but now we need to *show* that's who we are."

The guy was dazzling—handsome, yes, but charisma leached out of him like radiation. Xander fought to keep it at bay. "So you're the president of the frat or something?"

Ting. There was the smile again. "No. Risk manager. Very low on the totem pole." When Xander huffed dubiously, the smile ratcheted from charming to *lethal*. "My fraternity is important to me. For how it reflects on me but also what it means to my house brothers and to the national organization. For the idea of what Greek life means to the college."

Was this guy real? "I assume you're a poli-sci major."

Goddamn, but the soft chuckle was worse than the smile. "Double major in economics and marketing with an English minor. I'll be taking the LSAT this fall."

Business, and he was going to be a *lawyer*. Which meant he was going to be a *business lawyer*. Xander stifled a grimace. He supposed that made sense with the stuff on the back of the business card. "So you're helping me as part of your senior project?"

"No. You *are* my senior project."

This time Xander couldn't step on his horrified reaction. "Your grade depends on how well my show goes?"

"First of all, your show *will* go well. That's become *my* job, to ensure that happens. What *my* advisors will look for is how well did I understand and serve my client. If this were the real world and you hired me, the whole purpose would be for you to focus on your art while I helped draw attention to it. It will be the same general principle here, with more attention paid to your review board instead of sales made. Using your connections, your personal networks, and of course at core your art, this could be a brilliant exhibit."

That would have been funny, except the acknowledgment of what a farce this was only made Xander more sour. "I hate to break it to you, but I think you've been punked by the art department. I have no network. No connections. I go to class, I paint, I talk to my cats. I don't even have friends."

"You have more of a network than you think, and I can help you identify it. Classmates. Peers. Students interested in your work."

Holy shit was this guy in for a rude awakening. "*Nobody* is interested in my work."

Skylar's smile was close-lipped and tilting, and Xander kind of wished for the ridiculous megawatt back. "If you recall, at least *one* person is interested. I can find you more. I *will* find you more." He leaned forward, blue-green eyes glinting. "In fact, above and beyond any paperwork, senior project, or application—I promise you, here and now, that whatever list of professional goals you write out for me, I *will* make happen. That's what I want you to have by our next meeting, and I want it to be big. I want you to *try* to stump me."

"You have no idea how impossible your job is going to be."

"You have no idea how much I love overturning impossible."

The smile was getting on Xander's nerves. Under his skin. Into the soft places in his belly. Hardening that weakness, Xander lifted his chin. "Fine. If you want to look like an idiot, I'm not going to stop you."

Skylar winked and reached into his suit coat. He

passed over another card.

Xander took it and tucked it angrily into the vest pocket of his shirt.

Chapter Three

By Memorial Day weekend, Takaketo, New York, was practically a ghost town.

It always amazed Xander to see how *much* the city shrank—though calling it a city was a generous move, only something someone from his hometown of rural Pennsylvania would do. With students, Takaketo was thirty thousand people. Without them, it was more like twenty-four thousand.

For Xander, who'd grown up in a city of nine thousand, both versions of the college town were pretty substantial. For the editor of the student magazine, born and raised in Brooklyn, Takaketo was a joke, and he wasn't happy to be staying. Jacob Chen usually spent his summers helping his family at their bodega or deli or whatever their restaurant was called in the city, but it had closed, so now he was here in Takaketo working three part-time jobs.

When Jacob called Xander to ask him to help the rest of the staff pack up and haul the boxes because they were being moved from Tori Hall, Xander had braced for Jacob to be a total bear. But outside of grumbling about how the college had no respect for such an established institution like *Lucky 7*, Jacob was in fairly good spirits. It probably helped that his best friend, Cory Brandon, the print and layout guy, kept cheering him up. As they finished their work and got ready to go their separate ways, they talked about how they were going to make things great no matter what, and about how they hoped when the construction crew opened up the building, they found a shrine.

Not every student at Benten College believed in the myths of their academic institution's founding, but it was practically a job requirement for members of the *Lucky 7* staff. The legend, as Xander had been told, was that in the 1870s a group of rich, eccentric friends from New York toured Asia and fell in love with Japan. They came home full of half-baked Shinto beliefs and a passion to start a Japanese revolution in the US. When their efforts to instill Japanese philosophy didn't take, they decided what they *really* needed to make their ideas catch on was an academic institution to further their interests, and thus Benten College was born.

Except by the time the college was actually founded, it was the late nineties, they'd grown older and more eccentric, and in the case of several of them, significantly poorer. The few who still had money had held on to it by being *less* mad with their ideas, and they insisted the college had to appeal to the masses. Compromises were made. In the end, Benten College was just another run-of-the-mill academic institution, except that this one was radical enough to accept men and women. All Eastern traces were gone.

Unless you knew where to look.

Xander had never seen one of the hidden shrines, but he'd searched for them. What self-respecting art student at Benten hadn't? He wanted to see one, half for the lore, half for hope of some kind of legacy artwork. That *would* make construction at Tori Hall worth it, if one turned up.

He doubted one would show up, though, because in all his years at Benten, he had yet to see any. The college was rich with Japanese culture, though bizarrely low on people of actual Japanese heritage, and it had always been that way. Occasionally in the college's history they'd had Japanese instructors for the Japanese language and culture classes, and there were Japanese international students when the college recruiters did their job properly, but mostly the college was a bunch of rich white people, a handful of people of color, and an explosion of Japanese culture that made no sense when you looked at it from the outside. Not much from the inside, either, to be honest.

Xander didn't care. In fact, he was *one of those,* as the frat boys liked to whisper, one of the geeks who came armed with a love of manga and anime and rushed to sign up for the Japanese language courses because he wanted to read his favorite series without having to download pirated scans online. He'd always felt more at home in the envelope of Japanese pop culture than he had in his own, and the idea that he could go to a college that celebrated Japan, even in a quirky way? Bring it the hell on.

And outside of his encounters with the frat boys who came here because they couldn't get into their Ivy League first-choice schools, Xander's experience at Benten had been excellent. Capping it off with a shrine find would be perfect, yes, but he wasn't going to push his luck. He'd accept simply surviving his BFA.

Right now, though, Xander's dreams extended no further than getting a shower, but when he arrived at home, a note from his landlady was on his front door.

Hey, kiddo. Need some help with an order for a shop. Could I borrow you for the evening? Will pay your usual rate plus a meal and conversation.—P

Pamela Stolarz had been a professor and celebrated modern artist back in the day, and she'd been married to one of Benten's most famous Japanese literature and language professors, Takahiro Oshiro. She'd bought the convoluted old Victorian house she lived in with her husband's life insurance money when he passed, and named it the Palace of the Sun because she said it had the best view of the sunrise in town. The fact that it sounded Japanese and reminded her of her recently departed and beloved spouse didn't hurt anything, either.

But Pamela was lonely in her huge, ramshackle house, and though she made a brisk business selling her folk art at events and collecting commissions through area shops, she had difficulty keeping up because of arthritis in her hips and shoulder. So when she found out Xander's scholarships didn't quite cover all his costs and he needed a more economical place to live and a part-time job, she offered him a deal he couldn't refuse. She dictated to Xander what she wanted set up, he did the heavy prep work and even some of the base painting, and then she did the artwork she loved to do. In return he got to live in her attic apartment with a steal of a deal on his rent and utilities.

She was already there waiting for him when he arrived in the garage, standing in the middle of a stack of cement slabs. She smiled as she heard him enter. "Good afternoon, honey. How are you?"

"I'm well."

She didn't look up from her work, but she nodded at a large box sitting on the bench beside her. "Another package came for you from your mom. It said *perishable,* so I brought it out of the sun. I assume it's cookies again."

Xander saw the familiar red-and-white label and sighed. "She just sent a box two weeks ago." He took in the sight before him, assessing. There had to be at least fifty six-by-twelve two-inch-thick cement slabs stacked on wooden pallets. "Do you want to paint them yet, or are you still thinking about what you want to do?"

"Still thinking. I don't think I have enough time to do anything with them for the June show, but we could make some nice hay with them for the fall festival, and of course Christmas."

Pamela—and by his turn, Xander—made bank on folk art at Christmas. "You're the boss. Tell me what you want done, and I'm your guy Friday."

"That you are." She patted his shoulder. "All righty. Let's start with the fence pieces you brushed down yesterday. If you could give them a nice white patina—not too much, just enough to give me a surface, that ought to be enough to keep you busy."

It did at that—her instructions were vague, but Xander had both enough experience with what Pamela wanted and enough artistic sensibility to understand what she meant by a "nice white patina"—she wanted that distressed look that would make it seem as if the fence pieces had been once painted white and then left out in the rain to peel away over time. In fact, what he ended up doing was using a thin layer of white house paint and sometimes scraping away bits with the edge of a trowel—this was all work she could do herself, but why should she, when she could pay him to do it for her?

When it was time for dinner, Pamela had a bowl of soup ready for him, and a sandwich, which he ate on a stool while he watched her work on some smaller boards he'd prepped for her the week before. Her artistic style was markedly different than his, and her folk art style wasn't the same as some of her oil paintings he'd seen in the house, but folk art paid the tax man and kept her in trinkets. "Plus it keeps me social," she was fond of saying.

Xander curled his lip over the rim of his spoon just thinking about being social at a folk art show. She'd tried, many times, to get him to help her sell her wares, offering him more of a cut if he came along, but he'd always declined. Not his cup of tea, he told her. Over and over.

"So." She smiled at him as she paused mid-brushstroke. "My day has been full of exciting blood work and doctor's appointments. What have you been up to today?"

He finished chewing before he replied. "Helping the editor of *Lucky 7* pack up our supplies. We have to move out of Tori Hall." He frowned. "Blood work? Is everything okay?"

"Just routine checkup stuff. Nothing to worry about. I forgot they were renovating Tori Hall this summer." She waggled her eyebrows. "Maybe they'll find a shrine."

"Have you ever seen one?" She'd worked at Benten for twenty-five years. She might have.

"Takahiro and I looked, but we never found anything. We used to take *Lucky 7* staff on hunts, back in our day—he was their academic advisor, you know. But we never got anywhere."

Xander didn't even know who their academic advisor was now. "Do you honestly think the shrines exist?"

"I want to believe they do, so yes. Belief is powerful and important. Without it, we're nothing but ants crawling across the dirt." Her face took on a faraway, sad look as she continued to paint. "Takahiro always used to say that. I'd roll my eyes at him when he did, and now here I am, saying it for him."

Pamela talked about her late husband a lot. Xander

didn't mind, except that he hated how lonely Pamela sounded when she did. "I wish I could have met him."

"Oh, you've met him. We were soul mates, he and I. He's with me every day. He's just invisible now. Nagging me to stop being such a sad mouse and enjoy the life I have left." Her lips pursed, and she painted with a touch more terseness. "To *which* I tell him I'd like him to try being the one left behind and see how he handles things." She rolled her eyes. "Though he'd only wave his hand at me and tell me I'm doing fine. Takahiro was type A, like you. Maddeningly calm."

Pamela believed in the Asian blood type personality system and referred to it often. Xander, not so much. "I'm not calm."

"You are, though. You're calm and you avoid confrontation, as much as I, a type B, seek it out. And look, I knew I could erase that scowl, at least for a second. You were plenty cross when you came in here. Did they threaten to make your manga digital again?" When that brought his scowl back, she laughed. "Oh, there I go, ruining my own work."

Xander swirled his spoon in his soup. "I understand it would be easier for everyone else, and cheaper. But it changes my work in ways I don't like. Mostly I want them to wait one more year to switch so I don't have to deal with it."

"Unfortunately life likes to hand us challenges on its timetable, not ours." She glanced at him over the top of her glasses. "Not to get your back up, but wouldn't it be a good skill set, to learn how to use the digital software?"

"I already know how to draw digitally. I'm getting my BFA. I've had four digital drawing courses, and I own a drawing tablet of my own. It's not that I don't know how to do it. It's that I don't like it. It's not the same feel as marker or pencils, and I don't like that I have to look at the screen while my hand moves on the pad."

"Fair enough. Well, I wish you luck in your campaign of resistance."

Xander *hmpfed* and picked up his bowl to drink the remainder of his broth. He had a feeling he was going to need all the luck he could get.

Chapter Four

FIVE HOURS INTO background research on Xander Fairchild, Skylar was ready to admit it would have been wise to do this work *before* rashly promising his new client the moon.

"You're going to be wasted in law," everyone in the frat teased him, insisting he should open a business where he made marketing plans for people. Privately, Skylar agreed with them about being wasted in law, though he didn't want to make marketing plans for a living either. But his future career was a cauldron of regret he had no desire to stir.

He had a full pot with Xander Fairchild as it was.

Normally when doing this kind of thing, either for class or for practice, he worked up what he called a zip sheet: a digest of facts about the client, assets and liabilities, and his best prognosis for a plan. He gleaned the details from internet searches, company or client history, interviews, social media culls. He couldn't get anywhere with Xander's except that he'd gone to Mason City High School in Pennsylvania and that over the years he'd won several art contests. Most of those were elementary and middle school, but there'd been one in high school and a few here at Benten. Skylar wrote those down, but for facts, this was about it. After some *intense* digging, he was able to verify Xander was confirmed at Bethlehem Lutheran Church in Mason City, Pennsylvania.

No Instagram. No Twitter. No Tinder, no OKCupid, no Facebook, no Pinterest, *nothing*. Not even DeviantArt, which seemed to be some kind of graphic art showcase.

Skylar did get some hits from Benten itself, of course, from the mundane to the shocking. Xander had been in the requisite Benten art shows as part of his standard curriculum, which Skylar noted on his zip sheet as pertinent but not very helpful. There were a few minor awards and achievements from within the art department Skylar found as well.

And then Skylar found the *Lucky 7* website, where a small, three-line bio with an angry amine avatar said that Xander Fairchild was the head *mangaka* for *The Adventures of Hotay & Moo*.

Skylar couldn't help it, he gasped, and he…well, he put his hand over his heart.

He'd been reading the student magazine since he was a freshman, and so had Unc. They discussed it every time a new issue came out, arguing over the Shinto references and debating where the plot would go next. *Xander drew that?* The very thought made Skylar's heart beat faster.

He felt ridiculous for not putting two and two together before, but he hadn't gone to the website and looked up *who* drew the manga. Which was unlike him, honestly. But *Hotay & Moo* was a guilty pleasure, an escape from the strict path of his life, so he supposed it made sense that he'd only immersed himself in the story and not explored further. The dots were connected now, though. His guilty pleasure was drawn by Xander Fairchild.

He didn't know how to put that in his zip sheet, but…damn, he kind of wanted an autograph.

Skylar forced himself to move on from *Hotay & Moo* and get back to the business of hunting down information that would help him build a profile on Xander, but it quickly became clear the only way he'd get that information was to interview the man himself. Except Skylar felt if he showed up to start that process with nothing flashier than *I know you were raised Missouri Synod Lutheran and won an award from your public library*, his recalcitrant subject would shut down and give him nothing.

Skylar was desperate. He was on fire with the thrill of uncertainty, of impossibility. He dug deeper. And deeper. He found a thin network of people who had to be classmates of Xander's in high school and stalked *them*. Not their present but their past, their deep, social media archives. He hunted *their* profiles, combing through everything like a madman, looking for a crumb, a hint, an anything.

At two in the morning, he found it, and he was almost sorry.

He nearly missed the nest of threads. It was on Facebook in 2011, bleeding into 2012, in a series of conversations between twenty people, exchanges it was clear he only saw part of. At one point adults had intervened, which was when the public conversation ended. The initial exchange remained, and it was damning.

There wasn't one post that did it—they were subtle but persistent jabs. Little digs where the way they kept saying *Xander Fairchild* made Skylar think they'd tagged him but the account was now gone. Mocking his clothes. Suspecting a fart in class as coming from him. Essentially Xander's peers made it clear he was their scapegoat for teenage angst in every way, every form. Consuming the comments in one sitting, it was clear Quasimodo looked like a golden boy compared to the Mason City teenagers' construction of Xander Fairchild. Yet *only* in such a condensed read did it seem horrific. The comments were distributed over months and scattered across profiles. Of course, Skylar acknowledged grimly, *Xander* would have received them all.

Then, after the start of the year in 2012, the comments took a turn.

Xander Fairchild is a faggot.

Xander Fairchild wants to suck cock.

I saw Xander Fairchild looking at my ass. OMG, barf.

If I catch Xander Fairchild drooling at me, I'm punching him in the face.

Then all comments ceased.

Skylar closed the window, leaned back in his chair, and shut his eyes. No social media, Xander had said. *No friends.* Skylar had thought, maybe, he had an introvert on his hands. He suspected he still did. Now he acknowledged he had a *damaged* introvert.

He spun his chair sideways to study the painting on his wall. Maybe it was conceit or affectation after reading those horrible posts, but the painting that had captivated him for a week turned abruptly haunting and sad. That was indeed a man in the foreground, staring out at a…sea. Of feelings. Of rage, of sadness, of longing. Beautiful, terrible longing. Viewing it in the dim light of his desk lamp only intensified the aesthetic.

He'd dug deep in a pile of bones, so of course he'd found skeletons. He feared he'd never be able to look at the painting again without feeling guilty for violating Xander's privacy. Obviously the guy had left social media because he wanted no association with it, and he had good reason to make that decision. Yet if Skylar *hadn't* stumbled onto this boil, he'd have accidentally lanced it in attempts to nudge Xander out of what seemed like a ridiculous refusal. Skylar had his arguments all ready. Some of them he'd still have to use, as the art department made it clear they expected some social media promotion.

Knowing what he knew now, though, Skylar would never push Xander the way he'd originally intended.

He brushed his teeth and climbed into boxers, then lay in his bed a long time, staring at the painting.

His phone buzzed, and he glanced at it—Carolyn again. Frowning, Skylar turned the phone over.

He put in his earphones, logged into his tablet, and queued up a show, watching until his eyes started closing and he couldn't read the subtitles, at which point he gave up and let sleep claim him. When he slept, he dreamed of painted whorls that chased him into darkness, chattering at him in languages he couldn't understand. He was in high school again, running down a hall, looking for something he couldn't find, until he finally escaped to the roof, where he stared at the sunset and wept silent tears while his uniform tie whipped in the breeze.

At seven in the morning, he woke feeling disoriented and jumbled. But as sleep sloughed away, it revealed an idea formed in the back of his mind. He stared at the ceiling for a half hour, letting it expand and fall and rebuild itself.

At seven thirty he got up, padded downstairs to get a mug of coffee from the Keurig, and woke his computer from its sleep. He opened a new zip sheet template and filled it effortlessly, a profile he'd never share with his client, the deep analysis which would help him create the actual zip sheet he'd take to their coffee meeting on Sunday.

Xander Fairchild, 21, Bachelor of Fine Arts junior. Paints in oils.

NOTE: Also is a manga artist.

Born in Mason City, Pennsylvania. Attended

Bethlehem Lutheran Church, Missouri Synod.

NOTE: Missouri Synod not LGBT accepting. Bullied online in middle/high school, possibly in real life as well.

NOTE: RL bullying impossible to confirm without direct question, but likely, given facts about bullying in general.

CLIENT GOAL: To have successful art show via effective marketing and promotional campaign, particularly via social media.

ASSETS: Client is talented visual artist. Has won awards. (verify GPA, other flair)

LIABILITIES: Client is antisocial and resistant to social media promotions and direct contact with public. In fact, direct engagement will likely upset client and possibly affect his ability to work.

DIAGNOSIS/PLAN: Client must be aided in all steps through professional promotion and with a careful hand. Client must be schooled in all aspects of social engagement, not only to maximize potential but to eradicate unease in said social situations.

Marketing and promotional manager must convince client to enter these lessons. Most likely means of doing so is to become his friend.

Skylar sat back and sipped his coffee as he reread what he'd written. Xander had serious walls to climb, and only a genuine, honest attempt to breach them would work. Once that had happened, Skylar would have the Herculean task of convincing Xander he could trust other people too, helping him find them. And he'd have to lead him into even the most basic social media exchanges without letting on he knew exactly why they were land mines.

Skylar smiled around the rim of his mug. *God* but he loved a challenge.

When he set the coffee cup down, his gaze fell on the fat LSAT study guide, and some of his good mood deflated. Unbidden, the image of his father materialized in his mind's eye, glowering and judgmental, demanding to know why Skylar was fixating on a mousy art student instead of doing his best to ensure he got a high enough score to get into Yale Law.

Skylar pushed the manual and mental image aside, shifting his gaze to the painting hanging on his wall. He focused on the fat brushstrokes, on the nebulous figure staring out at the wild sea of color.

Then he took another swig of coffee and dove back into Xander Fairchild's zip sheet.

THE DAY XANDER met Skylar Stone to hear the marketing plan he absolutely didn't want yet decidedly had to endure, they met at the Kanahe Trail Java House. Xander intended to arrive half an hour early to stake out his favorite table by the fireplace, but he got distracted with a sketch and suddenly he'd had to work to avoid being *late,* forget early. Which meant he remembered to run a comb through his hair at the last minute and tossed a flannel on over his painting T-shirt instead of dithering over what to wear. He wasn't sure if he should bring anything, so he chucked a steno book and a few functional pens into his satchel and took off.

When he arrived at the coffeehouse, it was overflowing with patrons, and it looked as if every table was taken. There was space at the other end of one of the couches, but Xander didn't have words for how much he did *not* want to have the conversation while trying not to accidentally snuggle Skylar. He was so busy scouring for empty seats he'd overlooked he didn't see Skylar approaching until his greeting made Xander startle.

"Thanks for coming." Skylar held out his hand for Xander to shake, which he did, awkwardly. Skylar wasn't wearing a suit this time, but he hadn't rushed a comb through his hair and thrown on a flannel, either. He wore cargo pants that somehow still managed to look dressy, and a close-fitting T-shirt Xander was sure he'd have a wet dream about later.

Xander nodded at the full seating area. "Sorry, I was going to come early and grab us a seat, but I got caught up."

Ting. There was that damn smile again. Xander noticed Skylar smelled like a magazine again too. "No worries. I got us a seat in the second study area, by the fireplace." Skylar indicated the line for placing orders. "What can I get you?"

It quickly became clear it'd be easier to let Skylar

buy him a drink than talk the guy out of it, so Xander settled on a café au lait and a croissant. Skylar ordered a sugar-cookie latte, and when they both had their drinks, he led them to the table, which was pretty much where Xander had wanted to get a seat.

"I tried to do as much advance work as I could." Skylar passed over a three-hole-punched folder with professional-looking headers and notes as well as some blank spaces Xander assumed were for questions. "I'd like to conduct an interview with you today so I can finish fleshing things out and give you a few different proposals. I also want to make sure I understand the breadth of what the department wants of you. I don't want to conflate my expectations from *my* studies with the actual needs of your exhibit."

This guy was so intense it made Xander exhausted simply watching him spin like a top. He pulled at the edge of his croissant as he sorted out a reply. He settled on, "Okay."

Ting. "Fantastic. Let's start with some basics. Where are you from?"

"Mason City, Pennsylvania."

"And you're twenty-one? Or twenty?"

"Twenty-one. I'll turn twenty-two in December."

"Oh?" This smile was less *ting* and more regular human. "When? Hopefully not too close to Christmas. I'm January fourth, and it's always some sort of pathetic Christmas afterbirth."

That weird visual made Xander's lips quirk a smile against his will. "December thirteenth. It's not much better on the other side."

Skylar lifted his mug and gave a sad salute before sipping the foam. "If it's okay, I need a little info on your life before college. We won't use much, but I need something for the postcard."

"Postcard?"

"Sorry—that's not literal, just my shorthand for this kind of information. This would be the kind of stuff you'd put on an About page on a website, what we'd pull bios from for interviews and promotions. We want a broad postcard to build that from—nobody but you and I will see this full version. And yet this is a selective self-history. If you chain-smoked your way through high school and cursed your family farm, we don't say *that.* We spin that into something a little more palatable. Packaged, if you will." He put down his pen and turned over his hands so his palms extended like an offering. "For example. You and me, sitting here drinking coffee, I'll tell you I'm the only child of two aggressive, successful people, and there are moments that's great and moments it's so much pressure I can't breathe. On my postcard, though, I talk about how living in Greenwich, Connecticut, watching my father practice law and my mother run her own company, I was instilled with the desire to help others and succeed in business. My bio is much more polished than that, with buzzwords tailored to whatever I'm aiming at."

Xander was going to need a Tylenol before this was over, he could already tell. "You have a bio? Why?"

"I have several bios. Some are brief ones on social

media and networking sites. I have some information loaded on generic hosting services, but I have my own website as well, because I want my own flagship space where I can build my brand. Stand out from the crowd a little."

"I don't have any websites. Or bios. Or postcards."

Ting. "I know. That's why I'm here, to help you figure out which ones you want. Or more to the point, what kind of presence will be something you're comfortable maintaining and what will satisfy the requirements of your department and promote your show. So." He took up his pen once more. "Don't fluff it up. Tell me how you'd describe your precollege life."

Xander picked at the croissant again. "I have three younger half brothers. They're my mom's. She's remarried, my birth father isn't. They divorced when I was two, and it was a mess, but it's better now." He sifted through his sea of experience, searching for a nugget he could offer up. "None of their professions particularly inspired me in any way. Mom's a secretary part-time at a dentist office. My stepdad is a machinist. My real dad is a real estate agent in California, but I don't have any contact with him outside of birthday cards with twenties in them."

"Why did you become an artist?"

"I don't know. I always doodled, and art was my favorite class. My aunt bought me an oil painting set for Christmas one year, and I liked it, so I kept buying canvas and new paint with my allowance, as well as sketchbooks and markers and so on. Took art in high school. Lots of art. A whole year of independent study."

"That's unusual, right? To take that much art?" When Xander gave a kind of shrug-nod, Skylar pressed on. "Why did you take so much art? What was the driving factor?"

It was independent study and meant I didn't have to be with anyone else in class. Not saying that. "I've never...been much of a people person. And I do like painting. So I used independent study to be by myself and work."

"Perfect. Okay, give me a minute, then tell me what you think."

Skylar scribbled on his notebook, pausing twice to sip his drink. Xander watched him awkwardly, unsure what Skylar was doing and what *he* was supposed to do in the meantime. He drank his coffee, studying the shadows and highlights of Skylar's face, absently plotting the colors he'd use to paint him. Debated brushstrokes to catch the perfect falls of his hair. The crisp folds of his clothes. The smooth perfection of his skin.

God, the guy was *too* perfect. Xander wanted to draw him, paint him, uncover the parts of this guy he didn't want the world to see. Because the more he studied Skylar Stone, the more Xander wanted to find the flaws. Would they ruin the beauty, or crack him open to reveal a treasure all the more breathtaking?

Xander's fingers itched to put down the sketches his mind was already mapping out. The shape of his ear. Line of his neck...Xander could lose himself shading that for an hour.

God, he wanted to run his finger down it, memorize the curve…

Xander cleared his throat and focused on his coffee.

After five minutes Skylar put down the pen, lifted the legal pad slightly, and read aloud. "'Xander Fairchild grew up in picturesque Mason City, Pennsylvania, the eldest of a boisterous family. When his aunt gave him the gift of an oil painting set for Christmas, he discovered a creative escape and nurturing space in visual arts. The opportunity to take intensive art classes and several courses of independent study allowed him to enrich and practice his skills, leading to—'" Skylar paused, glancing at Xander. "What I'm hoping I can say here is that you won some awards. If not, I can spin it in another direction."

"I won a few, I guess. They weren't particularly fantastic, though."

"Doesn't matter. Any scholarships?"

"Yes, but they're not anything important. Just the standard ones Benten hands out for grades."

Skylar waved this away. "No worries. But *anything* you can think of that singles you out, tell me. Even if the scholarship or award wasn't directly related to art. If you won some big thing everybody in art knows about, we'll trumpet that, but if not, we're basically giving you some flair."

Xander wrinkled his nose. "This is like that movie. *Office Space* or something?"

"Right. Except it's not a joke. You need shiny things

to wave at people. We're taking the initial steps of crafting your brand. This is the you that isn't exactly you. It's not lies, it's not bullshit, but it's not you spreading your shirt open and showing your naked chest."

Even though Skylar had specifically said that *wasn't* what he was doing, Xander pulled his shirt a little tighter. "Is this really necessary? All I'm supposed to do is put forth a good-faith effort in advertising my show."

"This isn't simply advertising your show. This is laying track for postgraduate shows you might have. This is the foundation of a *career*."

This was so much bullshit. "I won't have a *career*. Not in hosting shows. Not like this."

"But that's just it." Skylar tapped the legal pad with the tip of his pen. "This postcard, these bios, this plan—it exists so you don't *have* to be this person. Not all the time. Not all the way. The Xander Fairchild we create here is your shield. He takes the dings so you don't have to." The *ting* in his smile eased into something gentle, pretty. "You can focus your energy on making more great paintings."

The smile got to Xander, so he prickled. "Anybody ever point out you'd make a great snake oil salesman?"

"In fact, they have." He poised the pen over the pad. "Just a few more questions, and then I'll work up your prospectus. Okay?"

What choice did he have? Xander slumped over his coffee and stared glumly at the legal pad. "Fine."

The rest of the interview was more of the same,

Xander barfing up his mediocre background and Skylar spinning it into something shinier. He had to admit, the finished product wasn't bad. It would look great on a flyer and on his space on the department website, which was currently a blank square with *coming soon* in faded gray beside a generic profile silhouette. He wondered if he dared ask Skylar to help him get a decent headshot.

"I'll email you some branding worksheets. If you could at least wrestle with them a little before we meet next time, that'd be a big help. But don't worry if you get stuck. They're just something to nudge you toward thinking about packaging yourself." Skylar leaned back in his chair as he sipped his drink. "Which brings me to my next question. When would you like to get together next?"

Xander shrugged, rubbing his thumb along the rim of his mug. "Whenever. I'm usually free after five, except when I have studio time. Then I'm out at seven." He paused, remembering Pamela and her whims. "Unless I get called in to work."

"Why don't we meet after your studio time, barring a call from work? I'm assuming that puts you at one of the art buildings, and they're near my fraternity. We could find somewhere in the department and use my room as a backup."

It'd be a cold day in hell before Xander entered a fraternity, especially Delta Eta Sigma. "The Java House is fine."

"Sure. Wherever you're the most comfortable." Skylar removed the stylus from the side of his phone and dragged it around on his calendar. "Would Thursday work for you, or do you want more time to go over the worksheets?"

Xander had no idea how long he'd need, only knew the sooner he dealt with this unpleasantness, the sooner it'd be over. "Thursday's fine."

"Great." *Ting.* "You've got my information. Call, text, or email if you need anything at all. I'm utterly at your disposal."

With a grunt, Xander scooped up his empty mug and left the table. After dropping his dishes into the tub by the coffee bar, he hefted his backpack onto his hunched shoulders, tucked his head down, and began the trek back to his apartment.

It wasn't as bad as he'd imagined it would be. He didn't enjoy any of it, and he doubted he ever would, but he thought he could endure enough to get through. After all, how long could it take to get a social media campaign set up?

Feeling moderately hopeful for the first time ever about his project, Xander hiked his backpack higher on his shoulders and rounded the corner to cut through the south side of campus. He was behind the science building when he heard a familiar, shrill voice shouting his name.

"*Xander Fairchild, stop right where you are.*"

Xander turned around, frowning as he squinted across the sidewalk. It was Zelda, the closest thing he had to a friend, if you were liberal with the definition. "Zelda, what's wrong—?"

He cut himself off as Zelda came closer, and he saw the image on the screen of the smartphone they were holding out.

Zelda glared at him, shaking the phone in Xander's face, which had an Instagram of Skylar smiling at Xander (who was scowling) at the coffee shop on it. "Explain to me what in the *hell* you were doing at Java House having coffee with a fucking Greek?"

Xander's gut twisted, wondering who had taken the picture and why, what they'd captioned it with, who had seen it, how many people were laughing—he shut his eyes and took a deep breath, doing his best to stop the avalanche. "It's a long, stupid story."

"Tell me all about it." Zelda tucked their phone into their pocket and linked arms with Xander, frog-marching him toward the art building. "I *love* long, stupid stories."

Chapter Five

XANDER TRIED TO explain to Zelda about the BFA exhibition, about Peterson and the Delta Eta Sigma vandalism turning into a public service project. But Zelda wouldn't let him get through the sentence before they had their phone out again, flashing social media pages at Xander faster than he could register them.

"Do you understand who you just put your project in the hands of? Do you have any earthly idea? No, you don't, because you're so far offline you're in 1989. *Skylar Stone,* Xan. His sophomore year, he was the youngest president of Delta Eta Sigma in the history of Benten. He's been president of like seven different clubs. I think he has six majors or something."

"He told me he had two."

This earned him no points from Zelda, who waved their phone again. "*A Greek,* Xan. The Greek of Greeks. He's dated half of the Tau-Kapps, though never for very long, and only the richest, prettiest members. I saw him with Carolyn Hawthorne, *president* of the Tau-Kapps, just a few weeks ago, when I was protesting an event. *He* was her fucking date to that shitshow. I've heard rumors he's dated a few guys too, but even there only fellow

Greeks, and only the *prettiest* gay Greeks. Disgusting."

No, what was disgusting was how the thought that Skylar might be bisexual made Xander's heart flutter with hope. He said nothing, though, because he did not have a death wish.

Zelda finally put the phone away. "Do you know where he's from?"

The coffee shop conversation rewound in Xander's mind. "Greenwich, Connecticut?" When Zelda's eyes widened in cold fury, he held up his hands. "*Sorry,* I thought you were asking, I swear!"

They aimed a finger at him. "Are you *attracted* to this jerk, Xander?"

Oh, fucking hell. Xander shook his head and frantically filtered a full formal denial carefully. Zelda was a proud aromantic asexual, and while they of course didn't object to other people having relationships or even pining for them, they absolutely did have strong views about people pining after Greeks. "No. No, Zelda, I swear, and if you'd let me explain—"

Zelda was not in the mood to let him explain. "Do you know what that means, when someone is from Greenwich? *His* part of Greenwich?"

Xander didn't, but even if he'd done a research paper on the damn place, he'd have shaken his head and waited for the next part of the lecture.

Zelda put their hands on their hips and tipped up their chin in triumph. "He's a *one percenter.* He's a one percent of the one percent. His mother owns a company. His father is a partner in a Manhattan investment law firm. He wasn't born with a silver spoon in his mouth because silver spoons aren't good enough for people like him. His was platinum." They sneered and gestured vaguely in the direction of Greek Row. "*He* is a snake because he's a smooth talker. They call him Silver Stone. He always gets what he wants. Everyone loves him. And if you tell me you do too, I'll empty your drawer right now and smash every one of your brushes."

As threats went, it would have been a terrible one, except Zelda had made it a thousand times before and had yet to carry it out. The only one worse would be if they promised harm to his nibs, though those he kept safely stored at his apartment. But if Zelda was threatening his supplies, it was code they were serious about something, so he took the situation seriously.

"I don't love him, no. I find him annoying on the whole, to be honest. But the department saddled me with him, and he *is* giving me good ideas for the requirements for this stupid social media crap."

Zelda folded their arms over their chest. "*I* would have helped you with the stupid social media crap. I can't believe you didn't ask me."

Xander suppressed a shudder. This was the one blessing in Peterson's dictate that Skylar help him, that Zelda wouldn't have a chance to. Zelda loved social media far too much and was always trying to drag Xander kicking and screaming onto any and every platform they could manage. "Well, what's done is done. This is his grade too now, so we'll all make the best of it. I'm kind of hoping we can do it over the summer and have it locked and loaded by the time classes start in the fall." He sighed. "I suppose he'll go home, though, which means to do that I'll need to learn Skype or something. Gross."

"Oh, no. Skylar Stone famously never goes home over summer term. And I still think you're wrong. He has to have more than two majors."

"He only told me about the two." Xander felt weird, knowing more about Skylar than Zelda, and he vowed to let them be right about the next fact, even if he'd heard differently from the source himself. "I'm glad he'll be on campus. Saves me navigating tech, and I'll be able to get the stupid social media requirement set up for sure. He'll have his project done and so will I before we're officially seniors."

"You still have to actually do your show." Zelda nudged his portfolio on the table. "Have you decided what you're going to do? Painting or drawing?"

"Painting, probably. I don't know what yet." But he wasn't worried about that. He never stressed about art projects. Those always seemed to come to him at the right moment.

"I figured. Speaking of drawing, though. You skipped the last *Lucky 7* meeting, and you shouldn't have, because some shit went down. I know what you're going to say, and I don't want to have the argument, but I thought you should know that Cory supports the move to digital. Be ready."

Xander's whole body went rigid. Cory was the layout and printing specialist for *Lucky 7.* If *he* had taken up the digital crusade, Xander was fucked. "I guess it was inevitable. I just hate the way it prints. I know you don't notice the difference, but—"

"You misunderstood me. Cory wants to do a digital *edition.* No print."

Holy. Fucking. Shit. "What the *hell*? This is the first I've heard of this. What the *fucking shit*—"

Zelda shut him down with a glare and an index finger. "I *said*, I don't want to have the argument."

"Jesus *Christ*, Zel! No print *at all*? It's *not the same.* I assume this has to do with saving money—"

"—it does—"

"—but manga isn't like a newspaper or regular magazine. It's harder to follow when it's digital. It doesn't have the same look and feel, either. The saturation is different. The whole *experience* is different, both for the reader and the artist."

"Hey, remind me again of the logline under *Lucky 7*'s masthead?"

Not this shit again. "Don't get cute, not with this."

"*Forming new straight lines.* Times change, Xan. And printing budgets get cut, especially when readership falls."

This was ten thousand times worse than having to join social media. "So you're telling me it's already been decided?"

"Unless you can invent us a new budget for the fall semester, yes. I'm sorry. He's run it by Jacob, and Sara's on board too."

Xander wanted to puke. "You know even less people will read us now. *Lucky 7* is as good as dead. This is a new straight line right into the fucking garbage dump."

Zelda looked as grim as he felt, but without the anger, only resignation. "Maybe you can get your brilliant new lab partner to save *Lucky 7* when he's done launching your BFA show." When Zelda saw the thoughtful expression on Xander's face, they leapt off the table. "*I'm kidding.* Jesus. Don't scare me like that."

"I care a lot more about that manga than I do my stupid show."

"I know. And that's messed up, by the way, those priorities. Which is your answer right there. You should do a manga show for your BFA."

Xander laughed. "Good one."

Zelda wasn't laughing. "I'm serious. You can't use Hotay or Moo, obviously, but it's not like they're the only characters in the world. Make up new ones."

"It doesn't work like that. Even if we assumed I could convince the art department to take manga art style seriously—highly doubtful, by the way—please remember I *borrow* Hotay and Moo. They arrived prepackaged. Do you even understand the history behind them? I couldn't write something as awesome as them in a million years. I can't write anything. I paint and draw things already there. I can draw them in realistic style or manga style, but I can't make them up out of thin air."

"Then find something that exists and make that into a manga and turn that into your project."

"Oh my God, I'm not going to explain the creative process to a goddamned communications major. I'm fucking *not*."

They threw up their hands. "Fine. All I'm saying is if you feel this passionately about it, the odds are good this is where you should put your efforts."

Xander didn't want to argue anymore. "Point taken. Can I go now? I have all these stupid forms I have to fill out for Mr. Greek, and I still want to paint."

"Whatever. I have to catch the bus to the airport anyway. But you're keeping me updated on this project stuff until I get back to town."

Zelda was from Maine, and they had to go home to help with the family business until the second week in July, after which time they'd be back on campus to torment Xander with what passed for them as friendship. "I'm not joining social media just so you can stalk me."

"No, you're joining social media for your senior project." Zelda patted him on the shoulder. "I'll be sure to look for you and friend you right away."

Grumbling, Xander hiked his backpack onto his shoulder, grabbed his folio from the table, and hurried out of the building.

SKYLAR THOUGHT THE meeting with Xander had gone pretty well. Not quite as perfectly as he'd wanted, but that was okay. Room for improvement was just fine.

He'd fired the worksheets off to Xander before he

left the coffee shop, pulling out his laptop and joining the Java House's Wi-Fi to send the files to Xander. He'd also taken a moment to type up his notes from their meeting as well, filling out Xander's postcard and fleshing out his own observations in his private notebook.

> *Reluctance regarding the project remains intense, and even my best efforts to show empathy and make connections barely penetrate. Repeated, more subtle connections essential for easing Xander's barriers.*

Thoughts about Xander lingered as Skylar drove back to Delta Sig. *Reluctant* had probably been the wrong adjective to describe Xander. *Hostile* was a lot closer. Skylar wasn't sure he'd ever met anyone so suspicious and pessimistic. He understood *why*, given what he'd dug up about the guy's past, but… Well, he wanted to argue that no one bullied him here at Benten, but the truth was he couldn't say that wasn't happening with certainty. Having his mural spray-painted certainly didn't help anything. Even if there hadn't been any incidents here on campus, Skylar conceded Xander's past might make him unwilling to let anyone get close enough to hurt him.

Years of resisting, with just cause or not, had to have made for some pretty thick walls. And now the art department wanted at least three social media holes in his battlements.

There had to be a way in, though, some topic or issue related to Xander he could use as a springboard for the social media campaign. Skylar just couldn't find it. He'd almost brought up *Hotay & Moo*, and he felt ridiculous that he hadn't been able to get over himself enough to do so. He'd actually *choked* at the thought. The rational part of his brain had formed the idea of bringing up the manga as an achievement, and the fanboy Skylar hadn't known lurked inside him had squealed and tackled the rational brain, muzzling it quick before it could so much as bluster its way toward the subject. It unsettled him just thinking he had such an element in him, and he decided it would be best that he never bring up the manga at all. If Xander did, he'd deal with the subject when the time came.

Maybe Skylar should start hanging around the art department more often. If he was going to find an answer to unlock Xander, the odds were he'd find it there in the man's home base, and Skylar had a great excuse with his project. It might not be a bad strategy to ask for office space. A shelf in a supply cupboard and a card table in a lounge would be more than adequate.

This idea percolated in Skylar's head through the rest of that day, and on his way to an LSAT cram session the following day he swung by Dr. Peterson's office to formally make the request.

He didn't have to sell the idea very hard, because Peterson beamed and nodded as Skylar made the pitch, then fell over himself to fulfill it. "I'd be happy to find you some space. It won't be much, but I can get you a drawer or two for supplies and put you on the rotation for office hours without any trouble." His smile widened, lighting his gray eyes. "I must say, you're an example to your fraternity, Mr. Stone." His smile dimmed a bit as he continued. "And I'll be honest, it's a relief to hand Xander Fairchild off to you. He's a gifted artist, but he's reaching Van Gogh levels of antisocial temperament."

"It's my pleasure to help both him and the department. Though now that you bring it up, I've been meaning to ask—does he have some acquaintances here in the department? I'd like to begin by integrating his local network. Even if I have to reach out to people who have gone home for the summer—I thought I could start by hooking them up to his social media accounts, for example."

Peterson grimaced. "This is what I'm trying to tell you. He doesn't talk to anyone. There are a few individuals from the communications department he talks to because of *Lucky 7*, but that's about it for students. It's the only part of the college he participates in at all outside of classes. He barely speaks to the faculty. On the rare occasion there are group projects, he either does an alternate project himself or stands in the back of whatever group is asked to absorb him by the professor. He glowers at anyone who tries to connect with him, but he never gets in so much as an argument with his peers. He's as skilled at staying out of the way as he is at painting and drawing. Though, he is known for giving good advice to fellow artists, when they can get him to give it. You have your work cut out for you, getting him to socialize enough to promote a show."

Skylar understood this truth more and more every day. "His work is incredible, though. I should think this more than makes up for an artistic temperament."

"Twenty years ago? Maybe. But everyone has talent these days, and even exceptional people need a megaphone to be heard. I'll be honest. I don't think he's going to be able to navigate a career in the visual arts. Maybe he'll be able to sell his work on the side, but..." Peterson shrugged, then smiled. "Come on. Let me show you to your space."

The area Peterson led Skylar to was a cubicle, Skylar's assigned drawer the bottom slot of modular white shelving. He was introduced to the student secretary, who helped him schedule some office hours between his other cube mates' claimed spaces and his own burgeoning calendar. Given that it was the summer, the place was mostly empty, though it seemed a number of art students lingered to work on their BFA projects, like Xander. They were eager to talk to Skylar and hear his ideas for implementing social media strategy and were grateful for his help.

*Un*like Xander.

Skylar roamed the halls, quietly injecting himself into conversations, introducing himself as the liaison between Delta Eta Sigma and the art department. He passed out cards, explained his theories of social media navigation, and gave a few casual pointers to interested parties. And whenever he could maneuver it into conversation, he asked about Xander.

Almost no one knew him, and those who did had nothing much to say.

"He's that junior, right? Well—senior now? Works in oils?" Deanna, a graphic design major, wrinkled her nose as she tried to dredge up more intel. "I've had a few classes with him, but I've never talked to him. He doesn't seem to like people very much. Though he did help a friend of mine with the color scheme of her painting, and she said it saved her grade. And his mom makes the *best* cookies."

Camden, a senior photography student, had a similar story. "Sat beside him in seminar last term. Let me borrow a pencil a few times, gave me some offhand advice about composition that made a huge difference in the way I approached my work. Impossible to deal with, but he's a brilliant artist. Never comes to any department events unless he's required, and he hangs out in the back, like he's waiting for his sentence to be up." His face lit up as he added, "The *cookies*, though."

Camden was the fifth person to bring up Xander's mother's cookies, and Skylar decided he had to get more information. "I keep hearing about these cookies. I'm going to have to look out for one of those boxes, clearly."

"They're *amazing.* Xander's mom makes them and *mails them* to him every few weeks in this huge box, and he brings them to the art department. It's like, you can be having the worst day ever, and then you see that box coming and you know everything is going to be okay. She makes all different kinds of cookies, but they're all good. I mean, I cried once when I had a snickerdoodle, because they reminded me of my grandmother."

Skylar couldn't believe this. Antisocial Xander brought cookies from his mother for the art department? Every two weeks? "Why does Xander give the cookies away?"

Camden held up his hands and shook his head. "Dude. I don't know, but I don't ask. He never eats them, that much I know. He doesn't even open the box. He drops it off and leaves."

This information gave Skylar more questions than answers, but it was certainly interesting.

The only real lead Sky got at all was from Eden, who'd done a group project with Xander sophomore year. "He's super nice, once you get to know him, but it's hard because he doesn't let anyone in. I tried to get him to hang out with our class, but he always had an excuse why he couldn't. It's like the more you try to get him to join you, the harder he pushes you away. I think he's probably the most antisocial person I've ever met."

Antisocial. Over and over again, that was the word people used to describe Xander Fairchild. Some called him a snob, but most simply had no opinion. They thought his work was pretty good, but otherwise Xander might as well have been a ghost in his own building.

As if to prove this observation, Xander appeared. Clutching the strap of his backpack, hunched forward, hair in his eyes, Xander made no eye contact, but Sky could see his gaze flicking back and forth across his path. No one seemed moved by his appearance, however. The only acknowledgment of his presence came from a large group who had to shift to the side and narrow their spread across the traffic path, though Xander skulked as close to the rail overlooking the atrium as possible.

When his scan took in Skylar, Xander faltered and slowed his walk, his focused expression morphing into a glower tinted with wariness.

Skylar smiled and offered a quiet wave.

Xander's scowl deepened and he shifted closer to the rail.

Antisocial? Skylar was starting to think that was the understatement of the year.

Skylar was about to approach Xander when a girl came up to him. She had a Tau-Kapp pin on her bag, something Skylar noticed because she was holding it with clear intent to make sure he saw it. "Skylar?" Her smile widened and she tilted her head to the side. "Hi. It's Amber. We met at Carolyn's party?"

Oh, hell. Skylar saw Xander scuttle farther away. "It's nice to see you again, Amber. I'm sorry, but I need to—"

She shifted to block his view of Xander, her expression going from hyper-friendly to slightly intense. "I was hoping we could get together sometime."

Fuck. Skylar didn't glare at her, but he was firm nearly to the point of curt as he replied, stepping around her to trail Xander. "Now's not a good time," he told her, and cut around a group of freshmen.

But by the time he got to the atrium railing, Xander was already gone.

WHEN IT WASN'T raining, Xander generally ate his lunch near the hospital behind Benten's art campus. He sat on an old stone bench which was slightly sloped, as one end had settled into the ground over time and one had not. The tree the bench was beneath had a tendency to drop twigs and, for most of the fall, annoying little seed things that stuck to people's hair. He wore a hoodie during seed season, propped the edge of his backpack under the side of his ass affected by the lopsided seat, and all his problems were solved. No one ever took his spot. No one ever asked to share it.

No one, that was, until the day Skylar Stone sauntered up the hill, perfect smile glinting, hand waving a greeting.

"Fancy meeting you here." Skylar stopped in front of Xander, slipping his hands into the pockets of his chinos. He looked like an Abercrombie ad, oxford shirt untucked but not sloppy, brown chukkas rugged but not rough, an olive cardigan draped over his leather messenger bag.

In his three-year-old jeans, Keds knockoffs with flapping soles, ragged plaid shirt, and tee splattered with paint and stinking of turpentine, Xander looked like a reject from Goodwill. He grimaced at Skylar and nodded a greeting he hoped telegraphed he wanted to get back to eating his lunch in peace. "Hi."

He wasn't surprised Skylar perched on the downward slope of the bench, but he did resent him for it.

Skylar ignored Xander's glare and glanced around. "Wow. This is an incredible view."

It was, in fact. The trees framed the main campus buildings perfectly, with or without leaves, and the hill made a highly pleasing vista. The view was the *other* reason Xander sat here. But he didn't want to make small talk. He wanted to get rid of Skylar.

"Yes," Xander said, and went back to his sandwich.

"Takaketo is beautiful, especially the campus areas. I think the river helps a lot. Greenwich doesn't have anything like that. It's pretty enough, but I prefer Takeketo, I'll admit." He stared a few seconds more, sighed happily, and turned to Xander. "How's the homework I gave you? You haven't contacted me, so I assume everything's going well. File open okay?"

Xander hadn't so much as opened the email Skylar had sent him, let alone any files. He still had two days until they were supposed to meet. "Fine." He took a larger bite of sandwich.

"I've started a preliminary proposal, making a list of social media sites for you to consider, as well as some general advertising schemes. I'll tweak them, of course, once I get your information."

Xander continued to chew, willing Skylar to say, *Well, nice to see you, I have to get going,* and leave. If he didn't, Xander would have to come up with a different avoidance tactic. He was almost out of sandwich.

Skylar in fact said nothing at all, not for quite some

time. He seemed content to sit and soak in the sights of the crisp, slightly muggy summer day. Xander squirmed a little beside him, annoyed at himself for enjoying the way Skylar's scent mingled with the smell of earth and bark and tree. It wasn't unusual for Xander to be mildly attracted to a hot guy, but they usually didn't sit beside him and try to make small talk. It unnerved him, to the point he considered inventing an excuse to leave, except his lunch was still half-eaten and it would be obvious he was leaving to avoid Skylar.

He wouldn't mind being rude in the abstract, but in the specific he couldn't do it. Part of it was the old terror. He understood intellectually Skylar had no interest in bullying him, but his reptile brain kept whispering this was like the old days, when the popular kids would crowd him and pretend to be his friend, right before they stole his bag or his lunch or his gym clothes or dumped a trash can over his head.

He doesn't stink like a magazine ad today, though. This observation eased Xander for reasons he couldn't articulate.

Skylar shook his head, gazing across the river. "I don't do this enough. Sit and absorb the world around me. I always mean to, and then I never do. That's my biggest sin, not stopping to smell the roses. I think I should take lessons from you."

Xander couldn't help the snort of derision that escaped him. "That's probably the worst idea anybody has ever had."

He tensed, hating himself for saying that, hating

Skylar in advance for the nosy, probing questions which were inevitable after such a comment. But Skylar laughed in the same self-deprecating manner, then went quiet for another minute. Xander was starting to relax into the silence when Skylar spoke again.

"I can't stop staring at the painting you gave me."

Xander was back on alert, but he couldn't make himself say anything, dismissive or encouraging. He waited to see what else came after that comment.

There was plenty. "It changes every time I study it. It's as if my mood affects it. Not just what I see in it, but how bright or dark the colors are. I worried at first that meant I was losing my mind, but I asked the other guy staying for the summer in the frat house, and he said the same thing. He wanted to know if you had another painting he could buy from you."

Nothing on earth could have stopped the quiet wave of pleasure this remark gave Xander. "That's what art does. Speaks to deep parts of us, usually ones we can't access any other way." He gripped his sandwich tighter as he ground the sticky gears of his manners. "I'm...glad you were able to see yourself in mine." He ignored the part about the total stranger allegedly wanting to buy his art, assuming it was nothing more than a line.

Skylar smiled, not his *ting* but the gentler one that made something behind Xander's balls tingle. "Me too." The smile turned regretful as he rose. "I'm ashamed to admit that even though I should probably sit here for another hour and bleed off more tension with your beautiful view, I need to get back to the LSAT studying making me stressed out in the first place. I was taking a walk to clear my head and happened to see you. I'm glad I did."

The comments about his painting and the way Skylar had managed to hint Xander was responsible for the *beautiful* view combined and made Xander a complete and utter idiot. "This bench is always open. Nobody sits here, because of the slope. But it's fine if you sit on the edge of a book or a bag."

Terror kept Xander's blush at bay at his bold offer. Skylar didn't notice his panic, only grinned. "I bet you sit here every day."

Now the blush crept up, hot, awkward fingers stealing across Xander's neck and cheeks until they reached his ears. "Pretty much. I'm here every day from quarter after noon until a little before one."

Why did you tell him that, you moron?

Skylar's smile widened, still no sign of that fake *ting*. "Like I said, I should be taking lessons. But I won't show up unannounced and poach on your private time. You were here first, after all."

"I don't mind." *God, why can't I shut up?*

Skylar seemed as surprised as Xander at the comment. At the *offer*. Xander wanted to take it back, tamp it down at the very least, but he was so busy trying not to throw up his sandwich he could only stare.

Skylar didn't laugh. He looked at Xander the way he had when he talked about Xander's painting. "Well. In that case, I'll try even harder to make the time."

He did leave then, which, thank God, because Xander didn't know what other kind of idiocy his brain would cook up. He simply watched Skylar leave, heart swelling like a fool's. Which was ridiculous. Skylar wasn't flirting with him. He was being friendly with the sad sack he'd been assigned to help, making the best of an awkward situation.

All the same, once Xander was home later that day, he inked out a panel of the view from his bench, which he'd done before. Except this time he added a man in the center, hands in his pockets, cardigan over his bag as he stared across the campus, a riot of emotion spilling like leaves around him.

Chapter Six

SKYLAR DIDN'T SHOW up Wednesday for lunch, and Xander kicked himself for feeling disappointed. It was stupid to have looked forward to it. He felt a little glum throughout the afternoon, but he felt better by the time he was back at his apartment for dinner, safe at home with Hokusai and Hiromu. He brushed Hiromu, threw a crinkle ball for Hokusai, and gave them both too many treats. They thanked him by snuggling up on either side of him that night, though not until they'd play-fought on the floor beside the bed for twenty minutes.

Thursday he woke early as usual, eager to sketch the morning away. That day, unfortunately, he had to forgo his favorite indulgence because he still hadn't filled out Skylar's social media forms. He spread them across the table and glared at them over the top of a cup of coffee, occasionally shifting his ire to Hokusai, who was convinced the papers were there for his amusement.

They certainly weren't fun for Xander. In fact, they were confusing, panic-inducing torture.

What makes you special? Who is your audience? Where do you see your career headed? Xander wanted to write *nothing, nobody,* and *nowhere.* He was seriously considering writing those answers down when his cell phone rang.

It took him a minute to find it, because he hadn't plugged it in since the last time it rang, and it was buried in a pile of junk mail on the kitchen counter. He caught himself hoping Skylar might be the one trying to reach him, which meant he was angry at himself all over again when it—of course—turned out to be his mother.

He glanced at the little readout that told him he had a low battery, then hunted for the charge cord while he spoke. "Hi, Mom."

"Hi, sweetheart. So glad I caught you. How's everything going?"

"Fine." He booted Hiromu off a pile of clothes in his bedroom, ignoring the cat's wounded look as he searched for—and didn't find—his charge cord.

"Did you get the care package I sent you?"

"I did. Thank you."

"Were the cookies okay? Did they get broken? I tried to pack them well, but you never know with the post office."

As usual, she'd wrapped them in individual parchment sheets, put four cookies at a time in quart Ziploc bags, put *those* in gallon bags, then put everything in bubble wrap and peanuts in a big box with FRAGILE, CONTENTS PERISHABLE written all over the outside, stamped with hearts. He hadn't eaten any, but the secretary had opened it while he was in the room. "They were fine."

She sighed in relief. "Good. I'm so glad. Classes going okay? How's your senior project?"

He had no idea how to explain Skylar Stone. "Everything's fine." He still couldn't find the cord, dammit. "How, um, are you?"

"I'm doing fine. Your grandmother called me this morning, talked my ear off for an hour about how upset she was over the neighbor doing something to her hedge. Goodness, tell me if I ever carry on like that." Then she proceeded to carry on for twenty minutes, just like that.

He found the cord as the phone began to beep its low battery warning, and he spent the rest of the phone call tethered to the outlet in the kitchen, listening to his mother explain the two-for-one bread sale at the grocery store and other inane bits of trivia drifting in and out of her mind.

Then her conversation turned to her husband and Xander's half brothers.

"Nick is taking the boys fishing this weekend. The whole house will smell like fish for a week, and I don't want to talk about the garage."

Xander didn't want to talk about Nick or his half brothers, but he couldn't tell his mother that. "I hope they have fun." Which was a lie. He hoped their boat capsized and they all drowned.

Okay, he hoped their boat capsized and they came out of the water on some distant shore where they were alive but never heard from again.

She continued to tell stories about her youngest

boys and her husband, and Xander kept quiet, picking up a pen to doodle angrily while she spoke. He listened to her chatter because even when it was about his stupid stepfather, he found the sound of her voice soothing.

But then her idle chatter shifted into something serious.

"Also, I meant to tell you. Nick said the transfer might be a little late this month."

Xander sat up straighter. "Wait—what do you mean, *a little late*?"

Her tone shifted from chirpy to distressed. "Honey, I don't know. He only asked me to tell you it was late."

"Mom, I pay rent with that money. Buy food. Pay my bills. I need to know when *late* is. Also, *why* is it late?"

She was seriously anxious now. "I don't really know. Something about a big expense coming up."

Xander shut his eyes and took a deep breath, reminding himself his mother was not the enemy, only the enabler. "Well, my rent is due on the tenth, and by the twelfth I'll be completely out of money and unable to eat. Just so you're aware of what his big expense costs me."

"But you have a job—"

"I have a *part-time* job with unstable hours, and I'm a full-time student in his last year of school, with a major project hanging over my head for the fall. I have to produce a full body of work for a show, which means I have to buy supplies, Mom. Paint and canvas. It's not cheap. This wasn't in our agreement. It wasn't what I planned for. And they're not going to accept a note from you saying you had an expense as an excuse for why I don't get my project completed."

"Xander, you don't have to be mean."

He rubbed his temple. He didn't want to be mean to her, but he was stressed and hurt. Once again the floor had been yanked from beneath his feet, and he was pretty sure it was because his jerk of a stepfather wanted to take his nasty half brothers on a fishing trip. Or it might be straight up to fuck with Xander.

Xander rolled his gaze to the ceiling and worked to keep his voice flat. "I have to go. Bye, Mom."

He hung up before she could start in on her rationalizations of Nick and make Xander angrier than he already was. He closed the phone, stared at it in impotent rage and disappointment.

Then stilled, realizing the phone was blinking at him. It said 1 UNREAD TEXT notification on the tiny, pixelated screen.

He had a text? Nobody texted him. His mother didn't like them, calling them too impersonal, and Zelda emailed after they'd learned the hard way he'd never answer a text. He assumed this was from them, trying again.

Except that stupid part of him that wouldn't shut up thought, *Maybe it's from Skylar.*

He almost didn't read it, but he decided in the end it would be a better punishment to show himself it was Zelda or a wrong number. He glared at the readout as he fumbled through the buttons, trying to remember how to call up text messages.

His breath hitched as he saw, in fact, it *was* from Skylar. The number matched the one on the business card he'd taped to his fridge.

Sorry I missed you at lunch yesterday. Can I join you today and bring lunch from Breadgarden, my treat?

Xander put the phone down and backed away from it slowly.

He didn't know how to respond. Should he say no? Probably. He didn't eat on the hill on Thursdays, since he didn't have studio time until two. And he still had the stupid forms to fill out.

Also, it was clear he was having some kind of Stockholm syndrome over Skylar because of their forced contact due to their projects. This wasn't good. He should back away before things got worse.

So, he should decline to go, or better yet, not answer the text and say he didn't see it, yes? Without the phone call from his mother, he wouldn't have.

That seemed the best course of action, so he followed it. He even buried the phone under the junk mail again, putting his back to it as he sat back down with the branding forms.

What makes you special?

Xander did his best to put his head in the game. He pushed aside his negative self-image and gave answers that wouldn't make him feel like a poseur but would get him off the hook. He wrote that he used a blend of Cloisonnism and Fauvism, leaning on abstraction but leaving enough recognizable subject matter so an untutored viewer didn't feel lost, but that his earliest influence was Hokusai, and he felt the artist's style still bled through to the base of all his work. What he wanted to say was his biggest influence was Hiromu Arakawa, but since she was a manga artist, he knew that wouldn't go over well with the department.

He remembered how Skylar had said Xander's painting had invited him in, and he wondered if he could write that down, that his paintings invited people in.

He recalled also what Zelda said about how passionate he was about manga, and told them to get the hell out of his head because he could *not* do a manga-themed BFA show.

He glanced up at the clock. Eleven. He usually went to lunch at 12:15.

He wondered if Skylar was annoyed he hadn't replied to the text.

He forced the distractions aside and tried to answer question two.

Who is your audience?

This question always annoyed him. He wanted *everyone* to be his audience. Or at least he wanted *anyone* to be able to be his audience, if they wanted to be. But he always assumed no one would give a shit about his paintings, which was why this show was such a kick in the groin.

Once more, he thought of Skylar and his reaction. So he wrote that he wanted his audience to be people who didn't always feel they understood art, as well as those who did appreciate it. He wished he could say he got that kind of reaction from *Lucky 7*.

Goddamn, but he was still angry about the magazine going digital, so angry he was tempted to stop drawing *The Adventures of Hotay & Moo*, but he knew he couldn't do that. He was already afraid the manga would die out when he graduated. What was he saying, he *knew* it would die. Sara was talented, but talent wasn't the problem. People just didn't give a shit anymore. Couldn't they wait, then, to make the damn magazine digital? Why did they have to do this to him during his last year? Was there any way to stop the change, short of winning the lottery and paying for the printing costs?

And his fucking rent and painting supplies?

Eleven thirty now.

He should reply to Skylar. It was rude not to.

Fine. He was rude. Anyway, he had work to do.

Where do you see your career headed?

Xander chewed on the end of his pen. He honestly had no idea. He'd just wanted to do art, and he didn't know what else to do, so he was going to graduate school so he could keep doing art. It'd be cool to be an art professor, but he'd seen how many people had applied to the last opening at Benten. Also, he'd have to talk to students all the time, which would suck. Mostly he wanted an office and access to all the supplies. So probably not a professor, the more he thought about it.

Once upon a time he'd wanted to be a manga artist, but how the hell he could be a manga artist while living in Pennsylvania, he had no idea. He had no intention of going to Pennsylvania ever again after graduation, but he was sure he couldn't show up in Tokyo with his two years of Japanese, declare his intent to be a manga artist, and be welcomed with open arms. Also, he couldn't write any of this on the form. So he wrote *art professor.*

Okay, if he were *really* honest, he wanted to draw and paint, depending on his mood, but above all he longed to reach people who needed to be reached, to move people. He wanted people to react like Skylar had to his painting the day they'd met. But that was conceited, right? And impossible to write down. But that was all he could think of to say.

Quarter to noon. Too late to reply to that text now. Skylar had likely already made other plans. Probably with his girlfriend. A guy like Skylar would have one. Maybe two.

He thought about what Zelda said, about the rumors of Skylar being bi.

The idea was too tantalizing, so Xander pushed it away. *No.* Also, it didn't really…fit. Not that Skylar would ever cruise a guy like Xander, but…no. It didn't feel right to him. He would have a plastic girlfriend. A sorority girl who majored in English and clipped dresses from *Modern Bride*, cutting out her head and Skylar's from photos and putting them over grooms and brides in happy poses.

Except that didn't feel right either, for some reason.

Whatever. Who cared who Skylar would date? Not Xander, that was what mattered. Xander didn't date either, and he didn't want to. He didn't like people, just cats and art. He didn't have lunch dates, platonic or otherwise.

Xander pushed the junk mail off the phone and glared at it again.

The fact remained it was rude not to reply.

What if Skylar was going to show up anyway? Bring lunch in case Xander didn't see the text?

The image of Skylar walking up the hill, a bag of fragrant Breadgarden soup and sandwiches and a drink tray in his hands, smiling until he saw the empty bench, made Xander pick up the phone. He texted awkwardly, fumbling to turn numbers into letters, hands shaking as he hurried to correct mistakes, Skylar's disappointed face still lingering in his mind.

hey sorry just saw this. sorry I missed you.

He stared at the phone, cursing himself for waiting for a reply, belly doing acid-laden somersaults as a return text appeared.

Not a problem. Didn't realize your lunch was early today. I'll make a note and try to catch you next time.

Xander almost let it go. Except he felt like he had to say something, he was a shitty liar, and…well, he was also a complete idiot.

I haven't gone yet. I just mean it's obviously too late now.

Skylar's replies came fast, but then, he was clearly typing on a smartphone, not some piece-of-shit flip phone circa 2008.

It's not too late at all. You've made my day. What

can I pick up for you at Breadgarden? I'm standing outside of it right now. I can get our orders and head straight over.

Oh shit. *Oh shit.* Xander tried to figure out how to say he wasn't going with as few words as possible so the awkward typing was less awkward, and then his insanity took hold of him again, and he typed *ok* and hit send.

He tossed the phone onto the counter like it was on fire. He covered it with the mail again, and also with the pile of unfolded dishtowels. He left the kitchen and paced his bedroom, Hiromu sitting in the doorway judging him quietly, Hokusai sitting on the bed swiping his leg as he went past.

He'd agreed to go to lunch. He'd failed to give his order, but he knew better than to think that would stop Skylar. He'd probably show up with *options.*

He dashed around the apartment, rifling through his closet floor for a moderately clean shirt and pair of jeans, rubbing a dripping washcloth over his head, and scraping a brush through his unruly hair in hopes he could tame it enough to look human. Slipping into his tennis shoes, he stared at his bike in the corner, aprons draped over it, tires visibly flat.

With no other choice in front of him, Xander grabbed his keys and backpack, swore, and burst through the door, tearing across town as fast as his shaking legs could take him.

SKYLAR ARRIVED AT the crooked bench at 12:20, ready to

apologize for being late, only to discover Xander wasn't there either. He frowned and pulled his phone out, wondering if he'd missed a message. It turned out he had.

sorry late b there soon

He tapped back a reply. *No worries. See you when you get here.* Then he sat on the bench, stared out at the river, and exhaled a slow, happy breath as he drank in the view. He was so lost in his reverie he listened to the heavy breathing and sharp footsteps on brush for several seconds before his brain suggested he might, possibly, want to see who was running toward him so quickly.

It turned out *Xander* was running, looking like a racehorse run seven laps longer than he should have gone. His hair was matted with sweat, his face flushed, slender chest heaving as he leaned on a tree and gasped for air. He'd been walking by the time Skylar turned around, but he had the look about him people got when they were trying to appear they'd been walking the whole time but were in fact nearly dead from booking like hell. Thankfully Skylar processed that before he made the mistake of commenting on Xander's bedraggled appearance. Instead, he smiled, held up the takeout bag, and shook it enticingly.

Xander offered the most fake, sorry excuse for a smile Skylar had ever seen, huffed a few more desperate breaths, and shuffled to the bench. He smelled of sweat, but it wasn't worse than Unc in the kitchen after a run. What did concern Skylar was the way Xander's hands shook, and the way he seemed like if he had the stamina left, he'd turn around and run the other direction.

The poor guy. Empathy washed through Skylar, followed by a renewed determination to save Xander. Or at least to teach him how to save himself.

Skylar set down the bag of food. "I got a smoked turkey with gouda, a vegetarian, and an order of hummus with veg. I love all of it, so pick what you want. Alternatively, if you can't decide, I had them split the sandwiches, and we could mix and match." When Xander mostly huffed and puffed, Sky passed over a bottle of water, uncapping it on the way. "Here, drink this. I'll lay the food out like a picnic, and you can decide what you're in the mood for."

Xander took the bottle, hand still trembling as he glugged the liquid into his system.

Skylar kept track of him out of the corner of his gaze, making a show of getting up, crouching behind the bench, and laying out the spread in the space where he'd been sitting. "We're so spoiled for great restaurants in Takaketo. I swear there's a new one every week."

Xander's huffs and puffs had slowed. "We don't have much in Mason."

"Mason—you mean Mason City?" *Yes, let's chat a little bit about home.* "You get back there much?"

"Not if I can help it."

"I heard from the art department your mom is famous for her cookies."

He'd known that was a potential land mine, but Skylar wasn't prepared for the way Xander's whole body tensed, how his entire system threatened to shut down. *Shit*, was that a miscalculation. He worried for a second Xander would bail.

But Xander didn't, thankfully. He only nodded and said, his tone flat and conversation thread-ending, "Yes."

Skylar cleared his throat and smiled, Silver Stone beam on full blast as he gestured to the food. "All right. Take your pick. And I promise, I'm happy with all of it, some of it, or however it shakes out."

Xander hesitated only a moment before taking the whole of the turkey sandwich. "Usually I just have peanut butter."

Having noticed that, this was why Skylar brought the vegetarian option. "I'm happy to provide a treat, then."

"I can give you money." Xander looked awkward, like he wasn't sure if he should have said that.

Skylar gave him a breezy wave. "It's a paltry exchange for your painting, but it's a start at least."

He didn't miss the way talking about Xander's art made his whole demeanor change—he was still guarded, but eager, too, like a starving man afraid to accept sustenance.

Skylar let him dig into the sandwich for a minute or so, but when the silence seemed too much, he pressed on. "I have to admit, I'm entirely jealous of your ability to create art like that."

"To be honest, usually it feels like a relief, because by the time I'm halfway through I'm convinced it's shit, and getting out of it is like escaping a portal of hell."

That made Skylar laugh. "Come on. You don't have to be modest."

Xander grimaced at his sandwich. "It's not modesty. I haven't created a project and not felt like I'd gone outside without pants since I was ten."

"But surely I'm not the first person to tell you your work is incredible."

"It's not that." He worried the crust of his bread. "I think most artists feel that way. You start excited about the idea, like a honeymoon phase. Halfway through it all gets real, and doubt creeps in. You have to keep pushing. Eventually you're done, and you have your work. But it's rarely this big, satisfying thing. Because you worry you didn't do it right, or stopped too soon, or went on too long, or that you've lost the spark that got you started."

Skylar considered this as he chewed a bite of hummus-laden carrot. "Okay, when I do a project, I feel that way in the middle too, but by the end I feel satisfied because I can see it's successful. I'm not saying I don't see where I could improve the next time, but I have a sense of accomplishment, for sure. You're saying you don't have any sense of satisfaction?"

He thought back to the writing he used to do, way back when, but decided against bringing it up. It would be too embarrassing, compared to what Xander could do.

"Maybe some, but not always, and not like you're talking about. Da Vinci said 'art is never finished, only abandoned.'"

Skylar raised an eyebrow. "I thought it was Paul Valéry talking about poetry who said that."

"Whoever said it, I cosign the sentiment. Art is never, ever as magical on canvas as it is in my head. I've come to terms with that, which I can tell you, took some time. But every finished project will be bittersweet because when I put the brush down, no matter how much other people like it, I only ever look at it and see the ghost of the idea I couldn't capture."

All the shakiness was gone from Xander now. He wasn't exactly happy, but he was definitely centered in a way he hadn't been before. Art truly was his zone—though maybe, Skylar thought, his own wheels turning, Xander's wider brush was the creative process. He slid a piece of cucumber through the hummus. "So talk to me about why you didn't like the painting you gave me. Were you too caught up with the failure to realize your vision?"

"No. The focal point wasn't strong enough, and I didn't have enough color balance. I didn't like the texture, either. It didn't do what I wanted it to do."

"But I *love* that painting. Does that mean I don't know anything about art? I mean—okay. I don't know anything about it. I've always wished I could draw, or even simply write."

He hadn't meant to say that. Hadn't he decided not to bring that up? But his recalcitrant mind flickered to the stories he used to write at the summer house, and he wondered what had ever happened to those.

Clearing his throat, Skylar pushed those thoughts aside. "I don't understand visual art. I admit that. But explain this to me…is your dislike of it an illustration of that failed vision, or is it something else?"

"No." Xander leaned forward a little. He was intense now, focused and arresting. "See, this is the magic of art. I can love or hate my own work, but the viewer is who turns it into something. I made that painting, but *you* gave it life. Art isn't real until it's viewed." He grimaced, lowering his sandwich, but even as he retreated, he still had his inner fire. "This is where I always get it wrong. I *know* I need to connect to people in order to understand my own art, but…I'll be honest. I hate people."

You don't say. Skylar laughed. "Maybe that feeds your art, though. Maybe you don't have to go to all the parties, just some of them."

"I don't want to go to *any* party, ever. I get nervous around people. I'd rather be by myself."

And yet you ran until you nearly had a heart attack, hurrying to have lunch with me. "Even hermits need a few friends."

"I'm a shitty friend. Ask Zelda. It's better if I stick to cats."

Zelda? Skylar wanted to ask about this Zelda person, but he knew better. *Not yet.* "You have cats?"

This turned out to be another point of entry, as Xander softened. "Yeah. Hokusai and Hiromu."

The names sounded…familiar. Sky took a shot in the dark. "Painters?"

A tiny smile. "A printmaker and a manga artist.

Both Japanese, as it happens. Hiromu—the cat—is a longhair, and a real softie. Gets her feelings hurt easy. Always wants me to hold her. Hokusai is an asshole, but he mostly gets bored. He can be good, when he feels like it."

Cats and art. Skylar wanted to ask about the cats' namesakes, especially the manga artist, but he tucked those points of entry away as topics to bring up the next time Xander started to shut down.

He considered, briefly, bringing up *Hotay & Moo*, but he had the same ridiculous fanboy flutter as the last time, so he didn't go near the subject.

He kept the conversation light—asked Xander how much time he spent in his studio, at home, and at the college. Once Xander was fully at ease again, Sky led him gently into a more back-and-forth conversation, laying bait for Xander to ask him about *his* major, his life at the frat house. Unsurprisingly, the latter made Xander sour again. "I couldn't imagine living with so many people."

"It gets tough at times, I won't lie. But when I need somebody, my brothers are there for me." Skylar hesitated, a shadow falling over that line he'd said so many times. "It's been a little tougher this year. The mural incident was a blow to our reputation, and the leadership hasn't been as on point as I'd like. Next year may be even worse. But I can't do much, because I'm only the risk management officer. Well—I'm not *supposed* to be doing much, but they keep acting like I'm still president." He realized he shouldn't have said that, and tried to sweep it under the rug with a smile. "Don't mind me. I just can't let go of the reins gracefully."

Xander cocked an eyebrow, his look saying, *I don't believe you, but whatever you need to tell yourself.*

Skylar's phone buzzed in his pocket, and he pulled it out to glance at it. It was only Unc inviting him to a party he absolutely wouldn't be going to, but the time caught him up short. "It's already one thirty?"

Xander jolted, panicked. "Oh, shit. I have to get going."

Skylar waved him on. "You go. I'll pack this up. But I'll see you tonight at seven, yes? At Java House? Or would it be more convenient for me to meet you at your studio this time?"

"I—I don't know." Xander ran a hand through his hair.

"Tell you what. Let's make it seven thirty, and I'll swing by your apartment and pick you up. Or we can stay there, if you've had enough running around town by that time." He flashed his phone. "Just give me a text and let me know what you'd like to do."

"Okay." Xander hovered, looking like he wanted to say something, couldn't find it, then hunched into himself and gave an awkward wave. "Bye."

Skylar waved back, projecting as much nonthreatening confidence as he felt Xander could take. "See you later. Have a great day."

He watched Xander go, then went about putting away the remains of their picnic. As his hands worked, so did his mind, rushing forward as it sifted and sorted everything he'd learned during lunch. He ruminated on it on the way back to Delta Sig, and when he got there, he gave the most perfunctory of greetings to Unc before hurrying to his room, opening his computer, and typing as furiously as he could. He ignored three texts from Carolyn—he wasn't in the mood to go anywhere with her or any Tau-Kapp.

Art is not finished, only abandoned. The quote rang like a bell in his head, tearing down everything he'd set up for Xander's project, and in the ruins he saw the glittering, terrible scaffolding of some art all his own.

Chapter Seven

ALL THROUGH THE afternoon, Xander tried to decide if he should meet Skylar at the coffeehouse, let him come to his apartment, or cancel the whole thing entirely.

He'd had the best time at lunch he could remember having since his aunt had taken him to every museum in New York City, which should have been a point in the guy's favor, but there was just something about him Xander couldn't trust. It was more than his being overly polished, that Silver Stone bullshit, though that didn't help anything. He hadn't *tinged* as much at lunch, but even so, Skylar wasn't…real, somehow. Every now and again Xander thought he saw glimpses of a guy he'd buy as legitimate, but most of the time as soon as Skylar's radiant beams had left the building, Xander felt uneasy in the afterglow. Like now.

As the time for their meeting drew closer, Xander felt more and more drained. He'd thought the best plan would be to go to the coffee shop again, but the idea of going out made him want to go to bed. Which took him back to canceling, which meant they'd just have to meet again later.

God, Xander wanted to chuck all of it and run.

As he batted Hokusai away from his dinner, he texted Skylar. *I'm feeling pretty beat. Not sure how much focus I have left.*

The text took forever to beat out with his thumbs and the numeric keypad, and he was admitting he'd need to invest in a phone with a keyboard if Skylar kept texting him, when Skylar replied.

I promise I won't take much of your time, but I'd really love to meet with you tonight. Our lunch inspired me like I can't tell you. I'm dying to show you my new proposal. You've made me throw out all my worksheets and reinvent the whole concept of your pitch.

Great, so he'd filled out those forms for nothing. He should have drawn, like he wanted to in the first place.

Skylar texted again. *Give me your address, and I'll be over in half an hour. I'll be out of your hair by eight, I swear.*

Xander texted Skylar his address, wolfed down the rest of his food, and dove into the shower.

He lingered under the hot spray, shutting his eyes and tilting his head down so the water ran in steamy streams over his face, cursing himself for feeling flustered now that he knew Skylar was on his way. This was not a fucking *shōjo* manga. He was not a goddamned romantic heroine—hero, whatever—preparing for a big scene with his crush. He'd admit he found the guy attractive, but that was it. There would be no love confessions, for Christ's sake. Why was he getting so worked up because the guy was coming over? He was here to discuss social media, not the starry pools of Xander's eyes.

Emerging from the shower, he toweled himself off, put on clean jeans and a T-shirt and socks, because bare feet around Skylar seemed weird somehow. Odds were good the guy would show up in a suit or something casual but highly fashion show. He did a pass through of the main area of the apartment and the bathroom, making sure he didn't have underwear somewhere random (he did), consolidating the dirty dishes to the counter and the sink. He fluffed the pillows and paced the living room, trying to think of what else he should be doing in preparation.

This wasn't cleaning up for his crush. It was polite to be tidy for guests, was all.

The cats watched him in mild fascination, Hiromu from the arm of the couch, Hokusai from his favorite stalking spot beneath the kitchen chair, pleased to discover Xander so distracted he kept walking close enough to be caught in a paw swipe.

In the last five minutes before Skylar was due to arrive, Xander swept the piles of junk from the small table in the kitchen where he usually kept just enough room to eat a bowl of cereal or reheated dinner. Jars of ink, old nibs, pencils markers, and of course any loose junk mail and letters from school were shifted to the burgeoning kitchen counter, an Amazon box by the door, and his dresser in the bedroom. He was putting the last of his markers into their case when the knock came.

Despite his half hour of scolding himself for being

ridiculous, his heart still skipped a beat when he opened the door and found Skylar there.

Traitor, he whispered to the organ.

Skylar smiled at him, but there was an extra sparkle to him this time, like he had something up his sleeve. It intensified as Xander awkwardly invited him in. "Thanks for letting me come over. I'm really excited to show you my new idea."

Xander hugged his belly, not sure what the etiquette here was. Old gears turned, clunking and grinding. "Um, do you want something to drink?"

"No, thank you." Skylar glanced around. "Would you rather sit somewhere comfortable, or at the table?"

Xander's only comfortable seating option was the couch, which was full of cat hair, and it sagged in the middle, meaning it would tip them constantly closer to one another. "The table is fine."

Thank God he'd cleaned it off.

The cats had scattered at the door knock, but Hokusai emerged to inspect Skylar as he took his seat. Skylar spied him and beamed. "Oh, the cats. Which one is this? Not a longhair, so it must be…Hokusai? Did I say that right?"

"Yeah." Xander watched Skylar lean down to navigate the intricate art of petting Hokusai. Skylar laughed when Hokusai batted at his hand, scritching under the cat's chin before creeping incrementally around his face to his head, at which point Hokusai submitted to the affection with mild surprise and eventual contentment.

Skylar glanced around the room as he continued to

pet Hokusai. "Where's the other one?"

"Hiromu? Under my bed, probably. She doesn't like new people."

Skylar looked like he wanted to say something but didn't. Instead, he gave Hokusai one last scritch and reached into his messenger bag. He withdrew a legal pad in a leather folio cover and took out the pen hiding in a slim pouch along the binding. He sat straight in his chair, but he leaned forward, his forearms on the table, framing the open notebook and setting his focus like a laser on Xander. "I want to pitch an idea to you, something more than simply laying out a social media presence. I want to help you create an entire social persona."

Xander pulled back in his chair. "A what?"

"A social persona. Another you, or rather a version of you, crafted to help you showcase your work and share it with people who want to experience it. I want to help you carve that version of yourself, hone it and practice it, and present it."

"Right, isn't that what we're doing? With the profile stuff, I mean."

Skylar shook his head, his blue-green eyes dancing with eagerness. "I want you to take it *deeper.* More than just online. You can *live* it, Xander. It doesn't have to stay in your profile. You can use the same principles we were talking about for your digital look to change your whole life."

Oh fuck, here they went again. The idea sounded like hell on Earth, but Xander could feel the Skylar

Stone tractor beam pulling him in. "You want to be my social media Pygmalion?"

Skylar frowned. "Pygmalion? I swear I've heard that before, but I can't remember where."

"There are several versions. The original is the Greek myth of the sculptor, Pygmalion, who falls in love with his creation, a perfectly carved statue of a woman. Aphrodite brings her to life and she becomes Galatea. The modern version is the play by George Bernard Shaw, and the musical and movie adaptation with Audrey Hepburn, *My Fair Lady*. Henry Higgins, a professor of phonetics, makes a bet he can get Eliza, a Cockney flower seller, to pass as a duchess at a party. He teaches her how to speak, how to hold her posture, etcetera."

Skylar brightened in understanding. "Right. I think I saw the movie once. They end up together in the end, and she humbles him a little, undoing some of his uppity and arrogant ways?"

"Well—it's unclear if they end up together or not. In the original play, Shaw resented how producers always put the two of them together. He didn't feel Eliza was emancipated if she stayed with Higgins. The musical and the movie made it ambiguous. If people want to imagine them together, they can, but Higgins doesn't exactly come all the way around to humility." Xander blushed hotly, worried he'd accidentally revealed his secret affection for Skylar. "What I meant was the idea of transformation. Which, I have to tell you, won't ever work, not with me. It's not as simple as changing my speech and getting me clothes without paint stains."

"I think transformation would absolutely work. Because I don't want to turn you into a mini-me or some rigid statue, some preset concept. I want to help you find a way to speak to other people the way you spoke to me today."

Xander combed over their lunchtime conversation, trying to sort out how exactly he'd spoken to Skylar. "I don't understand. I didn't talk any differently than usual."

"You absolutely did. You weren't shy or hesitant. You were articulate, confident, and engaging. You changed the way I think about not only visual art but the creative process in general. You made me realize the key to your success at selling yourself is *being* yourself." When Xander recoiled, Skylar smiled, a gentling gesture that made Xander tingle, despite his terror. "I want you to share that part of yourself with as many people as possible."

Mayday, mayday, mayday. "I don't think you understand how bad I am at dealing with other people. The only reason I keep talking to you is because I have to." He acknowledged how awful that sounded and blushed hotter than he had the first time. "I don't mean it like that."

"It's fine. And I *do* appreciate how little you like dealing with people. But that's exactly why I want to help you do this. I want you to be able to protect that part of yourself *while* you deal with people."

"That doesn't make any sense."

"It will. I promise." Skylar turned his palms up on the table. "Will you let me try to show you?"

If the devil came to tempt Xander Fairchild, he would come as Skylar Stone. "I don't know. What does *showing* me entail?"

"Let's start slow. And small. Give me a goal you have, something unrelated to the show. What's something you'd like to do but haven't been able to? Something simple but important to you."

Xander's panicked thoughts flopped around his brain like beached fish. "I don't know."

Skylar winked. "You don't need to decide right now. We've got time." He rose, gathering his folio, phone, and bag. "It's almost eight, and I promised I wouldn't take more than a half hour from your evening. I want to meet with you again soon, though. What openings do you have in the next week?"

Skylar wheedled not one, not two, but *three* meeting times out of Xander. When he left, Xander stood at the door, hugging himself, feeling as if someone had peeled him raw.

How did the guy keep *doing this to him*? And what the *fuck*, what fresh hell was this Pygmalion bullshit?

A furry brush of his legs and a nip at his ankle made him bend automatically, scooping Hiromu into his arms. He hugged his fluffy cat, shutting his eyes as he let his pet lick his face and snuggle into her favorite place at Xander's neck.

As the silver glow of Skylar dissipated, Xander's unease deepened, and the sense that something was not quite right about Skylar did as well. Xander tried to focus on that instead of his impending role as Eliza Dolittle/Galatea, but as usual he didn't really get anywhere beyond *something is slightly plastic in the State of Denmark.*

With nothing else to do with himself, Xander drew—and he ended up drawing Skylar. Again.

He tried to draw a proper sketch, but it felt even more fake than the man's smile, so Xander switched to manga style, and on impulse he drew Skylar as Henry Higgins and himself as a reluctant Eliza. As a drawing, it wasn't bad. Skylar was as hot in manga as he was in real life, and Xander was just as dour. But the image bothered Xander even more than their conversation the longer he stared at it.

He wasn't sure why, but all he could think when he looked at it was, *this isn't right.*

He tried again, casting Skylar as Pygmalion and himself as Galatea—the drawing was better this time, in part because he'd improved the design of Manga Skylar, but as far as actual subject composition, Xander disliked this even more. Skylar honestly didn't work as Pygmalion, and Xander sure as hell was no Galatea.

Hiromu jumped onto his desk and mewed at him, and Xander gathered her into his arms, frowning at the sketches as he stroked her fur. "Hush, it's fine," he murmured, crooning to himself as much as her. "It's probably going to be just fine."

SKYLAR DECIDED TO give Xander the weekend to acclimate to the idea they were about to get serious working on this social persona. Their next meeting wasn't until Monday, another lunchtime on the hospital hill. In the meantime, he put together a detailed plan of action with smaller goals and benchmarks, including a list of resources at his disposal. He had a vinyl portfolio ready to house each step in a sheet protector, but before he committed to assembly, he spread it across his desk and ran through the plan several times, both to refine his presentation of it and to triple-check for any speed bumps or wrong turns.

He worked on Xander's file until noon, but after a quick lunch, he reluctantly put his notes away and dragged out the LSAT books instead, submersing himself in the fantastically dull study guides until his eyes crossed and his neck cramped. God, but there wasn't anything worse in the world than studying for the tests, and he'd been doing it for six months.

He was due to take the practice test again soon, but he worried he wasn't anywhere near the target score he needed.

Skylar was about to start another case file when his phone rang. He almost didn't answer, but he glanced at the caller ID as a matter of course, and when he saw the readout, his heart skipped a beat. Dropping the notebook and pen, he picked up the phone.

"Hello, sir."

"Ellen told me you'd left a message for me."

Skylar had left approximately twenty messages and

forty texts for his father since the last time Leighton Stone had deigned to contact him, not that Skylar was counting. "Yes, sir. I wanted to let you know how my LSAT preparations were coming."

"Your tutor gives me a regular report. Is something not going well with the tutor? She came highly recommended."

"No—she's fine." Skylar's cheeks heated, and he cursed himself for feeling so flustered every time he spoke to his father. "I just wanted to let you know I was studying hard. I'm going to do well on this test. I'm looking forward to applying for Yale."

Why did he say that? He wasn't, in fact, studying hard. He had his doubts about how he was going to do, and he was terrified of Yale most of the time, unsure if he could handle it.

"Well, I'm glad to hear that."

The thin thread of praise yanked hard at Skylar's belly, making him yearn for more, inspiring him to clamor for more things to say, to keep that soft, interested tone in his father's voice. "Also, I wanted to give you some information I overheard at an event hosted by Carolyn Hawthorne's family. The new Republican candidate for the Senate was there."

"Oh?"

Skylar's heartbeat fluttered again, and he rode the high of Leighton Stone's attention as far as he could. He rattled off every detail he'd gleaned from the evening—and he'd made it his business to overhear as many interesting details as possible. Anything to keep hearing that tone in his father's voice. That flicker of intrigue, that delicious whisper of focus directed at Skylar.

"That's all very interesting. Thank you for passing it along."

"I'll let you know if I hear anything else. Whenever I'm at fundraisers with the Tau Kapp girls, I hear things." He regretted now how many phone calls from Carolyn and the others at the sorority he'd brushed aside.

"Oh, and speaking of fundraisers. Don't forget your mother's event at the beach house on the Fourth of July."

"Yes, sir. I have it on my calendar."

"Make sure you bring someone suitable. One of your usual Tau Alpha Kappa ladies would be fine."

"Yes, sir."

His father cleared his throat. "Ah—I have a client coming in shortly. It was lovely to talk to you, son. Keep up the good work. We'll talk again soon."

Skylar stared at the phone in his hand for several minutes after his father hung up, the final exchange ringing in his ears.

It was lovely to talk to you, son.

Keep up the good work.

He shut his eyes, burning the praise onto his heart. Telling himself it was enough, that he could live on it until the next time they talked, whenever that was. Even if it was a month from now.

He glanced up at Xander's painting, but he didn't look at it long. Somehow the figure seemed to judge him, to tell him he shouldn't be satisfied, that he shouldn't just want but *demand* more from his father—and Skylar couldn't handle those kinds of thoughts. Turning his back to the art, he opened his notes and tried to get back to work.

When his house mother, Ms. Mary, stuck her head into his room at five, he felt as if he were a zombie climbing out of a pile of sludge, and she had to repeat herself twice before he understood what she was trying to tell him.

"—Amber Adelson from Tau Alpha Kappa called and asked you call her back. I told her you were studying, but she insists I pass on the message." Ms. Mary pursed her lips. "You didn't tell me you were dating anyone, young man."

Skylar tried to give her a reassuring, slightly debonair smile, but mostly he was tired and not particularly caring about anything Amber had to offer. Except his father's phone call and admonishment for him to pass on more information was fresh in his mind. "Thanks for letting me know. I'll give her a call."

"If you go out, let me know, and use the alarm code to get back in. I'm heading to bed early tonight, I think."

Skylar wished he were too, but one way or another, he knew he wouldn't be. "I'll bear that in mind. Get some good rest."

He shut his door and locked it before digging out his phone and returning one of Amber's multiple missed calls.

"*Skylar.*" Her sugared voice set his teeth on edge

through the phone. "Thanks so much for calling me back. Oh my God, you're a *lifesaver.*"

Shutting his eyes, he pinched the bridge of his nose. "What can I do for you, Amber?"

"My parents are in town, and I need a date. They know I have a boyfriend, but…well, they'd never approve of my actual boyfriend. Carolyn said you'd be willing to stand in as my date for the evening." She paused, clearly for dramatic effect. "You do know my father is a lobbyist for the coal industry?"

Skylar suppressed a sigh. He didn't bother to force a smile into his tone. This game didn't have a need for them. "Text me the information I need to know about our fake relationship. I'll be by to pick you up at six."

He hung up in the middle of her teary thank you, not wanting to hear it.

Though he didn't really have time, he took a shower anyway, lingering under the steam, letting the hot water beat on the top of his head. He avoided his own gaze as he shaved, then again in the room as he adjusted his tie. He dusted himself in cologne, gave his nails a quick buff.

He didn't look anywhere near Xander's painting.

The evening went fairly smoothly, except for the part where Amber tried to kiss him her thank you when he dropped her off at Tau Alpha Kappa, and when Skylar let himself remember the way he'd had to sit there and look uncomfortable rather than argue when Amber's father had tried to engage him in first some racist, then homophobic, then classist views before rolling his eyes and muttering about Leighton Stone's son being a disappointment after all. That this story would get back to his father didn't upset him—this was nothing new. His dad wouldn't care about that, especially when he heard what information Skylar had picked up.

But that he'd sat there and listened to that garbage upset Skylar a great deal. He was ashamed of what he'd done, and he felt sick. Worst of all, he couldn't articulate why, since it wasn't different than anything he'd done a million times before.

He took another shower when he got home, and then, because he still felt dirty, a long, hot bath. He wanted to sleep, but it eluded him.

He lay in bed for half an hour, staring at Xander's painting, wishing it would tell him the answer.

He thought, for an insane moment, about texting Xander.

In the end, he propped his tablet on his lap, put his headphones in, pulled up Crunchyroll, and ate an anime.

His sophomore year a roommate had helped him develop his addiction to Japanese anime and coined that term. *Eat an anime.* Most people would say *binge*, but the roommate had laughed and said no, Skylar *ate* them whole, as if he were a starving man taking in nourishment. Especially when it was like this, late at night, with his brain chasing itself like a squirrel. He'd indulged in their then-shared Crunchyroll account as an end-of-day treat, and at first Skylar had simply joined him on occasion, amused by the ongoing sagas of the martial arts anime his roommate favored.

But then they'd tried *Blue Exorcist* on a wild hair, and though his roommate quickly lost interest, Skylar couldn't look away. He'd inhaled every episode available that same night, and he stayed caught up with new seasons to this day. Skylar had seen *07-Ghost* in the sidebar as a recommended show once he'd finished *Blue Exorcist*...and his addiction was born.

Unc was always trying to get him to read manga, arguing if he liked *Lucky 7* and watched that much anime, he'd like reading more, but Skylar kept declining the tour of his friend's collection. It wasn't just about the content. There was something about the cocoon of sitting in his bed with a tablet or laptop or even his phone, hooked up to headphones and shutting out the world. He refused to watch dubs, because he wanted to hear the beautiful sound of Japanese, a language he couldn't understand but loved all the same. Sometimes he was frustrated by his lack of comprehension. Sometimes he appreciated the disconnect and the isolation after a day of people demanding things from him. All he had to do while he streamed his anime was read the text at the bottom of the screen.

He'd learned, after several lost weekends, that he had to pace himself and be deliberate about when he let himself indulge. Sometimes, as a treat, he'd allow himself to keep up with certain series while they were airing, but mostly he restricted himself to times like this, when, if he were someone else, he'd go binge-drinking or would have tried to seduce Amber. Skylar didn't like to get drunk, and he had no interest in taking a Tau-Kapp to bed.

But he dreamed of a beachside hut with great Wi-Fi, grocery delivery, a month's worth of vacation, and a sudden influx of new anime.

The anime he'd chosen tonight was one he'd been saving for some time, a high-school set story where a young man had transferred to an elite private school from France (but spoke perfect Japanese) and had special abilities that were revealed as he teamed up with his new best friends, who were misfits like him. The antagonists were the stylish, popular group—yes, he thought, you need to watch out for them, they're sly devils—though in a manner that he'd come to learn was quite Japanese, the villains weren't simply villains, they were sometimes secret allies, and there was *another* group of villains, the teachers, who weren't teachers at all. And yet even though they'd been exposed, the students couldn't defy the teachers but had to work around them and offer them at least public respect.

Skylar was fascinated. In an American cartoon, the teachers would have been skewered on a pike and roasted by now, but he was fully prepared for these villains to be converted before the show was over, or redeemed in some way. He also loved the way everyone encouraged each other, always, to do their best, even as they often promised to defeat each other, sometimes in the same breath. "Do your best so I can defeat your best self" was the basic message whenever people were squaring off. And when people were down on their luck, they never used it as an excuse. They compensated and overcame their obstacles and encouraged each other in a way that was...well, Japanese. It was refreshing. It was addictive.

The cultural differences between Japan and America grabbed Skylar's attention as well. As was often the case, there were no parents whatsoever, and in fact several of the high school students lived on their own in apartments while their parents were "out of town" essentially for their entire high school lives. Skylar wished there were someone he could ask about this. Was this actually a thing? Did Japanese high schoolers have this much independence, or did they only wish they did? He thought of the many, many ways Americans were represented in Hollywood and how inaccurate that was compared to *his* experience, and yet he couldn't help wishing Japanese high schoolers lived exactly this way because it was so amazing. He hoped, at least, they had as many confrontations on the roof as they did in anime. He couldn't think of a roof he'd been on in his life. Why he was so invested in the roof aspect, he didn't know. But he was.

All he knew was that he could give up a lot of things in his life before he could give up his Crunchyroll and Funimation subscriptions. A *lot* of things.

The anime, tragically, didn't come to any kind of conclusion at the end of the season, and since season one had aired in 2012, it clearly never was getting a second. Groaning, Skylar cursed himself for not looking this up beforehand, then dragged his laptop closer to hunt down information on a potential manga, only to swear again. Yes, there *was* a manga—translated into French, German, Spanish, Thai, and not English. Goddamn it, he'd have to hunt around for scans, which he hated to do. He somehow always managed to end up with a virus.

He thought about starting a second anime, but it was four in the morning now, so he lay in bed, feeling irritated and sorry for himself, staring at Xander's painting once more.

He should have told Amber no. He knew that now. He felt foolish and dirty after listening to Amber's father.

What am I doing? Why am I doing any of this? He shut his eyes, his head swirling with images of LSAT study guides and his score, a red 165 blinking overhead while Amber's father sneered at him and Amber slid her hand into his pants and licked his ear, making him want to vomit. Skylar did his best to ignore them, kept trying to get Crunchyroll to load, but it wouldn't. All his laptop would do was show Xander's painting, Xander standing above it, arms folded as he glared at Skylar in disapproval.

Skylar woke in a cold sweat, his head throbbing, his bed vibrating as his phone buzzed insistently against the mattress. He started to ignore it, then on impulse flipped it over. His heart skipped a beat as he saw the caller ID, and he nearly dropped it in his haste to answer.

"Xander?"

There was a pause, a long one. "Did I wake you up? I'm sorry. It's just…I can't do this."

Skylar sat up, rubbing his eyes. "It's fine. You can't do what?"

"This Pygmalion thing. It's been freaking me out all night. I get that I need to do the social media part for my project, and I appreciate you wanting to help me with the…other and all, but I'm good, really. I want to stick to the original arrangement and that's it. Please."

It was clear from the haggard tone of Xander's voice he hadn't slept much, if at all, and that this truly was upsetting him. And the truth was, it shouldn't matter to Skylar one way or another. He had plenty to deal with. He'd taken on more than he should have as it was. He should agree to this and let the man move on.

Whether it was Amber, her father, the anime, or his nightmare, he couldn't say. All Skylar knew was that the last thing in the world he was going to do was let Xander go.

"I'll be right over," he said, and hung up the phone while Xander continued to sputter his objections.

Chapter Eight

GODDAMN SKYLAR STONE *anyway.*

Xander tried to thumb out a text to him saying he shouldn't come, but his hands were shaking and he kept fucking it up, so in the end he decided the adult thing to do would be to draw all his blinds, throw his deadbolt, and pretend he wasn't home. Except his deadbolt was still broken, and if Skylar pounded on his door too long, Pamela would come upstairs to see what was going on, and Xander would have to explain why he was hiding from the super-handsome frat boy who wanted to give him a makeover and help him improve his life.

Fine. Xander would answer the door, but he swore he would make this the fastest rejection Mr. Smiley had ever received, no ifs, ands, or buts about it. Xander would *not* get swept up in the charm offensive. He would put on a goddamned pink pussy hat and fucking *resist.*

Except when he opened the door to Skylar's knock, there wasn't any charm offensive. Skylar Stone looked…

Well, he looked like shit.

All right, he still looked amazing, but relative to

how he usually appeared, he looked like garbage. He wore sweatpants and a T-shirt—real sweats that had holes in them and stains on the waistband, and a T-shirt that had legitimately faded with too many washings, the kind Xander would never have expected a guy like Skylar to even own. He had the barest hint of scruff on his jaw—usually Skylar was completely clean-shaven, so it was a switch. In fact, he'd cut himself shaving, and he had a tiny nick above his jaw. Sexy as hell. His hair was rumpled, his unruly curls hidden beneath a red ball cap, and even that was a little rough around the edge.

God, Xander was fucked. He could have resisted Polished Skylar so much easier.

Xander sighed and opened the door wider. "Come in."

Skylar hesitated, as if he too had expected more of an argument. He kept trying to smile—or rather, he was smiling, but it was like he was fishing for a gear he couldn't find. The guy really was tired. And upset, if Xander read him right. He wondered about that.

Skylar put his hands in his pockets and surveyed Xander's living room. "I love your place. The space is so open and unique. It has its own air."

"Yeah, well in July the air is way too hot, and the landlady insists the breakers can't take an AC unit, so I have to keep my markers in the fridge." Xander suspected the line about the breakers was bunk. Pamela simply hated air conditioning and felt the whole world should too. Also it was a ploy to make him come downstairs and see her instead of hiding out. It worked, because it got crazy hot in his apartment.

Skylar glanced over his shoulder, raising an eyebrow. "Markers? In the fridge?"

Xander wished he'd learn when to shut up. He waved his hand. "An art thing. Don't worry about it."

Skylar rubbed the back of his neck and turned to face Xander. "Speaking of worried. About what you said on the phone. I'm sorry if I came on too strong. But I don't—" He winced and pinched the bridge of his nose. "Damn it, sorry. I didn't sleep much, and I'm not… I rehearsed this in the car, but…"

Xander rolled his eyes. "Okay, first of all, let's start there. I don't want you *rehearsing* anything with me, unless we start doing plays together. Just be yourself. Open your mouth, say words, and don't run them through a subcommittee first." Skylar looked at him like a hurt puppy, so Xander stalked to his drawing table, where he realized he'd left out a few sketches of Skylar. He tucked them away as casually as he could as he babbled on. "I know it probably sounds insane to someone like you, but I'm fine with who I am. I don't need to be remade. So like I said on the phone, we're going to stick to the social media stuff and—"

"*Holy shit,* that's new *Hotay & Moo.*" Skylar held up a sketch from his desk. His face was flushed. "I—I've been meaning to bring this up, but I didn't know how. You draw *The Adventures of Hotay & Moo,* yeah?"

At first Xander couldn't say a word. Not with Skylar looking at him like that, as if Xander were steak and Skylar a starving cowboy. Swallowing, he wet his lips and took a step back, until his butt pressed into the edge of the table. Blocking the sketches of Skylar, in case the man went hunting for more drawings. "Um. Yes?"

A whimper escaped him when Skylar grabbed his shoulders, and he gripped the table's edge and held on as Skylar shook him gently. "*Oh my God.* You have no idea how much I *love* that manga. My fraternity brother does too, but he reads every manga ever made, I think—I mean, I only read this one, and when I found out you drew it, I was going to say something but I couldn't figure out how. And it's like I just put it in a different part of my brain so it didn't get in the way of the social media stuff but then *here is an actual drawing* and I'm *totally freaking out*—oh, *shit*!" He let go of Xander with a yelp, pressing the sketch on the table and trying in vain to smooth it out. "I wrecked it, I'm so sorry!"

This was so weird. *Hotay & Moo* had one goddamned fan in the world, and it was…Skylar Stone? Also, where had this come from? Where was the smooth-talking guy who got Xander to do things he didn't want to do and then felt awkward about later? Who was this? A pod person? Had Skylar been drugged? What the fucking hell?

Skylar was still trying to fix the sketch, freaking out more now because he'd smudged it in addition to crinkling it. Xander took it from him as if he were removing dry gunpowder from a clearing full of campfires. "It's…it's no big deal. That's just a doodle. I can draw it again. See?" He pulled down a fresh piece of paper, uncapped a Sakura .45mm, and freehanded

Hotay and Moo sitting in onsen, Hotay relaxing happily in the hot springs while Moo sat on a rock above him, wrapped in his towel and complaining about something while Hotay ignored him. It took him less than a minute to rough out.

When he looked up to hand it to Skylar, Skylar was watching him like he was a god, and when Xander passed him the sketch, Skylar literally squeaked.

Like a fucking mouse.

Skylar Stone. The sleek Greek Zelda insisted was the Antichrist was standing in Xander's living room in shitty sweats with bedhead and scruff *squeaking* because Xander crapped out a *Hotay & Moo* doodle.

What. The shit. Was happening.

"*This is the best.*" Skylar held the piece of paper with both hands and nestled into the space beside Hokusai on the sofa, staring at the drawing in wonder. "I'm sorry I'm being a geek. I didn't know I was going to act like this until I saw your sketch on the desk. I can't believe you actually write my favorite comic!"

Ah, there went his ego. Xander couldn't help a wry smile. "I don't write the story. I only draw the characters. The *Lucky 7* staff agrees on the direction the characters should go and work together to write the plot. There's a lot of research into Shinto that I don't quite understand. I just do what I'm told and try to keep the characters looking the same."

"Okay, but I bet I know when you started drawing, and you know more about Shinto than you think. You can't tell me you haven't done *some* research." Skylar held up the sketch. "There are six things in this sketch alone that tell me you know what you're putting in there."

Now Xander felt like an idiot, because at best he'd put *two* deliberate Shinto references into the sketch. "Are you telling me you're one of those secret-Shinto apologists? Are you going to whip out a map and try to prove to me there are all kinds of hidden shrines on campus?"

Come on, tell me you're going to whip out a map. Tell me you're one of us.

It was a silly, desperate wish, but… Jesus, there was that look in Skylar's eye again. Except he wasn't hungry this time. He was…wicked. "Oh, I wouldn't whip out a map. I'd *take* you to one."

Xander's whole body vibrated, and it took every ounce of his self-control not to grab Skylar's arm. "*Shut. Up.* You haven't seen a shrine. Nobody has." When Skylar's grin only widened and his eyes began to twinkle, Xander couldn't stand it. He *did* grab him. "You're full of shit. *No way.*"

Skylar leaned in close. "Basement of my frat house."

Xander's heart sank. "Oh, for fuck's sake. That's got to be a fake, then."

"Why? Because it's in a fraternity?"

"*Yes.*"

Xander expected an argument, but Skylar only sighed. He sank into the couch, staring dopey-eyed at the sketch again. Xander indulged in watching Skylar be giddy over his work a little longer, but thinking about how different Skylar was reminded him of the reason he'd called the guy in the first place, and he decided this was the moment to get back to the topic at hand. "Skylar. I don't want to be your Eliza, or your Galatea."

Skylar glanced up at him, dopey smile lingering for a second. "Right—I had an argument for that. I keep getting distracted. Sorry."

Good. Stay distracted. "I don't want to argue. I don't want it. Period."

Skylar set the sketch carefully aside and gave Xander his full attention. Jesus, he could *see* Silver Stone creaking back into gear. "But listen, you don't understand, I'm really good at—"

"I'm sure you are. What you're not understanding is how much I don't give a shit about that. It's great that you see me as Eliza Doolittle, but the difference between Eliza and me is Eliza *wanted* to be remade. I don't. I know, you see me and think I'm some cranky antisocial curmudgeon, and you'd be right. But I don't *mind* being a cranky antisocial curmudgeon. Look." He picked up the sketch, waved it at Skylar, then used it to gesture toward his stack of half-finished paintings. "You profess to like my art so much? Well, this antisocial crankpot made all of it. So leave him alone. Help him fulfill his social media requirements, then…"

Xander trailed off, not knowing how to finish that sentence.

"Leave you alone?" Skylar suggested quietly.

Xander sighed and sat on the other side of Hokusai, though at this point the cat had enough of being ignored and got up, giving both of them dirty looks on his way to the bedroom.

"I just can't figure out why you care," Xander said at last. "It weirds me out."

For a long time Skylar didn't say anything. Xander kept trying to guess what he was going to say, waiting for Silver Stone Spin.

"I talk to your painting."

Xander cast him a sideways glance without turning his head. "For real?"

Skylar kept his gaze on Xander's ceiling and nodded. "Usually late at night. Sometimes I talk to it so much I wonder if I shouldn't call a psychiatrist. Except then I'd have to explain it to my parents, and that would get…awkward." His lips quirked in a wry smile. "Sorry, that's pretty cliché."

"What is?"

"That my parents are part of my problem."

"Well, I mean…same? I wasn't exactly going to mock you for that."

Skylar turned toward Xander. "You don't ever do that. Mock anything. Except yourself."

"Is there another way I'm supposed to do it?"

"Yes. Most people I know do it the other way around."

Now it was Xander who stared at the ceiling. "So explain to me again why it is you want to make me over into someone else?"

Skylar's soft laughter made goose bumps run down Xander's arms. "Touché. All right, Moo. You win.

Except I was looking forward to spending the summer pulling you out of your shell."

Xander twitched. "If you pull me out of my shell, you'll find out how pasty and gross I am." Belatedly, he realized what Skylar had called him. "I'm not Moo. Not even close. He's a warrior king, for Chrissake."

"*Wisdom* king." Skylar shifted his legs, and his knee brushed Xander's. "It's odd that they chose to call the character Moo. The shortened version of Fudō Myōō is Fudō, or more properly, Fudō-sama. Hotay and Hotei I understand, but Moo makes no sense. It would be like giving you Der as a nickname."

Xander had thought the same thing, when he'd read up on the legends. "I guess they were after something that sounded snazzier in English? There's a big book in the *Lucky 7* offices with the history of the seven gods of fortune, and we use it for details when we need them for the storyline, but the big stuff was set when we got there. Probably they just heard the two names and figured they could pick whichever."

"God, that's so typically American."

"It is funny in the manga, though, that such a cranky guy is named Moo."

Skylar smiled. "That's true."

They sat in silence, staring at Xander's ceiling. Xander couldn't help but notice their legs kept brushing. More accurately, Skylar kept brushing his leg. Xander was carefully keeping his still.

Xander cleared his throat. "I'm not Fudō-sama, or Moo. *You* could be Hotay, though. You happy sap."

"If you think I'm happy, you're not looking at me very hard."

Xander shivered again. He hugged himself so it wasn't obvious. "Maybe you came at this the wrong way."

"Oh? How's that?"

Yeah, how was that? "Maybe…maybe you had it backward. Maybe I'm not Eliza or Galatea. Maybe *you* are." *Jesus, shut up, you're so stupid.* "Maybe…maybe you secretly want to be a curmudgeon. Maybe you want *me* to give *you* lessons."

"Huh. Maybe I do." Skylar's voice sounded dreamy. Then dejected. "But I don't have anything to offer you in exchange. And I still can't find a way to pay you for the painting."

"You're still fixated on that? I don't require an equal exchange. I told you. I gave it to you. And if you seriously want curmudgeon lessons, I offer them for free."

Xander turned his head to smile at him to make it clear he knew Skylar didn't actually want curmudgeon lessons. Except Skylar turned his head at the same time, and he looked completely serious. And their legs weren't just brushing now, they were touching.

Xander stopped smiling.

The air between them changed.

The insanity that had swirled in the air ever since Xander had called to cancel the Pygmalion thing settled around them like a blanket, but it didn't lighten the mood at all. It lit a charge.

I feel like I could kiss him, Xander thought.

And just as quickly another thought rode in after. *Don't.*

Xander was used to negative thinking. Sometimes he felt like he'd personally invented it. This wasn't negative thinking, though. This wasn't a voice in his head telling him how dare he imagine he could kiss Skylar Stone. The whisper of *don't* didn't come from self-destructive thoughts. It came from something else.

It came from…

He didn't know where it came from. All he knew was that he was pretty sure he could kiss Skylar right now. And he was even more sure that he should not.

Confused, Xander sat up, rubbing the side of his face.

Skylar sat up too. He seemed self-conscious and unsure of himself, something Xander had never seen on Skylar before. "I'm sorry."

Tread carefully.

This was the same voice as the *don't.* Xander still didn't understand what was going on, but something about the voice and the way Skylar was acting felt important, so he didn't let himself get awkward, he simply rode it out.

"Nothing to apologize for. Like I said. If you want to hang out with me this summer and learn how to be a curmudgeon, you let me know. I have my part-time job, but other than that, I'm just putting together my BFA project. And we'll have our meetings to do the social media stuff, obviously. But I'm saying…I don't mind hanging out more, with you."

Skylar looked grim and haggard, much as he had when he'd arrived at Xander's door. "I have to study for the LSAT. No courses this summer, for a change, but I need to raise my score. Which I'm not sure I can do. But I have to anyway." He softened as he glanced Xander's way. "I want to hang out with you, though. If I can."

This was so weird. Xander felt like he'd met a million different Skylars in the span of a few days. Well, no. If he thought about it, there were only two. The incarnations of smarmy, *ting* Skylar, the one Zelda had called Silver Stone, the one who wanted to plan out Xander's life and turn him into someone he wasn't. And then there was the one he'd met tonight. The geek Skylar. The softer Skylar. The I-wear-sweats-and-things-with-holes Skylar.

Xander really liked the second Skylar. Like, he *liked* him.

You, sir, are in so much fucking trouble.

Xander cleared his throat. "That sounds rough, that studying." He tried to think of something inspiring or helpful to add, but he had nothing.

"I'm supposed to go to Yale, or a list of other impossible-to-get-into schools. But mostly Yale. I need a higher LSAT score than the one I currently have."

Xander frowned at him. "What do you mean, you're supposed to?"

Skylar shrugged, staring at the carpet. "My dad. It's where he wants me to go. Or rather, where the firm where he works wants me to go. They'll hire me once I pass the bar, if I graduate from Yale Law. I was supposed to do my undergraduate there, but I didn't get in. Big family scandal."

Whole lot of *supposed to* in there. Zelda would light this guy on fire. Everything in Xander told him to back away slowly from this conversation, except the tired set of Skylar's broad shoulders kept drawing him in. "Well, is that what *you* want to do?"

Skylar scratched his stubble with his index finger, still fixing his gaze on the carpet. "It's not like you're thinking. It's not that my dad is some Republican blowhard who browbeats me." He picked at a hole in the knee of his sweatpants. "My parents are liberals. Big ones. My dad works with Republicans but donates to all kinds of charities. My mom owns a business and uses her profits to help shut down sweatshops."

Okay, so no. It wasn't like Xander had been thinking. Except… "You still didn't answer my question."

He knew right away he shouldn't have asked, even before Skylar tensed, fists closing on his thighs. Xander didn't want to retract it, though, because Christ, who wanted that kind of life? He didn't care if the Stone family was the goddamned Justice League, he didn't want to join it. It sounded insane.

If Skylar honestly wanted that, fine. If he insisted on lying to himself about it, not Xander's business. But the hell Xander was going to sit here and be part of the bullshit.

Skylar started to get up, and Xander thought he

would leave. Maybe that's what Skylar planned. But then the *Hotay & Moo* sketch fluttered to the floor, and Skylar stopped, carefully picked it up, and sat back down again.

"How about a trade," he said at last. "What if you gave me curmudgeon lessons, and I gave you lessons on how to realize not all people are worth avoiding?" He nudged Xander's knee with his. "I wouldn't make you be *too* social."

Xander grunted, mostly to cover how his brain short-circuited at Skylar's body contact. "You're far too invested in dragging me out of my cave. It's annoying."

Skylar laughed, and the sound was so charming, so unaffected and arousing, Xander had to bite back a groan. "Maybe that's why I can't stop, because you find me annoying. Most people don't."

"I didn't say I found you annoying. I said your *efforts* were annoying."

"Usually my efforts work without issue. You're a challenge, Xander Fairchild."

And you're my wet dream. God, what was wrong with him? Xander wanted to ask him if he had a girlfriend, just to shut himself up. He wanted to hear all about the perfect sorority girl Skylar was seeing to shut down in advance any dreams he was going to have of kissing the guy.

Don't. Don't ask him. Don't bring up anything like that, ever.

There was that damn voice again. Xander still didn't understand, but he did more this time than listen to it.

He engaged it. Poked at that space inside him that seemed to see Skylar, the *real* Skylar, and asked it what he should do with Skylar now, how he was supposed to move forward from here.

Surprisingly, it gave him an answer.

Xander turned to Skylar. "I'll think about it. That's the best I can do right now. But in the meantime, there *is* something you can do for me."

He was nervous about this, but he was trying to trust that voice. And it had whispered that Skylar needed to trade to feel safe, and he also needed time, lots of time, with Xander to get to know him before he would open up. Curmudgeon though he was, Xander did want to see the rest of the Skylar he'd glimpsed behind the veil.

Skylar regarded him hopefully, waiting. "Yes? How can I help you?"

Xander felt a little wicked. He couldn't help himself. He wanted to see if the voice was right. *The bigger the favor, the more excited he'll get.* "It's okay if it's too much to ask."

Skylar sat up straighter, leaned forward. "It won't be too much. Just tell me. I'll do it."

It's going to be so hard not to kiss him. Xander leaned forward too, to prove to himself that he had the restraint. "For my project, I need a subject. I was wondering…would it be okay if that subject was you, if you'd let me draw and paint you? Would you be my model?"

For a brief flash of time, Xander saw all the way in.

Straight into Skylar as he opened like a lotus, and Xander couldn't breathe for the perfect, heartbreaking beauty and joy. Then the flower closed, and it was simply Skylar, smiling, beaming even, pleased as punch as he clutched the *Hotay & Moo* sketch and leaned back onto the couch. "I would *love to.* Thank you for asking."

"It'd mean we'd have to get together. Irrespective of the lessons thing. A lot. And you'd need to sit still for a long time. Though some of that time you could be studying. Also, I could work a little from photographs."

"Stop trying to make me say no, curmudgeon. You've just made my whole summer. The only way it could get better would be if you told me you were using me as the model for the hero in a manga."

Xander laughed. "Um...well, my friend *wanted* me to do one, but I don't know how to write an original story. Plus, I really can't see the committee buying that as a BFA project."

There was that hunger again. "You could write one, though?"

"I could *draw* one. If someone gave me the story and the characters."

He wasn't sure what went through Skylar's head there, but plenty must have, given the expressions that passed over his face. All Skylar said in the end, though, was, "I'd be honored to sit for you, anytime. We can talk about it tomorrow when we have our meeting. And any other time in text, of course."

"Yeah, about that." Xander fished his sad little flip phone off the coffee table and waved it in chagrined surrender. "Try not to be offended if my texts are crap. I don't have that great of a phone. It doesn't have a keypad or anything."

Skylar's smile wasn't tinging anymore. "No offense will be taken."

Xander saw him to the door. It wasn't awkward per se, but it was a...*charged* goodbye. They were both aware everything had changed. That they'd cracked into something good, but scary. Fragile. Something to be treated with care.

He vowed to not mess this friendship up, to not muddy it or screw with it in any way.

"See you tomorrow," he told Skylar, carefully tucking his attraction away.

Skylar's smile was a sunbeam. "See you tomorrow," he replied, and left the apartment.

But the sunbeam—and the glow of Xander's want—remained.

Chapter Nine

SKYLAR WASN'T ENTIRELY sure what had happened at Xander's apartment.

It hadn't been bad, any of it—it felt good, when he allowed himself to relax into it. But if he thought about it too much, he felt slightly panicked, for reasons he couldn't quite put a finger on. He told himself it was because he'd gone over without a plan. It was the first time he'd ever done that, approached such a serious situation without a battle strategy. That was the Stone cardinal rule, and he'd broken it.

But look where it got you.

He still couldn't believe he'd sat there and watched Xander draw *Hotay & Moo*. He was a little mortified at how he reacted—seriously, where had that all come from—but it had worked out okay. It wasn't very professional, but he'd seen the sketch, and...well, basically something had snapped in Skylar. Silver Stone flew out the window, and Geek Skylar had sailed to the surface.

To see Xander *actually draw*, though. To sit there and *watch him draw the characters in real time* had been nothing short of magical. Now Xander wanted to draw

Skylar, all summer long. It felt like a dream. Xander had even hinted he'd be open to putting Skylar in a manga, if someone gave him a story.

Well, funny that you should mention that.

Over the next twelve hours, Skylar shut down that voice every time it surfaced, and he had to shut it down a lot. Hoping they'd calm if he acknowledged them a little, he let his thoughts spin out in the shower the next morning as he got ready to meet Xander.

He'd never been a writer, exactly, but he *had* always enjoyed stories. He used to write all the time. When had he stopped? He wasn't sure. He simply had at some point. He'd stopped reading fiction too, outside of what was assigned for his classes. Somehow anime had snuck in, like a thief. Now Xander, and his art, were worming their way in too.

Or rather, Skylar had invited them in. Xander hadn't wanted to stay, though. And Skylar had gone over there, barely dressed, unshowered, to make sure he didn't leave.

That hadn't been about his art, though. That had been about Xander evading the Pygmalion bargain. Which...there was another question. Why did Skylar care about that so much? Why did he want to transform Xander?

Because when he relaxes, he's fascinating, amazing, and everyone should see that. He doesn't have enough confidence, and it makes me crazy. I want to help him find some.

While that answer was the truth, it wasn't the whole

truth, and Skylar couldn't find the rest of the answer. All he knew was that when he thought of spending the summer with Xander, he felt a thrill all the way to his fingertips and through his toes.

Skylar took care getting ready before heading over this time, shaving and wearing clothes that didn't make him look as if he'd dressed out of the bottom of his closet, which was precisely what had happened the day before. When he knocked on the door to Xander's apartment, he wore crisp khakis, his blue check button-down, and because he'd been nervous, a little L'Homme Libre. He was dressed to impress and ready to seal the deal.

Except as soon as the door opened, Xander started scowling.

"Ugh, you're back to being a magazine ad. And smelling like one too. I guess it was too much to hope for that you'd show up like you did yesterday."

Skylar faltered. Like he had—yesterday? Xander *wanted* him to look like a slob? He'd assume this was a joke, but Xander didn't appear to have much of a sense of humor today. "But yesterday I was a mess."

"Yesterday you looked human. For the record, I'm drawing you like that, not this." When Skylar opened his mouth to defend himself, Xander waved a hand at him and slung his backpack over his shoulder. "Whatever, it's fine. Let's get this over with."

Skylar didn't want to *get this over with.* He intended to enjoy the day, but it was clear he needed to make some kind of amends to Xander first. He felt disjointed, however, to find his preparations were what had undone him. "I can go change."

Xander sighed. "You're fine. Ignore me. Let's go."

"But I don't *want* to ignore you."

They were on the metal stairs leading out of Xander's apartment and down to the driveway below. Xander, ahead of Skylar, stopped and turned around, staring up at Sky with a strange expression on his face.

"It's comments like that throwing me off."

Skylar frowned. "What do you mean?"

"When you show up at my house looking like a Brooks Brothers ad, when you give me that plastic smile, I remember you're a Greek. I remember what Zelda told me about how you're a one-percenter and how everything about you is alien to everything about me. When you're like that, I know where to put you in my head: in the same place I put the rest of the Greeks and the kids with trust funds and lives that are nothing like mine. But you tell me you don't want to ignore me. Or you tell me you like my painting. Or you turn out to be a fan of *Hotay & Moo,* and then get the history behind the story better than I do. For all that Zelda is the anarchist trying to blow up my life because they think it's healthy to be constantly reborn, *you're* the one making a mess of my tidy hermitage."

Skylar grinned, even though he was fairly certain Xander meant this speech to be an insult. "I think I'd like to meet this Zelda."

Xander snorted. "They would eat you alive."

"That sounds like an excellent challenge. But not

one for today. Did you have somewhere in mind to pick up something to eat?"

"I packed a peanut butter sandwich." More blushing and a deeper lift of the shoulders. "I know it's my turn to get lunch, but my stepdad is a dick sometimes and deliberately forgets to transfer my allowance to my account." He cut a glare to Skylar. "If you try and buy me lunch two times in a row, Richie Rich, it's not going to go well for you."

Skylar frowned at him, bemused. "Richie Rich?"

Xander rolled his eyes, though the gesture seemed to be aimed at himself. "Sorry. I think it's some 80s cartoon or something. My mom said it all the time. She had a thing for pop culture. As you might notice from my name."

Sky was truly lost now. "I'm sorry, what about your name is pop culture?"

Xander gave him a look of disbelief. "You can't be serious. Xander? As in Xander, Willow, Buffy, and Giles? *Buffy the Vampire Slayer*?"

"Ah. Yes, I know it. Wait. You're saying…"

"That I'm named after Xander Harris, yes. My mother had a huge crush on him that never died. Married a man who looked like him, and boy was that a bad choice. That relationship ended in disaster, but she got a baby boy out of it, so she named her son after her childhood crush." When Skylar couldn't help a wince, Xander smiled wryly. "Yeah, well, I thought I had it bad until I met Zelda. They're named after a video game princess. They pointed out I could have been named

Link."

Skylar laughed, but it didn't escape his notice that Xander had, for the first time, talked about his mother in some detail without being tense. He couldn't help himself—he plumbed a little.

"Do you mind that she named you that way? For a character?"

Xander shrugged. "I mean, it fits who she is."

"Do *you* mind, though?"

Xander looked away, but he still hadn't tensed up. "I don't, I guess. It's an okay name. Most people don't even think to guess it's for a show, and if they do, they think that's cool. But it's not like I really have friends to think that through anyway. So it doesn't matter."

"Have you ever watched the show?"

There was the tension, but it was more of a shadow passing over Xander, a sadness on his heart. "We used to, before she remarried."

Skylar hesitated, but decided to press just a little further. "I don't mean to pry, but…are you estranged from your family?"

He hadn't meant to be quite that blunt—God, but he was off his game with this guy—but thankfully Xander didn't close up again, though he did speak quietly, his tone flat and slightly hollow. "Not estranged, no." He shifted his backpack higher. "More that we don't speak the same language. I've found it easier to avoid contact with them."

Skylar thought of the unopened cookie boxes. He wanted to ask if homemade snickerdoodles could somehow muddy communications, but he was pretty sure *that* would shut Xander down.

He rubbed his chin, staring at Xander's backpack. Never mind his family just now. Skylar had to figure out a way to buy the man lunch. "Do you have your sketchbook and pencils in there?"

Xander gave him an incredulous look. "Is that a serious question? Of course I do. I have three sketchbooks, two sets of pencils, and my markers. Always."

"Excellent. Then I'm buying lunch. *And*," he added quickly, as Xander started to protest, "as payment, you'll draw me something."

Xander glowered at him, but his shoulders settled back into their proper place as well. "Fine, but I'm picking the sandwich shop, then, so I don't have to draw the goddamned Sistine Chapel ceiling to break even."

The thought of watching Xander draw even a McDonald's value meal worth of a sketch had Skylar's heart beating faster. "Sounds good to me."

SKYLAR MAY HAVE dressed like an ad again, but Xander could still see glimpses of the man from the day he'd shown up unpolished. Especially when they were on the hospital hill. For the first few minutes, Skylar lectured Xander about smartphones and social media apps. Then the wind rustled through the trees, dislodging some white blossoms from a tree, and Skylar cut himself off mid-sentence to look up and watch the petals fall.

Xander didn't watch the flowers, too caught up in the transformation of the man before him. It was like a camera shutter, except it didn't flash, it stayed open, stuck in place by the movement of the trees and the wind. Gone was the plastic smile and the calculation. This was nothing but wonder and softness, and it pulled Xander in like a tractor beam. He'd buy all the smartphones in town, if Skylar would look at *him* like that.

The wind settled down, but the petals kept falling, and Skylar's expression didn't change, only morphed into an extremely happy smile. "I feel like I'm in an anime. If only these were cherry blossoms."

"I think they're apple. Which, honestly, is a lot more American." Xander tried to feel his way carefully across the soap bubble of this softer Skylar. "So. First you read my manga, and now you admit you watch anime."

When Skylar's smile faded into a guilty expression, Xander worried that had been the wrong approach, but Skylar didn't retreat, only changed his focus to tearing the edge of his napkin. "I do, yes."

"I don't watch as much as I'd like. I'll admit, I have a bias toward manga, but I feel that's acceptable, given that I draw it. Also, drawing anime and manga isn't the same thing. I feel sometimes if I watch too much anime, I screw myself up."

That snagged Skylar's attention again. "Really? How is that?"

"Well—I mean, drawing is drawing, but the biggest

difference is that anime moves and manga doesn't. Anime is short for *animation.* They get to actually move their drawings around—in fact, they have to. I must convince you my static drawings *could* move. It's not all that different than the difference between a novel and a movie script, I would think. The script is the blueprint for the movement the actors do, and the novel has to do it all, or make you think it's happening." Xander's ears heated as he felt his metaphor sliding away from him. "Or something. I don't know, ignore me. I don't know what I'm talking about. Like I could write anything."

But now Skylar was *truly* interested. He leaned forward over their mini picnic spread, all his junior corporate persona evaporated—this was a different shark emerging, and it made Xander's whole body tingle. "*No,* you're right. It's exactly the same kind of thing. God, I never thought about it. When I used to write, I'd sit there for hours, trying to find a way to show a sunset or a fight scene or a lovers' quarrel. I could see it in my head, like a painting, but believe me when I tell you that you don't want to see me with a brush. I'm not sure my pencil was much better, but sometimes I thought I came close to painting with my words. That's so brilliant, Xander."

The wind had picked up again, sending more apple blossoms down around Skylar's head as he smiled. He was always beautiful, and perfect, but right now he was so excruciatingly perfect that Xander felt he could crack. *He's straight,* he told himself, desperately.

Are you sure about that?

And is that what you should be thinking about at this moment?

Xander let out a breath. "Thanks. I try." His brain finally registered what Skylar had said. "Wait, you used to write? What did you write?"

Skylar blushed—actually blushed—and Xander felt his own cheeks heat in sympathetic response because the guy was so *fucking adorable*, blushing under the apple tree. "Oh, nothing much. Just silly stuff, when I was younger." He smiled what Xander could tell was supposed to be one of his charming Silver numbers but was, in truth, just more embarrassed adorableness, and nudged Xander's foot. "Okay, so, finish your food so you can pay me for lunch. I'm looking forward to this."

Xander grunted and stuffed the last of his sandwich into his mouth so he couldn't self-deprecate. He hated it when artists did that, and it annoyed him to discover the reason he hadn't been one of their ranks was because he was such a hermit no one ever gushed about his art the way Skylar did, not to his face. Hell, maybe no one ever did at all. Maybe Skylar was his only fan.

Maybe they were some sort of doomed muse relationship where Xander was in love with Skylar and Skylar was in love with Xander's art.

Actually, that wouldn't be a half-bad arrangement. He'd been getting himself off this long. Why fix what wasn't broken?

Xander dusted off his hands, wiped them on his jeans for good measure, and got out his supplies.

Skylar brushed his crumbs away too, tracking Xander's every movement. "What are you going to draw?"

Technically, Xander should offer to draw whatever Skylar wanted, since this was supposed to be his payment, but he was feeling punchy. "You."

It pleased him to see how much this startled Skylar, made him sit up straighter and fidget. "Me? Seriously?"

"I did tell you I wanted you to model for me. Why not start now?"

God, but the man was cute when he was put on the spot. "But…I'm not wearing anything special, and I'm not…prepared."

"God help us if you get more prepared. I want you to seem natural, so don't do anything in particular. Relax, and let me study you. It's my job to make the portrait interesting."

"But why do you want to draw *me*?"

Dammit, busted. Time to bluff. "Because it's fun to watch you get flustered." *Redirect, redirect.* "Okay. I brought along a few different mediums. Regular pencil, charcoal, or manga marker?"

He'd been pretty sure of the answer before he asked, but it was fun to watch Skylar's face light up. "Manga marker—does that mean you'd draw me as a manga character?"

Xander couldn't help smiling. "If you wanted. I don't *have* to draw manga style with my markers. I could also draw manga style with pencil, for the record. But if you yearn to see a comic version of yourself, I can make your dream come true."

All Skylar's self-consciousness bled away. "Yes,

please."

Xander smiled to himself as he pulled out his manga paper and his tin of markers. "Done. But if you want it colored, you're going to have to spring for a lot more than a sandwich. All my Copics are low."

He shouldn't have said that, but he couldn't stop himself. He yearned to see the hungry look on Skylar's face. "*You can do it in color?*"

It was like they were passing a crack pipe back and forth, and God help him, Xander couldn't stop. "Not just color. The good color, that rich, dark stuff like you see in your anime. Copic color. Japanese markers. My pride and joy. But they're pricey as hell. Twelve dollars for one marker, new, and the refills are five dollars each online, seven dollars in town." He tried to reel himself in, but there was no hope for it, not with Skylar looking at him like that. "I don't whip them out for just anyone."

There was the shark smile—no *ting*, something far, far more dangerous—and it didn't simply make Xander shiver. It made him want to lie in the grass and wait breathlessly for Skylar to do things to him. It made him bananas to admit Skylar wasn't flirting with him. Well, he *was,* but not in the way Xander wanted. Not in *all* the ways he wanted.

As he roughed out the drawing, however, that voice came back to him, that strange backseat whisper that kept nagging at his mental coattails.

It's not as simple a comparison as that. It's not that he isn't interested in you. He's interested differently in you. Pay attention.

Xander didn't understand that voice, in fact got more frustrated by it every time it nagged him, so he snuffed it out and focused on his paper. That is, he did until a Skylar-head-shaped shadow fell over it.

"I thought you were going to use marker."

The right side of Xander's mouth tipped up in a smile. "I will. First I'm roughing out my map. I can erase pencil. Marker, not so much." He flicked his fingers at Skylar's nose, suppressing a shiver when he accidentally grazed his skin. "Sit back. I need to check your proportions. This may be a comic drawing, but if it's going to resemble you, I need to see what you look like." He nodded at Skylar's legs. "Your feet, specifically, please. Your hands too, but also your feet."

Skylar laughed as he shifted his body so his feet were visible. "Why my feet?"

"Because the human body is like a puzzle, one part giving clues about the other. Your feet I need simply because they're always tricky to get right, but hands are critical. Your hands are exactly as big as the size of your face."

"What? No way."

"Check it and see, if you think I'm lying."

He watched as Skylar put his hand to his face and then gasped as he discovered Xander was, in fact, telling the truth. "That's insane."

"So I suppose you're going to lose your mind when I tell you your arm span is the same as your height."

Skylar did, and Xander stopped sketching for several minutes, giving a mini drawing anatomy lesson to a delighted Skylar, who tested out everything testable on himself as Xander watched, smiling.

"That's amazing." Skylar shook his head. "Who knew all this stuff?"

"Portrait artists." Xander picked his pencil up and began to sketch again.

This time Skylar didn't ask him any questions, and soon Xander lost himself to his work, first mapping out a rough concept until he liked his draft, then, at last, opening his markers and beginning the real work. He'd decided to draw Skylar as he was, in a way, sitting at his picnic, but what Xander couldn't get out of his head was the way he'd looked when the apple blossoms fell. That unbridled joy on his face. The true Skylar, unvarnished.

And because it had seemed to mean something to him, when he added the falling petals and the tree they came from, Xander made them cherry blossoms.

How long he worked, Xander wasn't sure. He only knew the drawing quickly stopped being something he did to humor the man he had a crush on and became art he took pleasure in making. He loved chasing down the little flicker in Manga Skylar's jaw—he didn't mean to put the stubble back in, it simply crept in on its own, starting as a shadow, then giving in and becoming a baby beard. The character had his hands up, fingers spread, mouth open in happy surprise as he tried to catch the petals falling all around him.

There were a lot of petals, and Xander felt compelled to put a great deal of detail on the cherry tree, and in the grass, and of course on Manga Skylar. Which was probably why his neck hurt so much when he finally put down the marker and why, when he glanced at his phone, it told him he'd been drawing for almost two hours.

"Oh my God, I'm so sorry! Why didn't you—?"

He stopped talking when he got a look at Skylar's face.

Skylar looked arrested. He clearly hadn't pointed out how long they'd been sitting there because he didn't know how long it had been, either. He looked gut-punched, but not necessarily in a bad way. More straight-up gobsmacked.

Xander couldn't take it anymore. "You know, nobody else looks at my art the way you do."

Skylar lifted his gaze to his, but he seemed drugged, like all he wanted to do was look down at the drawing some more. "Is that really how you see me?"

Didn't think things through, did you, Fairchild? "Um, well…yeah. That's how you looked to me when the petals fell. Except I wanted you to have cherry blossoms."

It was as if Xander had gut-punched him all over again. "That's the part that keeps getting me. How you changed the flowers. But I guess that's an artist's job, to be perceptive."

"You're not exactly blind to people's details, Mr. Stone."

"But I can't do this. I can't do anything like this." He touched the edge of the paper reverently, as if it might disintegrate under his touch. "*Could* you color it?"

Xander sighed. "I'd color it as thanks for the hungry way you look at my art, but I wasn't kidding when I said my Copics needed refills. My pinks especially, which are going to be critical for the blossoms."

"I'll buy them for you. Please don't fight me," he said, before Xander could try. "It's my own self-interest here."

"You don't understand how many markers I need refilling to color this one sketch."

"Not to be gross, but you don't understand that you could tell me it was one hundred markers at twelve dollars and I could order them for you on my credit card right now." He winced. "Sorry. That really was entitled. But I want you to color this. Badly."

It *was* entitled, yes, but it was also kind of hot, to see Skylar come undone over his art. And it was also a bit sexy to have money thrown at him like this. With nothing expected in return except a colored-in drawing.

Xander was developing a kink.

"Message received, Richie Rich. You want to go to Art Haus now, before I come to my senses, or order online where the prices are a little better?"

"Art Haus, definitely." Skylar sighed. "Here I was going to try to talk you into letting me get you a phone, but I'm buying you markers instead."

"Marker *refills*. For the record, I'd have never let you buy me a phone. And I wouldn't let anyone but you buy me refills."

The smile Skylar gave Xander rang in his head like a

bell. "Good to hear."

IT WAS NINE by the time Skylar made it home to Delta Sig. He came in the back door as quietly as he could, but unfortunately he didn't make it to the stairs before Mary came to find him, drying her hands on a towel and offering him a welcoming smile.

"Well, look what the cat dragged in. That must have been an amazing study session."

"Not a study session." Unc appeared behind her, munching on a cookie as he leaned in the doorway. "He was off working on his senior project, the overachiever."

No, he'd been at Xander's apartment, spellbound as he watched him color with his magical Japanese markers, then enjoying cheap ramen in his kitchen while he coaxed Xander into talking more about art, specifically about how he made the *Hotay & Moo* comics. The truth was, Skylar could have stayed there another three hours, but Xander had been the one to politely shoo him away, apologizing because he had to call his mother before she went to bed so he could get money before he ran out of food and toilet paper and had to have awkward conversations with his landlady.

"Otherwise I'd be happy to sit here and talk with you all night," he'd said, then looked embarrassed to have said it.

Skylar smiled at Mary and Unc, the gesture feeling stretched and strange on his face. All he wanted to do was escape and process the day, alone. "It was a long day, for sure. Think I'll go to bed early so I can start again tomorrow."

Mary frowned and pointed at the ratty folio he clutched in his hands. "Goodness, what on earth is that?"

"*Nothing.*" Skylar hadn't meant to speak so sharply and tried to soften his rebuke, but the way she looked at the folder made him tense and grip it tighter. "Sorry. It's…a gift from my client."

"That's nice." She patted him on the shoulder and winked. "You sleep tight, sweetheart."

Escaping up the stairs at last, Skylar went to his room, shut the door, and locked it. Alone, he spread the folio on his bed and unlaced the string keeping it closed. Drawing a deep breath, he opened the flap and pulled out the drawing that had cost him a seven-dollar sandwich, fifty dollars' worth of markers, a ten-dollar mat board, and a day's worth of LSAT study.

As the beauty of it hit him all over again, Skylar vowed he would pay triple that price again in a heartbeat.

"My job is to create movement in stillness." Xander's words came back to Skylar as he stared at the drawing, now mounted and matted, glowing in the light shining from beside his bed. Skylar didn't look away from the image, but in his mind's eye he saw Xander at the table in his kitchen, waving his hands to illustrate his point. "The potential of movement. I use your own mind to help me out—it *wants* the drawing to move, and if I set the lines just right, it will assume motion for me. Then it will realize there *isn't* movement, and that paradox will charm you, which is where your appreciation for my talent comes in. Theoretically."

There was no theory about it. Skylar was in complete awe of what Xander had done. The Manga Skylar sat spellbound, vibrant and glowing in his freshly refilled Copic ink—the color had added more than hue. Xander had done tiny crosshatches that somehow, along with the shading the black and gray markers had already done, made it seem as if Skylar's clothes rippled in the breeze. His skin had more shades and tones than should have been possible with the handful of markers he'd seen Xander use. And he *had* seen him use them.

"I don't usually let people watch me work," Xander had murmured. Then continued to let Skylar watch him anyway.

Skylar had tried to keep quiet and not bother him, but it had been too difficult. He was too enthralled. He kept saying things like, "That's incredible" or "How did you *do* that?" and when he asked questions like that, Xander would always explain, if he could. But most of the time Xander couldn't answer. "The magic of art," was his teasing reply.

The cherry blossoms still got to Skylar. That Xander had so casually made that switch—maybe it was a throwaway gesture to him, but he didn't know how many nights Skylar had lain awake, drunk on anime, tired of pushing too hard to meet everyone's expectations, and dreaming impossible dreams. Telling himself someday, perhaps for a vacation, he could go to Japan and see those cherry blossoms for himself. Hoping the dark voice inside him was wrong, that they truly were as beautiful as every anime made them out to be.

That's how you looked to me when the petals fell.

Skylar didn't know why it made him feel so uneasy to look at the expression on his manga self's face. He didn't know why that unbridled joy unsettled him so much, why he could neither look away nor at it somehow at the same time.

When he finally broke free of the drawing's spell, he got out his phone and checked his messages. A text from his mother's secretary about the fundraiser, reminding him she could still find him a date if he hadn't secured his own. Messages and emails from Tau Kapp and Delta Sig members wanting favors, following through on chains of events Skylar had set in motion weeks ago. Other people asking for help, wanting the magic of Skylar Stone for themselves. The only item that wasn't something demanding a piece of him was an email from Ellen with pictures of Chris's graduation photos and a thank you for the present he'd sent.

That message made him smile, but it made him sad too. He'd have liked to go to Chris's graduation, but he hadn't known if he'd be welcome. Did they want some rich white guy in the middle of their family event? Ellen would have let him come if he'd asked, but would she have *wanted* him there? He had no way of knowing, so he hadn't asked, to make sure he wouldn't be a bother.

Looking at the photos, though, he ached, wishing he could have been at least a little bit of trouble, even if only slightly to the side, out of the way.

Skylar stared at Xander's drawing some more, trying to recapture the happy feeling from the afternoon. All he managed, unfortunately, was that his chest tightened at the thought of that pressure and tension of those emails and texts enclosing around his joy.

Skylar laid the drawing on his dresser, shut off his lights, climbed into bed, and pulled his laptop under the covers, firing up Crunchyroll from muscle memory. But as the opening credits played, he stuck his head out, grabbed his phone, and punched out a text.

Thank you for today. I had a great time.

He couldn't quite bring himself to push the send button. He thought he should erase it and say something more appropriate, something encouraging about Xander's project or something joking about their joint Pygmalions, but in the end he put the phone back on his nightstand without texting anything.

Seven episodes later, he gave up trying to keep his eyes open and slid the laptop onto the window ledge, but he didn't sleep right away, his brain chasing itself.

I don't think Xander's giving me curmudgeon lessons, it whispered. *I think he's turning me into something else entirely.*

Except the warning wouldn't hold, burned away by the Copic-colored memory of Xander's manga drawing.

He's not turning you into anything. He's only chipping away your stone and showing you what's already there.

Chapter Ten

FOR THE FIRST half of June, Xander existed in a hazy, Skylar-filled dream.

He never did upgrade his phone, but he did let Skylar sign him up for six different social media sites. Initially Xander balked at this, since he was only required to prove he was active on three, but Skylar insisted he needed to get himself out there.

"Most of them end up duplicating themselves anyway, so they're not extra work, but they *are* extra followers. You *want* the sites like DeviantArt, though, and Tumblr, because they're how people will learn about you."

"Don't you mean steal my art?" Xander pressed his lips together and shook his head as he scanned the acres and acres of amateur art. "Honestly, *who* is going to come here to find my work? How will they see me in the middle of all this garbage?"

"Because I'm going to teach you how to get noticed, how to showcase yourself. How to stand out."

"Yes, because you *know* how much I love drawing attention to myself."

Skylar grinned and nudged Xander with his elbow,

making Xander's skin break out in gooseflesh. "We'll draw attention to your *work*, so you can sell it and buy more marker refills."

"And oil paint. And canvas. And ramen."

"All of these things, yes. But the first step is logging into the account. Which now you've done. Let's celebrate with lunch on the hospital hill. My treat."

Xander let Skylar buy him lunch that day without argument, mostly because he was shaken from the thought of all those online presences floating around, *existing*. It didn't help that when they went to his apartment afterward and Skylar made him log on again, he discovered exactly no one had friended him, anywhere. Not even Zelda had accepted his Facebook request. So much for their promise.

"This is pretty much how it's going to go, you know." Xander glowered at the screen. "You're going to be the only one who friends me. In real life and online."

"Not true. Not for long, anyway."

"Where exactly are you going to get these friends for me?" It was a point of order that had been bothering Xander for some time now. "I'm not kidding when I say I don't have any."

"But you keep mentioning this Zelda. Are they not a friend?"

Xander shrugged, averting his gaze. "I suppose. They're...an aggressive friend, but I imagine I have to count them. Probably I have to count the staff of *Lucky 7* as well, but I think they mostly tolerate me." He wrapped his arms around himself, feeling too exposed and awkward, but there was nothing to do but continue his confession. "People don't want to be friends with me. It's always been that way."

Skylar was quiet for a moment. He'd taken control of the laptop, fussing with the keys. "Were you bullied in high school, Xander?"

The question was somehow both unexpected and inevitable. Had anyone else asked, or even if Skylar had asked any other way, Xander would have refused to answer. But leave it to Skylar to find the right pitch and tone to lure Xander into a reply.

Except Skylar was going to find, he suspected, Xander's answer wasn't what he expected either.

"I was. And it was pretty brutal. But that's not why I don't have friends."

Skylar glanced up at him, curious. Inviting. Patient. "What do you mean?"

Xander uncrossed his arms and leaned back into his chair. "I was bullied, online and off. I was gay, and people knew. I didn't advertise, but people assumed, and they were right. It was a small town. People were bored and eager for a pecking order. Plus, my stepfather was shitty to me. You're an easy target when there's no one to protect you."

Pain flickered across Skylar's features. "I'm sorry."

Xander shrugged, trying to be breezy, but he felt wooden. He pivoted away from his family and back to hazing, which was so much more pleasant. "High school wasn't great, no. But I got through it. I survived. I retreated into my art, and it saved me. And now I'm fairly decent at art, so it's not a bad trade. That said, I didn't have friends even before the bullying. I've just never been the guy people hang out with. People annoy me. They get in my way. They want things. They misunderstand me. They mock me. They're arrogant and full of themselves."

Skylar raised an eyebrow. "And yet you like cats."

"They're honest about their arrogance and self-centeredness, at least. People lie about it. They want you to pretend it's an even exchange, but it never is. They want you to play this game of nice, and I hate it."

"So what about me? Do you hate being friends with me?"

Xander blushed and looked down at his lap. "No. You're different."

"Why? How?"

"I don't know. You just are." His blush became so hot his face felt like flame. "I don't want to talk about this anymore."

Xander sensed Skylar's hesitation again, and he knew another heavy question was coming. "About your parents not protecting you…it's not the same for me, but I feel like I understand that."

Xander's first instinct was to retreat into himself, but when he glanced at Skylar, saw the flush of his face, the echoes of pain, he couldn't. "You mean…with your dad?"

Skylar stared at the computer, though Xander suspected he wasn't seeing it. "It's not that he doesn't defend me, exactly. But he doesn't…" Skylar rubbed his cheek. "I feel sometimes as if there's nothing I can do, nothing in the world to get him to tell me I've done a good job or acknowledge I exist. Not even in a bored, disinterested way, let alone a proud way. And I can't stop trying to please him, no matter what I do." His gaze darted to Xander as he blushed. "Sorry."

Xander thought about letting it go. He almost did. It was his muscle memory, pushing people out. But…it was Skylar, asking to be let in.

Xander brushed his left thumb over the back of his right hand, and he kept his gaze there in his lap as he spoke. "My birth father left my life so long ago I never really knew him, but that's never stopped me from wondering what was wrong with me, what about me made it so he didn't want anything to do with me. Then my mom remarried, and my stepfather treated me like Cinderella, especially as my mom gave him new sons. He looks at me like he can't wait for me to be gone from his life."

"Doesn't your mom object to that?"

The question made the tight ball in the center of his chest swell. "She…doesn't like confrontation. She wants everyone to be happy and get along. It upsets her when we fight. I try not to fight, because they can't seem to understand me anyway, but that just means I lose."

"I'm sorry."

Xander shrugged. "I don't need any of them. I can make it on my own."

"But you shouldn't have to do that. I know you said you don't like people, but you should have *some* people."

"All they do is let me down."

"I won't let you down."

The vow hung in the air, poignant and slightly awkward. Xander ran a hand through his hair. "Anyway. The social media stuff is set up." His glance fell on his bookshelf, and he seized on the distraction. "Hey, I've been meaning to ask you. What manga have you read?"

"Not much, I'm afraid. I mostly watch anime."

Xander pursed his lips. "You need to fix that if you're going to write it. Have you read *Fullmetal Alchemist*?"

"No, I haven't. But wait, what do you mean, write? I can't write anything."

Xander waved this objection silent as he rose and crossed to his bookshelf, coming back with his box set of the twenty-seven volumes of *Fullmetal*. He plunked the heavy case on the table beside the laptop. "You need to read this. If you've seen the original anime, it's different. Even if you've seen the second version, *Brotherhood*, reading the manga is not the same as watching the anime."

Skylar opened the box set and ran his fingers down the spines of the volumes. "I haven't seen much of the anime. I saw parts of the early version and episodes of the *Brotherhood* one on Crunchyroll, but I wondered if I needed to finish the first one before I got into it."

"*Fullmetal Alchemist: Brotherhood* is the version that sticks true to Hiromu Arakawa's manga. The one that ran congruent to the manga's publication in the early 2000s is vastly different. I've seen both because *Fullmetal* is my favorite story and Hiromu Arakawa is a hero of mine."

Skylar grinned. "*Hiromu.* That's where your cat got her name."

Xander nodded. "Yes. She's a genius. Which is why I want you to read the manga, because while they're her ideas in the anime, you're not experiencing the art and story in her preferred medium. I have the art books too, which I could stare at for hours. I wish I could meet her. I have so many things I want to ask." He pulled out the first four volumes and handed them to Skylar. "Here. You can borrow these to get started."

"Oh—I don't want to take your books. I mean, I'll read them, but I'll read them here, or on the hill when we go to lunch. Or when you draw me."

Skylar was supposed to be studying, Xander thought, but he wasn't going to bring that up. "There are twenty-seven volumes. It's going to take you some time."

"But it's manga. It doesn't take me any time at all to read."

Xander recoiled as if Skylar had just dropped the books into mud. "*You have to take your time and look at the art.* It's not just about the words."

Grinning, Skylar held up his hands in surrender. "Yes, sir. But you see, that's all the more reason for me to read in your presence. How will I learn to appreciate the art if you're not there to show me?"

That's what Xander ended up doing. On sunny days they sat outside, sometimes on the hospital hill, sometimes at the state park. On rainy days they stayed in Xander's apartment on the couch, Xander sketching while Skylar read, except Xander kept stopping to point out particular panels, commenting on shading or composition. Skylar did read fast, too fast in Xander's opinion, but he did seem to appreciate the art as much as the story. Though he was absolutely into the story.

"I love this idea of equivalent exchange," Skylar said one day when they were at the state park. He'd led Skylar through the back trails to the ridge to show him the view. They were seated on the grass, overlooking the valley below, Skylar across from him, reading as Xander sketched him. "Everything about this story is that you give up something to get something. And it's true, that's how life works. Which is why you drive me crazy, because you don't let me give you things back."

"It isn't always how life works." Xander kept his gaze on his paper, but he was hyperaware of how Skylar sat, where his arms and legs were, how pretty his mouth was. How exquisitely beautiful all of him was, how soft and comforting he felt in Xander's sacred space, the place he'd never shared with anyone before. "Sometimes we give and nothing comes back. In fact, most of the time that's how it happens."

"But I'm *trying* to give to you, and it's like pulling teeth to get you to accept. You want to be the only one who gives, and it's not fair."

Xander shrugged, being especially careful not to

look up now. "I don't like to be in people's debt. It makes me uncomfortable."

"So you want other people to be in yours?"

He paused, arrested by the thought. "I don't consider them in my debt, though. If I give someone something, it's simply given. I don't expect anything back."

"That's hard on other people, Xander. When you give to people—to good people—they want to give back, and you need to let them. It hurts them when you don't let them give to you. Or help you. They want to interact with you."

Xander huffed and opened his mouth to say, *Nobody wants to interact with me*, but before he could, Skylar spoke again.

"*I* want to interact with you."

Xander's pencil stuttered across the page, and the rush of hot embarrassment felt like it engulfed his whole body. He picked up his eraser and cleaned up his mistake with a shaking hand.

"Fine," he replied, voice trembling. "You can give things to me. But just you." Somehow that felt worse, more exposed than anything he'd said yet. He cleared his throat. "Be quiet so I can draw you."

"All right," Skylar said with a gentle smile.

THE FUNDRAISER WAS looming ever closer, and Skylar still hadn't chosen anyone to take as his date. His mother's secretary had called him twice, wanting a name for the guest list, offering to pick someone for him, but Skylar couldn't bring himself to select anyone or turn over the task. He had a list of suitable women—from Benten and elsewhere, ones who understood the rules, who could play the game. They would fit the bill and then some. Whatever date appeared on his arm wouldn't assume they would associate beyond that night, though they'd likely be open to it if he suggested otherwise. Cool and practical. He had a list of interchangeable dolls, ready to be at his side.

His gaze fell on the painting on the other side of his room, and he thought, *I don't want cool and practical.*

Grabbing his wallet and his keys, Skylar left his phone on the desk and headed for his car. He needed to take a drive.

He hadn't intended to go to the state park, but once he was there, the rightness of the move seeped into him like water. A walk would do him good. He wasn't exactly wearing hiking shoes, but he didn't care. He wanted to go to the place Xander had taken him the other day. Ten minutes with the view from that bluff and his head would clear, he was sure of it. Then he could do what he needed to do.

Except finding Xander's hideaway was more difficult than he'd bargained for. He tried to get there via the main paths, but after twenty minutes he realized that route would never take him to the top of the bluff. He had to cut through the hiking paths, which were winding and circuitous, and it didn't take long for him to realize he was lost. Never mind where the bluff was—

where was *he*? Was this even a path?

Why, exactly, had he decided to do this without a phone?

He didn't see the branch until it was too late. One moment he was walking, the next he'd pitched forward, landing face-first in moldy leaves. Pain shot up his right leg. His face was full of earth, his hands too. His whole front was mud-caked, and after he spit out dirt and brushed his hands clean enough to function, he sat back and examined his shin.

Blood. The whole of his pants leg seeped with it, the tan fabric torn and blood-stained, and when he pushed the fabric up with a hiss, beneath it his skin was scraped raw, a long cut dripping steadily down to soak his sock. The sight alarmed him at first, and he worried he was trapped in the middle of nowhere, injured and unable to move, but when he pressed on the wound with a clean section of his sleeve, it seemed to slow, and as he tested weight on it, he thought he would be able to hobble to his car, provided he could figure out where it was.

He sat there first, waiting for the bleeding to subside, wallowing in his misery. And as he did so, thoughts bled out along with that coming from his cut.

I don't want to take any of those women as my date. I don't want my mother's secretary to pick anyone, either. I don't want to go to this event at all.

The only way I want to go is if I can take Xander with me.

That confession hurt inside his chest, and he shut

his eyes. Xander would never go with him. He shouldn't even ask. Xander would hate going to that kind of party.

He climbed to his feet, unsteady, but he managed to move. Slowly now, he headed east, using the sun to guide him. If he kept going this way, he should find the parking lot.

It would be fun to take Xander. The long car ride. They could talk about so many things.

He came to a stream—not a large one, but wide enough he couldn't leap over it, and deep enough that it came to his knees as he forged through it. It felt cool against his injured leg, and he hesitated in the middle, letting the water wash over him as he stared up at the sky.

The forest was beautiful. It had tried to kill him, but it was still beautiful.

He wished he'd asked Xander to come with him. Xander would have.

He would go with you to Connecticut. Ask him.

Skylar shut his eyes. What if he didn't want to? What if he said no?

What if he said yes?

Skylar opened his eyes again, staring up at the canopy of the trees. "This is dangerous."

Yes, it is, the trees seemed to whisper back to him.

He found the path soon after that, with signs clearly pointing to the parking lot and his car. The answer to his dilemma, however, lay firmly beyond his reach.

"THERE'S SOMETHING I need to ask you."

Xander glanced up from his drawing. Skylar had sounded funny, and he looked stranger. Embarrassed and nervous, which wasn't like Skylar at all. Xander wondered what was going on. "Sure," he said cautiously. "What do you need to ask me?"

Skylar rubbed his chin, and Xander couldn't help noticing he'd allowed a *tiny* bit of stubble to poke through. "I have a feeling I know what you're going to say, and it's fine, really, but…well, there's this thing. I wanted to know if you were interested in going to it with me."

Xander knew Skylar wasn't asking him out, but he had a thrill all the same. "What's the thing?"

"It's a fundraiser of my mom's. A lobster bake at our beach house. My dad won't be there, but a lot of important political people will, and she feels like it's better if family is there." Skylar wasn't just fidgeting now, he was blushing. "She asked me to bring a—someone."

Xander was blushing too. If this were manga, there'd have to be two panels, and they'd each have the crosshatches on their cheeks.

The *fuck* if that didn't sound like a date, actually.

"If it's not your thing, I understand—"

"It sounds great," Xander blurted out, overriding the 90 percent of his brain that was trying to make him scream, *No way in fucking hell, rich people baking lobster, are you kidding me, they're going to laugh me off the beach and you're going to lead the pack once you see how out of place I am!* But the 10 percent that seized control couldn't bear the thought of going to sleep that night. It honestly sounded like he'd been asked out.

By Skylar.

To a lobster bake.

What the fuck.

Now that he was committed, though, the panicked part of him began to hedge his performance in advance. "I didn't even know you could bake lobster, though. Also, I've never eaten it. Or been on a beach. Or to a fundraiser. It's possible, maybe probable, you're going to regret this ask."

Skylar still blushed, but he smiled now too. "Not a chance. And I hate to tell you, but the lobster comes in catered. If you tell me you want to order sandwiches and eat them in my room, I won't mind, and I won't tell a soul."

That was one worry down. "Okay."

"As far as the fundraising aspect goes, you don't need to do anything for that." He grinned. "Probably dress—what was it? More magazine ad. But mostly you can follow my lead. It'll be a good dry run, I thought, for the kinds of things you need to do for your BFA party."

Idiot, this was what he meant. Stop letting your fantasies bleed over. "Totally. Thanks for having my back."

"Plus you were my first choice when she told me to bring a date."

In the manga, Xander would have Xs for eyes and puffs of smoke over his head, he was so embarrassed.

Except Xander was also totally confused. It wasn't

so much that Skylar was sending mixed messages, more that Xander didn't understand how to read him. Or maybe it was that his own idiot lust was in the way. He reminded himself daily it didn't matter, that Skylar was a good friend and that should be enough, goddammit, that what Skylar didn't know about Xander's masturbatory fantasies was—well, it was fucking crucial at this point that Skylar not know about those—but even when Xander was able to keep his feelings in the friend zone, Skylar pulled shit like this. Xander couldn't tell if the guy was gay baiting or just that clueless, or if there was something else going on.

He tried *so hard* to ride it out, to bury his angst in his painting and let his unrequited emotions and his confusion feed his art. But when Skylar casually dropped that, by the way, they'd be staying overnight, and would that be a problem with the cats, because if so he'd spring for a sitting service—it was then that Xander caved and called Zelda.

They didn't answer, of course, but after the message Xander left, he knew he'd be getting a phone call soon enough. It took them about ten minutes, and they didn't waste time with a greeting.

"*What do you mean, you need help deciding if Skylar Stone asked you on a date or not?* What in the hell is going on down there? Jesus Christ, I can't leave you alone for ten fucking minutes."

Xander settled into his sofa, whereupon Hiromu immediately settled onto his chest. He stroked her fur as he tried to figure out how to start this conversation. "Hi.

How are you? Summer good so far? How's the restaurant?"

"Fuck my summer. Tell me what the hell is going on with you and Frat Boy. Why do you think he asked you on a date, and why is it unclear? Why did you not turn him down on his fascist ass?"

"Because he's not a fascist." Xander was no longer amused. "His family is liberal, you know."

"*I do know*, thank you. Trust me to do my homework, please. The Stones are *those* kind of liberals."

"A quick reminder that if you mention Hillary Clinton, we're going to have an argument, I won't get my question answered, and I won't speak to you until Labor Day."

"Listen, this time it's *germane*."

"It isn't, in fact. Because believe it or not, I haven't once discussed politics with Skylar and never intend to. I don't discuss politics with anyone."

"Well, then what *did* you want to talk about? Because I don't want to talk about your potential relationship, and if you even *sigh* in a sexual manner, I'm hanging up."

Xander shut his eyes and pinched the bridge of his nose. "I shouldn't have called. I knew that, but you've been gone awhile, and I let myself pretend you were someone I could hold a conversation with where I didn't want to run screaming into the woods afterward."

"For fuck's sake. I know you love a good mope, but this is intense even for you." They paused. "Oh. I get it.

You really are torn up about this."

"Which is what I've been trying to tell you."

"All right. I'll overlook the fact that his family is part of the cancer eating the world because I love you and want to see you happy, even though I don't understand how a Stone could ever make you happy."

"How generous of you." Xander settled deeper into the couch, earning a disapproving glare from Hiromu. "Though maybe that's a good place to start. I don't know that he's a very good Stone. I'm serious," he said, when Zelda snorted. "There's a side to him you don't know."

"If only you could see how hard I'm rolling my eyes at you right now."

"Shut up. He's…he's really different, more than I would ever have thought. For one, he fanboyed me over *Hotay & Moo.* And I mean he all but squealed. Made me sketch him something on the spot. He knew all about the secret shrine stuff and the seven lucky gods history. More than I did." He refused to bring up the potential shrine in the frat house, though he still burned with curiosity.

"So he likes art. That doesn't mean—"

"And then there's the Pygmalion thing. And the day he came over in his sweats and we ended up talking forever, and this whole time it was like I kept seeing this ghosted version of him. I even heard this voice in my head, like I had this mystery clue about him but I couldn't figure it out. Maybe I'm crazy, but—"

"*Slow down.* What Pygmalion thing? You were

watching the movie? Reading the play?"

"No. He wanted to teach me how to be social, like I was his Eliza Doolittle—"

"*Oh my fucking Christ*—"

"And then I said I didn't want to be remade. I just needed help with a few apps. But he said I could give him curmudgeon lessons, which, the thing is, I think he was serious. Except those aren't the lessons I'm giving him. I'm teaching him about art. And he's always telling me about how he used to write stories. Then I mention how maybe he could write again, and he backtracks hard and says oh no, he could never, but you can tell he wants to. Then ten minutes later he's telling me about writing again. And we're always together. We're supposed to be doing this social media thing, and we're doing it, kind of, but there's not much of it to do, and let me tell you how I'm not getting any Pygmalion lessons, either. I'm just drawing him manga doodles for sandwiches."

"You're—what?"

"It doesn't matter. The point is, I don't know what we're doing or why he's so interested in me. Obviously he likes me as a friend. I keep telling myself that's all it is. But every time I have myself convinced, he does something like invite me to his mom's beach house lobster thing *as his date* because *I'm the only person he could think of asking.*"

Long pause. "Whoa."

"Yeah. And I get a lot of smiles. And blushes. And a couple of times I think there's been unnecessary touches, but I may have imagined it."

"A reminder you're asking the wrong person about this. I'm not even one of those aces who enjoys reading about romance or sex. It just doesn't do a damn thing for me."

"Yes, but you have brain cells, and you know how to use deduction and problem-solving. *Help me.* Why would he be doing this? Why would I be so unable to tell if I'm in the friend zone or not? And why do I keep hearing that voice?"

"What voice? You mentioned that before too. Are you hearing things? Are you painting without proper ventilation again?"

"No." Xander buried his free hand in Hiromu's fur. "I don't know how to explain it. There's just…sometimes when I'm with him, especially when it's kind of…well, *a moment*, and in the movie version of my life I'd lean over and kiss him or he me or whatever, he doesn't look at all like that's on the menu, and meanwhile I'm sitting there dying because Jesus fucking Christ it's like I'm on a tractor beam and I need all my faculties to resist the pull. And sometimes when that happens, I hear this little voice. I mean, obviously not literally. But it's like when I'm painting, and I hear a voice that tells me to add red to the sky or put a figure under the tree, or don't add leaves, or keep working color into that sky because something interesting's going to happen—that kind of voice."

"Instinct, you mean?"

"Yeah, I guess. But instinct that gives good directions. And I always follow it. Except this is the first time I'm getting driving instructions about a person. And it's a weird direction."

"Well, what does your driving instructor tell you to do with Skylar? They probably have better advice than me."

"They tell me to wait. To be careful with him. And whenever I want to kiss him, they tell me not to. I know he doesn't want it, either. I don't think. Except sometimes maybe I think he does. It's…I don't know. It's like I'm holding spun glass in my hand. Which, okay, but I don't understand. I just…I wish I knew what was happening."

"I suppose it's out of the question that you do the obvious and ask him?"

"I'd rather go downtown to Scrugg's during happy hour, get naked, and do six rounds of karaoke."

"That's a hard no. Okay. Shit, dude, I got nothing. Except that I want one of those backseat instinct drivers. Sounds handy."

"I need some help figuring out how to play this. Do I keep bumbling forward the way I am?"

"Except didn't you call me because you couldn't stand doing it that way any longer?"

Fair point. "Okay, so…what else is there to do?"

"Besides doing the obvious thing and go talk to him?"

"Besides that, yes."

"Well…I'd say what's left is unpack this instinct voice thing."

Xander sat up straight, eliciting a yowl from Hiromu. "That's *it.*"

Zelda brightened. "It is? Really? Cool. I was totally bullshitting. I had no idea what to tell you to do."

"No, really, that's exactly what I need to do. What I get stuck on a painting or drawing, even sketches for *Hotay & Moo*, I try to focus my instinct like an antenna. I've never used it for something like this, so it might take me longer, but...that's a *great* idea. Thank you."

"I literally did nothing, but you're welcome." Zelda sighed. "I'm going to have to hustle my ass to town. There's no telling what kind of trouble you and Frat Boy are going to get up to by the time I get back."

"He got me on social media, which you've been after me to do forever. And you haven't friended me."

"Because you look corporate slick already. It's gross."

"It's my *grade.*"

"It's your *soul.* The welfare and wellbeing of the planet. The universe."

"My soul wants to be able to afford its next meal once my stepdad cuts off my stipend after graduation. As for the planet and the universe, I'm not entirely sure how my having a slick social media presence threatens its existence, but I'll shorten my shower and stop using plastic bags at the grocery store to compensate." He glanced at the clock. "And with that, I need to get going to work."

"Work with *Skylar*?"

"No, my actual job, thank you. And I really am going to be late, so I'm hanging up on you now."

Pamela was there when Xander got to the garage, but she didn't seem upset that he was a few minutes late. "Busy with your project again? Though I didn't see your friend's car, so I wasn't sure."

The subtle emphasis on the word *friend* made Xander fidget as he tied his apron on. "Skylar has to study for his LSAT. Besides, my boss is a hard-ass."

She chuckled. "Hmm, yes. But he's easy to look at, isn't he, that one?"

Xander poked at the bucket of brushes. "He's my friend."

"I didn't say he wasn't. Only pointed out he made for nice scenery. You should sketch him. Better yet, ask him to pose nu—"

"Would you look at that, these brushes need to be cleaned," he said too loudly. "I'll just take them to the utility sink and wash them, shall I?"

He didn't wash them, but he did splash water on his face, cold water, hoping to dispel the image of nude Skylar from his mind. It did not. He was still shaking, both from his imagination and the cold water, when he came back into the main room.

"You didn't used to react so badly to my teasing—good Lord, child, did you soak your head? You did, didn't you? Well, I'm sorry. You really are worked up over that boy, aren't you?"

Xander gave up. "I'm trying not to be. It isn't going well." He sat on a stool and used the hem of his apron as a towel. "I feel like a perv. I mean, shouldn't I be able to find someone attractive and not act on it?"

Pamela gave him a serious look. "Are you telling me you're making unwanted passes at him?"

"*No.* I mean, I can't stop thinking about him. Romantically. I try to keep it just friends, but my head won't play along."

"Silly. It's not your head that's the trouble. It's your heart. You're in love with him."

Sick fear spread across Xander's chest. "Yeah, well, he's not with me, so I'm fucked."

Then there it was, that instinctive voice inside him whispering, *I'm not so sure,* at the same time as Pamela in real life said, "Hmm. I'm not so sure about that."

Xander snapped his gaze to hers, his heart skipping a beat in hope. "What—what do you mean?"

She put down her brush and leaned against the wall of the garage, gazing at the reclaimed wood she was painting. "Well, I don't pretend to understand young people the best. But some things are the same no matter what the generation. That young fellow has affection for you of some kind, and it's not because you're helping him with a project."

Oh. Xander deflated somewhat. "He likes my art, is what I think you're seeing. And I think he has an artist's soul of his own, if he'd only let it out."

"*That's* clear as day, and good for you for pushing him out of his suits and into his passion. This is something else though, honey. His art isn't what's kindling the light in his eyes. Or, rather, it doesn't really matter what's lighting those fires. It's where the headlights are aimed. They're looking at you, always."

Xander held up his hands, managing to limit his blush to the tips of his ears. "Okay, but why does that have to mean he's *interested* in me? Maybe it's nothing more than a deep friendship. Like all those men with their asses sticking out of the hood of a car in *Life* magazine photos. Best friends, brothers-in-arms, that kind of thing. Maybe I'm polluting something pure."

"First of all, you know some of those asses were gay in those magazines. Second, if you're going retro, remember they had a different concept of sexuality back then. Rigidly defined roles and no blurred lines. My generation went through a lot of effort to mess those up so that yours could do things such as bring about marriage equality with a sudden wind and send transgender and nonbinary issues after it like a brush fire." She sighed. "Not sure how women got skipped over in all that, but I suppose in a patriarchal culture this was a better approach. I wouldn't have minded having a woman in the Oval Office instead of the nonsense we got instead, but then, while I was disappointed, I can't say I was surprised. But you hate it when we talk about politics, so let's get back to your shy suitor."

For once, Xander would rather talk about politics. "I honestly don't think he's my suitor. I think…I think he's not used to having a friend like me, maybe. For me, yes, it could be more, but not him. He's—straight."

God, but the word tasted like shit in his mouth.

And he didn't know why, but it felt false too.

Pamela clucked her tongue. "*Straight* boy like him dates a lot, does he?"

Xander's cheeks stained, and he picked up the bucket of brushes again, holding it against his body as he fussed with the bristles. "He's very busy."

"Makes a lot of comments about pretty girls? They catch his eye when they pass him?"

Xander stilled. "No." He turned to Pamela. "He doesn't look at guys though, either."

Pamela seemed pleased as punch now. "Because he's looking at *you*." She scratched her chin. "I wonder what blood type he is? I can't quite pin him. I've thought both B and A."

Xander had no idea what blood type Skylar was, but Pamela was wrong about how Skylar looked at him. Dead wrong. There was a difference in the way Skylar looked at him and the way guys *looked* when they were cruising you.

Men *looked*. Whether they were dating or not, looking for a partner or not—they *looked*. It wasn't cheating or offensive, or it wasn't intended to be. It simply was. Xander would lie on hot coals for one kiss from Skylar, one brush of his fingertips on his naked chest, but if the right guy walked by post-workout without a shirt, it would take willpower not to steal a glance and file images away for the spank bank.

Skylar never looked at Xander that way, ever. He didn't find him attractive. There were those flickering moments when they were doing art or something together, but that was a different look altogether.

Of course, Skylar never really looked at anyone, not like *that,* not to cruise. Xander rewound through every public trip he'd taken with Skylar, every walk to the sandwich shop, trying to find an instance where Skylar had glanced at someone. Anyone. He couldn't find anything. Granted, there hadn't been many times they'd been in public, because he was such a fucking hermit. But the few times they had been...

Was Skylar that much of a gentleman? Was that possible?

Or was he like Zelda—simply not interested in looking...at anyone?

The bucket of brushes clattered to the floor, startling him and Pamela both. "Heaven's sake," she said. "Are you all right?"

"I need to go to the bathroom. I'll be right back."

He didn't wait for her permission, and he didn't go to the bathroom. He went up the stairs to his apartment, but he didn't go inside, only paced back and forth on his balcony, muttering to himself and pushing his hands into his hair.

"*Idiot.* You've spent weeks telling yourself you should be happy being friends, and now the idea he might be an ace makes your stomach empty into a pit?" Zelda would kick his ass, and they'd have every right to.

That wasn't it. It was that he was so confused. That's what was making his stomach twist. If he *knew* Skylar was asexual or somewhere on that spectrum, he could place him in the same mental headspace as Zelda and everything would be fine. Well—not the *same* mental headspace. No one could be Zelda but Zelda. A similar concept, however. Once he knew, or even had a firmer assurance, everything would be fine.

Of course, Skylar might not be aromantic, like Zelda. He could be demi, too, or some other amorphous point on the gray spectrum.

Or he might be cisgender straight, Sly Silver Stone after all, and you're making shit up because it suits your narrative.

At this point Xander didn't care what the truth was: he simply wanted to know it so he could accept it and move on. The trouble was, how to get to the truth?

Then he realized—the lobster-bake thing. *Perfect opportunity.* Not only would there be enough men and women for Xander to be a proper judge of who Skylar flirted with and didn't, there was enough chance for him to see if, God save him, Pamela was right, and the whole thing had been Skylar's slow-burn romantic setup for Xander. He sincerely doubted that, but anything was possible.

He still wasn't looking forward to going to Skylar's family's beach house. He still feared he'd end up facing some amped-up version of his worst nightmare, or a remix he hadn't known to be terrified of. Thinking of watching who Skylar may or may not be flirting with made him queasy.

But the idea of knowing if Skylar was attracted to him, or anyone, heartbreak or no, was better than this chaos in his head.

He had to believe it, anyway.

Chapter Eleven

THERE WASN'T ANY way to dance around the issue. Skylar hadn't put in half the LSAT studying time he should have.

He wasn't taking the test until September, but it wasn't going to be easy to get the scores he needed, and every practice test he'd taken so far told him he wasn't anywhere close to Yale's standards. His tutor hadn't come out and told him it was going to be impossible, but her face made it clear he had a lot of work to do, and his failure to show up and put in the time wasn't helping his cause. Even when he was there, his performance was grim. She hadn't yet told his father how badly he was doing, but Skylar could tell that shoe was going to drop soon, because if she didn't spill the beans, at some point Leighton Stone would want to know why she hadn't prepared his son well enough. And Skylar was absolutely not prepared. He kept choking on the logic sections, and on the reading comprehension, of all things. He failed because he was nervous and the stakes were so high.

Or maybe it's that your heart isn't in it. You'd rather be across town in a quirky apartment arguing about manga and posing for a portrait.

Skylar dropped his pencil and stopped the stopwatch where he'd been pretending to keep track of how long it was taking him to compose the writing sample he wasn't writing.

He pressed his fingertips to his eyes, rubbed for a second, then rose, thinking what he needed was a change of venue. There had been interesting smells coming from the kitchen earlier. Perhaps if he were lucky, whatever Mary had been baking still had some leftovers. During the regular school year, no chance. But with only himself and Unc in residence, it was possible.

Indeed, he found Unc bent over the brownie pan, but he'd only trundled through two rows, and at the sight of Skylar, he grinned a chocolate-crumb-coated grin and pushed the tray his way.

"Sorry, man. I was going to save you some, I swear."

Skylar raised his eyebrows but said nothing, only tugged the brownies closer and helped himself to a large serving. As was always the case with Mary's baked goods, they were heavenly, and the simple taste of chocolate and sugar did wonders to chase away some of his troubles on the spot. "How was your day?"

Unc shrugged. "A day. Desk jockeying the student union isn't all it's cracked up to be. Though, that reminds me. That chick with big tits from Tau Alpha Kappa. What's her name? She got a nose job last year."

Skylar stared at him blankly.

"Aw, come on, man. *You know.* That girl." He mimed huge breasts with his hands. When Skylar still appeared unmoved, Unc sighed. "Anyway. I can't remember her name, but that girl, she stopped by the desk. Twice. Leaned over the second time and gave me quite a view. She wanted me to tell you she needs you to call her. Apparently she's left you several phone messages. She needs a date." Unc shook his head. "I will *never* understand how you get the tail you do."

Skylar did his best to shutter his expression. "*Ah.* That must have been Tabitha West. Unfortunately I can't help her out."

Unc's face was red now. "Are you *shitting me*? You're *turning her down*?"

He'd already turned her down twice—if she was going behind his back to go through Unc, she must be desperate for a date indeed. Skylar wiped his mouth with a napkin to hide his frown.

Unc shook his head. "How can you be so cool about it? Never mind that—how do you *do it*? You've always got girls running up and down the steps giggling and asking if they can see you, and you're always taking them out to fancy dinners—of course, I'd never do that. I'd go straight to the main course." He paused. "Is that where I'm going wrong?"

Skylar gave Unc an enigmatic smile. "I can't reveal trade secrets. You know that."

"*Come on, man.* I don't need all of them. Just enough to get tits girl to beg for me the way she does for you."

"To start, I don't call her *tits girl.*"

For whatever reason, tonight Unc wasn't letting it

go. "I'm serious, Sky." He came around to Skylar's side of the counter, brushing brownie crumbs off his hands. He glanced from side to side, as if making sure the room was clear, then lowered his voice. "Look…I've heard the rumors, and I don't mind if they're true."

A shot of ice water ran through Skylar's veins, but he kept his demeanor cool, only raised a bored eyebrow that would have fit in well in either of his parents' boardrooms.

Unc glanced around again as his voice became a whisper. "You know. How sometimes…sometimes you date guys too."

It was tough not to let out a breath of relief. "It is the twenty-first century."

"That's what I'm saying." Unc held out his hands. "I mean, I'm not into dick, but to each their own, yeah? We got gays in the frat now, and it's no big. Next thing you know we're gonna have a trans man. And I'm all for it. Equality. All the way." Unc waited a moment, basking in pride at his own inclusivity. Then his shoulders rolled forward, and he bounced on the balls of his feet like a little kid. "Now *come on,* tell me how you do it, *please*, Sky."

Clearly he wasn't getting out of this until he threw the dog a bone. Skylar sighed. "Fine. One hint. But that's all. Are you listening?"

Unc was practically salivating. "*I'm so listening.* Hit me, baby."

Skylar would love to, most days. "You have to give them what they want."

When he stood, Unc blinked at him in confusion. "What? That's it? That's your big secret? Come on, that's not—"

Skylar stopped him with an upraised hand. "That's *the* secret. I give them what they want. Of course, you have to know what it is. Sometimes I ask them. Sometimes they tell me. And yes, both of those are trickier than they sound. But central to the whole game is giving them what they want."

"And what about them?" Unc's grin was as lecherous as his wink. "They give *you* what *you* want, then?"

The question rocked Skylar, making him sway on his feet. It wasn't only because he was tired and unprepared to whip up a false front to Unc's omnipresent sexual innuendo. It was that the bald question was, for once, worth asking.

Had they given him what he wanted? Had any of them?

What do you want, Skylar Stone?

Skylar pushed the tray of brownies away. "I'm going to study some more."

"Aw, don't be mad. You know I'm just teasing. You're always such a funny one, Sky. I don't mean anything by it."

"I know." Skylar didn't know how to explain, though, that this didn't make the teasing any easier to bear.

Unc sobered and took a step closer. "I'll stop. I promise. But you gotta tell me what it is I'm doing wrong. I treat you like I'd treat any of the guys. You're my brother, you know that, right?" Unc stilled, and Skylar could see some idea, probably terrible, dawning. "Sky—bro, if you're gay, or bi, or trans or stuff, you know it's cool with me, yeah?"

Skylar wiped his hand over his face, but he couldn't get rid of his smile, not completely. He sighed and punched Unc lightly in the shoulder. "I'm not gay, or bi, or trans."

Unc looked almost disappointed. "Okay. But if you change your mind, I've got your back."

Skylar waved him off, laughing, and went back up the stairs to his room to study.

Thanks to Unc, however, all he did was stare at the study guides, his mind spinning the conversation on a playback loop, his reply to Unc's last query feeling like the statement most likely to damn him should his case ever go to trial. Without consciously meaning to, he ended up staring at Xander's painting, at the shadowy figure he so identified with, and he thought about both the emotions the painting evoked in him and the man who had engineered the art itself.

Then he gave up, put on his running shoes and shorts, and went outside.

It was too early in the evening, and his run made him sweaty fast, even in the shade. By the time he got to the hospital hill, he was a ball of sweat, and he collapsed on the bench overlooking the city with his chest heaving. His body dripped with perspiration. His hair sagged onto his face, his neck, into his eyes. He felt sticky and disgusting.

If Xander were here, though, he would stare, and he would make you feel beautiful.

Skylar shut his eyes, opening his mouth as his lungs fought to reclaim air. Very well. It was past time to think about this, to decide how to handle it. And was there, really, a better place to do it than their hill? He released a few more breaths, steadying himself, and then he let the voice he'd been so carefully shuttering whisper what it had been trying, for weeks now, to tell him.

You might not be gay, but Xander Fairchild is. And he's attracted to you.

And you are attracted to him.

Skylar shut his eyes tighter, his chest hitching and breath catching for reasons having nothing to do with how fast he had run or how hot it was outside. This was why he'd silenced that voice. He didn't want to think about that, not with Xander. He *liked* being with Xander. A lot. Couldn't they simply leave it alone? Why did they have to make it complicated? Xander hadn't said anything, certainly he must be fine with things the way they were—

He's not.

Neither are you.

Skylar rested his elbows on his knees, burying his face in his shaking hands. Why? *Why* couldn't being friends be enough? Why did it have to become complicated? He didn't understand. He'd thought he'd finally come to terms with himself, had almost swallowed a label, and now…now what, he was wrong?

Except that wasn't right either, because it wasn't as

if being attracted to Xander had radically altered him in some way. More like showed him a hidden door. That was everything about Xander, honestly. *Come play in this secret garden with me. Discover truths about yourself you never knew.*

The thing was those truths terrified Skylar. This one too.

Did Xander really understand about Skylar? He couldn't possibly. If Skylar hinted he were interested too, Xander would assume…and then Skylar would have to explain…

While Skylar shouldn't feel any shame in that, it didn't change the fact that Skylar didn't relish experiencing a negative reception, especially from someone he held in such high regard. He *needed* his time with Xander. What they had right now? It was enough for him.

Is it enough for Xander?

Skylar squeezed his fists so tight his nails cut into his palm. No. He was fairly sure it wasn't.

He had to find a way to tell him, but he didn't know how. Not when he couldn't figure out what it was he was supposed to say, what the truths were in his own heart. Not when every time he turned around, they were all changing.

Skylar stared across the sunset-lit skyline of the town and whispered the few truths he did have.

"You aren't Galatea, Xander. I am. But I don't know which parts are real and which parts are facade anymore, which ones are deeper truths you helped me uncover and which ones are false fronts I've used to hide the truths that are never going to change. Does that mean I'm going to end up alone? Does that mean I'm *supposed* to be alone?"

He shut his eyes again, a tear escaping down his cheek as heaviness settled on his heart.

"I just want to find a way to be with you that doesn't hurt you. Because I didn't realize it until Unc asked. No, no one's ever given me what I wanted."

He opened his eyes, turning his head to look at the space beside him, where Xander should have been. "Until you. You give me what I want without my ever asking for it—and almost always without giving you anything in return."

He placed a trembling hand on the stone bench, which was cool, despite the heat. "But what if I can't give you what you want from me?"

XANDER SPENT THE drive to Skylar's family's beach house envisioning ways he would embarrass his friend in front of his family and in general stick out like the awkward banana he was.

"Stop being nervous," Skylar told him when they stopped for lunch at a diner outside of Liberty. "My mom will love you."

Xander stabbed his fry into his ketchup. "You're only saying that."

"No, she will. She's always liked artistic types. I've often wondered how she ended up with my dad, to be honest."

"What are your parents like?"

Skylar's smile strained a little. "Oh, you know. They're busy. Lawyer and CEO. Always running. Hardly ever in the same state, let alone the same house. It's always been that way."

Xander blinked. "You mean—they didn't live together when you grew up? Who lived with you?"

"Nannies." Skylar's smile was almost a *ting* now, and it was weird to see it again after such a long absence. "My dad's assistant, Ellen, basically raised me. She and her family. Her daughters were my best nannies."

Xander didn't know what to say to this, because it was...weird. Skylar wasn't raised by his own parents? Was that normal with rich people? Xander felt weird complaining about his own parents now, because for all their issues, at least they stayed in his zip code. Well, not his birth father. Fuck him, really, but...*cripes.*

Searching for something to say to lighten the awkward, Xander seized on the first thing he could think of. "Do you have pictures of them? Ellen and her daughters, I mean."

He felt dumb as soon as he said it, but though Skylar looked surprised, his plastic smile melted away, and a real one replaced it, accompanied by a blush as he picked up his phone and thumbed through his photos. "I do. Tons. Ellen's always sending me pictures of the family. Here—that's Ellen, there, with her husband Tom."

Xander peered at the phone. A lovely, late middle-aged black woman stood proudly in a smart yellow dress with her hand on the chest of a brightly smiling black man in a gray suit and cream dress shirt with a burgundy tie. "She has a lovely smile."

So did Skylar, right now. He thumbed forward a few photos. "Here's a group shot with her children." He introduced Xander to Ellen and Tom's five children, told him how old they were, who they had married, the names of their children and showed their baby photos.

"Wow, you really have a great relationship with them, it sounds like," Xander said, when Skylar wound down.

Except that must have been the wrong thing to say, because Skylar's face clouded again. "Ah, well, they were only my nannies. We keep in touch, is all."

"Do you have pictures of your mother and father?" Maybe he shouldn't have asked that, but he thought it might not be bad to be able to identify them.

Skylar pulled up another photo. "This is from a fundraiser a few years ago."

Xander studied the glittering pair: the glowering, older, shorter gentleman and the tall, beautiful blond woman who looked as if she could be in her thirties—except as a portrait artist, Xander could tell she was, in fact, in her forties. "Wow. You look a lot like your mother. And you don't look anything like your father."

"People always say that." Skylar reached across his plate to steal one of Xander's fries. "Remember, only my mother will be at the fundraiser. Not that we'll see much of her. She's going to be busy wining and dining people."

"The whole weekend? Really?"

Skylar nodded, brushing salt from his hands as he chewed and swallowed. "The most important guests will stay the night, and some of the others will return in the morning for brunch. Everything about this party is business." He smiled wryly. "Everything about my mom's *life* is business."

"That's pretty much the polar opposite of my mom. She's a professional wife and mother. She has a job, technically, but all she cares about is making her family happy."

As soon as he said the words, a shadow fell over his heart, and he wished he hadn't said anything.

"That's right. I'm so jealous of your care packages. Do they have little notes in the box and everything?"

Xander sent more fries to drown in tomato and vinegar, stirring them until they snapped. "She sends too many. I give them away most of the time."

All of the time, but Skylar didn't need to know that.

Skylar made a scandalized noise, and Xander glanced up. Skylar looked like a wounded puppy. An adorable wounded puppy. "Well, give the next box to me. I've *always* wanted a care package." He leaned over his plate conspiratorially, anchoring his fork in his hot beef sandwich. "But you know what I *really* want?"

God, this guy was going to kill him dead. Yes, he knew what Mr. Anime Lover *really* wanted. "Someone to make you a bento."

Skylar blushed. "I just like the little lunches. They're so cute."

And you like the idea of someone giving you attention. Xander couldn't help noting that bentos were often given in anime to people characters had romantic interest in.

Did that mean Skylar was open to romantic interest, then? In general? Just romance, or maybe more? From Xander, or not? Only on Tuesdays?

Give me a map, dude. Forget the shrines. I want to know the way to you.

Xander forcibly derailed this train of thought before he wrecked himself. "Bentos are cute. Did you know they're everywhere in Japan? You can get them at convenience stores. Can you imagine, being able to get a lunch like that at a 7-Eleven?"

"I know. I really wanted to add a Japanese minor, so I could go on the spring break trip to Kyoto, but my dad would have had a fit. At the very least it would be cool to watch anime and not have to read the subtitles. Right?"

Xander thought about playing along, then decided in the long run he'd get caught and it would be crueler. He made a small bow over his plate. "*Hajimemashite. Boku wa Zandā Feachairudo desu. Yoroshiku onegaishimasu.*"

Too late, he realized this had been a tactical error after all. If he'd thought the looks Skylar had given him over his *art* were hungry... "You...you know Japanese?"

Xander had to swallow twice before he trusted himself to speak without his voice cracking. "Not tons, but some, yeah. I have trouble with native speakers, end up telling them *yukkuri, onegaishimasu* over and over—that's please slow down—because my oral Japanese isn't half as good as my written. I took Japanese I and II, but after that it's been self-taught so I could read manga in the original Japanese. Kanji is a real bitch, though, I'm here to tell you. And I'm way out of practice. I was gung-ho my sophomore year, but last year I was too busy and I'm afraid I've lost a lot." He read the expression on Skylar's face, held up a hand, and headed off the question before he could ask. "No. I can't give you Japanese lessons. I'm not good enough, and it would result in you knowing shit Japanese. You deserve better."

"Teach me that bit you just did, at least. What did you say?"

God help him, Xander could not resist this man when he pleaded like that. He sighed and pushed his plate away. "*Hajimemashite.* That's a greeting, like nice to meet you. And here's the thing with Japanese, it's phonetic, so listen to the syllables. It's spelled the way it sounds too, which is handy. Ha-ji-me-ma-shi-te."

Skylar planted his elbows on the table, and Xander got an image of Student Skylar. He was a sexy motherfucker. "*Ha*jimemashite."

Xander shook his head, his Japanese instructor's lectures rushing back. "No. This is your next lesson about Japanese: in addition to being phonetic, it doesn't have any kind of emphasis like we do. Well—okay, it does, but for our purposes right now what you need to know is it doesn't have the same kind of hard lean on one syllable that our language does. *Sky*lar. Japan*ese.* When you say *hajimemashite,* make sure you keep each syllable even. Try again." He clapped his hands in an even rhythm as he spoke. "Ha-ji-me-ma-shi-te."

Skylar clapped too, speaking each syllable to the beat. *"Hajimemashite."*

"Not bad. Okay. The next part is easy: I said, 'I am Xander Fairchild.'" He wondered if he should explain that he'd used a masculine pronoun and if he should go back and start him at neutral *watashi,* then decided to hell with it, throw him right into *boku.*

"Okay, but you said your name differently."

"Right. I used Japanese pronunciation." He blushed. "That was me showing off, I'll be honest."

"No, that was cool! I want to know how to do that, please."

They sat there another half an hour, Xander going against what he said and teaching Skylar his rudimentary, half-forgotten Japanese. They had to look up several things on Skylar's phone, downloading two apps and a dictionary so Xander could give him a better pronunciation guide. Skylar gave him his phone's password so he could continue to teach him while he drove.

"Explain the *yoroshiku* thing again?"

"*Yoroshiku onegaishimasu.*" Xander thumbed through the language app, looking for something cool to impress Skylar while he explained the phrase once more. "It's not really translatable. Mostly you need to remember it's what you say when you meet someone. I want to say literally it means 'please be kind to me' or something like that, but there's cultural stuff that goes with it which won't make sense to English speakers. Like how in Japan you say 'I will likely be a burden' when you go to someone's house, and it's just what you say. And the whole *itadakimasu* thing before a meal."

"*Yes.* What does that mean? I couldn't decide if it was a prayer, or what. They say it in all the anime, every time they eat anything! Even sometimes with juice boxes."

"It means…damn, let me look it up, because I can't remember, but it's not a prayer." Xander thumbed through the app. "Aha. It means, 'about to receive.' And at the end of the meal you say *gochisōsama,* which is more straightforward: thanks for the meal. But you need to say both. It's rude if you don't. There are a lot of dos and don'ts in Japanese."

Skylar was so starry-eyed. If anyone *did* want to romance this man, *nihongo* was the way to do it. Art, bento, boxes of cookies, and Japanese lessons.

Well, sailor, you could do all of that, couldn't you?

Xander was about to ask Skylar if he wanted to learn to count, having read through the numbers enough to feel confident about explaining the variants of four and seven and the others that had more than one way to say them, when the message-preview bubble popped over the top of the app screen.

Message: Tabitha West

Hey Sky I know you said you can't but I really need you for a date this weekend, please, I'll do anything. I promise the goods are off the charts.

The hamburger and fries lurched to Xander's throat as his stomach hollowed out, and Skylar's phone clattered to the floor.

Skylar glanced over, concerned. "Oh—you okay?"

Xander hugged his knees a moment while he fished for the phone, taking deep breaths to steady himself. *What the fuck. What the fucking fuck.* "Fine." He took another breath, schooling himself with reserve honed after years of acute harassment. *You don't sound fine. Fake it harder, or he'll figure it out.* "Okay, maybe not fine. I think I must have eaten something bad, though. Feeling a little off."

"Oh no, I'm sorry. Do you need to stop somewhere?"

Yes. A bus station. Except he had twenty dollars in his bank account. He could call Zelda and ask for help. They'd give it, but he'd never hear the end of it. Worth it?

Maybe.

Skylar winced as he got a look at the dashboard clock. "I didn't realize how late it was." He grinned, the real one that melted Xander, or had before he realized this was fake too. "It was worth it, though. I love the Japanese lessons. I'm so glad you could come with me this weekend. There's no one else I'd want to have with me."

Five minutes ago, that would have sent Xander over

the moon. But now all he could think of was that fucking text.

I'll do anything. I promise the goods are off the charts.

He turned away to face the window, hoping his face wasn't reflected in anything, because this fucking hurt. His heart lurched, threatening to break, but he steeled himself. Not now. Later for that. Not in a car, not with him here.

The whispering voice tried to speak up, tried to tell him he was overreacting, but he shut it down. How else was he supposed to read that text? It didn't get more goddamned black and white than that.

"Something's wrong."

Xander startled at the tension in Skylar's tone, almost forgetting to censor his expression before he turned. He knew better than to look him in the eye, carefully keeping his focus on the dash. "I told you. Upset stomach—"

"No. Your body language doesn't say sick. It says you're angry. You went from relaxed to closed off with no warning. What happened? What did I do? Did I say something?"

Shit, he should have thought of that. Xander wasn't used to bullshitting *Silver Stone.* He floundered, trying to recover. "No, I feel bad that I'm going to be sick at your mom's thing, is all—"

"The phone. Someone messaged me, didn't they?"

It annoyed Xander that the asshole sounded pissed, not chagrined at being found out. "Tabitha says she really needs a date. She'll do anything. You might want to take her up on it. Apparently the goods are off the charts."

"Fuck." Skylar's face screwed up in fury and...agony. He slammed his hand on the dashboard, startling Xander, and he swerved so hard the car beside them laid on its horn and flipped them off. "*Fuck.*"

Xander had no idea what was happening or how to react. He was totally lost now. What he did know was that he didn't want to die on the freeway in Connecticut. "It doesn't matter. It's not my business what you do."

"That's *not*—" Skylar swerved again, and this time two cars honked at them.

Xander made a tactical decision. "Hey—it's fine, okay? If you want to tell me about Tabitha, we can do it when you're not in a position to kill us both. Okay?"

Skylar was clearly *not* okay. Xander had never seen him this unhinged, not even that day he'd come over in sweats. "It's not what you think." He ran a hand down his face, looking ready to cry.

Part of Xander still wanted to hold back, hurt by what he'd seen, but the lion's share of him didn't need that instinctive voice anymore. If Tabitha herself were waiting at this lobster bullshit party with a herd of sorority girls to laugh at Xander for thinking he had a chance with her boyfriend, right now, here in this car, he couldn't stop empathizing with Skylar. Something was wrong here. There *was* more to this story.

Except *why* had she texted him *that*? Why did Skylar get texts like *that*? And why did he look so guilty?

Why the hell had Xander agreed to come five hours from home, where he couldn't run back to his hermitage when things went south?

Because you love him.

Yeah, well, look where love had fucking got him.

Chapter Twelve

SKYLAR DIDN'T KNOW what to do.

This was the second time in his life he was faced with a situation he couldn't Silver Stone his way out of, once again it was with Xander, and he had no idea how to fix this. His mind whirred like a top, searching for the words that would smooth this over, the explanation to erase the acerbic tone from Xander's voice, but no matter how he wracked his brain, he came up with nothing.

Not without telling him everything. Skylar *couldn't.* He didn't want Xander upset with him, but he *couldn't* tell him the real reason, not…not yet. Certainly not right before he had to put on a show for his mother. He couldn't bare himself like that and then put on a facade again so fast.

But he hates you. It's coming off him in waves. He's disgusted by you. He opened up to you beyond your wildest dreams, and now he's more closed off than he was the day you met him. You have to fix this.

His hands trembled, something he could hide while he was driving, but every time he lifted them from the wheel, he looked like he had Parkinson's.

Xander noticed. "Jesus. We're going to die on this goddamned highway."

Skylar's gut was so twisted he was nearly doubled over. "You're angry." *Shut up. That's not going to help, pointing out the obvious.*

"No shit, I'm angry. You're driving like an idiot." He glanced at the dashboard clock. "What time does your mom's thing start again?"

"Four."

"Pretty sure we're going to be late."

Yes, they were. And they were going to be later, Skylar decided, spying a turnoff to a beach he remembered from high school. He gripped the steering wheel tighter as he sent his mind through his mental database again, determined this time to find an explanation that would stop Xander from hating him without making him feel like a peeled prawn.

He couldn't come up with a goddamned thing, and now he was pulling into the parking lot. *Shit. Fucking shit.*

"What the hell? This is a beach, not your house. What's going on?"

Skylar parked the car, shut his eyes, and took a breath. "I need to explain. Before we get to the house. I don't like that you're angry at me."

"I'm not angry." Xander had never sounded more angry.

You can do this. Deep breaths. You can do this. But he couldn't take a deep breath. Only small, desperate ones. "I'm not dating that girl."

"Don't care. Not my business."

But I want it to be your business. Skylar pressed his hands together like a prayer and held his fingers against his lips. "Re…regardless. I don't…want you to think of me that way. That I would…"

"Would what? Date?"

Please stop being mean.

Skylar bit his lip to stop the words. Swallowed. He managed one deep breath, finally, then another. *Get your footing, man. You can do this.* "I told you before that my father has political interests. When…when I go on these dates, I'm not really going on dates. I'm gathering information."

"Hold *up.* You're telling me—you're saying that *date* was…what, some kind of spy mission?" He rolled his eyes. "Come on. I'm not stupid. Don't bullshit me. I don't fucking care. So you're dating her. Congrats. She sounds like a great time."

Xander practically spat the last two words across the car, and they landed like the knives they were meant to. They made Skylar desperate, made him lose the last of his good sense. "I'm *not* bullshitting you. I'm telling the truth. It's not a spy mission, it's more like…I don't know, fact-finding? It's always a trade. They need cover. Usually they don't come out and say it outright, but everyone knows what the arrangement is. A nice guy to put on their arm for some event or other, or to snow their parents—it's always something, and in return, I get to mill around an event where I can gather information for my dad—"

Xander's eyes went as big as his head. "Jesus Christ—you *whore* yourself to these fuckers?"

Skylar's stomach lurched so hard he seriously thought he might vomit. "No! No, I don't—It's not—"

"Oh, *please*. It's not whoring? Then what the fuck *is* it, *Silver Stone*? You're selling yourself, yes? I hope they're good lays at least. *Christ.*"

"*No,* I don't have sex with them—"

Xander rolled his eyes and folded his arms over his chest.

Skylar, heart in his throat, tears in his eyes, bile at his teeth, put his hand on Xander's arm and squeezed it tight, desperate to make him understand. "I *don't.* You have it all wrong—you don't understand—I don't have sex with anyone!"

Inside Skylar's head, all the glass in the universe shattered.

ONE SECOND SKYLAR was in the car, staring at Xander, his face white as a sheet, his eyes wide and terrified. Then Skylar flung open the driver's door and burst onto the beach, where he threw up his lunch, gasped for air, then dry heaved until he was too weak to do anything but collapse in a heap onto the sand.

Xander stood beside him, head swimming, no idea how to respond. He couldn't decide why Skylar had freaked out. He was fairly certain that's what this had been, total panic, but he couldn't be sure of anything at this point. It didn't make tons of sense to him—this was

Skylar's reaction to coming out as asexual? Or that he was a virgin still, which—welcome to the club? What the hell? No way, it had to be something more complicated. It had to be the batshit thing where he whored himself for his family's political bullshit—which, holy fuck. What the *shit* was that? It had to be that.

Except when Skylar finally recovered to the point of speech, it turned out, no, it wasn't.

"I didn't mean to tell you that." Skylar whispered this to the sand, kneeling over his pile of vomit, pressing the back of his hand to his mouth. "I didn't mean to tell you that. I've never told anyone. *Anyone.*" He rocked back and forth, like he was in shock. "Even when I took them on dates, when I wouldn't so much as kiss them, they didn't know. I made sure of it. They all thought I was a player."

Xander found this hard to believe. "*All* of them?"

"Yes. I gave them what they wanted—their favors—and they left happy. They didn't ask questions. People are ridiculously easy to manipulate. Except for you."

Xander couldn't decide if he was empathetic or annoyed. "This is a ridiculous reaction, to be honest."

Skylar's laugh was scary. "I don't think you understand how upside down I am right now. I barely have my own hands around it. I didn't realize how much I was hiding who I was, how bad it had gotten, until you." His breath hitched, and he doubled over, dry heaving again.

Xander crouched beside him, put a tentative hand near his back, then pulled away, unconvinced touching

Skylar was the best plan. Nuclear bombs seemed more stable. He didn't understand what was happening, but he *did* know he'd misunderstood everything—what that text had been about, why Skylar was upset…he wasn't even sure he knew anymore why Skylar had been so excited to bring him on this trip. What he did know was despite his hurt feelings, his confusion, his affection for the man in front of him hadn't changed.

And despite being certain he hadn't done anything wrong, he knew he'd still managed to be the cause of this deep, intense pain.

He put a hand on Skylar's shoulder. "*Gomennasai.*"

Skylar's shallow, panicked breaths skipped, and he turned slightly. "What?"

He increased the pressure of his hand, to reassure Skylar or steady himself, he couldn't say. "*Gomennasai.* I'm sorry."

Skylar reached over his shoulder to put his hand on Xander's. "You didn't do anything. This is all me. I'm the one who needs to apologize."

Xander didn't agree with him, but this wasn't the time to argue. Nor, he thought, glancing around at the small audience peering at them and whispering, was this the place. "Let's get back in the car. I'll drive. Tell me the way to the beach house, and I'll get us there."

Skylar looked ready to vomit again. "I can't go there. Not now. Not like this." He shook his head. "Not until I can pull myself together."

"How long do you need to pull yourself together?"

"I don't know."

Well…what now? "Where should we go, then, until you can figure that out?"

"I don't know."

Fuck. When Skylar melted down, he didn't mess around. Xander shoved his hand into his hair and tried to think. More people were watching them now. It was pissing him off.

Right, he was starting with that. He took Skylar by the elbow and hefted him to his feet. "We're getting in the car. And you're giving me the keys."

"You don't actually need them. It's one of those push-button things. They just have to be in the car."

Wise guy. "Fine. You keep the keys. I'm driving, is the point. You're sitting in the passenger seat. And you're not throwing up."

"I'll do my best."

Xander tucked Skylar into the seat, going so far as to fasten his seat belt for him, which in hindsight was a bit intimate, but Skylar had become as helpless as a baby, so he went with it. Once he was settled into the driver's seat, everything adjusted and his own belt fastened, he put the car into drive. "Okay. Now we have to figure out where to go."

"Not the beach house."

"Well, I don't know where it is, so you're in luck there." He glanced at the dashboard clock, did the math. "Do you want to head back to Takaketo?"

Skylar shivered. "No."

"What about a hotel?" He felt creepy suggesting it, but he couldn't think of anything else that gave them privacy and somewhere to go.

"They'll see the credit card charge and want to know why I was here in a hotel. Or more to the point, Mom's secretary will."

This was getting ridiculous. Never mind, this was well past ridiculous and into insane. But then Xander remembered the way Skylar had come apart on the beach.

I didn't realize how much I was hiding who I was, how bad it had gotten, until you.

"What if we tell them you got sick?"

Skylar lifted his head. "What?"

Xander was on the main road now, looking around for any hotel that seemed legit, but he cut a glance Skylar's way. "It's not a lie. You got sick on the beach. What if we told them you had the flu? It happens. People get sick. What if we told them you were almost here and threw up? That you pulled into a hotel—" Xander saw a likely suspect and switched lanes. "This hotel over here, and checked in so you didn't make any of your mom's important guests sick?"

"It's…not a bad idea. But I don't have it in me to lie right now. I wouldn't be able to sell it."

Xander pulled into a parking space, killed the engine, and held out his hand. "Call your mom and hand me the phone."

Skylar regarded him blankly.

Xander made an impatient motion with his hand. "Come on. Dial it. I'll take care of it. Trust me. I've been taking these social lessons. I've got moves now."

That made him smile a little. He punched in a number on his phone, wearily, and passed it over. "This is Patricia. My mother's secretary. I'd never call my mother for something like this."

That was all kinds of weird, but Xander didn't litigate that, not with the ringer going in his ear and a nagging voice in the back of his head asking if he had just written a check he couldn't cash.

A cultured, harried woman answered, not with hello, simply launching in demanding to know where Skylar was. Xander looked at Skylar's devastated, weary face—Skylar could clearly hear her, she was that damn loud—and something took over Xander.

"Yeah—hey. Um, sorry, this isn't Skylar."

The woman paused mid-rant. "Who is this, then?"

"This is his friend, Xander. I came with him for the weekend."

"Well, where in the world are you? And why are you using Skylar's phone?"

He decided the role to play here was *dumb friend*, since it was what she expected. "So, uh, we're at a hotel. I don't know where exactly? Not far from the beach I don't think. But Skylar got really sick all of a sudden. I mean, he threw up everywhere. It was pretty gross."

"What?"

"Vomit? He was vomiting." Beside him, Skylar had his hand over his mouth, trying not to laugh. "I guess stuff was going around his frat or something. Anyway. He's in the bathroom again. He says he's going to stay here tonight and see if he can get better by tomorrow.

But I dunno, man. I don't think puke's supposed to be that color."

"He *can't* stay at a hotel. Mrs. Stone is expecting him *tonight*. She's been looking for him for the past hour."

This time Xander's hesitation was legitimate. "You seriously want him to come to a houseful of guests when he has a contagious virus?"

Skylar raised his eyebrows. *Told you so.*

The woman on the other end of the phone was getting increasingly hysterical. "He needs to take some anti-nausea medication and tough it out. Look, kid, I don't know who you are, but—"

Xander was done playing. "I'm the guy who rode five hours in the car with him and just held his hair while he puked for the seventh time and told him no way, nobody would expect him to go to a party in his condition. I don't know what kind of flu you get, bitch, but anti-nausea medicine isn't a fucking cure-all. He's staying in a hotel tonight, because he's too weak to drive, I've got the keys, and now I've got his phone. So if you want him at this lobster fuckfest, you can figure out where we are, come kidnap us, and bring us to the party yourself. Otherwise you'll see him when he's got a fever lower than 103 and can at least keep down a saltine. Have a nice fucking evening."

He lowered the phone, fumbled for a second with the unfamiliar controls, then finally hung up on the woman shrieking obscenities into the car.

Xander placed the phone carefully on the seat between them, as if it might begin spontaneously shouting again at any second. They both stared at it for a few heartbeats, until eventually Skylar broke the silence.

"They're going to be angry with me."

Xander turned to look at Skylar, whose profile was backlit by the sunset. "I'm sorry."

Skylar shook his head. "No. Thank you. I think." He stared at the dashboard. "I mean…I don't know why that isn't upsetting me more. Usually I care a lot about what they think of me, but right now I don't. I'm a lot more concerned about what *you* think."

Xander froze, unsure what to say.

Skylar didn't seem to expect him to speak. He shut his eyes, taking long, slow breaths. "I feel lightheaded. Like I'm in a dream. If I think about it too much, I start to panic again. Telling you wasn't part of my plan."

Now Xander *did* know what to say. "Do you really think your orientation matters to me?"

Skylar's face flushed, and he waved his hands in distress. "It's not—I don't know what orientation you think I have—"

Xander held up a palm, trying to soothe his skittish colt. "I'm not labeling you. I'm saying it doesn't matter what you just admitted to me. I'm saying I'm hurt you'd think that would affect my feelings about you."

This attempt at reassurance, however, only seemed to agitate Skylar more. "But…but I told you…" He cut a nervous glance to Xander. "I thought…I thought you were…that you…?" His eyes widened, and he withdrew. "Oh God, was I wrong?"

Xander decided of the two of them, he was in a better position to be brave. "I'm attracted to you, yes. But that doesn't mean if you aren't attracted to me back, I stomp off in a huff. I'm not twelve. Honestly, I wouldn't even have done that at twelve. At that age I could never have spoken to you at all, *especially* if you were nice to me."

He kept waiting for *one* of these speeches to start soothing Skylar, but he continued to slide sideways into different agitations. "It's not…it's not as simple as that."

Xander rewound the last thing he'd said, wishing he hadn't babbled so much because he couldn't figure out what *that* wasn't so simple as. "I don't get what you mean."

God, but it was never going to stop being weird to see Skylar fidget and fret. "I mean… I mean that…it's not that I'm not attracted to you."

Xander went very still as the universe he thought he knew tilted sideways. He wiped his hand over dry lips. "You…you mean you're *not* asexual?" On cue, a mini Zelda began to scold him in his head about asexuals and attraction and how not all aces were aromantic, and he tried to cover his tracks. "I mean…or demi…or…spectrum…" Fuck, he was screwing this so bad.

"I thought you weren't going to label me." The quip was acerbic, and Xander blinked, unsure how to respond. Skylar sighed and rubbed his temples. "I used to think I was ace. Or rather, I told myself I was, because I wanted a hat to wear the same as everyone else. But even inside the privacy of my own head it felt off. So I told myself I was sexless. That I was nothing."

That's not how it works. That's not the way you describe yourself, not with that derogatory tone. Xander kept quiet, however, and let Skylar finish his story.

He looked pained, world-weary, but determined to see this through. "It didn't make me any happier, calling myself that, but it felt more accurate, or safer, or something. I don't know why. What I did know was I had to hide it."

Okay, so much for keeping quiet. "But why?"

"Because the world you slapped down on the phone tonight doesn't have room for whatever I am. Not in an open and honest way. So I tucked it away and tried to find a use for myself."

The dating. Xander winced. "Shit, I'm so sorry."

Skylar's laugh was bitter. "What, for calling me a whore? Where was the lie?"

"Yeah, still gonna feel like shit for the rest of my life for that, thanks."

Skylar tipped his head against the headrest. "I never enjoyed it. It always made me feel dirty after. I usually showered or bathed multiple times, and I never slept well. But I kept doing it, thinking at some point I'd pass on information that made it worth the effort. I was able to tell myself it was worth it, until recently. Until you."

Xander's heart broke and soared at once. He wanted to fold Skylar into his arms, but he hadn't entered that zone yet.

I didn't say I wasn't attracted to you.

His heart fluttered again.

Skylar drew his hand close to his body, fist to his abdomen. “Sorry if this is…too weird.”

Xander had never been so on tenterhooks in his life. “No, please.” He wanted to touch Skylar’s arm so badly, but he didn’t. Didn’t even touch the armrest between them. He kept his hands still, his whole body as immobile as possible, as if Skylar was a wild animal he dare not spook. “Please…it’s not weird.” When Skylar remained quiet, he thought maybe some tit for tat would help. “I thought you were handsome the day you took my painting, but I kind of resented you for it. I was attracted to you in the way I’m attracted to any hot guy, but I’d never have told you. You could have openly cruised me and I’d have told you to fuck yourself.”

Skylar blinked at him. “You’d have turned me down, seriously?”

“Hell yes.” His face went hot as he realized what he was about to confess, but again, he was never going to get anywhere without laying down his own cards. “I…haven’t been with anyone either. Though for different reasons than you.”

For the first time since his accidental confession, Skylar seemed like his old self: confident and put together, except this time there was an extra brightness to him that made Xander melt internally into a huge puddle. “You’re serious, aren’t you? You didn’t say that to make me feel better?”

Xander shut his eyes on a slow blink and swallowed in self-defense. “Um, hello, do you think I could lie about something like that? And blush this hard over it?"

"I don't know, you were pretty slick with Patricia."

"I could never be slick with you."

He realized the double entendre in what he'd said, yelped in dismay, and covered his face with his hands as his skin burst into flame.

Skylar laughed, and Xander mumbled into his palms about how this wasn't fair. Then he froze because he could feel Skylar's hand on his thigh, his breath brushing against his ear.

"It was when you drew me in the cherry blossoms. That's when I started to realize I felt more for you." Skylar withdrew his hand as Xander lowered his, but he remained close to Xander as he confessed the rest. "At first I was confused, then a little scared. Of what it meant that I'd been wrong about myself. Mostly, though, of what it would mean if..." his voice hitched as he went on, "...if you couldn't be patient with me."

Xander turned toward him slightly, speaking even more softly. "You mean, you're worried what happens if something starts between us and I want to go further sexually than you do?"

The tension was coming off Skylar in waves. "I don't know where the edges are for me anymore. But yes. I worry about that."

"You don't need to."

Skylar clearly didn't like this answer. "Why not? It's hardly fair to you."

"So you're saying it has to be unfair to you?" Xander gave him a *be serious* look. "What about me, exactly, gives you the image that I am a rampaging sex maniac? I just told you I'm a virgin. And I'm not a cranky hermit because of that, either. That's a lifestyle choice. And frankly, so is the virginity. So yeah, if my choices are with you but with a different kind of sexual experience or not with you, I'm going to give *with you* a try, all right?"

"Even if it's really limited?"

"Even if."

Skylar regarded him with hope and suspicion at once. "Because if this were a television movie, right now we'd be kissing. And I'm not ready for that."

"Not to put too fine a point on it, but you legit vomited half an hour ago. I'm not kissing you until you brush your teeth."

Skylar drew back, eyes wide, putting a hand over his mouth. "Oh my God, does my breath—?" He exhaled against his hand, frowned. "It's fine. Isn't it?"

"Yes, but the part to focus on is you have something you're fussy about, and so do I. And to be honest, I would be too freaked out to kiss you even if you hadn't decorated the beach with your stomach."

Xander wasn't sure it was entirely a positive how easily Skylar slid back into his confident mode. "Why in the world would you be freaked out?"

"Because I would be, all right? I guess that's my way of saying I'm not ready, either."

"But why *freaked out*? It's just me." When Xander gave him a death glare, Skylar tipped his head back and laughed, a trill that reverberated through the small interior space and down Xander's spine. "So, what, you're saying if I *did* make a move on you—"

"—after you brushed your teeth—"

Skylar blushed, some of his smoothness eroding away. "—after that, yes. You're saying you'd reject me?"

Xander did his best to push past his internal freak-out to give the matter serious consideration, but discovered there was only more internal freak-out. "I think I'd try not to let you know I was nervous, which would make me more nervous, and then you'd probably get super smooth or something, and then I'd snarl to keep you from noticing I was *exceptionally nervous,* and it would end in a mess."

Skylar wasn't laughing anymore. "Except I couldn't ever do that. There is no Silver Stone, not in that department. A girl kissed me once in junior high, and I'm still not over it. It was on that beach where we just were, in fact. I don't know when I'll be ready, to be honest."

Xander wasn't freaking out anymore. In fact, he felt a small thread of...anticipation. Hope. "You know...this could work." Except even as he said that, he felt the same pull of longing he'd been denying for a month now, the one his instinct had been warning him to resist. And now he knew why. He sighed. "It *is* hard not to touch you, though."

"When did I say anything about you not touching me?" Skylar held out his left hand in the space between them, splaying his fingers. "By all means. Please don't hold back."

Xander all but recoiled. He was angry, rattled. "You can't just whip it out like that, for fuck's sake. That's not what I mean by touch you."

"Well, what do you mean, then?"

Jesus, he never would have guessed the slick magazine ad could be this clueless. "Forget it. You have sufficiently killed the moment."

Now Skylar looked wounded. God, they were a pair. What idiot had thought this could work again?

Skylar, apparently, because he wouldn't let it go. "Don't. I'm serious. I want to know."

"I don't really know what I meant, all right? Just that I want to touch you. A lot." This time the blush started from the center of his chest and ran up his face like a rash. "Fuck. *Please*, drop this."

"Xander." Skylar's voice was a siren's lure. He held out his hand again, this time with the same gentleness as his speech. "*Onegai. Onegai…shi…*"

The parking lot faced the setting sun, and Skylar was cast in warm fire, his cheeks stained with blush, his skin lit by the refracted light against the clouds. He was beautiful and perfect, achingly so.

He has never felt attraction for anyone. Until you.

Xander couldn't trust in that. Or rather, the thought gave him no comfort. But Skylar's softness did.

"*Onegaishimasu*," Xander finished for him, surrendering.

Pinning his elbow to his side to keep his arm from trembling, he reached for Skylar's hand.

He didn't grab it or even lace their fingers together,

though that seemed to be what Skylar anticipated, the weirdo. No, Xander didn't want to *hold* hands. He wanted to *touch* Skylar's hand. So he did. He traced along the sides of Skylar's palm. Down the center of his wrist. Ran his fingernails gently up the center, teased up to the tips of Skylar's fingers.

Skylar gasped, shivered, nearly pulled away.

Xander paused, glancing at him, breaking out of his own trance for a moment of self-consciousness. "Is it too much?"

Skylar shook his head, but he looked...breathless. "It's...it's not what I expected, is all. But...but it's good."

Xander searched Skylar's face for a sign he was taking one for the team. "You're *sure*?"

Skylar nodded, unable to take his gaze from the place where Xander's fingers hovered over his own. "It makes me...dizzy. I feel like I'm being tugged. And spun around. It's almost too much, but it's...good." His cheeks stained red. "Would...would you do it again?"

In a heartbeat.

Xander moved more boldly this time, though he still kept his touch light, since it clearly thrilled Skylar. His blood rushed in his ears, his heart thumping at his throat as he forced himself to move slowly, carefully adjusting the pressure so he wasn't tickling, not quite, but still ghosting over Skylar's flesh. Because he was starting to live for those tiny gasps Skylar gave, the quivers his long, slender, manicured hands made under his. Xander felt a rush, but he felt calm too. Like he was a hunter with all the time in the world to pursue his prey.

Except Skylar wasn't his prey. *Partner.*

Play with me, Skylar Stone.

"Turn your hand over."

Was it wicked of him to like that Skylar trembled so much? He took extra time to gentle him, smoothing the back of his hand, folding their fingers together briefly so he could stroke Skylar reassuringly. Except Skylar didn't seem to want reassuring. His breathing was quicker now, and when Xander didn't pick up the pace again, Skylar took over, leading the tease against Xander's hand.

It sent his nerve endings sailing, made him heady and breathless too, but nothing quite like it did for Skylar, so he quickly turned the tables, and soon he had Skylar quaking once more, shifting in his seat, making gasps and whispering, "Xander," every now and again as he was caressed.

They were building toward something, Xander could feel it, a tightness in his chest that made him want to lean in closer and press his forehead to Skylar's and turn up the friction. But his whisper of instinct was back in action, and he heeded it without question. Instead of following the foregone path to the pinnacle, he eased them slowly down, despite the fact that he had to coax Skylar into going there.

When Skylar resisted, trying to push him back into play, Xander deflected with a teasing brush of his thumb alongside Skylar's. "Hey, Skylar Stone. You know what you just did? You just made out in a car."

Skylar went still.

He withdrew his hand from Xander's, pressed it against his mouth.

His eyes went wide, and he turned his gaze for a fraction of a second to Xander's. The look was so raw, so full of emotion, Xander couldn't breathe.

Skylar shut his eyes, not tight, but enough that a few tears leaked down his cheeks. When he opened his eyes again, he took Xander's hand in his once more, firmly. Drawing it to his mouth, he brushed a chaste, reverent kiss against his knuckles. "Let's go home."

Now Xander was the shaken one, Skylar's simple kiss burning all the way to the center of his body. "You mean to Takaketo? Tonight? Now?"

Skylar nodded. He let go of Xander, wiping his eyes with his fingertips. "I don't want to see my family. I don't want to be in a hotel where they could find me, or where I might feel guilty and decide I should go over and see them in the morning. I don't want to go to the fundraiser, even though I know it's going to end in a lecture for me at some point. I want to get away from them right now. I can't escape forever, but I can for tonight. Will you help me? Please?"

"Okay." Xander tentatively captured Skylar's hand again, this time simply lacing their fingers together. "Hey...no more dates with people for favors, okay?"

"No more dates for favors." Skylar squeezed Xander's hand gently. "Can...can I have one with you, though?"

Xander's heart fluttered, grew wings, and sailed lazily into the sky. "You can have as many as you want."

Chapter Thirteen

IT WAS TWO thirty in the morning when they pulled into the city limits for Takaketo.

They'd taken turns driving, but Skylar had been the pilot for the last leg, and he'd convinced Xander, finally, that it was okay for him to doze off, that Skylar was wide awake and in no danger of inadvertently joining him in a nap from his position behind the wheel. The twenty-ounce container of convenience store cappuccino had gone a long way to helping him on that front. But the truth was, Skylar's swirling thoughts were ammunition enough to keep him awake.

Since traffic was nonexistent as he wove his way to the northwest side of campus, Skylar stole liberal glances at Xander as he drove. At his face, quiet and serene in sleep.

At his hands, curled up against his chest.

Skylar's heart beat faster when he thought about how Xander had caressed him in the hotel parking lot. He hadn't seen that coming, that Xander would want to touch his hand in such a manner, or that he, Skylar, would react the way he had. Plenty of other people had touched his hands, and he'd never thought anything of it. Girls attempting to flirt with him had stroked his hands, he was almost sure of it. Maybe guys had too. A lot of people flirted with Skylar.

Why was Xander an exception? Why, when Xander touched him, smiled at him, did Skylar feel giddy and nervous and excited? Why did he spend so much time thinking about how he could get it to happen again?

It was a good thing, yes? He'd felt with Xander like he'd been able to be himself, but more importantly, he didn't feel like some kind of sexual freak. He understood, intellectually, he wasn't the only person who experienced attraction differently. Gray sexuality. Asexuality. It was a spectrum, he knew, but that was about it. He hadn't looked deeply or thought about it much past the initial glimpse into his research. He'd been young, tense, and…perhaps a bit proud. He remembered thinking, *I'm not like that. I'm not one of those.*

He winced. Very well. He'd been more than proud. He'd been an ass. But he'd been afraid. He still was, if he was honest. But he was also eager. Eager to explore this…this whatever this was, this part of himself, this new element. So long as Xander was there, he was willing to open the door.

He was aware it would be difficult to shut later. That he would, in fact, need to shut it, and be the Skylar his family wanted him to be. But right now he couldn't think about that. He told himself it would be fine, and he overrode all the voices warning him he was ushering in something he couldn't stop.

He *was* fine, at the moment—but he wasn't ready to see if he was fine when he was left to his own devices, alone in the darkness. He wished now he'd have booked them in a hotel room. Had he done that, Skylar would have been able to go to sleep with Xander in the room beside him. Not in bed beside him—the thought did give him a thrill, but it also made him panic and break out in sweat—but perhaps in a nearby bed. And then they could have breakfast together. And talk some more. They *had* planned to spend the weekend together, yes?

Could he still do that?

What would be the best way to ask?

To start, he'd have to wake him up, so he began there. "Xander." He put a hand on his shoulder, shook him gently. "Xander, we're back in Takaketo."

Xander roused blearily, for a few seconds clearly unaware of where he was or what had happened. It was adorable, and Skylar would have enjoyed it lingering, but soon Xander blinked, rubbed his eyes, and yawned himself into the moment. "Right. Sorry. I totally zonked."

"It's fine." Skylar swallowed an urge to clear his throat and mentally scrambled for an overture. "I was wondering…since our return is a little unplanned…" He lost his courage and drew a breath, trying to regroup.

Xander filled in the breach, not understanding what he meant, but saving him nonetheless. "Yeah, I'm going to totally freak out my landlady. She sets an alarm for her part of the house, and she's used to it if I come home late during the school year, or even if she knows I'm working on a project, but with her thinking I'm gone? I should wake her up. Which will suck, but I don't know what else to do."

Skylar wanted to purr. *I do.* "Come stay with me. We have plenty of room."

The last of Xander's sleepiness fell off as he held up both hands and backed against the passenger door. "*No. Way.* The hell I'm going to your damn frat."

While Skylar had expected this reaction, it didn't annoy him any less. "There are only three people in the entire house. Myself, the house mother, Ms. Mary, who is a complete marshmallow, and Unc."

Xander lowered his hands and raised dubious eyebrows at Skylar. "*Unc.* Seriously?"

Skylar smiled, nostalgia washing over him as he called up the origin story. "Back when we pledged—he and I are both seniors this fall—he was friendly with everyone, and helpful, but in a way that wasn't always caretaking. He wasn't a mother hen. He was your favorite uncle who teased you and made you forget you were nervous. I can't remember who started calling him Uncle Jeff. He might have named himself that. At some point he became Unc. And then that's all he was, and all he's been since." Skylar sat up straighter, hit by a sudden epiphany. "*He* is your Hotay. Jolly jokester, always up for an adventure."

Xander did not look amused. "A frat boy is *not* my Hotay."

"You tried to call me Hotay, and I'm a frat boy."

Xander grunted and turned to face the window, arms folded in front of his body.

Skylar buzzed now, alive with the thought of not only taking Xander to Delta Sig but introducing him to Unc. But Xander wasn't sold on the idea yet. *Think, Stone. How are you going to seal this deal?*

He wracked his brain, rifling through *Lucky 7* issues, seeing if he could use some kind of *Hotay & Moo* hook. He sifted through the original source material too, through the seven gods of fortune, and of Fudō Myōō.

When he found the bait, he almost slammed on the brakes, he was so excited and overcome by how obvious the answer had been all along. He gripped the steering wheel, drew a breath, and said as calmly as he could, "If you stay overnight with me, I'll take you to the basement and show you the shrine of Benzaiten."

Xander shot him a glare, but Skylar knew he had him. "There's no shrine. Especially not to Benzaiten."

"Come over and catch me in my lie."

Xander stared straight ahead and bit hard on the inside of his left cheek. Then he sighed. "Fine. I will."

Smiling wide enough he thought his face might break, Skylar aimed the car down the street that would take them to Greek Row.

XANDER REGRETTED AGREEING to go to Skylar's fraternity as soon as the house appeared around the corner. It sat on a hill, imposing in red brick and white pillars, overlooking Gama Auditorium like it was a sanctuary of the gods. Which Xander was sure the occupants of the house felt it was. He hadn't even passed through the gates—*the fucking driveway had gates, with a passcode Skylar entered on his smartphone*—and he already wanted to run.

"Relax," Skylar murmured as he put the phone into the drink holder and sailed through the blockade as it parted for him. "I'm telling you. You're overreacting."

Xander wrapped his arms around himself and glanced back and forth, waiting for drunken assholes to burst from the shadows and from behind clumps of greenery. "You're sure there's no one here but this Unc guy? And the marshmallow mother?"

"No one else is here. Unless Unc has an overnight guest, in which case we won't see him, because he'll be otherwise occupied. I doubt that's the case, though, because he struggles in that department. He lacks a certain…subtlety in securing a date."

"The more you talk about this guy, the more I'm sure I'm going to hate him."

"You might take a minute to warm up to him, but Unc will win you over eventually. He always does."

Xander vowed to under no circumstances raise his temperature to this guy above that of an icicle.

Skylar parked his car in the back of the house in a long garage where he had his own individual door. He pulled it closed and hit a keypad tucked into the frame of the garage as soon as they had their bags from the trunk, and as they headed for a side entrance, he punched at an app on his phone.

"Turning off the alarm. Give me a second." He hovered over the app a little longer, then nodded, put it away, and reached for a set of keys. "Okay. We might luck out and everyone will be asleep, but the odds are—"

"Stone, what the hell—well, *hey*. You brought a friend home!"

Skylar glanced over his shoulder, a rueful smile on his face. "As I was saying, the odds are good Unc is still awake."

Xander stood behind Skylar on the landing of a set of stairs, where their choices were go down into a basement or up into what appeared to be a kitchen or mudroom area off a kitchen. The man addressing them was above them, halfway down the stairs, and damn Skylar if he didn't step to the side so the bleach-topped buffoon grinning as he towered over Xander could get at him more easily.

The man stuck out a not-insubstantial hand. "Jeff Turner. Pleased to meet you."

Xander tried to keep his expression flat, but he was fairly sure he scowled. "Xander Fairchild." He made no remarks about his enjoyment level over their encounter.

Unc raised his eyebrows at Skylar. "Wait—is this—this is *the guy*? The one from the project? Who draws *Hotay & Moo*?"

Skylar nodded at Unc but turned to speak to Xander. "Unc is another fan."

Xander tucked his hands under his armpits and cast

a suspicious glare at Skylar. *I don't believe this shit for a second.*

Skylar held up his hands and let an intense Unc fill his space.

"I fucking *love* that manga." Unc guided Xander down the stairs, and somehow there was no way for Xander to do anything but follow his lead—it was that or trip. "You took over our sophomore year, right? The drawing style was different when we were freshmen. It was fine, but I like the way you draw them better. And you've really improved in the last year especially. I can't wait to see what you do with it next."

They were in some kind of lounge area now, a huge open space with a bar and sectional couches, plus a pool table and several smaller study tables. And a row of what sure as hell looked like restaurant booths in the back. Unc led them to the nearest sectional, where a spread of study guides and notebooks were littered everywhere—but also a stack of manga.

Including *Fullmetal Alchemist.*

Xander scanned the stack—volumes five through fifteen—and couldn't help slide his gaze to Unc. Surely these weren't *his.* But then he remembered Skylar saying something about his fraternity brother who read manga.

Oh, *shit.*

Unc stuck a pen in the side of his mouth and grinned around it, looking like a cat with the canary. "I know, total old school, right? But I can't help it. I go for the classics when I'm stressed. I'm reading *Attack on*

Titan, obviously, but it's unfinished, and that makes me anxious when I'm trying to study. I need to be able to close the narrative. Sky told me you had him reading *Fullmetal,* and I needed to revisit it again."

Xander could see Skylar smiling knowingly off to the side, behind Unc. He tried to renew his vow to stay icy to this guy, told himself a lot of people read *Fullmetal Alchemist.*

But not that many read it for stress relief. And talked about narrative closure.

"I named one of my cats after Hiromu Arakawa."

Unc grinned. "That's awesome. What else do you read?"

Xander kept his arms pinned to his belly, his gaze on the stack of manga volumes. "I haven't had time to read lately, but I wore down every copy of manga and comics the Mason City library had in high school, and I bought the *Fullmetal* box set with Christmas money. I love the way Arakawa-sensei drew the series. She was my gateway into manga drawing style." He glowered. "But I don't read *Attack on Titan.* I don't go in for the gore and death and fighting manga."

"Sure, sure. But…you read *Evangelion,* right? Or you've at least watched the anime?" When Xander winced, Unc all but turned into an offended Southern miss. "But…*Evangelion.*"

"Sorry. Not my thing."

"Okay, so what *is* your thing? You can't have stopped reading entirely. I gotta know what *Hotay & Moo*'s artist is into."

Xander wasn't sure why he was reluctant to confess. Probably because he knew he was three more conversational exchanges away from caving and at least tolerating this guy. "*Noragami.*"

"*Yesss.*" Unc did a fist pump. "I knew it. I totally see shades of Adachitoka in your work. But I wasn't sure if that was me reading into it because both *Hotay & Moo* and *Noragami* have Shinto echoes." He flopped onto the sofa, sprawling with one leg over the armrest, patting the space beside him with one hand and gesturing to Xander and Skylar with the other. "Sit, both of you. I don't know how far you drove tonight, but it was hella far, I know that much, because I saw Sky Instagram from way the fuck over in Liberty at lunch. You don't have to talk about that yet, though, because I want to hear more about this manga stuff."

"He came to see the shrine," Skylar said as he sat. He did so elegantly, Xander noticed. Xander couldn't stop tracking Skylar's hands now. Watching his fingers open and close around things.

Remembering the way they felt, the way touching them made Skylar gasp.

"*The shrine.*" Unc's booming voice startled Xander out of his erotic thoughts. "We totally have to see the shrine. I gotta hunt down the key, though. Do you think it's in Vernon's room?"

"I don't need to see the shrine." Xander sank deeper into the couch, noting it was incredibly comfortable. He could sleep here, until six or seven, when Pamela would wake up. Then he could go home.

"He doesn't think it exists," Skylar said.

"*What?* Oh, now we really have to see it."

Xander glared at Skylar. *Thanks.*

Skylar winked at him, and Xander's body broke out in goose bumps.

Unc was on his phone, thumb-texting like mad. "I'm seeing if Reynolds knows where the key is."

Skylar tucked his feet beneath him on the couch and leaned onto the cushions, propping himself up with his elbow. "So who is your other cat named after?"

God, but Skylar looked good, lying there so relaxed. "Hokusai? He's an incredibly prolific Japanese artist who spawned the Western Impressionist painting movement. You know of him, though you may not know you do."

Unc glanced up at Skylar briefly from his phone. "That wave poster in Bedler's room you like so much? That's Hokusai."

Xander side-eyed Unc, having a hard time believing the guy who really did look like a total fuck-off was this much of an expert on Japanese culture. "Well done."

Unc shrugged. "I'm sure you know tons more than me about him. I'm what you call a generalist."

"I do like that painting," Skylar said. "Though it scares me at the same time."

Xander tried to shut up, he really did. But it was like holding back…well, a wave. "It's not a painting. It's a woodcut, so that's a print. And you shouldn't see the wave as scary. That's not what he was saying."

Skylar lowered his arm and twisted his body to

frown at Xander. "But it's a *tsunami.* It's *swamping boats.* It's overtaking a *mountain.*"

Xander shook his head. "No. It's doing none of those things."

Skylar stared at him openmouthed. "It is so. I've seen the painting. The print, whatever. I've looked at it dozens of times."

"I've seen one of the original prints live and in person, and I've written a twenty-five-page paper on it and Hokusai's other Fuji prints. And I got an A."

Unc put down his phone and chuckled as he rose. "I'll be right back. Bedler left the poster in his room, I'm almost sure of it."

He hurried up the stairs, humming to himself as he went. Once he was out of earshot, Skylar tipped his head to the side and widened his eyes at Xander in silent question.

He sighed and reached for the top volume of *Alchemist.* "I don't *love* him. But I don't hate him."

"I told you. He grows on you." Skylar moved closer, not quite touching, but near enough that Xander's heart beat faster. Xander flipped through the pages, part of his brain registering nostalgia for the familiar panels, but mostly he was aware of how close Skylar sat. He drew a deep breath and without meaning to leaned closer.

Skylar's hand brushed his thigh before resting on his own leg. "You can't tell me I smell like a magazine. I never got a chance to put on cologne."

Xander blushed, heat spreading from his chest into the trunks of his legs, down his arms. "You don't."

Skylar tensed. "If you tell me I smell like vomit..."

"No." Xander shut his eyes, inhaled again, slowly, trying to put words to the scent. But words weren't his forte. "I can't name it. But it's...you."

Skylar leaned closer, intensifying the scent, making Xander's heartbeat quicken and drift into the base of his throat. "Could you...draw it?"

Xander ducked his head, smiling. His jaw trembled, though, when Skylar's fingers brushed his, sending electricity down his arm, through his veins. "Skylar." He gasped, shivering and shutting his eyes when Skylar coaxed his hand open, teasing his fingers back. Xander tried to resist, tried to object. "He's coming back any second."

He waited for Skylar to point out the obvious, that nobody but they knew touching hands was making out, but Skylar said no such thing. He also didn't continue his light touches, instead lacing his fingers between Xander's, as if asking for an anchor.

"He knows." Skylar squeezed, tentatively, and swallowed hard before continuing. "I can tell by the way he's watching. He thinks there's something between us. I don't know if he'll say anything while you're still here—I wish he would, because you'd shoot him down."

Xander drew back to look at him, affronted. "Why do you think I'd do that?"

"Because of the way he'd do it. He'd tease you, and you'd get grumpy at him—I can't explain it, you'd smooth it somehow. Or maybe that's me being hopeful. All I know is at some point he's going to waggle his eyebrows at me and say, 'So, changed your mind after all, huh?' and then I have to either lie or tell him the truth. And I don't want to do either one."

Xander stroked the back of Skylar's hand. "What do you mean, changed your mind?"

"He asked me the other day if I was gay. In a manner of speaking. And I told him I wasn't." Skylar glanced at Xander, looking worried, as if this statement would upset him.

Xander wasn't upset. He did, however, tread with care. "Do you identify with a specific orientation?" When Skylar tensed, he stroked the back of his hand some more. "It's all right not to, you know. I only wanted to know, so I didn't misidentify you."

"You're not upset because you're gay, I said I'm attracted to you, but I…"

"There are definitely people who feel they must run around and police the way everyone else speaks about themselves, who think there's a right and wrong way to be queer and gay and gray and everything that isn't straight cisgender. Me, I'd rather ignore the arguments and paint, but I do prefer to know how *individual* people identify, and I try to get it right when I talk to and about them, because it's polite. Beyond that, I figure, none of my business." He felt that said it all, honestly, but in case Skylar was still worried… "As far as you and me go, does it matter what label you have or don't? Does it change something?"

Shutting his eyes, trembling slightly, Skylar leaned into Xander's side. He tilted his head so it rested against

Xander's temple. "Where have you been all my life?"

Xander's heart swelled, soaring inside his body. "Pennsylvania. And Art Building West."

"Found it!"

They pulled away from one another at Unc's call, though Skylar's hand lingered on Xander's until the last possible second, he couldn't help noticing.

Unc came into the room. "The poster was simple to get to, but I got the key too—in Vernon's underwear drawer, if you can believe it. The guy has no imagination." He had the framed poster tucked under his arm as he hustled down the stairs and over to the sitting area, spinning a key on a string on his other hand. "Honestly, if you think about it, he should have given it to one of us for the summer, or Ms. Mary. I never even thought of it until just now. Because aren't you supposed to keep it clean? I remember them carrying on about it when they showed it to us as pledges. Anyway." He plunked the poster frame on the edge of the coffee table in front of Xander and Skylar. "I want to hear about this painting. Woodcut thing. Start there. What do you mean, it's a woodcut?"

Xander missed Skylar's hand, but he still felt the pressure of it humming against his skin. "I mean that you're looking at a print. That every version of them, they're all prints. He drew the designs for the print, then he and his assistants carved the design out of a woodblock so they could print that image en masse. So there are original *prints*, and then there are prints made from when the woodblock had aged—you can tell the difference by the wear on the edges of the boats, and the color. The color is also key. He couldn't have done the print without Prussian Blue, which had just been invented."

Unc sat on the edge of the coffee table. His eyes sparkled, and he grinned. "*Yeah.* This is great. Keep going. I know you've got more."

Xander could go on for an hour about Hokusai. "He made the print because he was broke. It was part of a series about Mt. Fuji—everyone focuses on the wave, but the focal point is the mountain. And it isn't a tsunami. It's just a large wave."

Skylar scooted forward on the sofa, shaking his head as he gestured to the white tips of the water, to the boats underneath. "The wave is a monster. It's engulfing the mountain, the men in the boats. Look at them. They're terrified for their lives."

"No, *look* at them." Xander pointed to the men, pressing his finger to the plastic coating of the frame. "And think about the culture he produced his art in. The time. This is the Edo period. Japan had been cut off from the rest of the world for centuries, but they're about to lose that isolation forever. Hokusai can feel it. Everyone can. That's what the wave is. That's the monster. That's the terror. But they're not letting it break them. That's not the way Japan works. Those fishermen aren't quaking. They're *hunkering down.* They're going to ride out that wave. And that mountain? This print is in point perspective—which, incidentally, is why westerners love it so much. It's what we're used to. Usually ukiyo-e prints didn't use it, not the way he did. That mountain isn't in the path of the wave. Look at it again. The mountain is the anchor. I told you, it's the focal point. It's the thing that will keep the fishermen, and Japan, stable. This wave is going to come, it's going to change everything, but the mountain will remain. They will be okay. That's his message."

Unc had slid to the floor to get a better look at the poster, still propping it up with one hand. "Holy shit."

Skylar sat quietly beside Xander, staring into Hokusai's sea. Xander couldn't tell what Skylar was thinking. So he kept talking.

"Hokusai is the reason we have the Impressionist painters. His work—especially this print—was exported by the Dutch and seen by the masters we know in the west. He made a print of a wave crashing onto Kanagawa, but what ended up happening was his wave washed from Japan onto the rest of the world, and it's still cresting. So maybe it was a tsunami after all. But it came *from* Japan. Not onto it. Fuji still stands."

Skylar pressed his hands together as if in prayer, holding them before his lips, still staring at the print. "You're incredible, Xander. You truly are."

Xander ducked his head, feeling the blush stain his ears. "It's only art history."

"You *two*." Unc ruffled each of their heads in turn, and Xander held his breath, ready to be called out on their relationship—did they have one, then?—but Unc only stood, stretching, and sighed. "Okay. You guys ready to go see a shrine?"

Skylar rose, offering a hand to Xander. His eyes shone with excitement. “I can’t wait for you to see it. *I* can’t wait to see it again. I haven’t been down there in years, and we really don’t open it up for anything else.”

“There’s a committee who cleans it, but neither of us has ever been on it.” Unc rubbed his hands together. “Let’s do this.”

Xander followed them, unsure if he should let himself get caught up in their eagerness or not. “I still can’t believe there truly is a shrine. In a fraternity, of all things.”

Unc glanced over his shoulder. “You really are down on frats, aren’t you?”

“He really is,” Skylar answered for him.

Xander glared at them both.

Unc grinned. “That’s all right. We’ll show you otherwise. Starting with our amazing shrine.” He led them through a narrow door down a winding set of stairs into a basement hallway. “Wait until you see it. It’s got the red-gate thing and the whole bit, and the little roof. The pledges hang up prayers too. It’s the best.”

Then it should be on the main campus, Xander thought, but said nothing, only continued to follow. It *would* be cool to finally see a shrine on campus after all this time, even if it was in a damn fraternity.

Unc fiddled with the key. “Get ready to have your socks knocked off,” he said, and pushed open the door.

Skylar reached around the corner to turn on the lights, and the three of them stepped into the small chamber.

Unc was right. The shrine definitely left an impression.

Unfortunately, it wasn't the one he'd intended.

Chapter Fourteen

THE SHRINE TO Benzaiten in the basement of Delta Eta Sigma was, in a word, a travesty.

Xander was at best a passing expert on what Shinto shrines should contain, but he was fairly certain beer bottles didn't figure into their decoration, nor empty chip bags or other bits of garbage. What had once been carefully hung prayer requests on the peg wall beside the main body of the shrine were in tatters on the floor, and everything from the altar itself lay smashed throughout the room. The red gates—*torii,* to name them properly—were knocked askew, and Xander suspected he knew who had done this handiwork, because he recognized the lines of the penises scrawled onto the pillars. They were the same as the ones on his mural.

While Xander was disgusted with what he saw, Skylar and Unc appeared about to be sick. At first they simply stood and stared, dumbstruck, and then they gestured with helpless rage as they moved about the carnage.

Unc swept his arm across the room, then pressed his fingers to his lips as he shook his head. "What the *fuck.* I mean—*what the fuck.*"

"They were just down here cleaning last month." Skylar's voice was carefully controlled, and Xander thought he was getting a glimpse of how the man performed in his leadership role. "I saw them. I watched the cleaning committee come down, do their work, then go back up the stairs. It was the last they'd be down here before the big preparations for the fall pledges, but they were down here. And none of them would have done this."

Xander wondered if he should point out about the graffiti, but Unc got there before he had to. Unc gestured to the penis art. "It was those fuckers we kicked out. Everybody knows where the key is. They went and got it, had themselves a goodbye party, and now it's too late to do shit."

Skylar's gaze went hard and cold. "You think so? All we've done is enter the room. We've touched the doorknob. I'll have Ms. Mary call the police right now, get in here and dust for prints."

"You do that, and I'll call the leadership committee. Let's get this ball rolling and nail the bastards."

It took an amazingly long time to get the ball rolling, and it involved the three of them giving interviews to earnest police officers who Xander was surprised would come over in the middle of the night to investigate a desecrated fraternity shrine, but then he looked around at the way the walls of the frat breathed money and decided someone had called in a favor. He didn't think it was Skylar, either, given the way he swayed on his feet, ready to keel over from exhaustion, but nevertheless he didn't complain, only kept on working, first answering the officers' questions, then getting on the phone with Unc and fielding an hours-long conference call with first one set of fraternity officers and then another. It seemed this shrine was important to many members of Delta Eta Sigma, and everyone had an opinion on how this matter should be handled.

Xander was impressed with how Skylar dealt with the other people on the phone, all of whom seemed like bags of dicks, but Skylar smoothed them out even though he yawned around his cups of coffee. When he caught Xander drooping on the couch, he excused himself and led him up the stairs.

"You need to lie down," he insisted. "Let me show you to my room."

Xander's heart skipped a beat. "I can wait for you."

"There's no need. I have no idea how long this is going to be." He used a key to open a door at the end of a hall. "Make yourself at home—you can sleep in my bed."

This time it was more than a beat that Xander's heart skipped. He felt ridiculous. Skylar had confessed, basically, to being gray in the car, and they hadn't kissed, only had the hand make-out session, but even so, Xander panicked. He wasn't ready to lie in a bed beside Skylar, even if that was all they did.

His panic must have shown. Skylar smiled knowingly and caught Xander's hand for a brief caress that sent shivers up his spine. "Sleep in my bed. When I come up,

I'll make a blanket nest on the floor."

"That's not right—"

Skylar silenced him by stroking his face, letting his thumb catch Xander's lip before he lowered his hand. "I said, sleep in my bed. I'll sleep on the floor."

Arrested, all Xander could do was shiver for several seconds. When he got his voice back, it broke as he spoke. "What—what was that? I thought…" He trailed off and touched his lip. This was all his melted brain could manage.

Skylar looked ridiculously pleased with himself. "You thought when I said I had a narrow interest in sex it meant I was shy? That I didn't know how to use charm against you when I want to seduce you into doing what I want?" He chuckled and leaned in close enough to fill Xander's senses with his scent. "Oh, Xander."

Xander backed into the doorway, telling himself he felt woozy because he was tired, and not because Skylar was melting his mental circuitry. "You're not fair."

He braced for more onslaught, but what he got instead was Skylar crowding him with slight hesitation, resting his forehead on the doorway beside Xander's ear. "I'm sorry about the shrine. I'm sorry you were right about fraternities after all. More sorry than I know how to tell you."

Xander couldn't agree with him on that point, not when he was so clearly brought low by all this. "I'm not saying I'm gung-ho about all fraternity members. But it's clear the assholes who did that don't represent you or anything you believe in."

Skylar's cheek brushed Xander, and he couldn't stop a shiver, nor could he help leaning into Skylar's half embrace. "Are you gung-ho about *some* fraternity members, then?"

Fishing. He was fishing for compliments now, the bastard. And fool Xander, he was going to let him. "I'm all right with a few, I think, yes."

"Have you decided you don't mind Unc after all?"

Xander couldn't tease, not after the pain he'd seen on the man's face in that shrine. "Unc's a good guy."

A touch on his arm, his wrist. "Any other Greeks you find tolerable?"

The man didn't need a pole. He was reaching into the creek with bare hands. Xander bit his lip to stop a smile. "There's one other I don't mind, yeah. But he sure keeps me up late."

Skylar captured Xander's hand, stroking it tentatively as he rested the side of his head against Xander's. "Kiss me good night?"

Xander trembled as Skylar's fingers made love to his skin, as the heat of Skylar's body surrounded him, pressing him into the door. Skylar shifted and turned with their touches, and Xander held still, gasping out loud while Skylar kept quiet, focused on undoing Xander. It made him feel vulnerable and exposed, even as he didn't want Skylar to stop.

That was when it hit him that Skylar was the aggressor this time, holding him close. And if Skylar held him much closer, he was going to discover…

"You don't need to be nervous," Skylar whispered into his ear. "But if you want, I'll stop."

Xander didn't know what he wanted. He nuzzled Skylar's cheek without realizing what he was doing, then stopped, feeling unsure. That was the trouble, he decided. "I don't…I don't know what I'm doing. What…what's okay. What isn't. With you."

Skylar kept stroking Xander's hand, a rhythmic, steady petting that Xander thought might drive him out of his mind. "What is it you want?"

Xander sagged. "That's just it, I don't know." God, he felt dumb.

Skylar didn't laugh. He only laced his fingers through Xander's, no longer stroking, only holding him close. "Do you want me to hold you? Because I want to hold you."

There went his heartbeat again. "Y-yes."

"Like this? Maybe a little closer?"

Oh God. "Yes."

But Skylar didn't move closer. "But you don't want me to hold you on the bed. That's too much."

The very idea made Xander both excited beyond words and too terrified to speak. He shook his head. Then realized that was ambivalent. "It's too much. Right now."

"What about here, against the wall?"

Xander thought that sounded perfect. Except… His cheeks were on fire as he spoke. "You'd feel something extra."

He could feel Skylar's smile against his cheek.

"That's not a problem for me. Unless it upsets you that for me that happens differently."

"No, I'd never be upset about that."

"And I'd never be upset about the opposite being true for you. So I don't see anything stopping me from crowding you against this wall. Do you?"

Xander let out a shuddering breath. "No."

Then he shut his eyes as Skylar stepped in close, pressed their bodies together, and…

And.

Xander wanted to bury his face in Skylar's shoulder, but he also would rather die than do that, because…well, he wasn't ready to. Funny, he hadn't realized how much he wasn't ready to do with Skylar, with anyone, until Skylar made his confession in the car. God, after all these years of hearing Zelda's lectures, was *he*—

Skylar shifted against him, and Xander gasped as his body shivered and responded to the friction. His libido helpfully suggested what Skylar would look like naked, what he might taste like in his mouth, on his neck, down the center of his chest.

No, Xander wasn't asexual, or gray at all. But as those lustful thoughts made him tremble and blush, as even Skylar's simple strokes down his arm and across his fingers made him quake, he had to admit he was…

"*You're* shy," Skylar whispered, nuzzling his ear. Reading his mind.

Xander swallowed. "Sorry."

"Don't apologize." Skylar laced their fingers together, drew Xander in close enough that there would be no hiding the evidence of Xander's arousal. And Skylar's lack thereof. "I find your shyness very attractive."

"Oh," Xander said, because he didn't know what else to say.

"I want to date you, Xander. I want to help you with your project, and sit for your paintings, and write a manga with you, and I want to date you."

Xander wondered if he had somehow gone to sleep already and was dreaming. "Okay. And do your LSAT studying somewhere in the middle of all that, I assume?"

Skylar sighed. "Yes. And that too."

Why is it you're going to be a lawyer again? Because I've never once heard you say you want to, or that you love it at all. But Xander didn't say this. "You should get back to your phone call."

"I should," Skylar agreed.

With one last caress of Xander's hand, one more touch of his cheek, he was gone.

Xander fell into Skylar's bed and lay there spinning, drowning in sheets that smelled of the man who had sent him reeling so, all the while staring across the room at his own painting in the moonlight, the one he had been trying to throw away when he'd met Skylar in the first place.

Life, he decided, was sometimes incredibly strange.

BY THE TIME Skylar came to bed, it was dawn, and

Xander was out cold.

Skylar had been exhausted and ready to roll into the spare comforter he'd grabbed from the hall cupboard, but once he saw the form outlined in his bed, he couldn't help but linger, letting the image burn into his brain. His mind called up the feeling of pressing Xander into the wall, of the heady way Xander had trembled, going quiet. Skylar knew he would get drunk on that sensation for a long time. That he would be chasing down ways to find new versions of it again.

He couldn't stand on his feet any longer and did climb into the comforter then, but he lay as close to the bed as he could, wanting to be near Xander, wishing there were another bed in the room so he could look at him as he drifted into sleep. If only he didn't have a single and could scam on a roommate's bed. Because it was easier to draw up the memory of Xander's soft expression when he could see him, even in the shadows.

As much as Xander seemed to react to Skylar's touches and physical presence, Skylar was moved by Xander's reactions. By the way Skylar's touches made him change.

You're being dangerous. You're going to upset everything too much.

Skylar stared at Xander's painting in the dim light of dawn, unable to see it and yet aware of every stroke of the brush, every nuance of the paint. *I know. I can feel the world crumbling around me. But I don't want to stop.*

He slept fitfully, uncomfortable on the floor, bothered by the business with the shrine, unnerved by the track his thoughts had taken, and he woke at ten with five hours of sleep in him, knowing he was going to feel like a zombie all day. Xander was still asleep when Skylar got out of bed, but he barely had a cup of coffee poured in the kitchen when his guest came in after him, delightfully rumpled and, bless him, adorably shy and grumpy all at once.

"Hi," he said, looking like he was trying to find an excuse to bolt for his apartment.

Skylar passed him the mug of coffee he was holding with a smile and deftly cut off his escape. "Good morning. Come have some breakfast. You'll be sorry if you miss Ms. Mary's cooking. Then we'll get showered and go back to your place. If you're sick of me, I'll leave you alone, but if you're up to it, I'd be happy to sit for you." He knew they were alone and no one else was in earshot, but he stepped in close, mostly so he could feel Xander shiver as he put a hand on his shoulder and whispered in his ear. "You can arrange me however you like."

"When did you turn into a monster?" Xander murmured. But he leaned into Skylar all the same.

When you heard my confession and insisted it didn't matter, then taught me to make out with you by holding your hand. Skylar executed that move now, delighting in the fact that Ms. Mary or Unc could walk in and they wouldn't realize what was happening. Xander would know, though, and he'd be even more flustered, making the encounter that much more delicious.

What a *wonderful* kink.

"Oh my God, *stop*," Xander whispered, breathless. Except he didn't pull away.

Skylar felt like a god. He did stop, though, but not until he'd placed a kiss on the back of Xander's hand. "Let me take you to the dining room."

Ms. Mary and Unc were already seated, talking to one another, but they greeted Skylar and Xander as they entered the room. Ms. Mary gave special attention to Xander, shepherding him through the buffet line of food. She was talking him into letting her prepare him a custom omelet at the omelet bar when Unc pulled Skylar aside.

"Vernon and the rest of the council are making arrangements to get back here and assess the damage themselves, and meet with the lawyer. Two of the national representatives who are former Benten graduates are coming too. This thing is rippling like crazy. I mean, I knew the shrine meant a lot to the brothers, but this is intense." He frowned. "The problem is, though, that the fall leadership isn't exactly the best to tackle this. I'm not technically part of the leadership, but I'm roped into this now. I don't mind, because the shrine is important to me. But I worry how this is going to be handled."

Skylar stroked his chin, which sported quite a bit of stubble at this hour of the day. "They won't be able to save it. Not like it was. The sacred mirror is smashed, the *magatama* too. How can you get a new sacred mirror?"

Unc frowned. "A Shinto priest, I guess?"

"Right—where the hell will we find one of those?"

Unc ran a hand through his hair. "Good thing I didn't want to study today anyway."

Skylar didn't take that guilt temptation, reminding himself if he'd stuck to his original plan, he'd be in Connecticut. He was surprised his mother hadn't called him. He was sure it was just a matter of time before she—or someone—did.

These thoughts filled him with unease, so he pushed them aside and focused on joining Ms. Mary and Xander in a discussion about art on campus, both the odd-seeming modern pieces Xander insisted were important and visionary, and the more standard, visually easy murals and statues placed here and there.

Afterward they helped her clear the table and the buffet, then retired upstairs to shower. Skylar showed Xander how the bathroom was set up and where he should leave his things—it was adorable how he flushed and got nervous, as if Skylar might jump him in the bathroom. Skylar didn't, obviously, but he did wait to shower once Xander was finished, despite there being six other showers in the room where he could have taken care of his own business. He lay on his bed instead, hands behind his head, drinking in the faint scent of Xander.

He thought of him as he showered, of how good it felt to be with him, to tease him and try to draw him out. *This* was the real Pygmalion, except he didn't want to share this Xander with anyone. He didn't want to own him, or control him, but the thought that Xander would be soft and tender only for him, compliant only for him, surrender his sullen crankiness only for him…

Skylar gasped, shuddering as the ripple of pleasure rolled through him, then drew breath again as he realized what alterations that gasp of pleasure had done to him.

It wasn't that Skylar had never been erect before. Of course he got hard. But it had always been as if a switch had been thrown, his body announcing it was time to ejaculate, a chore to be taken care of. Sometimes he indulged it, mostly he waited until the impulse faded away. He found it annoying, troublesome. He had, in the past, been jealous of others who felt attraction to other people, whose desire of mind and body had no trouble uniting, but eventually he'd decided simply masturbating to get the job done was efficient and he shouldn't bother with what other people were doing with their private time.

It was, without question, thoughts of Xander sending a rush through Skylar now. Not because Skylar thought of his body. But because Skylar couldn't stop thinking of *him*, of his reactions. Of the special regard he'd given Skylar. No one had given this to Skylar before. It wasn't as if his life had been empty without this sensation, but it was not unlike going into a confectionary filled with delicious gourmet chocolate. No one could eat this every day.

But now that he'd tasted it, he didn't mind indulging a bit more…

Skylar trembled as he took himself in hand beneath

the spray, still not entirely sure of his decision, ready to stop at any time. He *wouldn't* sully those perfect thoughts of Xander. If this made them feel tainted, dirty, wrong, he would end it. He took it slow, stroking himself languidly, letting his mind's eye find the counterpart that fit. Imagining himself touching Xander didn't help him. Laughing with him, talking with him…yes, that was all right. Being drawn by him worked quite well.

What if Xander drew him naked?

The thought sent another thrill through Skylar. It was all too easy to see himself seated in Xander's apartment, or better yet in the art studio, soft light aimed on him while Xander hovered at the edge of the shadow, bent over his paper and staring hungrily at Skylar as he drew his form. Skylar chased this image. Yes, and Xander wouldn't make the situation sexual, either—his hunger wouldn't be for Skylar's body. It would be for the art, for the form. Part of him would want to admire Skylar as a partner, but he'd make himself see him as a subject to draw, to sketch, and he'd get that cool artist's eye. He'd roll his eyes all over Skylar, taking him in. Then when he was done, he'd show Skylar, and Skylar would end up seeing a side of himself he didn't know he had. It would be beautiful and open.

It would be their space. Just theirs. And Skylar would be safe inside it, as would Xander.

He came with a sharp cry against the shower wall—it wasn't a monumental orgasm in a porn-shoot sense, not that Skylar had much of a frame of reference there, but for Skylar the entire experience was so epic he had to sit on the bench outside the shower for several minutes before he could finish toweling off. He'd never done anything like that, ever. Oh, he'd gotten off in the shower more times than he could guess. But not like that. Not while thinking of someone, of doing things with someone. Not while letting go like that.

Out of habit, he hadn't brought any clothes with him, and so he had to go back to the room wearing only the white towel cinched at his waist. Maybe that forgetting had been subliminally done, because he couldn't help tracking Xander's reaction to his nearly naked presence. He wasn't disappointed. Skylar knew women and men alike found him attractive, but now the only thing that mattered was that Xander did.

The evidence was in the focusing of his pupils, the working of his Adam's apple. The way his gaze couldn't stay on Skylar's face but kept straying to his chest, lingering on his nipples, dipping down to the slope of the towel, trailing the V line of muscles at his Adonis belt. Skylar wondered if any water still lingered on his body. He wished he had spare time to work out, to give Xander more to stare at.

Skylar hadn't known he enjoyed being regarded like this. He suspected it was another thing that was only for Xander, for the two of them. Xander needed to drink this in, and if his expression was an indicator, at some point he wanted to touch as well. Skylar wasn't sure about the latter yet. This, however, he already knew he craved. This look on Xander's face. This hunger.

God, but he could wrap the two of them in a bubble and chase these feelings for a year. Put them in a cottage on a beach, give Xander all the art supplies he wanted, and the two of them could simply exist, exploring and teasing and…and…

No. He'd been wrong. He did want to touch, a little. Right now.

He sat on the bed beside Xander, moving carefully, but even so, Xander drew back, panicked.

"Skylar—dammit, you're going too fast."

Skylar almost apologized, but he stopped as he realized Xander's expression belied his words. He decided to take a different approach. *Come out and play with Pygmalion, Galatea.* Or was it the other way around? Skylar was losing track of who was who in their play. "Am I too fast, or are you too nervous?"

There was that blush Sky loved so much. "Both." Xander waved his hands in irritation at Skylar's chest, looking both hungry and annoyed. "How am I supposed to know what to do? Is it okay to touch you? Really? Because Jesus, Skylar, I want to *touch you.*" His whole face went beet red. "I doubt you want what I want. And I don't know how to draw the line."

Skylar could appreciate that. But he was nothing if not a problem solver. He took Xander's hands in his. "Then here are some rules, for now." He placed Xander's hands on his shoulders, loving how cool they were, how they trembled. "My shoulders, my arms, my face, my hands, even my back—touch that area as you like. If you want to touch my chest, I'm not against it...but maybe for now, let me drive. I'll hold your hand, move it to where I'm comfortable."

Xander's pupils had gone dark with lust again. It was such a good look on him. "How...how does this work for you? Is this...curiosity? Are you taking one for the team? Or do you actually enjoy it?"

Part of Skylar wanted to keep his discovery to himself, but he realized that wasn't fair, especially since Xander was going to worry about it so much. He did his best to put the feelings into words, capturing one of Xander's hands as he spoke. "I enjoy it, but not the way you do, I'm pretty sure." He slid Xander's hand to his throat, feeling a soft shiver as he watched Xander experience his own reaction.

Xander's gaze flicked up to his. "That—you reacted there, though. To my touch?"

Skylar shook his head. "To the way you looked at me while you did it. To the way you felt while *you* touched *me*." Now it was he who blushed. "I don't know how to describe it properly. It's not about the physical sensation. It's all happening in my head."

Xander studied him a moment, tilted his head, then smiled, a lovely, slightly shy smile. "So you're saying, you like it when I touch you and react to you, because while I get off on your body, you get off on my reaction to your body?"

Skylar wanted to swim in Xander's smile. "Yes. I think that's about right."

And here came back confident Xander, the one

from the car. The one who had pointed out to Skylar he had just made out with someone for the first time, for real, in his own way. Xander slid his hands down Skylar's arms, then up again, then massaged one shoulder cap while the other played with the slope of his neck, thumb running along his chin. His touches were still somewhat tentative, but he was gathering himself now. Aiming for a goal.

He kept brushing his fingers along Skylar's jaw. "I love this stubble. I hate knowing you're about to go shave it off."

That had been Skylar's plan, yes, to shave. "It's so messy." But Xander liked that?

"It's sexy. I have…dreams about this stubble." When Skylar pulled back and arched an inviting eyebrow, Xander shook his head. "I'm not telling you. It's too embarrassing."

Oh, now Skylar *had* to know. "I promise not to shave it if you tell me."

Xander panicked, attempting again to withdraw. "Oh my God, no."

So it was something a little bit dirty? With his stubble? Skylar couldn't begin to guess. He felt cocky and played a wild card. "I promise to *do* your dream, or something similar, if you tell me."

Xander simultaneously panicked harder and relaxed. "You wouldn't do it." He hesitated, then added, "I don't think."

This was, Skylar decided, a most wonderful game. He hoped they got to play it often. "Let's find out." He put a hand on Xander's thigh, just above his knee. "Please."

Xander flushed, trembling. Aching. Nervous. Desperate. It was like a fine wine. Skylar felt like a vampire.

Xander's tongue darted out to wet his lip. "This is what you mean, isn't it? You like this. Pushing me. Making me…like this. Making me tell you."

Skylar's whole body was hot. He wasn't erect, not in his body, but his mind pulsed, a second skin inside him breathing, itching to respond to Xander. "Yes." He slid his hand higher on Xander's thigh, the skin inside him tightening as Xander gasped. "Do you like it when I make you tell me?"

"Yes." A whisper, a beautiful confession—then on the heels, an aching one. "But I worry I'm going to admit I want something you don't, or can't, and I'll feel ridiculous."

Ah. Skylar's hand on Xander's leg squeezed reassuringly, his heart pulsing with tenderness. "Don't ever feel ridiculous. If you want something I can't give you, if that happens"—*when it happens, let's be honest,* he admitted—"we'll work it out. Without guilt or recrimination. For either of us. How about that?" When Xander shut his eyes and nodded, Skylar stroked his cheek. "Now—please, tell me, what it is you wanted. We won't do it now. But I want to know. Because maybe I want it too."

Xander drew a deep breath, keeping his eyes closed and leaning into Skylar's hand as he spoke in almost a whisper. "I want…I want you to press me onto the bed, or a couch, or the ground, and rub your stubble against my neck. And cheek. And throat. And shoulder." He bit his lip, swallowed, and kept going. "And…and push against me. With your whole body."

Skylar broke out into gooseflesh. That certainly was advanced cuddling. But if he was getting thrills from Xander's reaction describing it… "Are we wearing clothes in this scenario?"

"Either…either way…it would end…messy, on my part." Xander ducked his head and covered his eyes. "Jesus, I can't believe I said that."

"I'm glad you did." Skylar laced their fingers together, leaned into Xander's cheek. "That will take some working up to. But some of it can be arranged in the meantime."

"You don't have to."

"But I want to."

Xander shivered. He kept going soft, all his usual prickliness gone. "How did we get here? Yesterday morning I was in a car with you, determined not to let you know how attracted to you I was. Now I'm in your bed confessing my sexual fantasies to you while you're in your towel."

"Tabitha West. I need to send her flowers."

Xander's grip tightened on his. "Don't you dare."

Skylar's heart ached, happiness and yearning mixed with a swirl of…fear? "Don't leave me," he whispered.

Surprised, Xander put his free hand on his back. "I won't."

"I want to stay with you today. Please."

"Of course."

Skylar had thought about teasing Xander with his stubble, of playing the game a little more. Somehow, though, Xander's possessiveness had stopped it all. He left him with a smile instead, gathering his clothes and taking them back to the bathroom to get dressed.

He'd forgotten his phone in there, and he saw his mother had called him. Normally the sight would fill him with joy, the thrill of being noticed. Today he deleted the message without listening to it, afraid it would burst his bubble of joy.

When he emerged from the bathroom and went downstairs, Unc and Xander were both in the living room.

"What, you're growing a beard now?" Unc asked, clearly shocked.

"Just a little stubble," Skylar replied, stroking his chin, keeping his gaze on Unc but watching for Xander's blush out of the corner of his eye.

He wasn't disappointed.

Chapter Fifteen

XANDER COULDN'T TELL if he was eager or terrified at the prospect of Skylar following through on his promise to fulfill Xander's secret beard-kink fantasy, in whole or in part, and the fact Skylar had come downstairs *with the beard* had him so frazzled he hardly knew what to do with himself the whole time he packed his things to head back to his place. It was clear too this was Skylar's goal, or part of it. Because this was *his* kink. Unsettling Xander.

The bastard.

"If I'd have known what a monster I was going to unleash," he muttered, then trailed off, unable to finish the sentence.

Skylar, hands in his pockets as he leaned in the doorway, didn't let him off the hook. "You'd have what?" He sounded amused. Not quite smug, but it was a razor-thin margin.

I need Zelda backup, STAT, Xander decided, and said nothing else as he followed a chuckling Skylar to his car.

Except it turned out Xander's offhand wish was a little too prophetic, because when he pulled into the

Palace of the Sun, an all-too-familiar car sat in Pamela's driveway. It wasn't only Zelda's car, either, back in town earlier than scheduled. Jacob's clunky station wagon was there too. The driveway was full with so many cars, Skylar had to park on the grass by the painting shed—and as he killed the engine, the entire *Lucky 7* crew came around the corner. Jacob, Sara, and Cory, with Zelda leading the pack, arms folded in front of their body and Pamela trailing along behind, looking confused and a little weary as she wiped paint off her hands onto a towel.

"Where in the hell have you been?" Zelda made the demand as Xander climbed out of the car, pointedly ignoring Skylar. "I've called *and* texted you. A million times. We're having a crisis. *Epic* crisis."

"Sorry, I was out of town, and then I was at a different crisis. But I'm here now." Xander held up a hand before they could launch into a tirade. "First, guys, let me introduce my—friend, Skylar Stone."

His ears heated over his hesitation, and he knew it damned him, that Zelda had caught it and was going to grill him later, but everyone else simply stepped up and gruffly shook Skylar's hand, falling quickly under his charm as he did his thing. He was a lot more approachable with the baby beard, Xander thought, and he'd worn jeans and a polo today—still pretty Rich White Kid, but he didn't look like he'd come out of the boardroom, which was something.

The only holdout to his silver smile was, naturally, Zelda, who wore a black T-shirt with white block letters reading RESIST splashed across the front, and they broadcast the message with body as well as attire. It seemed to unsettle them, though, when their brusque attitude only made Skylar more liquid and therefore more pliant, able to slide under their skin.

Eventually, though, Skylar backed away, turning to Jacob, who he somehow had pegged as their leader without being told. "I don't mean to intrude on your business, but what happened? Don't tell me this has something to do with *Lucky 7.*"

"It's everything to do with *Lucky 7.*" Jacob gestured angrily in the direction of the college behind him, the spires of the administration building visible through the tops of the trees. "They didn't just cut our budget. They *decimated it.* They moved us into *a cubicle.* We have to go digital, there's no choice, but they're not even giving us *equipment.*"

Xander was in such shock he couldn't speak. Skylar, however, somehow morphed into a suit without so much as putting one on. "How exactly are they justified in doing this? Did you petition a complaint to the student council?"

Sara blinked at him as if he had landed from Mars. "They're all on break. How would we do that?"

"That's why they did it now, the bastards." Cory looked ready to commit murder.

Skylar waved a hand. "They have phones, and they answer them. So do any number of student organizations."

Jacob snorted. "Nobody gives a shit about *Lucky 7.*

No one will help us."

Skylar gave him a smile that promised interesting things were about to happen and which, goddamn it, made Xander weak in the knees. Skylar held up a finger to Jacob as he pulled out his phone, but as he turned away to make the call, he winked at Xander. "Hey," he said into the phone. "It's me. Things calming on the issue there? Great. I need you where I am. Immediately. I'll text instructions." He paused, nodded. "Yes. I'll explain. Do me proud, please. Ah-huh. Yes. I will. See you shortly."

He hung up, texted furiously for a second, then turned back to the group with a winsome smile. "Sorry about that. I have an idea, if you'll indulge me. A friend of mine is coming to help with the details, but in the meantime—would you like to all hear it, or Jacob, would you prefer to consult with me alone first, before I bother the rest of your staff with something you'd rather not engage in?"

Xander ducked his head and bit his lip to hide his smile. Goddamn but Skylar was a silky little fish. You couldn't raise a comment in a lab better designed to puff up Jacob Chen's ego and get him to say—

"I think it'd be best if you told me first. This is *Lucky 7* business, no offense, and while I'm sure you have great ideas…"

Skylar held up his hands, still smiling. "Say no more. I completely understand. You show me where you'd like to talk, and I can lay things out for you in ten minutes, fifteen tops."

The two of them walked off toward the garage, and Xander braced himself for Zelda's onslaught.

It came as soon as Skylar was out of earshot. They pulled Xander to face them, sputtering and gesturing at Skylar and Jacob's retreating backs. "What—what the hell? What just happened? Why is he here? What—" They stopped, color draining from their face. "Oh. *Oh, oh.* This was the *weekend.* The lobster thing. But wait, you shouldn't be…"

Xander cast a helpless glance at Pamela.

Pamela smiled and took them each by the hand, putting herself between them. She nodded at Sara and Cory as she led Zelda and Xander toward the house. "Come on. I think it's time I played hostess properly. Xander, you'll help me make tea. Zelda and Cory, perhaps you could clear my table for me, and could I convince you, Sara, to lay out some cookies on a plate? There's some over there, in a box Xander left from his mom. We might as well do this up properly."

Pretty much nobody gave a fuck about tea or cookies, but everyone, Xander included, was at a loss of what to do, so everyone nodded and agreed, and that was how they all ended up in the house, having tea. It was oddly relaxing. Xander had made tea with Pamela a million times, but never with a crowd of people.

"How did they all end up here?" he asked Pamela in a whisper as he released a handful of leaves into the heated pot.

Pamela shrugged and emptied the hot water from the steaming kettle over the tea. "I think they were looking for you, but between you and me, mostly I suspect they were hunting for a place to gather. Zelda was muttering something about a fight with their mother, and Jacob has lost his apartment lease. He's staying with Cory for now, but if his landlord finds out, I guess that's a problem. That nice Sara is having trouble too. Her elevator has been out for two weeks, from what she says, and she has such a hard time with the stairs." Pamela put the kettle back on its stand and glanced over her shoulder at the table, a wicked twinkle in her eye. "I'm thinking of asking them if they want to move in. But I thought I should check them out a bit more over tea first."

Xander fumbled with the teacups he'd been pulling down from the cupboard. "What, *all* of them?"

"Why not? I have the room. Though I don't think Zelda will say yes."

No, Xander didn't think they would. Thank the gods for small favors. He wasn't sure how he felt about having more neighbors. But then he felt like an asshole, because clearly Sara and Jacob both needed rescuing the same way he had needed it. And Pamela certainly wouldn't mind more people around.

Funny how he'd always groused about being asked to socialize, and now that he had competition for Pamela…

She patted him on the shoulder and took the tray he'd prepared to the table, stopping to praise Sara on the way for arranging a perfectly *lovely* tray of cookies.

"So tell me," Pamela said as they all sat around her

table, now clear of random bits of junk mail and art supplies and gleaming with its natural oak finish, "where are the three of you from? I know all about Xander, and he's mentioned everyone on the staff, but I'd love to hear your stories."

They exchanged glances to see who would go first. Unsurprisingly, Zelda nominated themselves.

"I'm from Maine. My family owns a camping resort near Cape Elizabeth. I was originally planning to stay there and help out, but I'm back in town for the summer now."

Xander frowned. "What happened?"

Zelda looked coldly murderous. "My mother."

Pamela selected one of the cookies from the tray with a smile Xander knew was anything but innocent. "Do you have somewhere to stay?"

"I'm crashing with a friend."

"Hmm," was all Pamela said. For now. Then she turned to Sara. "What about you, dear?"

Sara smoothed her long hair away from her face as she sipped her tea, then launched into a tale Xander knew well. "My family lives in Poughkeepsie. My mom teaches at Vassar, and my father plays in the Hudson Valley Philharmonic. We moved to the States from Argentina when I was eight. I'm a citizen of the US now, though." She raised her left wrist, flashing the brace half-hidden by her sleeve, which Xander knew she wore long to hide said braces. "I have Charcot-Marie-Tooth disease, which is why I have the braces. It's not too bad right now, but it's not curable and it'll get worse as I get older, possibly. Probably. It's a neuromuscular condition. So I have to be careful with my body and my stress level, as that can exacerbate things."

Pamela had been nodding empathetically through Sara's story, but here she put down her tea and interjected. "You poor dear. It can't be easy to keep stress down in that building of yours. Between the stairs and the construction noise?"

Sara shrugged, a very Sara type of gesture. She twined a strand of her long, dark-brown hair around a finger. "There's not much for me to do. Sometimes life is unsatisfying."

"That, unfortunately, is most certainly true." Pamela turned to Cory with a smile. "And you, sir? Where did you land in Benten from? Oh, and what do you do for the magazine? Sara, you didn't give me that information about yourself, or you either, Zelda."

Zelda shrugged. "I do this and that. Officially I think my job is listed as assistant editor, but mostly I do what needs doing."

Pamela turned to Sara. "And what about you, dear?"

Sara had a mouthful of cookie, so Xander covered for Sara. "She's the head researcher for the manga, but she's also the *mangaka* in training. She helps me with backgrounds and screentones, and she's getting ready to take over when I leave."

"How *exciting*. So you're an artist too? How lovely." Pamela shifted her focus to Cory. "Now let's hear your story."

Cory cleared his throat, shifting on his seat and resting his forearms on the table. "I'm the layout guy, and the printer. I guess I'll have to be digital now, but I can do that. I was getting ready because I saw this coming. I do some tech stuff too—I'm kind of the jack-of-all-trades around the house. So is Zelda, but they're more metaphorical problem solver and I'm the this-is-broken-Jacob problem solver. I'm at home with tools and gadgets, but I like the research aspect too, and I don't mind helping out there."

Pamela beamed. "You're just like my late husband. He *loved* to tinker. I still have a garage full of his stuff. We didn't live here, mind you—we had a place east of town, but I couldn't stand to live there without him, so I sold it and moved here. I brought all his things, though, so he's still everywhere if I look for him."

Sara smiled over her cup rim. "I love the name painted over the door. *Palace of the Sun.*"

"Yes, well, it gets the best sunrise in town." Her smile turned melancholy. "Also, Takahiro always told me we would live in a palace one day. But it's too much room for just me. I have Xander upstairs, but…" She tapped her finger on the edge of her teacup, then shook her head with a smile. "I'm sorry, Cory. We were hearing your story."

Cory, who was naturally quiet and shy, looked like he'd been hoping to get off with what he'd already reported. He ran a nervous hand over his short black curls, ducking his head a little as he spoke. "Not much more to tell. I'm from Queens. My mom works in an office. My dad works as a manager of an auto repair shop. I'm here on a scholarship. Well, two of them. One for academics, one for minorities."

"How fascinating. How did you end up at Benten? Did something specific draw you here?"

Cory's cheeks stained with a blush. "I came here to hear Obama speak during his reelection campaign. Mom got us in the ticket lottery and we won. Since we're a mixed-race family, they put us on the risers behind him while he spoke, for optics and stuff. And then here's my mom, whipping out an essay I'd written in English class—'He's mixed like the President' she kept telling everyone, waving my essay at staffers, and they took it, and someone read it. Then afterward…I don't know why, but they took us to a room and we waited, and I got to meet him, and the president of the college too."

Xander's mouth fell open. He'd never heard this story. Sara looked stunned too.

Only Pamela had her wits about her enough to prompt for more. "My goodness, what an honor that must have been. Was he wonderful? Of course he was. Was he what you hoped for?"

Cory's expression became dreamy, almost youthful. "He…he was…like my dad. But he was the president. And my dad was there too, wiping his eyes, and Obama shook his hand, asked him about his favorite basketball team. They talked about the Knicks. And then he asked me where I wanted to go to college. Obama, I mean. The president of Benten—it was a woman at the time, I forget her name—said she hoped I'd consider coming here. And then the next year when I went to apply for colleges, she wrote me personally and invited me to apply for the scholarship."

Pamela leaned back in her chair, cradling her teacup in both hands, smiling. "That's a lovely story. Just perfect. And have you been happy here, I hope?"

Cory shrugged, some of his glow fading. "Yeah, mostly. Lotta white kids here. I mean—it wasn't so bad…before. But now that Obama's gone, all the politics getting so bad…I dunno." He shrugged again, staring into his tea. "Maybe Hillary wouldn't have done what I wanted, but she wouldn't have done this. I wouldn't have had to see people get this ugly."

Xander tensed, worried Zelda would make a derogatory Hillary comment, but they only curled their lip.

Sara shook her head. "I think we were always going to get this ugly. No one person created this. We had it in us all along."

"This is true. But I do wish we could have exorcised our demons more gracefully." Pamela sighed and put down her cup, but she had a twinkle in her eye. "Well. When you're finished with your tea, would you like a tour of the house? Oh, and by the way, do you happen to know your blood types?"

They didn't know them, but Pamela said that was all right, she thought she could guess. Xander steered her away from Japanese blood personality typing, knowing how she could get, distracting her by starting the tour.

As he'd predicted, the tour quickly became a real

estate pitch—what he hadn't seen coming, though, was that Pamela was luring Cory and Zelda as well as Sara.

"How high is your rent again, Cory? My goodness, that high? I don't charge Xander half that. And see, if I were to rent this room on the second floor, say, to two people, I wouldn't charge even that because it would be shared kitchen space. If my renters were willing to help with fix-it jobs though, things change. Zelda, isn't this a perfect space? Private, but with an amazing view? Now—Sara, what do you think of this room? It's supposed to be a conservatory, but I want to clear it out because all I do is fill it with junk. I don't need any of this stuff. Don't you think this would be a lovely bedroom? It's almost a suite, really. And on the main floor too. I never use this bathroom here around the corner, and it's a full one. I use the one upstairs—master bath, you know. And, of course, the one by the kitchen. What do you think, would you be interested in it?"

By the time Jacob came back to the house, Zelda had made plans to collect their things, Sara had already called her parents to approve the arrangement, Pamela had called her lawyer to draw up leases, and Cory pulled Jacob aside the second he entered the living room, ready to tell him all about the sweet deal they were about to fall into. Skylar came into the house shortly thereafter, and Xander went up to him, ready to tell him the whole crazy story, but before he could open his mouth, he saw Skylar wasn't alone.

"Unc?"

Unc winked at him, patting him on the shoulder as

he followed Skylar into the room. Xander came with them, frowning.

"Everyone," Skylar called, using his Silver Stone voice, but toned down, "I'd like to introduce you to a friend of mine: Jeff Turner. He's a fellow Delta Eta Sigma member, and likely member of the governing council for the fall."

Unc smiled as he went around the room, shaking everyone's hand. Everyone but Zelda, who kept their hands tucked tight against their body, regarding both Unc and Skylar with open suspicion. While everyone else circled around to meet the newcomers, Zelda hung back, saying nothing but making it plain they weren't happy.

Unc was strange, though. He was and wasn't himself. Apparently he had his own Silver Stone—Silver Unc? Jingling Jeff? He wasn't as good as Skylar, but he could decidedly swing a room his way when he wanted to, and he was doing it now. Charming each member of the *Lucky 7* by turns, and Pamela too.

"Dr. Stolarz, your house is *amazing*. Did you do the restoration yourself?"

She laughed and made a shooing motion at him. "Do I look like someone who can hold a handsaw? No. It came already done. I spent a ridiculous sum of money on it. My Takahiro and I were meant to take our epic trip to Japan after his retirement. We went a million times with students before he retired, but we wanted to go once just the two of us. Sadly, he had a heart attack before we could even get on the plane. So there I was with all our money and a broken heart, and I saw this house and decided to hell with it, I deserved it."

"You absolutely do. And is this all your artwork? My God, it's incredible. I hope you'll give me a tour of it later?"

"I will give it to you with a glass of my husband's twenty-five-year-old whiskey, you charmer."

He laughed, captured her hand, and kissed it. Then he worked over the rest of the room.

Jacob, apparently already a fan, helped. "These guys," he said, in full editor mode, taking command in front of the fireplace and gesturing to Skylar and Unc, who had moved themselves carefully to the side, "they're going to go with me to President Hardin tomorrow and try to get us a better arrangement. But even beyond that, Jeff says the frat will help pay for some supplies, so long as Xander signs off on it."

Zelda looked *murderous* now, but Xander was too distracted with his own problems, alarmed at the mention of his name. "Wait—what does this have to do with me?"

Skylar leaned over him, putting a hand on Xander's shoulder, sending shivers through him as he spoke. "You never did let Delta Sig give you or the art department any real compensation for the mural. I convinced the council *Lucky 7* is connected enough to count. They're eager to consider the debt repaid and save face."

Xander had no idea this was still a thing anybody gave a shit about. "Sure, fine, go for it, what do I care?"

Skylar squeezed his shoulder—and deftly, so no one

else saw, gave his nape a quick caress as he lifted his hand. "I think for the sake of appearances Xander should come with us when we make our case, given the connection to his mural and the fraternity."

Sara folded her arms. "If Xander goes, I want to go. I think we should *all* go." She pointed at Pamela. "I think Dr. Stolarz should go too."

Pamela laughed. "Please, all of you. I'm Pamela, full stop. Except to President Hardin. But why do you think I should come?"

Jacob had what Xander thought of as his wild eyes on. He aimed an excited finger at Sara, then Pamela. "*Yes*. You're right. She's emeritus faculty, and her husband advised us. Well, not *us*, but the magazine—God, Sara, you're brilliant."

Sara leaned back, unfolding her arms, her expression saying clearly, *I know*.

Xander didn't look at Zelda, but he could *feel* the glare at the back of his head. God, but he was going to hear about this. It didn't matter that he wasn't saying anything. He'd brought Skylar here: ergo, this was his fault, in Zelda logic.

Cory scratched his chin. "Okay, so we all go. What are we demanding, exactly? They can't magic a room for us. What are we going to do for workspace? What are we going to do for equipment?"

Pamela gestured to the outbuildings. "You can have the space above the garage. It's heated, and if you're willing to do a little work, you can divide it into offices or make up cubicles. You're all about to move in here anyway."

"Good. *Good.*" Jacob had wild eyes *and* he was pacing. He hadn't even had an energy drink. This usually was when Xander went and hid in the art room. "Okay. So what about equipment? Do we ask for a new printer? Find somewhere big enough for our old one?"

Zelda spoke up from the back, their tone cold and flat. "The old one broke, remember? They threw it out."

Cory held up both hands. "Guys, I'm telling you. This is why we need to go digital."

This argument woke Xander out of his quiet. "I want it printed."

Skylar straightened and frowned at Cory. "You were thinking of not having any print copies?"

Jacob answered for him. "It's the money. Print costs."

Unc wasn't having this either. "We'll find you the money for printing. Even if you have to reduce your print runs and up the price—sometimes you can make scarcity work in your favor. I'll write you up a prospectus."

"I still think we need to have the drawings be digital," Cory said, refusing to let go of the thread.

Xander wasn't giving up either. "I don't *like* drawing in digital."

Cory pressed his hands together and crouched in front of Xander, not going on his knees but decidedly getting into a begging position. "I swear to you, I can keep your work looking good if I can just get the right equipment."

Skylar and Unc swept in like a pair of eagles. "What equipment do you need?"

They sat there for hours, first in the living room, then at the dining room table, Unc taking notes while Skylar ramped Jacob up until he was practically on the moon, he was flying so high, spitting out ideas and wish lists, Cory and Sara getting into the act too. Almost everyone had things they wanted but Xander and Zelda.

Xander didn't like how quiet Zelda was being. He'd fully expected an explosion by now, and the fact that there hadn't been one yet wasn't a good sign at all.

He couldn't worry too much about Zelda, though, because he had his hands full with all the questions Skylar kept pelting him with. "What does *Lucky 7*'s artist want? More Copics?"

Xander opened his mouth to say he didn't want anything, but Sara spoke for him instead. "He wants a Microsoft Surface Studio."

Xander turned to her, looking at her like she was high. "I want a what? I don't want it. Whatever it is, I don't want it."

Sara ignored him. "Somebody with a smartphone, Google it, play the video, and put it in front of his face."

"Look, I don't *want*—"

Skylar stilled him with a touch on his shoulder. "*Forming new straight lines.* Watch the video, Fudō."

He'd spoken quietly, but Unc heard him and grinned. "Yeah, he is Fudō. That's hilarious."

"Who's what now?" Jacob asked, still amped up on his own juices.

Xander wanted to crawl under the table. "Shut up. I'm trying to watch a damn video."

He didn't give a fuck about the ad for a goddamned computer, but the hell he was going to let Unc and Skylar explain how Xander was a stand-in for Fudō Myōō. He glowered at the screen as it assembled the monitor like some sort of nuclear launch. Jesus. Pretentious much?

"If he's Fudō, who's Hotei?"

Xander hunkered over Skylar's phone, glowering harder. Goddamn Unc. "Nobody is anybody. Shut. Up."

"He said I was, but I don't think so."

And goddamn Skylar too. Xander wondered when this stupid video would end. All it was doing was spinning a monitor around as if it were a car in a showroom. Was someone going to come out and lie on it in a bikini? If it was a guy in a speedo, he might be interested. If the guy in the speedo came with the monitor.

Cory shook his head at Skylar and Unc. "Seriously, what are you two talking about?"

Skylar, to Xander's dismay, explained how he thought Xander wasn't unlike Moo from *Hotay & Moo*, though he also pointed out it was an odd shortening of the name. The staff laughed and agreed, enjoying calling attention to the obvious that both Moo and Xander were grousing hermits, except for their associations with Hotay.

Xander fumed and watched a woman on the screen press the monitor flat to the desk, or nearly so. Oh.

Well, that was a neat trick.

Unc scratched his chin. "Yeah, Skylar fits in that these two have become two peas in a pod, but he's not Hotei, not the god or your character Hotay. I bet we could find another member of the *Shichifukujin* for him to be, though."

Cory frowned at him. "The what?"

Unc looked severe. "You work on *Hotay & Moo* and you don't know *Shichifukujin*? The seven gods of fortune?"

Xander opened his mouth to explain Cory was their background guy, there to make sure machines worked and things showed up on time, though he was also filing away the name *Shichifukujin* to look up later because he'd never heard that one—and then the woman in the ad started drawing on the screen.

"Oh my God. What the—what?" Then the woman added a wheel-like object to the surface of the monitor, turned it, and all the colors shifted subtly with each click. Xander straight up got an erection. He whimpered and bent double over the phone. "*Oh. My God.*"

Sara patted him on the back, leaned over, and whispered in his ear. "Form new straight lines." Then she straightened and spoke to Skylar. "He wants one."

Xander wanted to have sex with one. "This can't be real. This isn't real? It can't...*Oh. My God.*"

Skylar sat beside him, sliding an arm around his waist. Xander didn't blush or object, too drugged by the idea of such a thing existing in the world. If the kind of pen pressure they were displaying here was accurate, the work he could do...*the things he could do...*

Skylar's thumb brushed his side. "Xander, would you like one of these computers?"

Forming new straight lines. It was the first time he'd actually wanted to embrace his magazine's motto. He wanted to make straight lines, and curved ones, and circles, and everything on this goddamned machine. "*Fuck yes.*"

"Done. Sara? Would it be convenient for you to have two?"

Sara laughed. "The president is going to shit when he sees the price tag for *one.*"

"Not material at the moment. Would you like one as well?"

"To be honest, a set of Surface tablets for the rest of the staff would be more appropriate, excepting whatever Cory needs."

"Will you make me a list of what you'd like to have, including software?"

"You bet."

Skylar withdrew his hand so he could talk with Jacob and Unc. Xander stayed where he was, replaying the video over and over, fast-forwarding to the part where the woman drew on the screen and blew his world open to new possibilities.

Chapter Sixteen

SKYLAR THOUGHT THE meeting with Hardin went well—the man was annoyed at being bullied into giving away money, but Skylar and Unc were a force to be reckoned with, and so were the *Lucky 7* staff, and Pamela too. Xander's glower was formidable, and Zelda seemed to come with some kind of invisible battle axe. Hardin acknowledged the bind he put them in, and with the greasing of the wheels from Delta Sig, he began to bend. But not without a fight.

"I don't understand why the two of you are so invested in this," he kept saying, gesturing to Unc and Skylar. "This isn't your type of thing, this little newspaper."

"It's a *magazine*," Jacob corrected.

Skylar smoothed him over. "A literary magazine dating to the founding of the college. Jeff and I are both avid readers of the serial manga taking up most of the contents these days."

Then, from nowhere, Xander said, "They're going to join the staff as well, both of them."

Everyone in the room turned to him, surprised to hear he'd spoken. Hardin blinked at him, then at Skylar.

"You can't be serious."

Skylar had no idea how to respond. Xander, apparently, did. "Skylar is going to be a staff writer for the manga. Un—Jeff is on tech support. With the new equipment, we'll need him."

Unc's cheeks flushed with pleasure. "Well. Yes. I suppose you will."

Skylar didn't know what to say. He stared at Xander, trying to decide if this was some kind of joke for Hardin's benefit, except Xander looked serious as a heart attack.

Hardin scoffed. "Your father, Stone, would have some things to say about you taking on such a ridiculous charge."

Beside Skylar, Unc stilled, underscoring the sick feeling Skylar had. Before he could so much as sort out how to react to it, however, Pamela pushed out of the shadows of the room.

"Frank Hardin. I'm sorry, did I hear you incorrectly, or did you just threaten a student?"

Hardin sputtered. "Of course I didn't, I would never—"

Pamela waved him silent with a bored hand. "Good, good. Then why don't you go back to telling them how you'll give them whatever they need? They've done all the work for you, even freed you up more adjunct office space because they're doing their work in my garage. Unless you think I should ask my lawyer if I should be billing the college?"

"No, no. This will be fine." Hardin fell over himself

to hurry the meeting to a close.

Outside the office, once it was over, everyone hugged each other and patted one another on the back in celebration. But Skylar pulled Xander aside. “Why did you say that about us being on the staff?”

Xander had a devilish expression on his face. “Because I think you should be on the staff. Duh.”

“I’m *totally* in, yo.” Unc high-fived Cory. “I will be your bitch. You tell me where you need me and I’m in. Goddamn, I can’t believe I get to work with you guys! Do I get to help look stuff up too?”

Sara groaned. “Oh my God, you’re *required* to. That’s the most annoying part, all the research. This is why they give it to me, the flunky.” She made puppy eyes at Skylar. “Do you really want to write for us?”

Skylar glanced around the staff members’ faces, unsure what was happening. “I—I would *love* to, but I don’t have much experience—”

“He’s written a lot before, just not lately.” Xander nodded at Unc. “So seriously, how *are* you with research?”

“Dude, for this shit? I’m all fucking over it. Skylar is too. He’s being shy because he’s Sky.”

Skylar blushed. “I’m not being shy. I’m simply saying I don’t have the qualifications—”

“You said you wanted to write a manga with me.” Xander raised his eyebrows and crossed his arms over his chest. “Well? Here’s your chance.”

I don’t really have the time. That was the true objection, the one he should have said. The one he needed to say. But Skylar couldn't, not when Xander stared at him, daring him to say no. Reminding him of what it felt like to be with him when he created. Of how much he wanted to be a part of that.

But could he truly be a part of that? Did he have it in him?

Skylar swallowed nervously, glancing around the faces looking at him expectantly. All but Zelda, he noted, who stood off to the side, looking as if they'd like to slice him into ribbons and put him under the microscope for further study. Which, now that he thought of it, was what he'd expected and was overdue. Why hadn't Zelda been more forceful in the meeting? He'd expected more opposition from them, given what Xander had said.

Not something to worry about right now. He let out a breath. "I'll…I'll give it a try."

Everyone cheered, and Pamela declared they had to come back to the Palace of the Sun where she would make them all a feast, which turned out to be that she ordered pizza. It was good pizza, though, and Skylar enjoyed sitting in the living room and laughing with everyone. Pamela served him jasmine tea, which he hadn't had before but discovered he loved, and he sipped it as he listened to Cory and Jacob and Sara plan how and when they were moving in, to Pamela and Unc as they discussed how best to clear out the garage attic to set up office space. Apparently Zelda was joining the Palace too, though they weren't part of the joyful planning. They were off in a corner with Xander having an earnest discussion—from the way Xander kept glancing Skylar's way, Skylar had a feeling the discussion was about him.

He wondered if he should go over and inject himself in the conversation, cut off some of the drama at the pass.

Before he could make a decision on that front, his phone rang. A glance at the caller ID told him it was his father.

Skylar couldn't say why he decided to answer. Perhaps it was to get the confrontation about his missing the fundraiser over with and out of the way. Perhaps it was because he was unsure how to handle Zelda yet, and in that moment his father seemed a safer outlet. Whatever the reason, he excused himself, stepped onto the front porch, and took the call.

"Yes, sir."

"Well. It's good to know you're not dead after all, as your mother was starting to fear."

Skylar leaned against a support pillar. "Sorry about that. I came back to campus and landed in a small crisis at the fraternity."

"This begs the question, of course, as to why you went back to campus at all. You were told to attend your mother's fundraiser with a suitable escort. Instead I'm pulled out of my own schedule to reprimand you for not only failing to show and ignoring attempts to reach you but for allowing the inappropriate punk you nearly arrived with to speak rudely to your mother's assistant."

Skylar shut his eyes and tipped his head back. "I'm sorry."

"You're sorry? Well. Isn't that helpful. I'm so glad I left my golf meeting to hear you tell me how *sorry* you are."

Skylar bit his lip to keep another *sorry* from slipping out.

His father continued, acid dripping from each word. "I certainly hope this is some kind of aberration and not an indication of how you've been spending your time this summer."

Skylar felt sick. It was, in a way, exactly that. "I'll do better, I promise—"

"Do not waste my time with promises. Show me some results, son. I'm counting on you. Your mother is too. She was looking forward to seeing you."

Now Skylar felt horribly guilty. If it weren't too late, he'd get in the car and drive to Connecticut right now. "I'm sorry. I know it doesn't solve anything, but I am."

"You can't afford distractions right now. Whoever that was you brought with you, the one who spoke so rudely to Patricia—get rid of them. They're no good for you."

Skylar stilled. He felt queasy with shock—and fear. "I—" He couldn't say anything else.

Get rid of Xander? The idea was completely unthinkable.

His father continued. "Your job right now is to study for that test and to get the highest score you can. Between you and me, I don't care that you missed the fundraiser, and I could give a damn if you find dirt on the President himself right now. That test, however, is another matter entirely. Buckle down and eliminate everything that keeps you from getting the best score you can on the LSAT. Keep your nose and the Stone name clean. Be the son I raised you to be. Do you understand?"

Someone laughed inside, a sharp trill, and it made no sense, but the sound, combined with his father's words, felt like a punch to Skylar's gut. As if the air, the words, the pain all swirled and combined, and for a second he couldn't catch his wind.

Eliminate everything that keeps you from getting the best score you can.

Whoever that was you brought with you...get rid of them.

Be the son I raised you to be.

Skylar drew a shallow breath. *But it wasn't you who raised me, really, Father.*

Even this defiant thought, though, couldn't help him shake the aching need to curry favor from his father, to please him and find a way to get him to say, "Good job, son." Yet for the first time in his life, as Skylar spoke to his father, there was a warring yearning, another pull of desire. Even as he longed to hear his father tell him he was good, his mind offered up an image of Xander, glowering, arms folded in front of his body.

Skylar wanted Xander too—wanted him with a pull stronger than the one drawing him to his father. He didn't want approval from Xander. He simply…wanted.

"I said, Skylar, do you understand me?"

Skylar cleared his throat, shaking off the image of Xander. "Yes, sir. Of course."

"Good."

With that, Leighton hung up.

Shaking, Skylar lowered the phone and let his head fall all the way back against the pillar.

"Hey."

He righted himself, masking his emotions as best he could, heartbeat quickening as he wondered what had been playing across his face, what whoever this was had seen.

It was Zelda. Alone, and from the look on their face, they'd maneuvered things so Xander wouldn't be rushing out to interrupt them. Not until they'd finished saying whatever was on their mind.

Great. *This*, in fact, fit the shark Xander had described. Leave it to them to strike Skylar right when he had no defenses left.

Skylar tried to push himself into Silver mode, to charm them the way he knew he needed to for Xander's sake. But the weekend had spent him, his father had bled him, and all he wanted right now was to go to Xander, to lose himself in his arms.

The fastest way to get to that point, he decided, was through this individual. He dropped his shields, put his hands in his pockets, and met Zelda with a flat smile. "Would you care to go for a drive?"

They snorted. "Not if you're driving."

"I have absolutely no desire to do so. Do we want a pretense to get ice cream or coffee, or are we simply leaving so Xander can't stop you from demanding some answers?"

Their eyebrows went higher, and the corner of their mouth lifted. "Look at you go. Huh. Well, are you buying?"

The impulse to be polite tried to kick in, but weariness overrode it, and Skylar almost snarled. "No. If you're going to interrogate me when I already feel wrecked, *you're* buying."

"Bitch." Zelda laughed. "Don't make me like you. Get in the car. I'm the piece-of-shit Chevy on the end."

They walked toward the car, but Zelda peered at Skylar's phone as he pulled it out to text. "Phoning a friend?"

"Texting Xander, so he knows where I am. I don't want him to worry."

"He doesn't answer texts."

"He answers mine." Skylar finished his message, hit send, and tucked his phone away. "I suggest you hurry us out of here. If he reads that *now*, you won't make it out of the driveway."

"Jesus, I'm not kidnapping you."

"Oh, you're not?" But he couldn't help smiling a little as he said it.

They drove aimlessly, quietly at first, and Skylar didn't mind. He sat back and watched the road go by, willing it to pull his father's conversation out of his head. It didn't work. It kept echoing.

"That your dad you were talking to?"

Apparently it echoed all over the car. Skylar nodded. "My father, yes."

"You call your father *sir* often?"

"It's how he prefers to be addressed."

"Your father's an asshole."

"He can be that, yes. He does good things too."

Zelda hissed through their teeth. "Boy do I hate that. *Justification.* 'This is wrong, but here's why it's okay to be wrong this one time.' Bullshit. Right is right. Wrong is wrong. Our world is so fucked, and it's all because of people like your dad. Blurring the lines. I want to punch everyone like that in the face. Make them pay for what they've done to us, to the whole world."

"Bishamonten."

"What?"

Skylar had his eyes closed, and he smiled. He wished Unc were here. This was a fun game. "In the *Shichifukujin* you're Bishamonten. The god of war. Of order and law. Remember when Jeff and I were assigning everyone roles from the Japanese pantheon? He's Hotei. Xander's Fudō Myōō. You're Bishamonten."

"*You're* weird." They sighed. "But you're not an asshole."

"Thank you."

They rode in silence a while longer. This time Skylar broke it.

"You've been friends with Xander a long time?"

"Since he came to Benten looking like a grumpy mouse nobody else was going to take care of."

They hadn't come up in his background research, though. Interesting. Skylar wondered how he'd missed them.

Zelda tapped their thumb on the wheel. "I'm willing to acknowledge you're not who I thought you were. But that doesn't change the fact that if you're just using Xander, I'm going to gut you. I don't care how much damn money you stuff in your mattress."

"I'm not using Xander. I wouldn't ever do such a thing." He thought of Tabitha and his string of previous dates, glanced at Zelda to check the murder in their eyes, and decided to add, "Not to Xander."

"So you admit to using other people."

Skylar nodded reluctantly. "Not…consciously. Not with that intent. But yes. It was Xander who pointed it out to me, what I was doing."

"How it was fucking wrong?"

"How it was hurting my chances with someone like him."

More steering wheel tapping. "So you *are* gay."

Skylar shut his eyes, breathing slowly as he fished for how to play this. He didn't know. All he had was his truth, now. "No. I'm not."

"Bisexual, then."

"No."

Predictable as the setting sun on the road ahead of them came Zelda's fury. "So you're what, gay baiting him? He's the magic gay who turns you queer? Which is legit, by the way, sometimes one person flips your switch for you, but then you *fucking own it*, you don't stand there and *no homo* them—"

"I didn't say I was straight."

The words startled him as much as they did Zelda. They shut them down, but the words stirred him up, made him want to climb the walls of the car, leap onto the roof and into the wind. But there was nowhere to go, nothing to do but sit with his confession, and try to remember to breathe.

This time when Zelda spoke—after a lengthy, almost painful silence—their voice was still sharp, but it had softer edges. "So you know, none of this is jealousy. I'm total protective parent over him, nothing more. I'm aroace."

Skylar kept breathing as best he could manage.

Eventually Zelda spoke again. "How about you? Got a term you prefer?"

Skylar choked on bitter laughter, turning his face to the window. *Breathe. Breathe. Breathe.*

This time the silence wasn't as cloying, but Skylar was tired now. He wanted to go back to Xander. He wanted to sit in the Palace of the Sun and listen to everyone plan.

He wanted...something else, but he couldn't figure it out. He was too tired.

"I'm not going to push you." Zelda's voice had lost all its edges now. "Xander told me you two were good—he *insisted* you were, and he's going to be super pissed at me for interrogating you. Especially if I take you back looking like I punched your kidney. Which, for the record, really sucks, because I *wanted* to punch your kidney. If you're going to look like that, at least let me, all right?"

Skylar wiped his face, dislodging tears he didn't know he'd shed. Felt the stubble of his beard, thought of Xander—and tears pricked his eyes again.

He drew in a sharp breath, pinched the bridge of his nose, but it was too late.

"Hey." He felt the warmth of Zelda's hand near his thigh, not touching. "Do you need me to pull over? I'm heading back, but I can stop. Do you want me to call him?"

Skylar shook his head. He wiped his eyes, but when he stared up at the car's ceiling, the tears kept coming anyway. "What do you care about rich assholes like me, Zelda?"

"I told you. You're not an asshole." Their voice became almost tender. "And I care a whole hell of a lot about hurting aces."

Skylar couldn't tell if he laughed, sighed, or cried out to the universe. All he knew was that something in his soul, something so tight and small and terrified, broke free. Said, *fuck this shit,* bounced around the car, and started to talk.

"I don't know what I am. I thought I was aroace, once. But the term felt like a straightjacket. I thought maybe it was because my family wouldn't like that choice."

"It's not a choice."

"*I know.* But at the time… My head wasn't in the right place. In so many ways. I couldn't tell if that meant the label felt wrong because it was wrong or I was. So I decided I wouldn't be anything. I would be *useful*. I'd be whatever anyone wanted me to be."

"Oh my *God*. Jesus. *Fuck*, Skylar."

The empathy bleeding from caustic Zelda's tones hit Skylar like knives. He let the cuts come, let the puss bleed out. "Everyone was so happy for me to be who they wanted me to be. Everyone was happy, that is, except…"

"Except your parents."

So cliché. Except… "And Xander. My parents wanted more. Xander—he wanted nothing."

Zelda chuckled. "Oh, *that's* how he got to you. Makes all the sense, now. He's your kryptonite. You want to please everyone. He's impossible to please. That's why you about looked like you wanted to dry hump him when you were setting him up for that computer. You *were* dry humping him. That's sex for you. Getting Xander Fairchild to soften in your hands." When he withdrew, looking uncomfortable, they waved a hand at him. "I didn't say it was bad. I was just working it out. Didn't mean to get into your pants. So to speak."

This was an odd conversation, and a bit more intimate than Skylar would normally prefer with someone he barely knew, but he'd never sat with someone who so casually acknowledged their asexuality before. It was like a drug. He couldn't stop. "I do…have a little attraction. Sexually. And arousal. It's different, though, I think, than most people's." He paused. "Is this okay to talk about?"

"It's on the edge for me. There are some other aces I think you'd do better to connect with, but for now, let's roll with this. I'm a little sex averse, so if we could pull the curtain of decency on any specific details, that would be great."

Good to know, because Skylar had been ready to go straight down that road. He diverted to another line of questioning bothering him. "So...how does it work, then, if I *do* feel attraction? I mean...does that make me an ace, still? I thought..."

"Look, there isn't any one definition for asexual. It's a spectrum for a damn reason. Though if you start using the label and share it with civilians, be ready to be compared to starfish."

Skylar blinked. "I—what?" He turned to Zelda, ready to hear the punch line to the joke, but they weren't laughing.

In fact, they screwed up their face and pitched their voice high as they role-played what was clearly a commonly asked stupid question. "'Oh, you're asexual? Like starfish?'" They glowered. "And if you point out that no, starfish *reproduce* asexually, they start arguing you should change your label because it's confusing. Demisexuals get it too. I have a friend whose cousin argued for an hour with her that demisexual had to do with philosophy, and another had her mom telling everyone she was a demigod. Then got mad when she corrected her, because how was she supposed to know? Fucking allosexual privilege."

"I don't really know if I'm demi or ace or some other kind of gray or what, though. Thinking about labels makes me crazy, to be honest."

"That's fine. You don't need to use the labels if you don't want to. I like them. A lot. You might change your mind later—that's also okay. You might change your mind about which label you like. Again, this is fine. Basically you make all the rules and everyone else is going to agree with your rules or I come and drop-kick them."

Skylar couldn't help smiling at that, but he did still have some concerns, and he wanted to talk them out. "Okay, but I do have to take Xander and his needs into consideration, and I'm not exactly sure how to do that. We're just getting started, so I'm kind of ahead of myself, but at the same time I feel like I don't know who I am anymore, so I don't know how to plan. I thought I didn't have this. Attraction, I mean. Now I wonder what else is going to happen. I didn't think I wanted to kiss anyone. Now I think I maybe want to kiss Xander. Possibly. But what if I'm wrong? And why am I thinking so much about this? Is this actually normal? Is there something wrong with me?"

"*Yes*, you're normal, *no*, there's nothing wrong with you. Stop that damn train, all right? You've passed all your physicals, yes? You've been this way your whole life? This is who you are. Oh, it's possible some asshole will do a study and tell us all about our brain chemistry and offer a fucking purple pill to *fix* us. Fuck that bitch before he even gets here. You'd be a different person if you'd spent your high school years fucking everything that moved, or even if you were slightly motivated. It's the same as Xander."

Skylar shook his head, thinking of the libidinous way Xander ogled him. "He's not ace."

"No. But he's reserved and caustic and cranky and a fucking hermit. You were going to spend the summer turning him into a social butterfly, from what I gather. What a nightmare if you could have managed it. You realize that now, right? His social media pages you made him make me want to puke, by the way. They're not him at all. *He* is human leather. You called him Fudō Myōō? You're right. He's a wisdom king, fighting in his own strange way. You can't corrupt him. He sees things as they are. I love him so much for that. Because he's so bitter, and then he paints such beauty. What if the people who run around 'fixing things,' fitting everyone into molds and binaries, could make him happy? They could, you know. I bet a heavy antidepressant would even him out but good."

"He's not depressed."

"Doesn't matter, right? Or rather, it depends on who defines what depressed is. Remember, there's still places in the country where people get taken by *good families* to doctors for *treatment* for the simple crime of being queer. And nobody stops them."

The thought made Skylar want to vomit. "There's nothing wrong with Xander. He doesn't need fixing. In any way."

"Exactly. Don't fuck with who he is, if he isn't broken. He's cranky, but he's a good person, and he makes great art. You're a good person too, and you're more than functional. Don't fuck with who *you* are. You have low sexual desire. Almost none, from the sounds of things. You've discovered a slightly different kink that aligns with Xander, and that's great. Chase that happiness. This world is a nightmare full of pain. You found someone you can make beauty *with.* Don't question how it happens or worry you aren't doing it the right way. Call yourself demi or an ace or gray, or refuse to take a name. It's all up to you. Call yourself the man who loves Xander Fairchild, the grumpiest, most antisocial asshole who ever lived. The one who made Xander love someone back."

Skylar wanted to cry again, but he was too spent. Also, there was a shadow over him, his father's phone call, echoing in his ears. He could see the Palace of the Sun outlined in the distance, against the purple of the twilight sky, could see Xander standing on the porch, waiting.

"My father…I don't want him near this. Near him."

"What would he do? What could he, real talk, actually do?"

He thought of his father's warning for him to stay away from Xander. He'd never heard his father actually give a warning before.

Of course, Skylar hadn't ever been inclined to ignore a warning, either. The thought terrified him, but the idea of turning away from Xander was like shutting out the sun. Inconceivable.

"I don't know," he said at last. "I'm afraid to know."

Zelda sighed. This time when they reached across the seat, they took his hand and squeezed it. "What did you call me? That god of war?"

"Bishamonten."

"This god badass?"

"Extremely."

Zelda nodded. Laced their fingers through Skylar's. "Consider Bishamonten officially on your team."

XANDER WAS READY to do battle with Zelda as they came up the driveway, his whole body lit up as he prepared to tell them off for doing exactly what he'd said not to and taking Skylar away to interrogate him. The air went out of him, however, as he saw the way the two of them were walking together. The way Zelda had their body turned toward Skylar, checking him like a bodyguard. The way, when Skylar swayed briefly on his feet, Zelda caught his elbow and righted him before anyone but Xander noticed, reassuring him quietly.

Goddamn, but the two of them hadn't simply gotten along. They'd fucking *bonded.*

Had Skylar come out to them?

All signs pointed to *yes,* given the way Zelda approached Xander with Skylar as if they were returning a comrade in arms. They inclined their head at Xander, a small apology, then checked back on Skylar. "You all right?"

Skylar smiled at them, a real smile, one that made

Xander jealous because he'd thought this kind of smile was only for him. "Yes. Thank you."

"I *will* get you those names." Zelda caught Xander glaring and rolled their eyes. "For *fuck's sake.* You know I'm not going to poach."

"You know it doesn't work like that, Zelda." Skylar sounded pleased.

Zelda waved goodbye to them both, casting one last glance at Skylar, and ducked back inside.

Skylar slipped an arm around Xander's waist. It wasn't a subtle move—they were outside, and they were alone, but they were also in full view of the others through the window, if anyone chose to look out. Xander couldn't help glancing around. "People can see us."

"That's my hope, yes." Skylar pulled Xander a little closer to him. "Is that all right?"

Xander's heart felt like a drum, its beats reverberating through his body. "If you claim me in front of my friends?"

"If I claim you in front of anyone. Everyone. I like the way it makes you blush. But I also simply like you. And I want everyone to know." Skylar nuzzled Xander's hair briefly with his lips. "Is it all right?"

Xander melted into his side, shutting his eyes. "Yes. It's fine."

Skylar stroked his side, resting his chin on Xander's hair. "I want to go upstairs with you. To your apartment."

Are we going to make out? A dumb question. The

way Skylar stroked him, the tone of his voice? Yeah. They were going to make out. The real mystery was, how would they do it? It wouldn't be that they opened the door and Skylar pushed him to the wall, ramming his tongue down Xander's throat. Once upon a time that had been the stuff of his fantasy. Now, that sort of thing occurring in real life would jar and upset him, because it wouldn't be Skylar. But whatever happened, it would be sensual and intense, and Skylar would wring Xander like a washrag before they were done.

Xander had to swallow before he could reply. "Yes. Let's do that."

As they wound their way up the stairs to Xander's place, questions nagged and eventually bubbled to the surface. Xander didn't turn around, choosing instead to ask them of the stairs ahead of him. "What happens when school starts in the fall, Skylar? Will you still want to claim me in front of people?"

"Yes."

That answer, frankly, shocked Xander, and he turned around to see if Skylar was joking. He wasn't.

Xander frowned at him. "You seriously are going to come up to me on campus and—" The mental image flashed, of him in a quiet spot, bombarded by Skylar and a harem of giggling sorority girls and glaring frat boys. He backed up a step. "Oh, *hell no.*"

Skylar stayed where he was, penning him in tight with both hands on either side of the railing. He didn't laugh or even smile. "Hell yes. Or is it *you* who is ashamed of *me*?"

Low blow. "You're honestly going to let them all think you're gay?"

There was an odd steel about Skylar's expression. "Let them think what they want. I don't care."

Skylar looked serious, but Xander couldn't help pushing back. "You care a hell of a lot and you know it."

"I care more about you. About myself. I don't want to live like that anymore." His shoulders sagged. "Please, Xander. I don't want to fight. I want to be with you."

Now Xander felt like shit. "I'm sorry." He took Skylar's hand, prying it off the metal rail. "Come on. Let's do some sketching."

This, as he predicted, put some life into Skylar. "Of me?"

"Of you." Xander teased Skylar's hand, turning it into a light kiss of fingers. "I thought maybe I could talk you into showing me some skin tonight."

They were at the door now, and Skylar crowded Xander into it. "Oh? This is different. And exciting. You want to draw me nude?"

"Well, not precisely nude yet." Xander unlocked the door and let them inside, catching Skylar's hand and leading him into the main room. Hiromu was perched on the counter, looking sullen beside her empty food dish, but Hokusai was nowhere to be seen. Xander put food in the dish for the cat before he got out his sketchbook and supplies. "I would feel uncomfortable. Because I want to actually draw you, not turn this into a porno introduction. Also…"

“Also, you’re shy.” Skylar ran a hand down Xander’s arm and moved to the center of the room, where he began unbuttoning his shirt. He’d worn a suit to face down Hardin, and he still had it on. “All right. How far down do you want me to go?”

Xander watched Skylar’s long fingers work his buttons, hypnotized. *All the way down. On me.* He cleared his throat. “Start with your shirt off. Dress and undershirt. Please.”

“Teach me that in Japanese.”

Xander’s brain was pudding as he watched first Skylar’s suit coat come away, then the panels of his cotton shirt open up, one button at a time. “There are a lot of ways.”

“Teach them all to me, then.”

His shirt was open now, and he’d moved onto the cuffs. “*Onegaishimasu.* That’s the main one that I taught you already. You can shorten it to *Onegai.*”

“Mmm. But there are others?”

One cuff was done. The second was giving him trouble. “*Kudasai.* It’s used with te-form verbs. *Please do it for me.*”

The cuff came free, and Skylar shrugged out of his shirt. “Ah, such as, *strip to your underwear for me, kudasai.*”

He took the white T-shirt clinging to his skin with both hands, tugged with a smooth motion, and peeled it from his body.

“*Sō desu ne,*” Xander whispered.

Skylar tossed the T-shirt onto his growing pile of

clothing and arched an eyebrow. "Another way to say *please*?"

"No. That's more something you say when you don't know what else to say."

Skylar grinned. "Well, you have me as you wanted me." He hooked a thumb in his waistband, tugging it down ever so slightly. "Sure you want to stop?"

Xander wanted to get to the floor and bury his face in that waistband. Except…he also didn't. He swallowed and licked his lips. "Can I ask you a question? I promise it's not to start a fight."

Skylar stayed where he was and kept his thumb in his waistband. "Sure."

"I don't—I really don't want this today. I couldn't do it. But…sometimes my fantasies of you are…pretty erotic. Mostly of"—his cheeks flamed—"me sucking your skin. Or…you. Or you me. But then I wonder, do they need to stay fantasy? I guess I just want to know."

Skylar's expression was hard to read. "Would it upset you if I said they would have to? That I couldn't do that?"

"Of course not. It's why I asked, because I wanted to know."

"But what do you mean, 'of course not'?"

This was a weird conversation. Xander tried to mentally map the minefield, but it was hard with Skylar's incredibly attractive chest staring at him. "I mean, of course not because if you can't do that, then I find something else to get hot over you about. There are roughly a billion things about you that turn me on.

What, you think I'm some kind of asshole who would stop wanting to be with you because you didn't want me to suck your dick? Jesus. I haven't even *kissed you on the mouth* and I'm so far gone for you—" He cut himself off, not having planned to confess so much.

Skylar honed in on that too. "What if I can't even do that? What if I can't kiss you on the mouth?"

"Why does this matter to you so much? Where is this coming from?"

"I don't want you to find me lacking! I don't want to come this close to you and then find out if I would have bent, just a little—"

Something inside Xander snapped—he could almost see it, and it was a tiny, red-hot rubber band. "*Hai.* Take off your clothes, all of them, Skylar-san, *onegaishimasu.*" When Skylar only stared at him, he clapped his hands twice. "*Hayaku.*"

Skylar faltered. "All?"

A flicker of doubt rose in Xander, but the wave of red in him snuffed it out. "I'm going to draw you." He paced a circle around Skylar, already mapping him with his artist's eye. "I want to see all of you. Every line and curve. I'm going to draw you as I see you. As I feel you." He spied his manga markers on the edge of his desk, felt the rush, and went with the impulse. "It's going to be a manga drawing. A big one. It's going to take some time. This won't be like our other modeling sessions. You'll need to get comfortable. Be ready for a long session. Watch for cramps. Take breaks, get hydrated."

Skylar's breathing had changed. He'd gone softer

too. For once Xander was in control. "Okay."

The rest of the clothing removal wasn't as charged as the first half, even though this part contained the aspects of Skylar Xander had yet to see and most coveted. He did allow himself a moment to appreciate the beautiful curve of Skylar's backside, the slope of his hips and lower back. Before he turned around, though…

"Do you want a sock?"

Skylar glanced over his shoulder. He was blushing. Xander memorized it so he could sketch it. "Seems silly."

"Not if you're shy. A lot of male models wear one."

The blush was replaced by a sharp look of jealousy. "Have you seen a lot of naked male models, then?"

Xander smiled slowly. "I have. I'm a BFA student with an emphasis in drawing and painting. Naked men and women to the point they look like blobs of flesh, I'm afraid."

"Hmm. Is that all I am right now? Another blob?"

"No."

Skylar held still, waffling. "It's not the sock or not. I just feel…very exposed. Which is obvious, but…"

Xander thought he understood what Skylar was saying. "The balance is off. Hold on." He set his sketchbook down, stood, and tugged his own shirt over his head. "Better?"

Skylar turned a little more to get a good look. "Hmm. Maybe?"

Xander undid his pants. "I'm not going full monty,

because if I sit here bare-assed, it's all I'm going to think about. But I'm willing to go to my skivvies."

"I think I'd appreciate your skivvies." Skylar cleared his throat. "And...a sock for myself. *Ku..kud...*"

"*Kudasai.*"

"A sock, *kudasai.*"

Xander went to his room and came back with a clean tan sock, and handed it to Skylar. It was long, and Skylar held it up by the end, raising an eyebrow. "You're a little optimistic."

Xander laughed. "It's the only tan one I have. I don't want it to pull focus."

Skylar put the sock on the organ it was intended for. "You plan to spend a lot of attention around my groin area?"

"I do. I find it beautiful. I can't wait to draw it."

He ran his hand down Skylar's arm, noting the way it made him shiver. Xander kept stroking, keeping his touch light, soothing.

Eventually Skylar gasped and flinched, covering his sock with his hands, which had...started to rise. "*Oh.* That's—that's very..."

Xander smiled. "Nice?"

Skylar looked taken aback. Slightly hungry, slightly apprehensive. "It's that sustained, light touch. From you. If it were harder or had more intent behind it..."

Ideas began to pop inside Xander's head. "Hmm. We'll have to try drawing on your skin sometime. Or maybe simply using a paintbrush. But not today." He patted Skylar's shoulder and stepped away. "Today I'm going to draw *you*. Come sit over here on this pile of cushions, and face my easel."

Skylar sat. He was used to sitting for portraits now, but Xander hadn't been kidding, this was a marathon session, and it had a thread beneath it like no other. Xander had set up a pair of mirrors behind Skylar, to help him get a better view of the whole, and it gave him a view of himself too as he worked, and Skylar's body posture. How nervous he was.

It showed, to Xander's surprise, how confident *he* was.

He'd watched himself work before, for self-portraits, but he'd never seen this. Never seen himself this strong and confident. It made him feel sexy and powerful. It gave him a big head, made him reckless.

Made him say, as he sketched Skylar, "Tell me about the rest of these seven gods. If you're not Hotei, who else might you be?"

The question was a good one, because it relaxed Skylar somewhat. "Hmm. Well, I already told Zelda they were Bishamonten."

Xander laughed. "God of war. Good call. Okay, that one's taken." He smoothed the line of Skylar's hip. "And Unc is Hotei. But keep telling me about the others. There are seven. That's two. Who are the other five?"

"There's Ebisu, the laughing god. His origins are the most Japanese. He's the god of prosperity and wealth. Loved by fishermen. In his origin story he was born without bones."

That wasn't Skylar. "Who else?"

"Daikokuten is the god of commerce and prosperity. Cooks, farmers, and bakers consider him their patron god. He's also known as a demon hunter."

Also a no. "Next?"

"Jurōjin is the incarnation of the southern polestar, the god of the elderly and longevity. He's based on a real person and has a very long head. Loves wine. Very cheerful."

"You really know all of them by heart. Okay, who are the last two?"

"Well, one is kind of an either/or. One of the gods can be either Fukurokuju or Kichijōten, depending on if they're male or female. This is a hermit god who can resurrect the dead. Patron saint of chess players. Known for wisdom, wealth, longevity, and happiness." Skylar shifted his foot, flexed his ankle. "Then the last one, of course, is Benzaiten. Our school's patron goddess, also known as Benten. Patron of arts and artists. Goddess of talent, beauty, and music."

Bingo. The rush of rightness flowed through Xander, and he knew he had the center of the piece now. His breathing slowed, his body took on a stillness which was, he supposed, its own kind of arousal. An artist's arousal.

Let me make love to you, Skylar.

"Shift onto your elbows, please, and widen your hips. Use the pillows behind you to prop yourself up if you need to. But open your knees."

Skylar moved into position, but he trembled a little. "That's…a rather exposed posture. Pretty erotic."

"You're an erotic subject, and it's an erotic piece." He kept his gaze on his paper, flicking it up to Skylar when necessary, losing himself in the zone, but when he looked up once, something felt off, and the expression on Skylar's face pulled him out, made him stop. "Are you okay? Do you need a break?"

Skylar shook his head, but he seemed...hesitant. "You're so...different when you work."

"Different bad?"

"Just different. You really are only seeing me as a blob of flesh."

Xander shook his head. "No. Okay—I'll grant I'm not looking at you the way I do when I'm admiring you. But I'm not looking at you the way I do my usual subjects, either. I'm highly aware of who I'm drawing right now. Of what I want this portrait to say, to whom I want it to speak."

Now Skylar softened. "You're drawing for me?"

"Everything I've drawn lately has been for you."

The air was charged now, but in a way that allowed them to be comfortable in the silence while Xander worked. Occasionally he urged Skylar to shift and put blood in his limbs, take a drink, and then eventually he told him he could get up.

"You're finished?"

"No. But I don't need you for this part." He glanced in the mirror, checking his image, but Skylar had stepped into it. "Could you move to the right, please?"

Skylar had wrapped a blanket around himself. "You're drawing yourself?"

Xander nodded. "Go get something to drink." A howl came from the kitchen, and he added, "And feed Hokusai, please."

It took him another half hour to finish the sketch, at which point Skylar was dressed in Xander's sweats and wanted to see, but Xander refused. The fire of the piece burned in him—he'd thought of making it a simple drawing, doing it in Copic, but he wanted to paint it now, and he wanted to be alone, so he sent Skylar to bed, pulling him in close and making out with his hand, caressing his other arm and shoulder, promising it would be worth it if he would wait.

Once he had the living room to himself, he set up his easel, his paints, turned on his stereo, and lost himself.

He'd never done this before. Never painted manga style. It was odd, but it worked surprisingly well. He got off on the sharp black strokes—did them in marker, so they'd stay—then brought in his brush and smoothed the color over the canvas, watching it spill and soak into the white.

Benzaiten, he thought as he painted, his mind calling up her desecrated shrine. *I know he isn't you. But he is worthy of you. Please look kindly on him, and take care of him. And please consider my work a humble offering for all you have done for him, and for me.*

It was dawn when he finished. The record had ended long ago. His shoulders ached. His fingers were cramped. His body was splattered with paint, and he was cold—something he didn't consciously acknowledge until he crept down the hall and climbed into bed beside Skylar.

"You're like ice." Skylar shivered as he wrapped his body around him. "You smell like paint. I like it."

"I'm done. You can see it." Xander's body turned to lead. "But not yet. Let me sleep first."

Skylar pinched his backside. "Not a chance. I've waited all night for this. I've barely slept."

Xander groaned, but he relented, getting out of bed. The fire was out of him, doubt creeping in. "I'm not sure of the composition. The color might be off too."

"Shut up and let me see my damn painting." Skylar tugged him, blanket-wrapped, down the hall. He flipped on the light. "I want—*oh my God.*"

He stopped in the doorway.

He let go of Xander, took three steps forward, put his hands over his mouth. Sank to the floor, where he sat on his knees and stared.

Xander's stomach was a queasy mess now. "Is this bad?"

Skylar pointed at the painting, his finger shaking. "That…that's Benzaiten's shrine. The one that was in Delta Eta Sigma—except it's not wrecked. But you never saw it this way. How…?"

That's what he was upset about? "I'm an artist. Imagination comes with the job description."

"But that's *me* lying in her shrine. Like I'm the body of the god! And…and that's you at the *torii*, and you're…" He pressed his hands to his cheeks. "You're Fudō Myōō."

Xander hoped to hell—or heaven, or wherever—this wasn't sacrilegious. "It's called *Fudō Myōō Comes to Remove Benzaiten's Obstacles.*" He took a step closer, waiting for Skylar to see the rest.

Skylar leaned in, squinted, then froze. "*Xander.*"

This part of the painting was the one Xander was sure about. "It was tricky, coming up with images to represent conventional sexuality without wrecking the composition. So I decided Tabitha and your old dates owed me one last favor. Good old carnal images of men and women wrapped around her—your—wrists and ankles." He gestured to Fudō's sword. "I mean, he's not going to hack them or anything. More dislodge them with the tip. Unless someone gets feisty. Then all bets are off."

Skylar had tears running down his cheeks, and he spoke in a whisper. He couldn't look away from the painting. "What did I do to deserve you?"

"You told me not to throw away my work. You chased me down and made me open up. Enough to see things I needed to see." Xander stepped closer and put a hand carefully on Skylar's hip. "This is how I make love to you, Skylar Stone. I make you take off your clothes and spread your legs for me. I get you to tell me stories of goddesses and turn you into one. I turn your deepest fears into the most beautiful painting I know how to create, and then I stay up all night to give it to you." He rested his nose on Skylar's shoulder, nipping him smartly. "The very idea I need to slobber on a body part to do it is insulting."

Without turning around, Skylar found Xander's hand and laced their fingers tight. "What happens if I tell you that I love you?"

Xander shut his eyes, smiling into Skylar's skin as his heart soared. He squeezed their joined hands tighter. "I'll tell you that I love you back."

Chapter Seventeen

IT WASN'T THAT Skylar moved into Xander's apartment, exactly. But as he explained to Ms. Mary when she commented on how seldom he was at Delta Sig, with all the construction going on because of the shrine renovation, he couldn't study there.

He didn't tell her how little he was studying at the Palace of the Sun or anywhere else, and he worked hard not to let her, his father, or anyone else know.

He still went to his tutoring sessions, where he appeared in his suit and what Xander would grumble and call a plastic smile. He did his best to prepare enough so his tutor didn't report to his father that he wasn't doing anything at all, but the truth was, essentially, he was doing the bare minimum required not to fall on his ass in the sessions, and he put a lot more effort into charming the tutor—female, straight, attracted to him—than he did the lessons. It paid off, because he didn't get any more phone calls from his father, and he got the impression that so long as he kept charming her, she'd make sure his reports were glowing.

But it was a lot of work, and it made him feel slimy, even though he was doing it expressly to protect his time with Xander. He feared what would happen if the tutor ever flirted with him in front of Xander, though she lived out of town and they met in the conference room of a private club of one of his father's friends. He was finally able to relax after one tutoring session when he witnessed Danielle getting into her boyfriend's car and realized this situation was the same as the Tau Kapps: She was flirting with Safe Skylar who wouldn't try anything but was so good for the ego. It made him feel better, but the guilt and sick feeling didn't go away, nor the impending sense of dread.

Because this was a game, he knew, that he couldn't win. Not studying was not studying. Posing for Xander and reading manga wasn't going to get him a good score on the LSAT. Eventually his father would find out what he was doing, and when that happened, Skylar had no idea what he was going to do.

He only worried on the drive from his tutoring sessions back into Benten, though, because as soon as he was back at the Palace of the Sun, once he walked into what were slowly becoming the *Lucky 7* offices, his tension eased—and when he saw Xander's grumpy face, fading into a smile at the sight of Skylar, all Skylar's cares disappeared entirely.

It helped that there was so much to get done to resurrect the *Lucky 7* offices in Pamela's garage attic. Unc and Cory had the tech end set up, with some help from Sara, who was teaching Xander the deep tricks of his new toy, helping him transition from paper drawing to digital. Jacob had his hands full, working all his jobs and wrangling with the printing company for the new arrangements, so Skylar offered to help, because the only other person was Zelda, and noble as their intentions were, it was like sending in a nuclear bomb to shift a cabinet to the left.

Then there was the writing. Xander hadn't been lying. There hadn't been a head writer position before because no one wanted the job. They were all more than happy to turn the task over to Skylar, though they promised to help him with research if he needed it. Never mind the fact that Skylar seemed to know more about their own lore than they did.

When he told them he wanted to include the full *Shichifukujin* in the storyline, their only hesitation was that they hadn't known the term meant seven gods of fortune. After that they said it sounded great, and he should go for it. They'd been milking the seven gods as side characters for years, they said, so why not make them regulars?

"I feel really nervous about this," he told Xander one night as they lay on Xander's bed, both in their underwear with a fan blowing over them because it was eighty-five degrees in the room, even though it was after ten o'clock. "I'm going to mess up the whole magazine."

"You won't mess it up." Xander swung over him, settling their groins together as he stared down at Skylar. "We'll write the stories together. Tomorrow we'll do some storyboarding. It'll be fine."

Skylar opened his mouth to protest, but before he could, Xander pulled a wide paintbrush shaped like a fan from the bed beside him and ran it lightly down the center of Skylar's chest.

Shuddering, Skylar moaned as gooseflesh broke out across his body. "*Xander.*"

"That's me." He ran the brush down Skylar's side, making him flinch and gasp. Then he ran the brush up the other side, across the lowest point of Skylar's abs.

The shivers rushing through Skylar became more intense. "I can't…think."

"Did you *want* to think?" He teased with the brush below Skylar's belly button. "Or did you want to put your arms above your head, bite your lip, and go slowly crazy while I run this fan brush all over your skin?"

Skylar put his hands over his head, arched his back, and closed his eyes.

This wasn't the first time they'd played the fan-brush game. Sometimes Xander sat on him the way he did that night, getting hard while Skylar got off, but other times Xander held Skylar's wrists with his right hand while his left ghosted invisible trails across Skylar's skin. They hadn't gotten naked with each other yet—the closest they came was when Xander painted or sketched Skylar, and that didn't count. They had, however, discovered what brushes aroused Skylar.

As in, literally.

Technically Skylar knew he was meant to be in the Benten Library practicing his law essays, but he couldn't, not when he could lie in a sweltering attic apartment, gasping and clutching at a blanket as Xander flicked a fan brush or an ox hair script liner against his navel. Over and over, touching nothing else, until Skylar canted his hips, chasing after his…erection.

He got erections now. With other people.

They weren't crazy intense, they didn't last long, and he certainly didn't ejaculate, but he *got hard.* It was so strange and wild and freeing that he often made rough, animallike sounds, tossing his head, mewling, grunting. He would have thought he'd be embarrassed. But it was all right, because he was with Xander. Xander understood.

At no time, ever, did Xander expect Skylar to take his moments of pleasure further. Xander refused to get off in front of Skylar, saying Skylar wasn't ready for that and neither was he. When Skylar occasionally felt guilty for this, Xander would point to the painting, still displayed in the middle of the living room.

"You aren't here for my pleasure. And you're still discovering your own. Maybe someday you'll be ready for more, but not now. I'm happy enough to be your vehicle."

Skylar threaded fingers in his hair, smiling and shutting his eyes against a wave of pleasure. "You're Pygmalion now. There's no question. I'm absolutely Galatea."

"No. I'm not creating anything. I'm only helping you set free what you've had in you all along."

Sometimes the game ended with a tender cuddle, lacing fingers and nuzzling noses. Sometimes Skylar felt brazen and turned the tables, literally flipping Xander over and giving him the body contact and stimulation he needed to get himself off—but as promised, they never went quite that far. That always felt like a razor edge, but that was why Skylar loved it. It wasn't about getting off for him. It was about undoing Xander.

He did that today, pressing Xander into the blanket—it was hot, sticky with their sweat, smelling of heat and dust. He pushed his groin into Xander's, let him feel his erection, which, as it always did, made Xander tremble and go soft everywhere except in the matter of his *own* space between his thighs. Xander didn't need a paintbrush to turn into a quaking pile of goo. He only needed a few slides of Skylar's body against his own.

"Please." Xander nuzzled Skylar's beard, teased Skylar's wrist, the back of his hand. "*Onegai.*"

Skylar gave him what he asked for. Slow, agonizing friction. Teasing fingers against his skin, grazing his nipples. And his beard—the stubble of his chin he rubbed everywhere. Ms. Mary kept clucking her tongue at him, asking if he was going to shave it off because he looked so nice clean-shaven, and Skylar ignored her. He was never shaving, because Xander loved this too much. It was *his* paintbrush.

Never had Skylar dreamed he could not only discover so much about himself, become so accepting of his orientation and sexuality, and find someone who not only patiently went with him on that journey but insisted it was his pleasure to be a part of it. To find their own way to their mutual enjoyment of each other together.

Delta Sig was rebuilding the shrine at the fraternity

house, but here in the attic of the Palace of the Sun, Skylar felt he was living Xander's painting every day. He came through the door, accepted his welcome by Hokusai and Hiromu, brewed some jasmine tea, and let his wisdom king lead him to paradise.

He decided, feeling cheeky, this should be the story of the manga, the arc they followed for the year.

"What if Hotay gets a call from Benzaiten?" He lay in Xander's arms one day as he said this, his boxer briefs on now that Xander was finished drawing him. "She's in some kind of trouble and needs help. All the *Shichifuku-jin* do, but Benzaiten is the one who asks."

Xander trailed his fingers down Skylar's arm, teasing his wrist. "Are you saying you want to have Moo and Benzaiten have a romance?"

"Maybe. But not right away. And not an overt one." He faltered, feeling his idea was weak, silly. "Never mind."

"No, no. Keep going. What's the conflict? Or maybe, what's the goal? Where do you see this ending?"

Skylar didn't know. He tried to imagine it. "Well, we don't want it to *end*, not completely. But it would be nice to see the arc finish, before we left Benten."

"So some problem arises that Moo needs to solve for the seven gods which can be seen to by the arc's end, but which doesn't tie up everything so much that the manga has to end." He tapped his fingers on Skylar's arm. "Hmm."

"Is that impossible, do you think?"

"Of course not. Problems are easy. Something gets

in the way, Moo solves it. He's the remover of obstacles. Obviously we have to make it a little difficult to remove them, but that's the gist. And with all seven gods to balance, that's enough right there."

Skylar wanted more, though. He played with the hair on Xander's leg. "What if to save the whole, he has to hurt the one? Or himself? What if there is a romance between himself and Benten, but to solve the problem he has to sacrifice something?"

"Huh. Well, that's *depressing*."

"It's reality."

"Yes, but…what if he only *thinks* he has to, and then it works out that they can have everything? What if it's by being part of the *Shichifukujin*, working together, that they can have their happiness? That's a good lesson for Western audiences. We're always taught to be the damn Lone Ranger." Xander poked the top of Skylar's head. "*You* need that lesson. I say we do this."

Skylar swatted his hand away, but he smiled. "All right, *how*? How would it work out that only the seven gods could save the day, but they wouldn't know at first? And how could it be tied to Fudō and Benten?" He bit his lip. "Is this even a good idea?"

"It's a great idea," Xander insisted.

They plotted for days. Xander showed Skylar how to storyboard, which felt like a revelation. Skylar wasn't sure if he wrote on his own he could make such organized outlines work, as his narratives always drifted out to sea somehow, but with manga, with a visual artist, there was no way. His narratives were nothing more than chunks, concepts Xander would rough out so Skylar would see how much text was needed, or more to the point, what his limits were. There wasn't time to wax poetic. He had to find the right phrase, right word to accentuate what Xander planned to draw. But Xander only drew what Skylar set up.

It was as if they danced together across the story, moving in perfect harmony with one another. Xander didn't mind that Skylar was still feeling his way. He patiently answered all Skylar's questions, helped him when he got stuck on a plot snarl, and best of all, seemed legitimately grateful to be illustrating his ideas.

"But I'm so clumsy at it," Skylar protested.

Xander shook his head. "You're passionate. You don't understand how important that is, how long I've been waiting for it. I would get so frustrated, pointing out there was nothing to produce without the plot and that I wasn't any good at making up stories, only illustrating them. So they would grumble and complain and help me make one. Not you. You wrestle with it, but your whole face lights up while you do it. Your whole spirit. My only complaint is that sometimes I want to stop storyboarding and sketch you. Or make out with you."

Blushing, Skylar leaned forward, ran his index finger down Xander's nose, then pressed their foreheads together. "I've totally neglected your senior project."

"You haven't. We have all those accounts set up. I've been working on my pieces for my show. It's fine."

It wasn't, though. Zelda was right, Skylar had set up

the entirely wrong approach for Xander. He didn't know the right one yet, and...and he didn't want to stop making a story with him to fix it. The same way he didn't want to study.

"Let's focus on the manga this summer." Xander stroked Skylar's beard. "We'll get serious in the fall. For now, let's enjoy this moment."

Skylar caught Xander's hand, laced their fingers together, and swayed them gently in the space between them, watching them glide.

I haven't been studying for the LSAT. I've been flirting with my tutor, even though it makes me feel sick, to keep my father off our scent, because I'm afraid if he finds out about you, he'll take you away.

He wanted to tell Xander. Wanted to explain how dangerous this was, how much it scared him. To tell him every time he opened his study guides he thought of storyboards for *Hotay & Moo*.

To tell him thinking of law school next year made him feel cold and dead inside.

To tell him that feeling was nothing compared to his attempts to imagine days where he didn't wake up and rush through his shower and throw on whatever clothes were handy so he could come over to this quirky Victorian house on a hill, to climb to the top and work with the man waiting for him.

He wanted to say these things, but he didn't. He told himself it was because he was afraid of what Xander would say if he found out about the tutor, and he didn't think he was wrong to fear that reaction. But the truth was, he was just as scared of the way he felt inside. Of the things he was letting go of, of the things he was shutting out of his heart.

Of the things he was turning his face toward and wrapping his arms around.

So in the end he said none of the things he wanted to say, only stroked the side of Xander's hand with his thumb and told him the idea he'd had for the next panel.

THE PALACE OF the Sun had gone from being a lonely old house to a bustling hive at all hours of the day and night. Sara had her own room on the first floor, but she only used it for sleeping, spending most of her time in the main living room or the kitchen. Zelda, Jacob, and Cory came downstairs more often than not.

Xander's mother's care packages never made it to the art department anymore, because now as soon as one of his housemates saw the familiar brown box with the red-and-white label and Xander's mother's handwriting sitting in front of the mailboxes, everyone started making doe eyes at him until he opened the thing and put it on the kitchen table.

"Are you sure you don't mind us eating all your cookies?" Cory asked, helping himself to four.

Xander turned away as he replied. "No, go ahead. She sends too many."

"Must be nice," Sara called after him, "to be loved so much that someone sends you too many cookies."

Xander didn't know what to say to that, so he said nothing. He wasn't able to mask his expression, though, and he knew as he rounded the corner onto the porch and ran into Skylar that not only had his boyfriend heard the whole exchange, he'd seen Xander's face as well.

Xander did his best to do damage control. He rubbed his neck and nodded at the stairs to his apartment. "Got a headache. Going to go take a nap."

Skylar said nothing, simply followed Xander up the stairs.

Shit.

In the apartment, Xander made one last attempt at escape. Dumping his backpack on the couch, he picked up Hiromu and headed for the bedroom. "Would you feed Hokusai? I'm going to lie down for an hour or so."

"Xander?" Skylar's backpack *thunked* softly beside Xander's on the couch. "Why don't you eat your mother's cookies?"

Xander tripped, dropping Hiromu, who leapt from his arms, glaring at him as she disappeared into the bedroom. He returned the favor by glaring over his shoulder at Skylar. "I don't want to talk about my mother."

He *wanted*, for the first time ever, to see Silver Stone emerge, but there was no *ting* smile to be found. In fact, Xander hadn't witnessed one in quite a while now. Skylar didn't smile at all, only stood in the middle of Xander's living room, patient and serious.

"I know you don't. But I think it's time you do anyway."

"Why?" Xander tried to make the question come out caustic, but he couldn't, and it only sounded sad. Tired.

"Because every time someone mentions her, you close off. I don't want to open a wound, but not talking about it doesn't seem to help either."

Xander stared at the open door to his bedroom. He thought about how easy it would be to go inside, to get away from this line of inquiry. He wanted to. He really did.

"Please, Xander?"

Shutting his eyes, Xander turned away from the door and sank against the wall. "It's complicated." His voice felt small and hoarse. "And it probably sounds ridiculous."

"I doubt that." Skylar didn't come closer or make any encouragements for Xander to leave the hallway. "Take your time. I don't have anywhere else to be."

"Like I told you, my stepfather makes me miserable. Which is common enough, and I could certainly handle that. But things got complicated when I was applying for colleges. Because my stepfather wanted me to go to a state school in Pennsylvania, and I wanted to go to Benten. I fought so hard. I *begged* my mother. I roped my aunt who lives in Wisconsin to lobby for me, and she gave me some money as well as browbeat my stepfather. In the end I took out a private student loan and got several scholarships, but my stepfather also had to put up some money because it costs *that much* to go here. Which is where all my troubles lie, because he's always threatening to take it away. And my mom doesn't do anything to stop him."

He curled his fingers against the wall. "I might not have come here if I knew everything I know now. The school's been good to me, but it wasn't the magical land of Japanese wonder and manga-tinged friendship I thought it would be. I don't know what I thought would happen, that we'd all get together in the cafeteria and swap manga or what, or that I'd suddenly want to talk to people or something, but I was definitely full of fairy tales when I applied, all of my dreams shit and nonsense, just like my stupid stepfather said."

"Not nonsense," Skylar countered quietly.

"Yes, nonsense, because none of my ridiculous hopes were real, and Benten is *expensive.* I mean, I thought I was going to show up and get a boyfriend, for fuck's sake. Mousy old me who's too grouchy and antisocial to talk to anyone."

"You're not grouchy. And you're not antisocial."

Xander startled. He hadn't heard Skylar move, but there he was, right beside Xander. Patient. Handsome. Earnest.

Too real.

Xander slid down the wall toward his room. "I am. Everyone says so."

"Not me." The hallway was full of shadows, but Skylar somehow brought his own light, his hair catching the thin reflection of sun from the other room, his blue-green eyes bright with tenderness. He followed Xander, not crowding him, but not letting him get away, either. "You're not grouchy. You're reserved. You're not antisocial. You're shy."

Xander's throat felt thick. *Stop.* He couldn't say the word.

He didn't want to.

He'd stopped trying to get away, but Skylar kept coming, moving even more slowly now, as if he were approaching a skittish lamb.

"Tell me why you don't open your mother's cookies, Xander."

Xander shut his eyes, startling when a tear rolled down his cheek.

"Because it hurts to see them," he whispered. "Because I don't want cookies. I just want…" He couldn't finish.

Her. I just want her.

Skylar closed the distance between them and gently, oh-so-carefully took Xander in his arms.

Xander sagged against him, allowed Skylar to envelop him, and let go. For a moment he thought he might sob—the waves of emotion rose up and rolled out of him, but they left him quietly, their only side effect that they made him shake.

Skylar continued to hold him, letting him ride the feelings out. When Xander had calmed, Skylar spoke again. "I have two other observations I'd like to make."

Xander breathed in the scent of Skylar, watching his own fingers as they traced along Skylar's collarbone. "Yes?"

Skylar stroked Xander's hair. "One, you *did* find your manga-heads at Benten, and you *did* exchange volumes with them over the dinner table. You did just that with Unc last night. And as for the other..." His hand moved to Xander's chin, which he held lightly as he tilted Xander's head far enough back to smile at him. "You *did* find a boyfriend. One who loves you very much."

Okay, *now* Xander was going to cry. "*Skylar.*"

Skylar stroked his cheek, his eyes sparkling with life and love. "I'd like to kiss you, Xander. If that's okay." He brushed his thumb over Xander's lips and added, with a wry smile. "With my mouth, I mean."

Staring up at him, Xander nodded, trying to remember to breathe.

He shut his eyes as soon as Skylar started to move—his heart beat faster and faster, and when Skylar's lips brushed his, he thought his heart had actually exploded. He gasped, tightening his hand against Skylar's chest.

Skylar responded by holding him more tenderly to his body and anchoring him to the wall so he could cradle Xander's face in his hands, tilt his head to the side, and kiss him again.

Now Xander did cry, big stupid tears that kept falling, and he kept trying to get away because he felt like an idiot, but Skylar wouldn't let him escape here anymore than he had at any other point since he'd run into him on the porch. They weren't deep kisses, nothing more than whispers against his lips, but they penetrated Xander more powerfully than the most Xrated lip locks he'd imagined when…

Well, when he'd dreamed of going to college and getting a boyfriend.

"Skylar," he whispered, still crying. He couldn't stop saying his name for some reason. He cradled his boyfriend's face in a mirror of the way his own face was being held and said Skylar's name over and over between the sweet, breathless kisses and his tears. "Skylar. *Skylar.*"

"Xander," Skylar whispered back.

And as Skylar pressed their foreheads together, twining their hands with one another in kisses that were much less intense but no less pleasurable, Xander felt the last of his sorrow and loneliness fade away.

THE END OF July and beginning of August before Xander's senior year of college were, when he looked back on the time years later, some of the warmest, most perfect memories of his life.

It wasn't only his slowly blooming relationship with Skylar. It was that Skylar was right, Xander *wasn't* antisocial, not anymore. He came home to find the house full of people and got excited about it, not annoyed. Zelda and Cory and Jacob weren't the only residents drifting downstairs to be with the others. On the rare occasions Skylar wasn't around, Xander hauled himself to the main kitchen or over to the offices, even if he had no reason to be there.

When Pamela commented on the change, he didn't

grumble or make an excuse. He only blushed and smiled.

Unc came over to the Palace of the Sun a lot as well. He said it was to help Cory with *Lucky 7* setup, but honestly that had been finished weeks ago, and until an official edition was ready, there wasn't much to do. So the two of them often drank wine in the kitchen while Unc made dinner. Unc was *always* showing up with a bag of groceries, and he'd put on an apron, turn on music, and start cooking. Xander knew this because someone would come fetch him. "Unc's cooking, you need to come down." Usually Skylar was with him, so they'd bring the storyboard they were plotting and work in the dining room until it was time to eat, and then all eight of them would sit around the kitchen table and laugh, eating Unc's food and drinking the wine from Pamela's cellar.

"Are you sure it's okay we're drinking all this?" Sara asked.

Pamela waved this away. "Takahiro would want us to. He was always bringing out bottles for company. He'd hate how I never had people over anymore. This? This he would love. I hope he's watching now and enjoying every moment."

They often drank to the point that they got ridiculous. One hot night Xander climbed onto the table and, wearing nothing but a pair of paint-stained cut-off sweatpants, swung an empty bottle around and christened each person in the room with a their *Shichifukujin* alter egos.

“You keep telling me I’m Fudō Myōō. That’s fine. I’m going to remove your obst-ch—obstacles now. You’re all gods.” He swung his arms expansively. “You’re the seven gods of fortune. *Tada.*” He pointed at Unc. “You’re Hotei. You laugh a lot, and you bring wealth and fortune wherever you go.”

Unc grinned and rubbed his belly, “I’m getting the Buddha belly to go with the name too, with all this wine and cooking. But I can’t say I mind. I love hanging out with you guys. This is the best summer I’ve ever had.”

Xander aimed his wine bottle at Pamela. “You’re Kichijōten. You’re wise, happy, and you helped bring us all back to life. The only thing missing was that you were always hungry, until the other gods moved in. Your soul was hungry. But now you’re fine. In fact now you only seem to nibble at food unless Unc is cooking. Because you’re satisfied now.”

Pamela looked misty. “I am satisfied. I love having you all here.”

Xander kept going, turning to Jacob now. “You’re Daikokuten. The god of wealth and food.”

Jacob glared at him. “I’m not wealthy. At all.”

Xander shook his finger. “Hear me out. You *are* food, though, with your family’s deli, or whatever, and the food service jobs you have, and the way you moved in here and immediately planted a garden. But now that you have Unc and Skylar, you’ve been using their financial advice and passing it on to your family. And it’s been helping, right?”

“Yes, but—”

"Plus you have a wealth of spirit. You're the one who keeps us going when we want to quit, when things seem hopeless. You're our king."

Jacob blushed, but he appeared moved.

"It's true," Zelda said from beside Jacob. "What he said. Every word."

Everyone agreed, and Jacob's chest rose, full of pride. A king indeed.

Xander kept going. "Zelda—you're Bishamonten. God of war and order."

They grinned and lifted their glass in toast. "Damn straight. Sky told me this one already. Except I hate the order part."

"You shouldn't. You can tear down the systems, but you have to put something in their place."

Zelda didn't say anything, but they looked thoughtful.

"And what about me?" This was Sara. She sat in the overstuffed chair, dragged into the kitchen so she could sit in it especially, because it was a bad pain day for her.

"You're Ebisu," Xander replied.

Sara lifted her eyebrows. "The…fish god?"

"The laughing god. The god of prosperity and wealth in business. He was born without bones, but he overcame his obstacles and loved his life anyway. He's the only god of fortune whose origins are purely Japanese too."

"Born without bones, huh?" Sara ran her hand down her brace. "Laughing god. Do I really laugh that much?"

"You do now," Unc pointed out.

Xander noticed that Unc's gaze lingered on Sara a lot, actually.

"That only leaves Sky and me," Cory said.

"Cory, you're Jurōjin. You're wise, you love your wine, and, well." Xander gestured vaguely at him. "You have a long head."

Everyone laughed. Cory did too, and he touched his hair. "I do?"

"Yes, but you wear it well." Xander and Skylar's gazes met, held. "As for Skylar, He's Benzaiten."

Everyone oohed and ahhed, agreeing that yes, that was perfect for Skylar. None of them knew how perfect, or knew that upstairs was Xander's painting, his finest as far as he was concerned, showing just how Benzaiten Skylar truly was.

They relished their new monikers, so much so that even beyond that drunken night they often took to calling each other by their god names in the privacy of the Palace of the Sun. Unc showed up one day with tiny keychains for everyone, clear acrylic rectangles with the seven gods inside, and he also got a blue Funko Fudō Myōō figure for Xander and seven tiny *Shichifukujin* to sit beside him on the main workstation in the *Lucky 7* office.

Xander couldn't help but notice that every time Skylar worked there Benzaiten ended up sitting next to Fudō.

They learned their blood type too, because Pamela insisted.

"If we're going to be Japanese gods, you need to know your blood type. It's very Japanese."

"To know your blood type and use it for personality typing, really?" Sara seemed dubious. Everyone did, except Unc.

"It really is a thing," Pamela insisted. "Some Asian employers try to use it, even though it's frowned upon, because certain blood types are favored over others, and it's not as if you can change your blood type. But *everyone* knows their blood type. They think it's strange that we don't."

Pamela got them all to a blood drive, and when they were back at the Palace with their ID cards and blood types listed in front of them, she looked at their little plastic cards and read their fortunes.

"No shock, Jacob's type O and totally competitive. But also a good leader. Zelda, you're also type O."

The two of them looked at each other startled—their expressions saying clearly they weren't happy about having to *share* a type, since that meant they weren't the best.

Cory, who was reading the printout Pamela had given him, grinned. "This says you would be good therapists."

Zelda snorted. "No thanks. But what are you?"

Cory smiled wryly. "Type A. I put others first, but I'm a good listener and make an excellent friend." He sighed. "Though I tend to bottle things up, which, *yes*."

Sara raised her hand. "Me too. That's my blood type, and also…yes, that's my personality. Isn't this *weird*, how it fits?"

"What's mine?" Unc asked. "My blood type was B."

"Oh, that's my type too," Pamela said.

"Extroverts," Cory read. "Great listeners, but at their own expense. Highly tuned to body language and read others intuitively. No problem expressing their emotions."

Pamela and Unc looked at each other, and everyone laughed.

"What type are you, Xander?" Sara asked.

He was lying on the couch, half in Skylar's lap. "A. Which you probably guessed." He tipped his head back to look up at Skylar. "I can't guess you, though. Pamela can't either. It's been driving us both nuts."

Skylar's smile was enigmatic over his mug of tea. "That's because, once again, I'm a unicorn."

Cory clapped his hands and pointed at him with one finger. "I got it—you're AB, aren't you?"

Skylar nodded. "Rarest blood type. Leave it to me, I suppose."

"Rarest and most *spiritual*, man." Cory kept reading. "You're rational and levelheaded, good at planning and organizing. Good at public relations. But good at education too. In case you decide not to be a lawyer."

This time Skylar's smile was…almost sad. And he changed the subject quickly, Xander couldn't help but notice.

They didn't talk about law school, or even the fall, outside of plans for the manga. They worked on the magazine, yes, but above all that summer the eight of them made amazing memories and deepened their friendships. It was as if they had stepped into a perfect, crystalline bubble of time and space where nothing bad could happen and everything wonderful would.

Eventually, though, August wore on, and signs of the school year starting began to appear once again. Skylar and Unc still came to the Palace, but they were drawn into fraternity business all too often as well. When Skylar would come over to see Xander, he seemed tense at first, until he shook off the mantle of whatever stress he'd worn over, but he had a cloak about him of constant worry, as if he feared something was coming.

Xander wanted to ask him if he was all right, if there was anything he could do to help. Except he knew the answer. No, Skylar wasn't all right.

And despite that he was supposed to be the remover of obstacles, Xander knew there wasn't a damn thing he could do for him. Not yet.

Chapter Eighteen

SKYLAR SHOULD HAVE loved the return of his fraternity brothers. Normally the bustle of filling the house was one of his favorite aspects of the school year—rekindling old friendships, preparing to start new ones. But this time, he didn't relish the chaos.

Some of it was that despite Unc's shepherding of the governing board, the tone of Delta Sig had taken a decidedly different turn. The newly elected officers were more interested in hosting parties than polishing the fraternity's image, and the new risk management officer didn't seem to care that they still had work to do in that department. Unc kept arguing for more responsibility, pointing out the national chapter was watching and that if they weren't careful they'd end up disbanded, but the rest of the officers only called him a worrywart and went back to plotting the most raucous rush week parties ever.

Unc was beside himself. He came to Skylar's room after a particularly contentious meeting, red-faced and fit to be tied. "I don't know where these fucks get off, but they're going to run us into the ground. Because if that brand-new shrine gets screwed over after the alumni did all that work to restore it, there's going to be hell to pay." He paced back and forth across Skylar's area rug a few times, then slammed his fist against the closet door. "*Goddamn* but this isn't who we are."

Skylar thought back to the spring, to how he'd run around begging for help with the mural issue. To the fall, when he'd been roped into being the risk management officer. To the year before, when he'd become president as a sophomore and everyone had been so impressed. *Was it impressive? Or have they been desperate all along?*

He shifted his gaze to Xander's painting, studying the ghostly man standing in the sea of paint.

I don't want to be desperate anymore.

Except he lived in desperation now, because every day the date of his LSAT test drew closer.

He'd begun to do more than simply snow his tutor now, his every waking hour crammed with studying he should have done all summer long, but of course it was far too little far too late, and even this marginal effort was poor at best. Skylar struggled to focus, and he couldn't find a place where his brain would willingly digest the material. At the fraternity he felt restless. At the library he felt anxious. In the living room of the Palace of the Sun he wandered around aimlessly, then inevitably went up the stairs to visit Hokusai and Hiromu while he waited for Xander to come home from working at the studio.

If Xander was in the room with him, he could work at least for a while. If Xander gave him the occasional touch or encouraging murmur, he could work longer. But it wasn't going to be enough.

"I should have been studying all summer." He confessed this one hot late-August night, a week before classes started. "I took a practice test the other day, and I'm not even close to the score I need."

His head was in Xander's lap, and Xander stroked his hair, gentling him. "There are parts you can't know how they'd score you, right? Essays and things?"

"Yes, but there are parts I know how I'll do now, and it's not good. I have to take the test the third week in September. I won't be ready."

"You can't put it off for later?"

Not without earning himself another lecture from his father and quite probably some kind of dictate he not see Xander again, this time with teeth. "No, I can't."

Xander's touch on his hair stilled, then resumed. "Do…you still want to go to Yale?"

Skylar shut his eyes. "Of course I do," he lied.

"Mmm," was all Xander said.

Skylar was sure Xander knew he hadn't told the truth. This knowledge made him feel heavy and weary. He turned so he lay on his back, opened his eyes, and looked up at Xander. "They're having another rush party tonight. Would it be all right if I stayed here?"

"You're always welcome to stay with me." Xander ghosted fingers along Skylar's jaw. "You need to put in an appearance first, I assume?"

He did, technically. But he didn't want to. "For a few minutes. The last one was completely jarring. They had a stripper. In our living room. And a wooden dowel and a bottle of lube, and I left before I could find out what they were for. They're bragging this party is supposed to be *better*, and frankly I'm terrified."

More strokes along his beard. "Do you want me to come with you?"

Skylar was so taken aback he sat up so he could gape at Xander properly. "Who are you, and what have you done with my boyfriend? Isn't a fraternity party your worst nightmare?"

Xander's jaw was set, and he had a determined look in his eye. "No, you being made uncomfortable about sexual situations around people you're not out to, is."

Skylar's whole face flushed, and for several seconds he didn't know how to respond. Eventually he managed to stammer a half-hearted, flustered, "You…you don't have to do that."

Xander took his hand, kissed the fingers, the seat of his palm. "I want to do that."

Skylar was melting from the inside out. Especially as Xander kept kissing his hand, slowly, as if he had all night to do so. "But how will you manage with so many people?"

"I'll use the social skills this amazing public relations person taught me."

Skylar had goose bumps from all the kissing. His voice broke when he tried to object. "I never taught you anything. All you did was paint me. And make love to me. I was a terrible teacher. I only gave you some social media pages that don't match your personality."

Xander paused his erotic assault enough to smile wickedly at him. "I watched you work the campus president. And Jacob. And me, when you wanted something. I took notes."

"And you think that will be enough?" Skylar shivered and shut his eyes, jerking as Xander's lips traveled above his wrist. "That's a little too much stimulation for me tonight, please."

Immediately Xander withdrew, smoothing the places his lips had touched with his thumb. When he spoke, he didn't sound troubled at all for being asked to stop. "Did I read you wrong, though? You seemed like you could use some sensory time. Do you want me to get the fan brush?"

This was too much. Skylar gripped Xander's wrist and squeezed. "You're seriously offering to go with me to the rush party? But first you'll get me off via paintbrush, to calm me down?"

Xander pressed his forehead to Skylar's and stroked his beard with both hands. Skylar stared at Xander's chin, at the stubble on the divot in the center.

"Am I going as your boyfriend or your friend?" He trailed a hand down Skylar's nape. "I'm okay with either way. I promise."

Skylar played with the hem of Xander's collar. "There's discomfort either way. So I should choose the truth, where at least I'm myself, yes?"

"Only you can decide that. It's in your own time."

"They'll assume I'm gay. I still don't know how to sort that one in my head, if I am or not."

"I don't know that it's important. Mostly I care that you want to be with me." Xander massaged the back of Skylar's head gently. "Perhaps we play it by ear?"

Skylar was hit with a fearful sense of loss as he thought of what his life would be like when Xander inevitably moved on to somewhere else and Skylar went to Yale. He felt cold, nauseated, and strange.

And sad. So sad.

Xander drew Skylar to him, tucking him into his body, wrapping himself around him. "I'm coming with you. Or you're not going."

Skylar buried his face in Xander's neck and focused on his breathing. "What's wrong with me?"

"Nothing is wrong with you."

"There's so much wrong with me." Skylar clung to him. "I don't feel like I fit anywhere anymore. I don't know what I'm supposed to do. How I'm supposed to be."

"You fit with me." Xander tucked him in tighter, as if to prove his statement. "You'll always fit with me."

And what about when you're not here? When I'm not with you anymore?

But he couldn't bring himself to ask that.

He kept thinking he would find a way to excuse Xander gracefully from the rush party, to prove it would be a quick in and out and he'd be fine on his own. Xander, however, ignored him. And he teamed up with Unc.

It was basically *Hotay & Moo*, the live-action version.

Unc was staying for the entire party, but not because he thought it would be a great time. He planned on filming and sending documentation of any infractions back to the national organization, hoping to head off a disaster that would end in the fraternity being disbanded. He was all for Xander playing Skylar's escort, though. To the point that when Skylar approached him privately to try to end-run the arrangement, it backfired. Unc doubled down.

"Not a chance. He's right. You need him there."

They were in the *Lucky 7* office, just the two of them, but Skylar glanced around nervously, fearing Xander might walk in on them at any moment. "It's only a rush party, for heaven's sake. I've been to a million of them. I'll dip in and out, make an appearance as a senior member, then leave. He's overreacting."

Unc shut his laptop and turned to Skylar. His normally sparkling eyes were sober, his expression serious. "Okay. We haven't talked about this yet. I don't know that you want to, and that's okay, but I feel like we have to, a little."

Warning bells went off in Skylar's head. "Talk about what?"

"You told me, before you showed up at the frat glowing and holding Xander Fairchild's hand, you weren't gay or bi. I decided you weren't ready to tell me and didn't think much of it. But then Zelda got up in my face about asexual rights and sexual-normative assumptions. I'm still not sure that's the right word, but I know what they mean. And they got me thinking about a lot of things."

Goddamn Zelda. Skylar held up his hands. "You're right, I don't want to talk about this."

"Hear me out a little longer, okay?" Unc rested his elbows on his knees. "They talked about how for some people sexuality is gray. Like it's almost not there. Or only there sometimes, or under certain conditions. Or how they can only develop a sexual relationship once they have a close emotional relationship."

Skylar wanted to end this conversation so much. "Why are we discussing this?" God help him if *Unc* brought up starfish…

"Because the more they talked, the more I looked back and felt like I understood you. Except if I brought it up, I knew you'd make that face you're making now, like you want to get up and leave but I haven't been rude enough yet for you to justify it."

"Why are you bringing this up?" Why *wasn't* Skylar leaving, that's what he wanted to know?

Probably because Unc looked so earnest. "Because I'm trying to tell you I support you. To apologize for all the years you had to stand by and watch the brothers be gross jerks and I didn't know it upset you."

Skylar opened his mouth to say being asexual didn't make him necessarily hate watching other people be sexual, that this wasn't how it worked—then he shut it, because while that was true, he *did* hate how the brothers always attempted to lure him into joining them. To the point that when he saw a stripper show up at a rush party, whether or not he was hosting, he got nervous, because he knew eventually someone would try to get prim Skylar Stone to let a half-naked woman sit on his lap.

Unc was clearly remembering this too. "All I can think of is last year with that woman who mashed her tits in your face. Everyone thought you were being a gentleman and a good sport. Except you weren't, were you? You were fantastically uncomfortable."

Skylar thought about lying, then gave in. "I took a shower for an hour afterward."

"And you were sick the next morning, you said." Unc looked pained. "Does it…repulse you? I'm sorry, you don't have to answer. I'm trying to understand. I only want to know, so I can help you. If you want help. In situations like the rush party."

Skylar picked at imaginary lint on his shorts. "With…Xander, and Xander only, certain things that are somewhat sexual in nature are acceptable, some of the time. But they're pretty mild by everyone else's standards." He smoothed his thumb against the fabric. "It's not exactly about sex for me, either. It's hard to explain. And…I don't really want to."

"Sure. Sure, it's cool."

Skylar said that…then kept talking anyway. "I'm not repulsed by sex, but I get tired of having it pushed at me. It would be like, for you, everyone assuming you were gay and always shoving cock in your face. You don't have anything against gay men, but it's not what you want every time you go out to a club, I assume. Maybe once would be tolerable, or a thrilling diversion, but after a while it gets to you. Especially if you feel like you can't tell anyone it's not what you want. That you'll be considered sick or a freak for it."

"I don't think that about you, for the record."

"I know."

"It's just, you look so tense. I thought I should reassure you or something."

Skylar looked down at his hands clenched in his lap. He unfurled his fingers, though it took more effort than he would have thought. "I'm not…used to talking about this. And now it seems like I talk about it all the time."

"Is that bad?"

"No. It's different." He glanced up at Unc. "I can't tell the brothers. Or rather, I don't want to."

Unc nodded. "Are you going to be open about your relationship with Xander?"

Everything kept circling back to this. "Let them think what they will about what it means about me, about my orientation. If they ask you, you can be vague." He rubbed his beard. It was comforting, because it made him think of Xander. "The frat, people on campus—they're not who I worry about."

"It's your dad."

Skylar tucked his thumbs inside his fists, stared at his knuckles. "My dad thinks he's a bad influence, because of the fundraiser. I shouldn't have let him talk to Patricia. But probably it wouldn't have mattered." He wiped his mouth, feeling his stomach churn. "I can just hear my father telling me Xander doesn't fit the image of a corporate spouse."

The air was heavy between them. “You’re thinking of things like spouses, are you?”

Skylar blushed. “I meant it as an example.”

“I don’t think you did, actually. But that’s okay. For the record, I think he’s willing to consider things that seriously too.”

“Yes, but it wouldn’t work, would it? Because I’m going to be some stuffed suit in a horrible law office and—”

“But *why*, Sky? Why are you doing it, when you so clearly don’t want to?”

Skylar stood abruptly. His heart beat too quickly, and he felt as if he were caged. He paced the edges of the room. “Did I say I didn’t want to?”

“You called it a horrible law office. I’d say that’s a sign that—”

“I’m frustrated, is all. Besides, life isn’t always about doing what we want.”

Unc rose, followed him. “Okay, you’re right—but it’s also not about suffering through things for no fucking reason. *Why* do you need to do this even though you don’t want to?”

“Because it’s a good firm, and we represent good people—”

“For fuck’s sake. It’s not a charity case. It’s a business. Your dad’s firm represents saints and sinners alike, whoever has the cash in their hand. And don’t counter with your parents’ charities. Those are mostly excuses to hang out and have parties. I’ve been part of those things for years. I know the drill.”

Why was Unc's argument making Skylar so angry? "I owe my parents. They've given me this education. This privileged life."

"Key word there, they *gave* it to you. It wasn't a contract negotiation." He snorted. "Though, with your parents, it probably was. My point is, you can do other things. You don't have to go to law school. Or you can go to law school but not *Yale* Law School. If you're determined to sacrifice yourself to a greater good, there are other ways you can get there. Plenty of them."

Skylar's head was starting to hurt. "How did we get from me telling you I could handle going to the rush party on my own to career counseling?"

Unc laughed. "I dunno. Sorry about that."

To Skylar's surprise, he found *he* wasn't sorry. He was still worried about Xander coming to the party, which Xander noticed and got annoyed over, which meant in the end when he came to pick him up he collected a very grumpy boyfriend who glowered at him while also appearing quite handsome in, of all things, a crisp, bright-blue polo and brick-red cargo shorts.

"I didn't know you even owned such things," he said, admiring the view.

"I do know how to dress up, thank you." Xander glanced self-consciously at himself, then at Skylar. "Do I look okay?"

"You look wonderful. Also comfortable, like yourself." Skylar even appreciated the scowl. It added a certain something.

At the party, Skylar worried about how they would

be received as they worked their way through the crush of guests—the crowd was 90 percent male, as this was meant to be a chance for the fraternity to interview potential pledges. If Xander was nervous, however, he didn't show it. He stuck close to Skylar, scowl firmly in place, scanning everyone who encountered them, like a bodyguard.

He hadn't shaved and had a bit of scruff around his jaw. He was handsome in his awkward, perfect Xander way. Skylar forgot to be nervous for him and simply enjoyed him, especially when the crush got thick and Xander captured his hand…and didn't let go.

"Yo, Stone!" A sophomore pledge wearing a hat with plastic breasts holding two cans of beer and elongated nipples as straws staggered toward him. He saw Skylar and Xander's joined hands and paused. "What the hell? This a new pledge? You hazing him or something?"

Xander's eyes went cold and steely. He laced his fingers through Skylar's. "I'm his boyfriend."

The pledge blinked. Repeatedly. Then laughed. "You guys. You're hilarious."

Xander grumbled and tugged Skylar away from the drunk, taking him onto the main floor.

There were more people here, some Skylar knew, most he didn't. Normally this wouldn't faze him. He'd weave amidst them, smiling, shaking hands, making connections. It was what he did. It was who he was. Except tonight, he couldn't do it. It wasn't because of Xander, either.

What was happening to him? Why was he looking at a roomful of people and feeling nothing but unease? Why did he cling to Xander's hand as if he couldn't handle it if Xander let go?

"*Stone.*"

A hand clapped him on the shoulder. He startled, then tried to cover his reaction, especially when it put Xander on ultra-glower. The president of the fraternity had come up to him. Raiden already had his shirt off and the red cord signifying his position as president of the fraternity tied around his head. His dark eyes glinted with trouble. "Ready to party, brother? Oh, and who do we have here? Are you pledging? You need a lanyard. I'll get you one."

"This is Xander," Skylar said before Xander could bite Raiden's head off. "He's here as my guest, not a pledge."

He wondered if he should have followed Xander's lead and been more declarative about their relationship, but it turned out there wasn't a need. Raiden's gaze fell on their joined hands, and he raised his eyebrows, then elbowed Skylar with an accompanying heavy wink. "Got it. Your *guest.* But look at you, you sly dog. You never brought one of your dates here before."

Xander leaned around Skylar and fixed Raiden with a truly god-awful smile. "Excuse us."

Raiden laughed as they walked away. "Stone, I think your date needs to get laid and lighten up."

"I'm sorry," Skylar whispered.

"Don't worry about it. Just tell me what else you

have to do here before we can leave."

Skylar wasn't sure. Normally these parties were a little raucous but had some form—there was a point at which the officers would stop and make announcements, old officers would be introduced, the house would be toured, and so on. Would that happen? He could see Unc across the room making his video, the riotous dancing, half-naked and in some cases underwear-clad young men swaying from too much beer. And the party had barely begun.

Jay, the vice president, got on top of the study table and clapped his hands. "All *right*. Pledges with blue lanyards, on your knees in the middle of the room."

The music still pounded, but the room erupted in cheers and chants as ten grinning young men waved at the crowd before taking their position in the center of the mob. Jay walked over to them, holding a portable mic in his hand. A spotlight had appeared from somewhere.

Skylar glanced at Unc. Unc was frowning, filming furiously.

Jay gestured to a corner of the room, where the other fraternity officers stepped aside to reveal a woman, draped in a shawl, though she let one shoulder peek through to hint she was not clothed beneath. She was voluptuous, heavily made-up, and from all indications appeared to be a sex worker.

"This wonderful young lady," Jay went on, "is here as our guest. She would like to entertain a few of our pledges for a half hour. But since we have more than two pledges here…" Jay grinned. "We'll have a contest. Gentlemen?"

Ten fraternity members, all of them the ones Skylar considered the less-desirable members, took their position in front of the kneeling pledges.

They began to undo their pants.

Skylar froze. His stomach lurched, knotted, turned over.

"The first two pledges to get their potential brothers off get half an hour in heaven with our lady guest." Jay tossed a wink over his shoulder at Skylar. "I should have offered you a shot in the game. Come on over and switch with someone."

The whole room turned to look at Skylar.

Everyone was staring at him.

Everyone waited for him to speak.

For the first time in his life, Skylar didn't know what to say. What to do.

"We're good, thanks." With that, Xander tugged Skylar's arm and began to plow his way through the crush toward the door.

"Come *on*." Raiden's voice echoed like thunder in Skylar's head. "What's wrong with you two? We're just having a little fun. You don't like fun?"

"Can't stand it. *Move.*" Xander was all but snarling now, and the party guests began to part like the Red Sea for him as he stormed forward.

Skylar didn't know what was happening, only knew he wanted to get out of there, to breathe air that didn't smell like sweat and beer, to be able to drop the mask he was so carefully holding on to his face and shudder in revulsion over the image of those young men who had been lured into Jay's game. What if that had been him? What if he had been trying to pledge? What if he would have had to choose between backing away and being mocked or taking it, literally—and what if he would have accidentally won? He wanted to throw up just thinking about it.

He wanted to cry.

Xander's grip shifted slightly, his fingers stroking his palm, a soothing gesture.

Just before they got to the door, Raiden swooped in, blocking their exit. "Guys, there's no need for dramatics. Stay. Enjoy the party. Skylar, you don't want our guests to think you're against the leadership of the fraternity, do you?"

The ice of that statement had barely penetrated before Unc appeared, his smile like a knife. "*Speaking of leadership.* You got your phone on you, Ray? It ought to be buzzing something fierce. I just sent a video of Jay's speech to the national president. He really wants to talk to you right now."

Raiden paled and fumbled for his pocket.

Unc nudged Skylar. "Go on. I've got this." He glanced at Xander. "You got him?"

"And I'm not letting go."

Unc held out his fist. Xander met the bump. Then he led Skylar around the council president and into the night.

XANDER GOT SKYLAR away from the fraternity house as quickly as he could. They'd come in Skylar's car, but it was in the back of the house, blocked in now by a million other cars. Plus, he didn't want to go one step closer to that place ever again.

He was never going to get the sight of those guys on their knees out of his mind. Especially the one on the end who'd kept glancing at Xander and Skylar's joined hands. Who had gone white with terror at Jay's announcement. Xander was counting on Unc not to let that nightmare of a "game" continue. His priorities were elsewhere.

Skylar held on to his hand as if it were the only thing keeping him from falling into the pit of hell. He didn't say anything as Xander led him out of fraternity row, but as they passed the auditorium, at the painted-over wall where his mural used to be, Skylar's legs buckled and they had to sit down while he rested his head on his knees.

"I don't understand. I knew the new leadership was weak, but...*why*? And why was everyone going along with it? That's not who we are, it's not..."

Xander spared a cold glance for the house on the hill, which was lit up and buzzing with sound even from this distance. "What normally happens at these parties?"

"*Some* drinking, possibly a little inappropriate sexualization of something or other, but never...never were potential pledges asked to..." He shuddered.

Xander switched which hand joined Skylar's, taking care never to leave him without contact, and rubbed his back in soothing circles. "Will they get in trouble?"

"I don't know. Probably a scolding from the national board. A reprimand not to do it again."

"Jesus, that's *it*?"

Skylar sagged against him. His grip on Xander's hand was so tight it almost hurt. "That's how it goes."

"If they so much as cause you to have a bad afternoon, I'm painting a caricature of them with tiny penises on the front door of that fucking frat. In the paint that's really hard to cover up." He slid his arm around Skylar, drawing him close as he kissed the hair above his ear. "Let's keep walking, okay?"

As they stood, Skylar glanced behind them sadly at the blank wall. "I did love that mural. I miss it every day."

"I don't. I thank the gods for sending the assholes who ruined it." When Skylar looked at him, startled, Xander winked and kissed his nose. "Because that's how I met you."

Skylar stared at Xander for several seconds, then reached up and stroked his cheek. "Sometimes I think about kissing you again," he said at last.

Xander's heart skipped a beat, lurched sideways. They hadn't kissed on the mouth again, not since that day. His gaze slid involuntarily to Skylar's lips. "You do?"

"I do." Skylar's thumb brushed the corner of Xander's mouth, catching the seam. "Sometimes I think about doing more than just brushing my lips over yours. It makes me a little nervous, but…excited too. I never thought I'd think about something like that. The problem is, I don't know if I'm ready to do more than simply think about it."

"I'm fine with either timeline." Xander laced their joined hands more firmly together, swayed them side to side. "I loved the kiss you gave me. I'd love trying another type of kiss too. But either way is fine."

A car went past, honking loudly, someone leaning out the window and yelling at them. Xander couldn't quite catch it, but he assumed it was a homophobic slur. It annoyed him, but it jarred Skylar. They moved off the main road as quickly as they could and into campus proper, where it was largely quiet, with only the Greek students and hopefuls returned. Mostly rush party attendees were milling about, laughing drunkenly, but as they went deeper into campus, fewer people were around.

"I wish we could go onto the roof of one of the buildings." Skylar pointed to the top of the science building, which happened to be nearest to them. "They always go up there in anime. I wonder if they go on the roof that much in Japan in real life? I hope so. It would be so disappointing if they don't."

"Well, I know the after-dark code to get into Art Building West. But I can't promise about roof access. I'm game to try if you are, though."

It took them half an hour, but they found a door that led to the roof. It was, however, not what they were hoping for. The roof's surface was full of asphalt pebbles, impossible to so much as stand on. They stood in the doorway nonetheless, looking out across campus.

"It's a pretty view," Xander remarked.

Skylar nodded his agreement. He kicked at the pebbles. "This is for insulation, I suppose."

"They should let us draw up here, though. Or eat lunch. Or something." He held on to the door and stepped onto the uneven surface, taking in the expansive wasteland. "I mean, it's a huge area, we could totally—" He stopped, squinting in the darkness. "Hey, there's something in that far corner."

Skylar climbed onto the rocks to stand unsteadily beside him and peer as well. "I see it. It's like...a chicken coop?"

"Nobody would keep chickens on this roof. Look, it's on the old part of the roof. I think they used to actually let people up here. Remember, this building is over eighty years old. It's been remodeled at least three times."

"Let's go over and see what it is."

They held on to each other and fumbled across the rooftop, laughing when they almost fell, though Xander doubted they'd find it funny if they landed on this gritty, sticky stuff. When they got close to the small shed, however, they sobered, because they both realized immediately what it was.

It wasn't a shed at all. It was a shrine.

Dusty, decaying, and unattended, it had been clearly ignored for decades or better, and yet it felt more poignant and real than the one in the bowels of the fraternity. Xander was sure he was being fanciful, but he thought he could feel Benzaiten here, at least a little.

Skylar reached into his pocket and placed something on the small, dusty altar. It was a nickel. He clapped his hands twice, held them in front of his face. He gave a nickel to Xander too.

Xander placed the nickel down slowly, trying to think of what he wanted to pray for.

Beside him, Skylar began to tremble.

Xander glanced at him. "Skylar?"

Skylar shut his eyes, shaking his head as he closed himself off. "I'm fine. It's just...been a long day."

As lies went, it was pretty bald, but Xander didn't press him. He did, however, know exactly what he wanted to pray for.

Please help me help him. He clapped his hands twice to get the god's attention and sent the prayer on its way.

Skylar ran a hand down Xander's back, and rested his head on Xander's shoulder. "Let's go home. Please?"

It took Xander a second to realize Skylar meant his apartment—that Skylar considered Xander's place his home. His heart constricted, then swelled. "Yeah. Let's do that."

Chapter Nineteen

As school officially started and campus life rolled into normal gear, it both amused and annoyed Skylar how few people believed Xander truly was his boyfriend.

People who knew Xander believed them—or rather, the people who got to know Xander through Skylar believed them. Skylar was still helping the art department out, though the way his fraternity was behaving he wasn't sure he should be doing *them* any PR favors. The art students, however, he didn't mind assisting at all, and they *loved* having him around. At first to those who hadn't met him over the summer, he was "that business major who helps with our social media stuff," but as soon as they saw him holding hands with Xander, teasing him, coaxing him into getting to know his fellow department majors—and succeeding in socializing him somewhat—he was Skylar, Xander's boyfriend. Especially when Xander started making him cute little bento lunches every day. The girls always sighed over the adorable shapes Skylar's boyfriend cut his vegetables into.

Skylar's boyfriend. He decided he liked that phrase a

lot.

But outside the art department, he was still Skylar Stone, Greek member and catch of the day, and no one believed he was dating, as one of the rather bitchy sisters from Tau Alpha Kappa put it, "a mousy art student who stinks like paint thinner." Those who'd been his former dates assumed it was a massive scam of some kind, that Xander had the mother lode of all political intel and that Skylar was simply milking him for as much as he could get.

"I swear to God, I'm going to make out with him in the middle of the student union stage," he grumbled to Zelda one day when they were having lunch together at a noodle bar off campus. Except even as he said that, he shuddered.

"It wouldn't be worth it. They'd think it was a stunt, for one, and it would upset Xander, because he'd know it was an act. Stop caring what they think. Stop caring about them, period." Zelda poked their chopsticks at Skylar. "Eat your food. You've hardly touched your ramen. Unc says you're barely eating at the frat too."

Skylar, who wasn't as adept with his chopsticks as Zelda, clumsily tugged at his udon but didn't put any in his mouth. "I don't have much of an appetite."

"When is the test again?"

His stomach lurched at the reminder. "Two weeks."

"Can we help you study?"

It was too late. He was cramming what he could, but he had his regular homework now too. And it was as if his brain refused to ingest any information about law.

He let the chopsticks clatter to the counter. "Everything is falling apart. I'm behind on my storyboards for *Lucky 7.* I haven't helped Xander with his social media as much as I should. I haven't *seen* Xander—"

Zelda's hand between his shoulder blades startled him. It was a brief touch, though, and more of a simple pressure than anything.

"Sorry." They put their hand back in their lap, but they regarded him with quiet concern. "Your shoulders were at your ears, and you were breathing funny. Xander said that helps you calm down, giving you pressure there."

Skylar sat up slowly, blinking as he digested this information. Both that they were right, that pressure did calm him and… "Are…are you guys *managing* me?"

Zelda folded their hands over their chest and gave Skylar a *you wanna throw down?* look. "Yes. Everyone is worried about you."

"I'm not going to do well on the test. At this point it's not even a question of whether or not I'll do well enough to get into Yale. I don't think I'll do well, period." Skylar pushed his bowl away and leaned into his hands. "They have my whole life planned out for me—I don't even know what they'll do if I don't show up for it. I honestly don't. Will they be furious? Will they ask me what's wrong and—?" He cut himself off and laughed bitterly. "Do you know, I used to beg for my father's attention? I used to whore myself out to Tau Alpha Kappa to get him to notice me. Now—"

He cut himself off, panicked, as he realized he'd almost spilled the beans about charming his tutor to Zelda.

Then he shivered, acknowledging how much he ached to do just that, to come clean. To end all of this. *If only it were that simple.*

Zelda put a hand on his arm and gently pried his hand away from his face. "You need to forget about the test. Tell your parents whatever you need to, but—"

"*I have to take the LSAT.*"

"*Why,* though, Skylar? Because you want to be a lawyer so badly?"

Because they'll stop me from seeing Xander. He almost told them, then, because he wanted to hear Zelda get angry and defiant, to hear them insist there was no way the two of them could be kept apart. But then the other reason he was afraid floated to the surface of his mind, and it chilled him to the bone, too terrible to speak out loud.

Because I don't know who I am if I'm not that Skylar Stone. I don't know what else I'm supposed to do if I don't go down the road they've paved for me.

Skylar drew his bowl of ramen closer to him, stabbed savagely into it with his chopsticks, and slurped at the noodles. They tasted like ash. They felt like lead in his belly.

Zelda watched him eat, looking worried. "Go stay at the Palace at least. Stay with Xander. He'll worry less if he sees where you are. Sara can feed you, and Pamela too. You'll sleep better. Feel better. Every little bit counts, right?"

Skylar had swallowed four noodles. He wanted to throw up. He pushed the bowl away again. "I can't ask him to let me move in."

"You could. But *you* don't have to."

He winced. "*Zelda.*"

"Tell me you don't want to go home to your own personal grumpy artist every night, and I won't say another word."

"It's not that—"

"Nope. To escape this, you have to say, exactly, 'I don't want to go home to my own personal grumpy artist every night.' Otherwise I'm going in."

Skylar understood now why Xander so carefully avoided riling up Zelda. "I'm not going to bother him with this, and I won't let you do it either."

Their eyebrows lifted. "You think this is bothering him?"

Skylar did his best to resurrect the old Silver Stone, to charm Zelda out of their plan, and when this failed to work, he tried distraction. He didn't know if he failed because he'd lost his touch or they were impervious or both. He was afraid to know the answer.

He decided he would catch Xander after his afternoon classes and head him off. Of course, he didn't, and he didn't get the notes from his seminar either, which meant he was going to have to ask someone for them and attract more attention.

He was hugging the far wall of the lecture hall as he left, avoiding as many other students as possible and wondering how he had come to this deep of a spiral when he ran into someone.

"Oh—sorry," he said reflexively, and then looked up.

Xander stood in front of him.

Skylar could only stare at him at first, so taken aback by his boyfriend's appearance in the business education center. In his classroom. He opened his mouth to speak, but he was so confused, he only made an incoherent noise.

Xander smiled, but it was a careful smile, full of concern. "Hey. Are you okay?"

"What are you doing here?" It came out too harsh, but Skylar couldn't filter anything.

Xander didn't seem to mind. He held up his phone—still that god-awful flip dinosaur—and showed a string of texts from Zelda. *Your BF needs rescuing, Moo, STAT. Also wants to move in with you but is too shy to ask. Call me.*

Skylar wanted to die of embarrassment. But Xander seemed so concerned. He put his phone away, and he kept looking at Skylar as if he were hunting for clues.

"I called them the second I got that text. They told me about your lunch date. How you didn't eat—again. How you really did say you wanted to come live with me." Xander's cheeks flushed. "Why didn't you tell me that? I'd love to have you in my apartment. I had no idea you wanted to be there full-time. Or is this Zelda blowing things out of proportion?"

The apprehension in Xander's expression undid Skylar. *No. They're only tearing down my walls.* "I did admit that. But I didn't tell you because…I don't know why. It felt like a bother. I wasn't asking out of joy, but desperation. I want to come stay because I feel so…lousy, and being with you makes me feel better. And that seems like such a horrible reason to move in with someone."

Xander shook his head in disbelief. "Why?"

"Because it shouldn't be that way." Skylar was reaching, grasping, and he knew it. He gave up and volunteered the real answer, staring at Xander's shoulder since he couldn't brave meeting him in the eye. "I didn't want you to have to rescue me. I don't understand what's happening to me right now, and I don't…"

He could feel people staring at him, knew they were whispering, wondering *what in the world happened to Skylar Stone?* He turned his face away from them, stared at the textured gray-green surface of the wall, and focused on breathing.

Xander touched his fingers, stroked the length of them. "Let me take you home."

Skylar kept his gaze on the wall, but he sank into the comfort of Xander's touch. "It's Thursday. You have class. And I do too."

"Let me take you home anyway." He rubbed circles in the middle of Skylar's palm. "Let me take you home, pamper you, and paint you. Then after dinner, we'll work on some panels."

"And your social media."

"And my social media. If you want to study for your test while I do that, you can, and if you don't want to, you don't have to. But what I really want is for Unc to come and get us, drive us to Delta Sig, and help us gather up enough things for you to stay with me, for the most part, until after the test is finished. After that, you can make whatever decisions you want. If you want to move in for real—out of joy, like you said—that's fine with me too."

Skylar shut his eyes, drew a deep breath. Nodded. "All right."

Xander laced their fingers together and led Skylar out of the auditorium and through the atrium of the business education building. He craned his neck at the architecture and lingered at the sculpture as they passed. "It's nice, but it's all a bit sterile."

"That's business design for you." Skylar winced as he saw the rain pouring down outside. "When did that start? I didn't bring an umbrella." He hadn't checked the forecast. Because he wasn't on his game, wasn't paying attention.

Xander pulled an umbrella out of his backpack, opening it as they passed through the foyer. "It's not terribly big, though. I'm afraid you'll have to crowd in close to me."

The mock teasing in his tone made Skylar smile for the first time that day. "Oh no," he teased back. "What a hardship."

They didn't speak much during the walk in the rain back to Xander's place, but there was no need. Simply being close to him was a balm for Skylar, and the shield of the umbrella and the steady patter of the rain around them reinforced the truth that while the rest of the world might be chaos, Xander was his shelter and his rock. He leaned into him, drinking in the smell of him, reveling in the closeness of him. Reminding himself it was Xander who had dropped everything to come find him. To help him.

Let him save you, perhaps, just a little.

So he did. After an afternoon of drawing and storyboarding, they called Unc and got Skylar's things, enough to allow him to stay at Xander's for the two weeks left before the test. Ms. Mary was concerned, but *she* at least understood how close he was with Xander and was all for anything that got him back on his feet, and officially excused him from all house meetings and anything else she could excuse him from. He felt bad leaving Unc to wrestle with the unsavory leadership alone, but Unc wasn't having any of it. "You've got enough on your plate, and I'm not an idiot. I've got this. You go fight your battles, and let Xander help you, all right?"

He tried. Xander bullied him into eating, studying, escaping into their manga. Skylar could tell there was more Xander wanted to say, things he was holding back. Three days before he was due to drive to Albany and take the test, those things came out, and they weren't pretty.

Xander took him to the state park to confront him, leading him through the hiking trails to the bluff, and they stood together on the ridge, Xander holding his hands as he said, "I think you should let me come with you to the test."

Skylar immediately got his back up. "That's ridiculous. I'll be there for hours. I have to get there stupidly early. It's a waste of your time."

"If I want to waste my time waiting for you, it's my business. I'm worried about you. I don't think this is going to go well. I want to be there for you."

Skylar huffed through his nose. "I *know* it's not going to go well, but thank you for reinforcing that."

"I don't mean the test." Xander released Skylar's hands and put his on his hips. "I mean *you*."

Skylar drew back. "What, you think I'm going to melt down?"

"Yes. That's exactly what I think."

Skylar's face was aflame. "I'm sorry I'm such a burden to you."

"Did I say you were a burden? No, I did not. I said I thought you were in trouble and I wanted to help." He threw his hands in the air. "Fuck this. Fine, so long as you're pissed at me—I don't think you should even take the damn test."

Skylar's chest grew tight, and the setting sun pierced his eyes. "I *told* you, I *have* to take it—"

"Why? *Why*, Skylar? Tell me. Tell me all about how you want to be a lawyer when you grow up. Tell me how it makes your heart sing, your soul light up."

Skylar turned his back to the sun, staring into the darkness of the forest, but he could still feel the heat on his back. "Not everybody gets to be an artist and love what they do."

"Sorry, but that's a bunch of shit."

Skylar staggered back.

Xander pressed forward. "I've watched you dance to your dad's fucking tune, and it's fucked as hell. There's no reason to do it. None. So if you go take that god-damned test, you better do it because you want it. Otherwise I have no idea why you're torturing yourself like this, and you don't seem to know either. If you can tell me, if you can explain to me why it's so important to make yourself sick over this, I'll support you every step of the way. I will choose a grad school based on wherever you want to go, because I'm in love with you, you messed-up asshole, and I don't want to lose you. But this? This is bullshit."

Skylar wanted to yell at him, and he'd been puffed up to the sky on *how dare you*'s until… "You…love me." He'd never said it so directly before.

Neither had Skylar.

Xander held Skylar's face in his hands. "I love you. I'm in love with you. I want you. I need you. I'm prepared to reorganize everything about my life for you." His thumb pressed into the corner of Skylar's jaw. "But not if all you're going to do is throw it away for people who don't even know who you are."

Skylar could barely breathe. "*I* don't know who I am."

"You're Skylar Stone. You're charming, kind, clever, helpful, beautiful inside and out. You don't give up. You bring people together, not because you want to use them but because you truly want to help people be better, to build good things. You help people find themselves. Sometimes you lose your way, but at the end of the day, you have a pure heart and the best of intentions. You're curious, you have drive…" He ran fingers down the slope of Skylar's neck. "You're sexy. In ways I didn't know sexy could be. You're romantic. You're attentive, caring, sweet—"

Skylar stopped his words with a kiss.

It was a simple press of lips. A soft, gentle pressure, the same as it had been the time he'd kissed Xander in the hall. But this time Skylar had so many emotions pent up behind the kiss, and this time…this time…

Overwhelmed by everything inside him, Skylar took hold of Xander's face, rode his fear, and deepened the kiss.

The impulse had swelled within him, and he'd followed it, wanting to know where it led him. He didn't take it very far, only the barest nibble against Xander's flesh. For most people, it wouldn't be considered much of a deep kiss at all. For him—for both of them—it was shattering.

He parted his lips over Xander's, deciding to take a little more.

He *did* shiver now, at the way Xander gasped and melted for him. He had gone from fire to a puddle of water with a mere brush of Skylar's lips, and *that*—that was Skylar's thrill. Pleasing Xander. Making him yield to him, making him respond like this.

How much would Xander melt down if he kissed him more? If he stole his tongue inside? Did he want to do that? He wasn't sure. Maybe he wouldn't ever want to. But maybe he would.

Either way is okay with me. It was what Xander always said, and finally, Skylar began to understand.

Either way is okay, so long as I'm with you.

Skylar pulled back, nuzzling Xander's nose. "I love you too. Very much."

Xander shut his eyes, gripping the shoulders of Skylar's shirt as he nuzzled back. "Please don't go to the test."

"I have to. I don't know what comes after the test, but I have to take it. I don't know why I have to, but I know that I do."

"Then let me come along, *please.*"

No. I don't want you in that world. That sounded insane even in his head. "I'm sorry."

Xander didn't press him any longer, but Skylar was well aware, that night and every day until the test, that his boyfriend was unhappy with him.

The day of the test he got up early—he wasn't surprised that Xander rose with him, but he was startled to find instead of having breakfast in the apartment he was dragged downstairs to have a full farmer's breakfast with the entire crew. Even Unc came over. They smiled and wished him luck, laughing with him, all but Xander, who followed him to his car and tried, once again, to get Skylar to let him come along.

"I'll sit in a coffee shop and work on my social media stuff."

Skylar shook his head. He could barely talk, but he

forced himself, smiling. "I'll be fine," he lied.

And then he drove away.

It was three hours to Albany, and at first he played music, but everything made him antsy, so eventually he turned off his player and listened to the silence. Except there was a rhythmic clink he couldn't figure out where it was coming from, and for half an hour that distracted him. When he stopped for gas and pulled his keys out of the cupholder, he found it.

It was the seven-gods keychain Unc had given him. He blinked at it, having forgotten all about it.

He put his keys in his pocket while he pumped gas and used the restroom, but when he was back in the car, he put the keychain on the seat beside him while he drove, and he kept closing his hand around it. The plastic cut into his hand, but he liked the feeling. It reminded him of everyone back at the Palace. Of how they'd gathered to send him off.

He wished Fudō Myōō were on the keychain.

He wished he hadn't been so proud. He wished Xander were here.

Why *had* he been so insistent Xander not come? Why had he been so determined to do this on his own? He didn't know, only that he knew he had to. Like this was his sentence he had to complete. Take this test, do terrible, and face the music. He didn't want anyone along for it. He didn't want to taint them with this ugliness.

Except the closer he got to the test center, the tighter he gripped that acrylic casing and the more constricted his chest became.

I don't want it to taint me, either, is the thing.

The only sound he could hear now was his breathing, short puffs of air punctuating the seconds as they ticked by. What *was* he going to do after the test? It was going to be abysmal. He hadn't studied as he should have. He was in a terrible mental state.

The keychain cut his flesh. The blood ran across his skin, and he exhaled in relief, as if it were leaching out poison.

He didn't want to take the LSAT.

He didn't want to go to law school.

He didn't want to be a lawyer.

He didn't know what he wanted to do, but it wasn't that.

He didn't know how he'd face his parents, what he'd say to his father, but he didn't want this.

You think I'm going to melt down?

Yes. That's exactly what I think.

Oh God, Xander was right. He was totally going to melt down.

Skylar gripped the wheel with his uninjured hand, squeezed the keychain tighter, letting the blood flow onto his khakis, staining them red. He could see the testing center up ahead. See the signage. He drew as deep a breath as he could, but it caught, and tears pricked his eyes. "Fudō Myōō, what do I do?"

He didn't even know if he was talking to his boyfriend or the god anymore.

I don't think you should even take the damn test.

Xander's voice, ringing in his head. His words from the other day. Skylar drew in another breath, let it out. He was stopped at a light now, but his next stop was the parking lot. "So what, I turn around and leave? I drove all the way here and I just give up?"

No. After all this time, you finally let it go.

A car behind him laid on its horn. Skylar startled and crawled forward, dazed. Whose voice was *that*?

What was he letting go?

I've watched you dance to your dad's fucking tune, and it's fucked as hell. There's no reason to do it.

That was Xander again. Except they were Skylar's feelings swimming inside him. Loneliness. Emptiness. Alienation, feeling as if nothing he did was good enough. That he couldn't connect with his mother or his father. That he didn't belong with Ellen and her family. That everyone everywhere in the world was part of something he couldn't be part of, and he was so afraid because he would never find a group to belong to, never find a partner, because he couldn't feel, couldn't join, couldn't—

The keychain knifed pain down his arm, shutting down that lie.

You have something you're part of. You have a group to belong to.

You have a partner who loves you, who sees you better than you see yourself and who loves you for who you are. Exactly who you are.

The world stretched, pulled, turned. Skylar saw the rooftop altar at Art Building West. The Delta Sig altar before it had been destroyed, when he'd pledged. The kitchen table at the Palace of the Sun.

Think carefully where you will spend the coin of your soil, Skylar Stone.

He cried out. Swerved from the entrance of the testing center at the last second, nearly hitting an Audi, setting off a cascade of honking cars. Sobbing, he ignored them all and drove around the corner to a side street, parked the car. Put the bloody keychain down, wrapped his hand in napkins from the glove compartment, and picked up his phone.

Xander answered before the ring had finished. "Are you all right?"

He could barely breathe, let alone speak, but he had to, had to tell him—"I can't," he whispered. "I can't take it."

"I'm coming to get you. Where are you?"

Skylar looked around vaguely. Houses. Cars. *Jesus.* "I'm so sorry."

"It's all right. Are you at the testing center?"

He shook his head. Drew a breath. "Next to it. On a street. Parked."

"It's okay. It's going to be okay. We're coming. All of us. Okay? We're coming."

"I don't know what to do. *I don't know what to do.*"

"You take deep breaths and you wait. Because I'm coming to take care of you."

The fear kept coming, bigger and bigger waves crashing on the shore. "I'm going to be alone."

"You will never be alone. Because I'll be with you."

Why did it hurt, sometimes, when he said that? "I'm falling apart—I'm not what I wanted to be for you, I wanted to be strong, wanted—"

"I've painted and drawn you all summer, made you the goddess heroine of my manga, and you still think that's what I see in you? I guess I'm going to have to get more gritty with my portraits of you. Maybe I'll paint directly onto you next time. Maybe I'll make you my canvas. Then you won't be able to do anything but look at what I see in you, because it will be painted all over you."

Under normal circumstances Skylar would have found that captivating, and part of him did, but mostly he was so tired, so lost. "I don't know who to be now, Xander. I don't know what they're going to do when they find out, and I don't know what I want to say or even feel."

"Be the man who was brave enough to know when he was making the wrong decision and stop before it was too late. Be the man who knew to call for help, who didn't suffer alone. Be the man strong enough to admit his fears so he could face them, not pretend they didn't exist." There was shuffling in the background. "We're in the cars now. I'm with Unc. He says he's going to push the speed limit to get to you. The others are coming at a more leisurely pace."

Why was everyone coming? Except Skylar didn't care. He was just glad. And tired.

"I think I want to nap," he said.

"Will you be okay where you are?"

He had no idea. "I think so."

"Will we be able to find you?"

"I hope so."

"Leave your ringer on. If we can't find you right away, I'll call you. Rest. Be safe. Call if you need me."

Skylar fell asleep almost immediately after they hung up. He put his seat down, shut his eyes, and drifted into strange dreams. He walked out onto a rooftop filled with that horrible asphalt gravel, trying to get to a shrine, but his father and mother kept pouring more gravel onto his steps. Ellen tried to help him up, but the rope she tossed him was made of photos, and every time he grasped it, it shattered, the images scattering across the rooftop, melting into the rocks.

Then Xander appeared, blue-skinned and ringed with fire, wielding a golden blade. He cut through the tar and led him by the hand to a gleaming shrine where Benzaiten embraced Skylar with open arms…and they merged, music playing, lights dancing. Children dancing. Something about that caught Skylar's heart, made him pause, and he thought, *Wait, there's something about that image…*

A rap on his window startled him awake. It was the real Xander, not blue-skinned, but very worried.

"Skylar?"

Skylar sat up, opened the door.

Xander had him in his arms before the door was fully opened. Hauled him out of the car, against his body, cradling him close. "Thank God. Thank God. I've never been so worried in my life. I'm never letting you do anything like that again. The next time I know you're doing something stupid, I'm going along whether you want me to or not."

Skylar let himself fall into his embrace, into his shelter, into his peace. "All right."

IT HADN'T BEEN Xander's idea for everyone to come along to rescue Skylar, but he hadn't been able to get them to stay at home. Zelda and Jacob had come with Xander and Unc, so Jacob drove Skylar's car with Zelda while Xander and Skylar moved into Unc's backseat. Pamela, Sara, and Cory were still en route to the scene.

The first thing they did was go to a drugstore and buy supplies to deal with Skylar's damaged hand. Xander had worried they should go to a hospital, but Zelda and Jacob had both agreed it looked superficial and that a good cleaning out and bandage should do the trick.

"Besides," Unc pointed out, "a hospital would trigger insurance, which would alert his parents."

Skylar said little through all of this. He leaned on Xander, resting his head on his shoulder and nestling into his side when Xander put an arm around him. But as Unc and Zelda returned with the supplies and Jacob applied the bandage, Skylar finally spoke.

"I want to tell my parents." He kept leaning into Xander, and his voice was quiet, but there was a confidence and a sense of peace about him now that hadn't been there in a month. As if something in him had broken free. "I don't know how to do it yet, but I want to confront them. I want to move past this. So I can go forward. If they disown me, they disown me. I just want it done."

Unc frowned at him. "Do you think it will come to that?"

"I don't know. I want to say probably not, but I can't say for sure. This feels like leaving the map. All the variables are unknown."

Xander stroked his fingers. "Not all of them."

Skylar turned his hand to capture Xander's. "I need to cut ties with things that weigh me down. I need to get quiet so I can figure out what it is I want to do. Because I don't have a plan now. I have no steps forward."

"We'll figure one out together," Xander promised.

For a moment Skylar looked pained. "There's something I have to tell you." He glanced at the front seat, at Zelda and Unc. "Once the two of us are alone again."

"Okay." Xander couldn't look away from Skylar's worried face. "You can tell me anything you need to."

This didn't seem to reassure Skylar. "I worry you'll be angry. But I need to tell you anyway, because it's making me feel sick, not telling you."

Now Xander was nervous. What in the world was Skylar going to confess? "It's okay. I'll listen to whatever you have to say."

Skylar squeezed his hand and didn't say anything else.

Zelda pulled out their phone. "Pamela and the others are almost here. Sara says there's a restaurant we could meet at not far from where we are. What do you think, Skylar? Want to sit for a minute with your squad, plan your future? Or at least have a nice meal?"

Skylar tucked himself against Xander's side. "Sure."

The restaurant turned out to be, of all things, Japanese. And not simply a sushi-bar strip mall—it was a full-on fancy kind of place, with a koi pond and curved bridge to get to the door, and a torii-style gate. The interior was beautiful, with elegant modern furniture, but the hostess led them to a small room off to the side which had traditional Japanese seating.

"I remember this place from Japanese class. We came for a field trip," Xander said, noting the sunken area before the rise of the room, and he held out his arm to stop Unc from going in before the hostess had to. "You need to take off your shoes for this room. And there's a way we're supposed to sit. I can't quite remember. It's like, most important person at…the head of the table, I think, and then the next important beside them facing the door, and then it goes around to the lowest ranking with their backs to the door. Except I have no idea how we assign that."

Unc clapped one hand on Xander's shoulder and the other on Skylar's. "Easy. The man of the hour is Skylar, and you're his right-hand man, Moo. The rest of us get first-come, first-served on the seats-of-honor business. And we just maybe don't tell the rest of them that the last one in is a rotten egg."

Their seating arrangement was Skylar at the head, Xander beside him, Unc beside him, Zelda on his right, and Jacob at the other end of the table. When the others arrived, they filled in the last side of the table. The waitstaff had already brought beer and sake, but now they brought sushi and tempura, edamame and miso soup. As they ordered their main courses, they chose things they would share, not eat individually, and Pamela gave lessons to everyone who didn't know how to use chopsticks.

Xander checked frequently on Skylar, who seemed to be doing as well as he could be, given the circumstances. His smiles didn't quite reach his eyes, but he *did* smile, sometimes. When people spoke to him, he engaged with them, and he wasn't putting on a show. He seemed raw, but real.

But what does he need to confess to me? Xander wished he could pull Skylar into the hallway and ask him right now. Was it something with his father? The test? Something else?

Something about their relationship?

Something *bad* about their relationship?

A had on Xander's knee startled him out of him out of his panic spiral. When he glanced up, Skylar was regarding him with concern. "Are you okay?"

Xander considered how to respond, then decided if Skylar was going to give him truths, he should respond in kind. He leaned in close enough, though, that it was only Skylar who heard his reply. "I'm a little freaked out about what you're going to tell me. Did I…do something?"

Skylar looked startled, then embarrassed. He too

leaned in close as he replied in a whisper. “You didn’t do anything. I did.”

Oh. Xander’s eyebrows raised, and he looked at his boyfriend, more confused than ever. What in the world had he done?

“I’ll tell you after dinner, I promise.” Skylar’s hand was still on Xander’s thigh, and he squeezed. “Okay?”

“Okay,” Xander agreed, trying not to wish the meal were already over.

Everyone else was blissfully ignorant of their angst, happily enjoying the meal. “This is the best,” Unc said, rubbing his stomach after he polished off his second plate of food. “Someday we should do this in actual Japan.”

Pamela sighed wistfully and wiped her mouth with her napkin. “I’d love to do that. The next best thing to traveling with my husband would be going with this crew.”

Xander glanced at Skylar and was pleased to find him smiling softly at his food.

“The only two here who know Japanese though are Xander and Pamela,” Jacob pointed out. “Plus we’d need money.”

“We could stay in hostels.” Zelda reached for another piece of sashimi with their chopsticks. “I don’t know enough about the programs to seriously suggest it, but we could maybe work our way through. I hear they’re always looking for English teachers there.”

“It’s a little more complicated than simply showing up and saying, ‘I’d like to teach English,’” Pamela said.

"But it's definitely a route one can take. There's the JET Programme, which is the most popular, but I know a few other, less-publicized options as well." She looked wistful now. "Oh, I would show you such a wonderful time, if we could take a trip together. I'd take you to Kyoto, to the shrines and temples. And Nara, to see all the historical places. We'd have to go to Tokyo too so you could have your excitement—you'd want to see manga cafes for sure."

"What are manga cafes?" Cory asked.

"Places where you can sit and read manga, for a fee. Shelves of it. There are couches and recliners, and there's Wi-Fi—they have everything. It's a great place to go if you miss the last train. But of course everything is in Japanese, so you'd best get learning to read."

She regaled them with stories of places she'd like to take them in Japan and things she thought they'd like to see through the rest of the meal. While the others were lingering over tea and dessert, though, Skylar took Xander's hand, and once they collected their shoes at the door, led him into the restaurant's garden.

It was a beautiful traditional rock garden, complete with benches and paths and overhanging trees which might well have been cherry or some other type that bloomed, but of course it was fall and the leaves were brown and falling. They drifted silently around the two of them as they wandered alone through the space, not holding hands but standing close together, until at last Skylar spoke.

"I have to confess something to you, as I said—

something that I did. At the time I convinced myself I was doing the right thing, but I admit now that it wasn't, and I need to tell you."

Xander couldn't begin to guess what was coming. He braced for impact. "All right. Let's clear all the air."

Skylar took a deep breath, let it out. "When I was studying with my tutor—or rather, when I was *failing* to study with my tutor—I Silver Stoned her so she wouldn't report to my father." When Xander only regarded him in confusion, Skylar cast his gaze miserably into his lap. "I…flirted with her."

Oh. Xander digested this, trying to decide if it made him angry.

Yes, it did. Though not, he suspected, for the reasons Skylar feared.

Before he could say anything, though, Skylar spoke again, full of panic. "I didn't *want* her, obviously—I wanted her not to tell my father, because he was threatening to pay too much attention to me if I didn't get my act together, and I didn't want to get my act together. I wanted to spend my summer with you and everyone at the Palace. But I still felt I had to take the test. I can't explain it. I don't know what I thought was going to happen. I think I'd convinced myself I could have the summer as an aberration and then go back to reality. Or maybe I was simply scared. Except none of this makes it right, what I did. It made me feel terrible too—both the flirting, which made me sick, and the fact that it was basically cheating on you, which made me feel worse—"

Xander put two fingers on Skylar's lips to end the

torrent of words. "Stop."

Skylar spoke against the fingers, his words muffled and desperate. "I'm so sorry."

"I know." Xander shifted his hand so he stroked Skylar's beard. "I forgive you. I'm sorry too—I'm sorry you felt those were your choices, that the only way you could have your freedom was to sell yourself yet again. I hope you feel safe enough now that those days are over. I hope, if you ever feel compelled to do something like that again, you come to me instead, so I can talk you out of it. Okay?"

Eyes shining with unshed tears, Skylar rested his face on Xander's palm. "Okay."

They stood there like that for a while, touching each other while the leaves rained silently around them. When they heard the voices of the others in the parking lot, the spell was broken, but Skylar wouldn't let Xander pull away.

"Do you know what I wish?" Skylar held Xander's hand tight as he looked up at the falling leaves. "I wish we could stand like this in Japan, under real cherry trees. Ones in bloom."

"We have real cherry trees in the United States, you know."

"The ones in Japan feel more real, somehow."

Xander smiled. "Then let's make it a vow. Someday we'll stand under cherry blossoms in Japan."

Skylar smiled back, and there was only weariness, no more shadows in his face now. "It's a promise."

SKYLAR ASKED IF he could stay at Xander's place a little longer, which Xander immediately said was obviously fine. But he also asked Xander another question.

"It doesn't have to happen tonight. I suspect it probably can't. But…all through dinner, I kept thinking about it. I should say, rather, I can't *stop* thinking about it. How you said on the phone that you would paint my body. Use me as your canvas. Would you please…do that?"

Xander's breath caught, and an electric bloom of anticipation expanded through him. "Yeah," he said, when he was able. "I'll…need to do some research first. Get some supplies. But…yes. I would *love* to do that."

Skylar turned his hand over, palm up. Spread his fingers, an invitation for Xander to lace theirs together. "I want to see how you see me. Plus, I want to feel it. The paint going on me. The brush moving on me. Your eyes on me, calculating, seeing me not only as your subject but as the art. I…I feel breathless just thinking about it."

Xander was getting there too. "Consider it done."

This was easy to say, but it wasn't quite as simple as he wanted it to be. Xander's initial thought was to use acrylic or tempera, since they were water-based and nontoxic, but research into body painting quickly taught him this was not the way to go. There were sites that helped him out, however, and after careful consideration of several mediums, he made his selections.

It cost him a pretty penny, though. He was sweating it a little, but he thought if he borrowed into his BFA allowance, he'd be okay. There wasn't much to do but pray to the gods that things continued to go his way.

So far, the gods *were* on his side, pretty much everywhere. His BFA project was going great. His social media campaign was practically superfluous. His greatest social media blitz had turned out to be dating Skylar, and his second greatest one was the first edition of *Lucky 7*. People really loved the new storyline with the seven gods, and it became normal for total strangers to come up to him and ask him what was going to happen, was Bennie going to be okay? And almost always on the heels of that came, "Are Moo and Bennie going to get together?" Though there were the occasional Hotay/Bennie shippers too. And apparently there were people who had been shipping Hotay and Moo this whole time, so for them Bennie as a love interest was a scandal.

He was going to ask Skylar about that one day when he came home, but he got distracted because Skylar was on the couch, draped in cats and reading Xander's copies of *Fullmetal Alchemist*.

Xander plunked down beside him, dislodging Hokusai. "I thought you finished. You're rereading already?"

"It's a wonderful series." He ran his finger down the center of a page. "I can't seem to leave this panel."

Xander looked more carefully at the page Skylar was on, seeing the words this time, not the art. It was chapter two of the first volume, just after Edward and Alphonse found out the philosopher's stone was fake.

They were preparing to leave, and as they did, Rose, the naive girl who had somewhat accidentally helped them expose the false priest, cried out to them on her knees, *What am I supposed to believe in now?*

Edward tells her, rather grimly, that she needs to figure that out on her own.

Xander put an arm around Skylar and pressed a kiss just above his beard at his jaw. "I think he's right, you do have to decide what to believe in yourself. But you're not Rose. And I'll stay here with you while you work it out."

Skylar kept staring at the page. "I don't even know what criteria to use to make the decision. I don't know where to start."

"Something that makes you happy. Something that makes you feel good."

Skylar's hands tightened on the manga. "It can't be that simple, that selfish. I don't *want* it to be. I want to help other people. I want to do good things *for* people. I want to be a part of something, Xander."

"Then start with that—those are part of the qualifications for what will make you happy. That's part of what you need."

He put his finger in the book to mark his place, closed it, and leaned into Xander. "I'm still scared, though. To leave everything behind. Sometimes I know part of what I want. But it means leaving so much of who I was, who I've been. Even if my parents support me—which they won't, not in the way I'd need."

Xander glanced at the calendar on the wall, his gut

knotting as he saw a week had already passed since the day Skylar had failed to take his LSAT. The results would be mailed in three weeks, he'd said, after which point Skylar's father would begin asking to see them. Skylar had estimated they had a month before things became pointed, six weeks before they became intense.

It was going to go by so much faster than they needed it to, Xander realized. He wanted to meet Skylar's parents, shake some sense into them. But he knew he didn't have the balls to smack down a Wall Street lawyer, a guy who played with kings and courtiers. Possibly literally.

All he could do right now was support Skylar through his grieving and his contemplation. Create with him. Cook with him, feed him manga and secret streams of anime only Zelda and their army of online hackers knew how to find. And all the while he gathered his supplies for body painting, practiced his techniques on his arms and legs and, swearing him to secrecy, Unc.

Until two weeks after Skylar's failed attempt to take his test, he was finally ready.

Chapter Twenty

"I THOUGHT, IF you were free, I'd paint you this weekend."

Skylar glanced at Xander from the manga he was reading over his bowl of cereal. "Sure, but I thought you were doing landscapes for your last BFA pieces."

Xander continued tapping on his phone. He had, begrudgingly, let Unc give him an old smartphone so he could keep up with his social media without using a computer, and had gone with Pamela to a few shows to earn enough money for a minor data plan. "I am doing landscapes. I'm not talking about using you as a model. I'm talking about using you as a canvas." He looked up then, a sly smile on his face. "I did promise to do a body painting on you, and I think I'm finally ready."

Skylar stared at him for several seconds, letting the implications of what his lover had just said to him ring through his psyche. Then he closed his book and set it aside. "So you would do what to me, exactly?"

"Paint on your skin. All of it. I ordered special paint that's not makeup but is kind of makeup-based, in a way. There are a lot of ways to do body painting, it turns out, but I had to search a bit to find one that would still let me use a brush on your skin. Because I knew for you that would be the part you wanted most. To feel me moving brushes all over your body. Marking you with paint."

Skylar was having a hard time breathing simply thinking about it. "Yes." He cleared his throat. "How—how long will it take?"

"The entire day. With a team of experienced painters it can take eight to twelve hours. With just me, as my first time, we're going to wake up, eat breakfast, get started at dawn, and go until the wee hours of the next day. Saturday, Skylar. All of Saturday, you'll be under my brush."

Skylar sat back in his chair, covering his mouth. "I don't…know if I can take that. I mean, I want to, but…"

Xander put down his phone and reached for Skylar's hand. At first it was a simple touch, but then he deliberately changed it, making the touch the kind that meant, between the two of them, a kiss, then a tender lovemaking. "Trust me to know what you can and can't handle. I've literally been working on this, researching and planning and thinking about it since you asked me for it. The kind of paint. The design I wanted to put on you. How much stimulation you could take. Have you noticed how much brush play we've been doing lately? How I keep pushing it, dragging it out, seeing if you can handle the pleasure of lying there, being painted on?"

How could Skylar *not* have noticed? It was getting to the point that even if Xander was painting for his project, Skylar would glance over, see the paintbrush, and sway on his feet. But... "You mean that was all *research*?"

Xander's smile was wicked. "Well, it wasn't *all* research. You do get terribly aggressive once we're done with brush play, and I benefit plenty from that. I can't wait to see what you do after a full day of it. I think you might turn into the Graysexual Hulk."

Skylar blushed, but he laughed too. And thought some more about what Xander was proposing. "All day. Wouldn't we both be exhausted? Cramped?"

"We'd have to take breaks, shift positions. I have a menu planned—things to eat that won't be too heavy but will keep us going and are easy to grab. I'd ask the rest of the Palace to please be busy elsewhere to give us privacy. Because I want you to be able to be loud if you need to."

Skylar startled. "You think...you think I'm going to orgasm from it?"

"Maybe. Or maybe you'll feel emotional. Or maybe we'll want to blast the stereo. I don't know what's going to happen—I feel like this is a powder keg, and I want us to be able to set it off in private. It's *our* keg. This is art, but it's ours. A show for two. And two alone."

Skylar already felt highly emotional. "That's a good point. Do you want me to talk to them? You've done so much of the rest."

"Absolutely not. This is my gift to you. You're the canvas only in this. Your whole role is to appear on Saturday and be painted on. To get good rest the night before. To shower and use no lotions or hair gels, no deodorants or perfumes. To walk out into this living room naked and ready to let me show you, on your skin, all day long, how I love you."

Skylar swayed in his seat. "I seriously don't know how I'm going to survive this. I'm weak-kneed and you're just talking about it. And you want to do this *all day*?"

"Yeah." Xander's grin was almost feral. "I'm so excited. There's literally nothing you could suggest to me that would be better to do with my Saturday."

Skylar knew better, but the little doubting part of him decided to test him anyway. "Not even if I said I wanted to spend it fucking you?"

Xander only raised an eyebrow. "One, I'd call you a lying liar who lies, because you would never want to do that. Second, sorry, but that's boring. Headfucking is so, so much more fun."

It was what Skylar had expected him to say, wanted him to say, and yet…so much more casual and confident than he'd ever dreamed. "You really don't mind, do you?"

"I've been trying to tell you that for some time now. I've been *showing* you that, in fact." Xander ran a finger down his nose, then booped the tip. "But it's all right. You don't know how to see through to what people are saying with their hearts. You're too conditioned to only hear the words and the promises they make with their mouths. You were overly social when I met you, but you're properly antisocial now. I fixed you up just like I wanted you, Galatea."

Skylar caught his hand, kissed it. "Oh? Was that painting a cunning trap for me, then?"

"Yes. I put it out every night to catch myself a man to take home and make into an image I prefer."

"How lucky for me, then, that I happened to come by."

"No. The lucky one was me." Xander laced their fingers, teasing his thumb as he rose. "Saturday morning?"

Skylar's heartbeat skipped a beat and quickened its pace. "Saturday morning."

The rest of the week, Skylar could barely focus, thinking of what was to come. He tried a few times to help Xander prepare, but he was apparently quite serious that Skylar would do nothing but arrive with his naked skin and his anticipation.

The only thing that dimmed Skylar's prospects for the weekend was the phone call he received from his father on Friday morning, the one he'd been dreading. He didn't answer it, even though he'd had his script all ready. That had been Xander's advice, once they'd set the date for the body painting: don't let his parents or any other nonsense from what Xander kept calling his past life get in the way of his upcoming pleasure. This included ignoring pressure from Delta Sig to explain why he had, for all practical purposes, moved out, and why he never attended Greek functions. He even left unopened an email from Ellen with an update on Marie, one he was fairly sure had something about an engagement in the subject line. Xander said he'd noticed Skylar was often sad after he read emails from Ellen, so no emails of any kind, not even Ellen's, were allowed.

"Nothing exists this week but your schoolwork and your upcoming session," Xander told him. "Keep my canvas clean, please."

Skylar did his best.

They had set up candles for Benzaiten in a makeshift home altar—it wasn't a proper *kamidana*, the Japanese Shinto home shrine, as it wasn't in the right place and it was too low, but Xander pointed out they really weren't Shinto anyway. "Form new straight lines," he said, and so they designed the altar the way that suited them best and created their own sacred path to their goddess.

Skylar's path was to brew her a cup of tea every morning when he made his own. He did it one day as an act of fancy, but it felt right, so he kept doing it. He was shy about it at first, thinking Xander would laugh, but Xander said it was a good idea and got him some incense as well, and said he'd be sure to keep the tea she liked in stock if he wanted to keep doing it.

Skylar said he did, and he thought Benzaiten liked jasmine, the same as he did.

So he made his tea, ignored the distractions, and kept Xander's canvas clean. He wished, as he went to bed on Friday night, feeling eager but light and unburdened, that he could stay this way. That he didn't have to pick up his troubles again on Sunday morning. That he could always be Xander's canvas and nothing more.

Xander woke him at six.

"Time to eat. I've made your breakfast."

He hadn't simply made Skylar breakfast. He'd brought it to him in bed, on a bamboo tray Skylar hadn't known he had.

It turned out he *didn't* have it—it was Pamela's, and he'd borrowed it for the day. But it was lovely, and so was the breakfast. Scrambled eggs, toast, sausages, and his jasmine tea.

"I put some out for Benzaiten already." Xander fed Skylar a bite of toast and wiped the crumbs from his mouth with a napkin. "I gave her some eggs and toast too, and I asked her to be with us today."

Skylar laced their fingers briefly as he chewed. "Thank you."

"Finish your breakfast, then go get showered. You can come out in your robe, but of course you'll take it off right away. No sock this time. I'm painting everything." He kissed Skylar's forehead. "I'm going to go get ready."

Skylar was practically vibrating with excitement, but Xander had already gone into Serious Painter Mode, so focused he was only partially present. It always turned Skylar on, but it was going to be different, he reminded himself in the shower, to have that fully aimed at him.

When he entered the living room, he found it transformed. The furniture had been pushed back, except for the stool Xander always used for sittings, the stool he sat on while he painted, and the ottoman, which he'd covered with a canvas drop cloth. Xander himself wore his usual T-shirt and sweatpants, and his painting apron. He had his brushes—all Skylar's favorites—set up on his little rolling table, but the paints lined up beside his plastic palette were not ones Skylar had ever seen before.

"Come on over." Xander waved Skylar to the stool. "We're going to start with your feet and legs, though I might not finish them first. I'm going to jump around a lot. And anywhere you have body hair it's going to be abstract, because the hair will be part of the painting. I could have had you shave, and I know you would have, but I didn't want to, stylistically. Your hair is part of you, so it's part of your canvas. Anywhere you're smooth, though, or the hair is short enough I can work with it, I'm going to do specific scenes." He rested a hand on Skylar's hip, making him startle then blush as Xander focused on his groin, as if he could see through the fabric of the robe. "I'm painting you everywhere. Your abdomen. Your groin. Your penis. Your inner thighs. Your ass. Everything." He looked up at Skylar, his penetrative stare making Skylar blush harder. "We'll wait for that. But remember, no one is around. Pamela took them to a hotel for the night, her treat. So you can have whatever reaction you want when we get to that part."

Skylar ran a hand through his hair, wondering how he was going to survive this. "What about you? What kind of reaction will you have?"

Xander smiled, some of his intensity fading. "Well, for me, I think this is a lot like how you get off on enjoying doing things to my body. You and I, we take our turns. Today I'm the one giving the pleasure. But this is still great for me. It's just a different kind of great. An artist's great." He stroked Skylar's beard, the gesture tender. "Are you ready, canvas?"

Skylar squared his shoulders. "Yes."

"Then take off your robe, sit on the stool, and when I come up to you, give me your right foot."

Skylar had disrobed for Xander dozens of times, but nothing had ever felt more intimate, more intense. It was more than simply that he'd never had his whole body exposed, more than missing a sock. It was knowing what was coming. That anticipation combined with everything else—when he sat on the stool, when Xander rolled up to him on a shorter one and motioned for his foot and applied the tiny brush to his skin—Skylar was ready to fly to the ceiling.

The brush came, the paint slid across his foot, cool and slick, a tiny line of bright white from his big toe and winding like a vein to his shin.

Skylar let out a breath.

Xander glanced up at him, smiling, then went back to his work, snaking another line from the pinky toe. "Feels great, doesn't it? I practiced on myself to get a feel for how it would go. Wait until you get a lot of it on you and it dries. It's like having extra skin. It moves with you. But when you get it wet, such as with too much sweat, it washes away. Magical stuff, this."

He kept painting thin white lines all over Skylar's foot, until it was nearly all white, except for thin patches of bare skin that peeked out between the vines. "What is it going to be?"

"You'll have to wait and see for that. And you will indeed have to wait, because this needs to dry." He put Skylar's foot on the floor and tapped his left leg. "Pop the other one up here."

He gave the same treatment to this foot, except its winding lines were blue-black. The working theme seemed to be that Xander was laying a foundation in certain sections, because after the feet he moved on to the shoulder caps, and the back of Skylar's neck, and his hips, and his knees, and the underside of his chin. He used all different colors, sometimes a multitude of them at once. Once those sections were done, they stopped for a break. To Skylar's shock, it was already almost ten.

"You've hardly painted anything, and that much time has passed?"

"That's why we had to start so early." Xander passed him a plate of cheese and crackers and a glass of water. They were seated with Skylar on the ottoman and Xander on a folding chair now, Skylar with a small towel of modesty over his lap, though he had a feeling before long he'd be giving it up.

"Do you think we'll be done in time?" Skylar asked him.

"There's nothing we have to be in time for. We can take until four in the morning. Six in the morning. And we might. I have coffee, tea, energy shots—*you* can doze if you need to. But I think it might start going faster here soon. There are sections where I'm going to layer on paint." He offered Skylar more water. "Oh, and I should tell you. You're a painting in two stages. There's going to be one painting, and then I'm going to wash that off and do a second painting. I had to get creative to make that work, but it was pretty integral to my vision, so I pushed until I could figure it out. That's what took me so long. Otherwise I could have been ready last weekend."

Skylar's heart was beating fast again. "Okay."

Xander dusted his hands off. "All right. Are you ready to go back in?"

The next section did go faster, and by noon a majority of Skylar's body had been painted in large blotches of color, though not all. Skylar was highly aware Xander had left his ass, groin, stomach, chest, forearms, and inner thighs untouched.

After a late lunch and a trip to the bathroom, that changed.

Xander had put on what appeared to be random albums on his stereo prior to this point, his indie bands and retro funk he loved so much, but now he played a playlist on Spotify that was all instrumental, and it seemed designed to put Skylar into a specific mood. It was, honestly, a little melancholic, yet still strangely sensual. Which made him tremble when Xander had him rest his hands on the edge of the kitchen counter, bend at the waist, and spread his legs so he could paint his backside and between his thighs.

"I'm going to talk to you while I do this," Xander said, "because this is pretty intimate." The brush trailed the line of his buttock, inside to his thigh, down to his knee. "It's going to get more intimate as we go on here, but the most difficult part won't be this, though you'll think that at first." A paintbrush touched the area just below Skylar's anus, making him gasp. "This is conditioning. This is the world telling you this is invasive. And funny enough, of the two of us, I'm the one who should be excited to see you naked and vulnerable. Part of me is, I suppose. But right now, you truly are canvas to me. I'm thinking about putting paint on you, not my mouth or my hands. And as we have discussed at length, I wouldn't do that to you. Not without a lot of conversation and consultation." He kept painting, running brushes across all of Skylar's most intimate areas, places even he hadn't seen. "Do you know, I like this better, sometimes? That this is how I get intimate with you, with my brushes and my art? I wouldn't have known to wish for that. But I love it so much. The same way I love you."

Skylar trembled, feeling dizzy. "I love you too."

It aroused him, being painted like this. More than he'd dreamed he could be. Some of it was the touch. Some of it was that it was Xander doing the touching. Some of it was nothing more than stimulation. Some of it was the surrender. Some of it was beyond his ability to understand how and why—maybe it was that this way, today, in this circumstance, he found everything sensual and sexual, that this was sexy to him. He didn't know, and he didn't have to know. He simply got to feel.

When Xander turned him around, for a moment he

was embarrassed of his erection, but of course Xander wasn't—he smiled at it, winked at Skylar, laced their fingers briefly, then continued to work. And as he had warned Skylar, it was different.

It was different, Skylar realized, because he could see, and because unlike the other parts he'd been able to watch Xander paint, this part he could tell some of what Xander meant to convey.

First Xander used a fan brush and drew intense, distinct lines of bright-red paint from the crease of Skylar's groin out to the sides of his thighs. This paint covered other paint in places, abstract whorls and streaks of colors on his legs—the red by contrast was sharp and defined, and thick whereas the other had been thinned out. To drive the point home further, Xander used red deepened with black to cast shadows on the other lines of red. While this dried, he took a flat brush dipped in black and approached, resting his hand on Skylar's abdomen as he began to paint his balls.

Xander bit his lip and glanced up at Skylar. "I'll confess. This part gets me going *just* a little."

Skylar had to shut his eyes, and he gasped against the sensation. "It's…hard for me to do anything but get going."

"Do you mind?"

He shook his head. "It's fine."

"It can be more than fine. If you want to enjoy it, you can. Make noise if you want."

He did have a bit of an urge to pant, to tug on Xander's hair—that was new. "I won't come, though. That I know."

"I know that too—you seem to think I've been somewhere other than on the other end of this paint-brush when we play together. Shout, though, if you like. Do what pleases you. This is your moment."

"I want…I want to pull your hair."

What actually pleased Skylar was the way Xander appeared surprised when he said that. A little abashed too. *See, you don't know everything.* "Ahh…sure. This next bit is all rough work, and I'm basically going to be worthless until I'm done painting your junk, so…yeah. Let's ride."

Skylar got pretty hard while Xander painted his cock and balls—every inch of them was covered in dull black, which seemed a little creepy and strange, but he wasn't the artist, and anyway, brushes on your dick felt good. They'd stayed away from genital play, but Skylar was putting that front and center on the menu from now on. Along with hair pulling.

Skylar didn't yell, but he did gasp, and whine through his nose, and breathe very, very heavily.

They took a break after that, though the break also consisted of the two of them nuzzling, Skylar rubbing his beard along Xander's neck and cheek, Xander panting against his chin. Their fingers laced, unlaced, trailed along wrists, danced together until they were in danger of abandoning their project and simply making out.

"I've got to get it together before I paint there the second time," Xander murmured as they went back to their positions.

"You're doing that *again?*" Skylar was going to die. Seriously going to expire before this was finished.

"Yes, but it will be different. You'll see."

Next Xander had him sit on the stool—his ass painting was dry now, and it wouldn't smudge, Xander said, unless he started sweating, and Xander had a million fans blowing on him and a cool pack under his tush. Now Xander painted his chest, and his abdomen, and his arms.

It took all afternoon and well into the evening, and it was something else.

The painting reminded Skylar of one of those Renaissance or medieval ones where there were a million people and just as many things going on—the ones with angels and devils and priests and cows and birds and shopkeepers and all kinds of odd details. Skylar didn't have any of those things…except he did. He had drunk fraternity brothers and sorority sisters hanging on each other and stripping their clothes off one another. He had a herd of lawyers severing each other's heads and ripping off ears and arms as they fought to get to a cold, gleaming tower made of fire that had a gaping demon at the top where all the lawyers leapt blindly into its mouth. He had what looked eerily just like one of his mother's beach party fundraisers, except the lobsters and the clams were climbing out of the ocean and carrying their roasted brethren away to burn them on funeral pyres, leaving burning coals in their places, and the party guests had no idea. They were zombies anyway; they couldn't notice a thing.

It was at this point Skylar started to cry.

Xander saw the tears, and with a gentle expression that said he'd known this was coming, passed him a tissue. "It's all right. I promise, this is just one phase. Remember, there are two parts to this painting."

"It's okay." Skylar wiped the tears away, glad Xander hadn't gotten to his face yet. "I see where you're going with this. And it's hard but…it's healing."

"I'm not really saying anything. That's not the kind of art I do. I paint and draw what I see."

The tears kept coming. "I wanted you to be a part of this. I kept trying to sell you this. No wonder you ran screaming. I'm just glad you didn't run screaming from me."

"This isn't how I saw you, ever. This is the canvas behind you. You're still coming." He pressed a kiss, careful to keep it dry, to Skylar's painted hip. "Let me know if you need to take a break. Otherwise I want to keep going."

"I want to keep going too."

Xander filled Skylar's torso with scene after scene of what had been his life. His absent parents. The people who demanded he perform for them. It shook him, gutted him—and then, as if reading his mind, Xander painted just that. Skylar, in the center of all of it, down his sternum and over his own heart and solar plexus, wearing a suit and smiling his Silver Stone smile, his guts emptied out across his body. Streaming into the hands of everyone surrounding him. Joining that red stain on his thighs. Constricting his blackened genitals—which weren't aroused at all. Not anymore.

"Is this how you see me?" Skylar could barely whisper. His heart felt like lead. He couldn't stop staring at himself. In horror.

"This is how you were, I think, when I met you. I couldn't see it all at the time. I could see this, though, the night we went to the fundraiser. This is what you showed me in the car. Except you didn't smile anymore, no more fake, plastic Skylar. I saw the real you, the one that had been flickering underneath." He started to paint on Skylar's forearm, a laughing Skylar like the one beneath the cherry blossoms. Then he painted another Skylar on the other forearm, but this one was pained, broken, sobbing. "That night I saw everything. I knew who you could be. Who you were trying to be. And I saw how it was killing you."

"*Xander.*"

Xander kept painting—the blotches across Skylar's body from before became, with slashes and dots, the lines of a suit, except with so many colors and with that nightmare on his chest, it was a rotten suit, as if he were a zombie too, decaying flesh. It was incredible how much it looked like a three-piece suit, complete with tie, had been put on him, front to back and all around, including shoes, but it made Skylar feel sick even before Xander declared the first part of the painting finished and put him in front of a set of mirrors so he could see it.

Skylar didn't want to see it. "Take it off," he whispered. "I hate this. I hate who I am."

"This isn't who you are," Xander said, "and you know it."

Skylar did, actually. The sick feelings twisted, turning to rage. New tears came, but didn't fall. "I hate what they made me," he whispered.

Xander undid one of Skylar's fists, held his hand. "Say it louder. Loud as you need to."

"*I hate what they made me.*"

Skylar stared at the mirror, at the horrible images, at the rotten suit. He clenched Xander's hand tight.

He screamed.

He sobbed.

He slammed his fist against the mirror so hard that it cracked.

"Go on," Xander said quietly. "Just don't hurt yourself. I bought spare mirrors."

Skylar looked at himself and Xander in the cracked mirror, and the wind went out of him. He simply cried.

"I hate what I let them make me. What I let them convince me to make myself." He buried his face in Xander's shoulder. "I don't want to be this anymore."

Xander kissed his temple, stroked his hair. "You aren't this. You were never this. I want to paint you now as I see you—I've done that a million times, but I realized I needed to do this first. To show you what I see other people trying to paint on you first. Because I think you keep trying to cling to this vision instead. Even though I think you've hated this for a long, long time. I wanted you to see it the way I saw it before you saw what I see you *as*. This isn't who you are, what you are. This is the suit they put on you. And yes, let's wash this nonsense away."

He kept Skylar in front of the mirrors as he worked, and he gave him another plate of food—a sandwich this time, and a cup of jasmine tea, along with more water and some fruit. While Skylar ate, Xander took a sponge and wiped his hard work—hours and hours and hours of it—away. Some of it remained, little echoes and smudges, but the lion's share of it was gone. Skylar was glad, but blown away as well.

"All that work, just vanished."

Xander smiled and shrugged. "It was never going to stay. This next one won't either."

"But you didn't even take a photo."

"Did you *want* to remember any of that? Or rather, do you think you can forget it?"

Skylar shuddered. "No."

"This one, I might take a photo of. But probably not. I like the idea of impermanence. That the painting is only for us and this moment. Besides." He smiled at Skylar. "I think we're going to be doing this again."

Skylar smiled back at him. "I think you're right."

This time when Xander began to paint, he used a thick, flat paintbrush, the one he used to prime his canvases. He was doing that now, it turned out—dipping into a vat of what Skylar had thought was white paint, but when it went onto his body, especially as it picked up the colors left over from before, it turned out to be…

"Gray?"

Xander nodded. "Yes. It worked out to be exactly the background color I needed, but...well, I appreciate the other echoes it gives my canvas too."

Skylar had the feeling he was going to be crying again.

He didn't right away. Mostly he marveled at how odd he looked with his body—*whole* body, neck and face and ass and balls and dick and thighs and toes and fingers and every single part of him—painted gray. As if he were a shadow or a ghost. They took another break then because Xander said it had to dry before he could go further. Xander smiled at him a lot now, Skylar noticed. As if it was getting harder for Xander to see him simply as a canvas.

Even though he literally looked like one right now. Even though he wore nothing but a sheet of boring gray. Somehow boring wasn't at all what Xander saw.

He didn't stay that way, though. First, black lines shot up from his feet, all around him—initially Skylar thought they were vines, but soon it became clear they were the trunk and branches of a tree. Then things began to grow on that tree. People, to start. The *Shichifukujin*, in various incarnations and occupations, and then their own seven gods, and the Palace of the Sun. And Fudō Myōō and Xander. Skylar and Xander together, everywhere—working on the anime, lying together in bed, Xander painting him, cooking together, walking together. A section represented their courtship, Skylar luring a cranky Xander out into the light. Then

Xander luring Skylar out of his suit.

A number of places showed Skylar standing innocently, talking to Pamela or someone and Xander watched him, from the shadows.

Skylar laughed a lot in these scenes. He was happy. He was always helping people too—a whole section depicted him playing hero to the art majors as they gazed at him adoringly, and Xander glowered jealously on the sidelines. That made Skylar laugh in real life. There were so many scenes of him helping people. He was Mr. Friendly, according to Xander.

This was such a better painting.

This was how Xander saw him?

This was beautiful.

This is who I want to be instead.

"I love this," Skylar said as Xander cleaned his brush.

"Oh, I'm not done."

Xander got out a small round brush and reached for the pink.

He began to paint delicate, beautiful cherry blossoms all over Skylar's body.

There was writing too—Xander explained each kanji to him, that they meant he was magnificent, sensitive, sensual, artistic, charming, loyal, steadfast—he lost track of the words, because while they were wonderful and the script breathtaking, it was the blossoms that did him in. *He sees me as a cherry tree. A blooming, beautiful cherry tree.*

Skylar sobbed.

"I love you," Skylar cried, trying not to spill tears because Xander was painting cherry blossoms across his face.

"I love you too, my *sakura*."

Skylar had watched enough anime to know that one. "Cherry blossom."

Xander kept painting. "I'm nearly done. Then you can get a look at yourself. I'll bring out the new mirror so you can see everything, all the sides. Do you want a photo too?"

Skylar shut his eyes, shook his head. "No. Because it can't ever match the memory. Nothing will ever be like this moment except for this moment."

Xander put down his brush, removed his apron, and took Skylar's hands in his. "I don't want to overcharge an already emotional day, but I need to tell you…I want all the moments with you, Skylar. Wherever you end up next year, whatever you decide to do, I want to be there with you."

Skylar could barely breathe. He squeezed Xander's hands as tight as he could. "But…you have graduate school."

"The world is full of graduate schools. If I'm good enough, I can get into any of them." His thumbs rubbed the inside of Skylar's wrists. "But there's only one Skylar Stone."

"What if…what if I told you I wanted to be a teacher?" He drew a breath, let it out. "In Japan."

Xander's eyes widened. Then he smiled. "Really? Are you serious? *Sugoi*."

"That's...*wow*, right?"

"Yes. We're going to have to up your language practice—and mine."

Skylar ducked his head. "Well, it's just an idea. And I wouldn't want to put mine over your grad school."

"It's not just an idea. I can tell by the light in your eye. You've been thinking about it and working your way up to admitting you wanted to do that."

"Will it work? I mean, I know Pamela said she knew of ways it could be done, but...does Japan even *want* someone like me? All kinds of people speak English. Probably a lot of people who already know some Japanese. What if I can't learn Japanese? You've taught me some, but not much, and I can't make the alphabet mean anything no matter how I stare at it. What if I can't, ever? What if—"

Xander pressed fingers to his lips. "Hush. First of all, I don't know anything about how many people try to teach English in Japan, but I will say I bet it's competitive. However, I also know *you* are unparalleled at meeting the challenge of that sort of thing. You can be pretty damn charming when you want to be, and I bet you kill at interviews too. But what matters at the end of the day is that you're willing to do the work, especially when it's something you believe in. And I'm here to help you. So is everyone."

Skylar's heart skipped a beat as he asked his next question. "Would you go with me, though? All the way to Japan?"

"All the way to the sun, if that's where you said you

were going." He kissed Skylar's fingertips. "Let me go get you your mirror."

He got the mirror, replacing the cracked one. Then they stood together, the artist and his canvas, and admired the view.

"I'm beautiful," Skylar whispered, clutching Xander's hand.

Xander laced their fingers together. "Yes. You really are."

Chapter Twenty-One

IT HAD BEEN Xander's hope that the body painting would be helpful to Skylar, but he hadn't been prepared for the floodgates it opened.

Skylar slept in his paint that night—it was almost dawn by the time they went to sleep—and though it was going to ruin his sheets, Xander didn't care. He wouldn't even throw them out. Every time he saw the stains, he'd think of that night and remember how incredible it had been. But when he woke, Skylar was already up, and to his dismay, showered. Dressed in what had become his new usual: polos and khaki pants, though since the morning was chilly, he'd added a cardigan. Benzaiten's altar was already lit, and Skylar was drinking his tea and squinting at a recipe book it looked like he'd borrowed from Pamela's stash as he bustled about the kitchen.

"Good morning." He smiled at Xander as he came in, then frowned at the book again. "I think I might need glasses, or contacts, or something."

"You'd look good in glasses." Xander sidled up to him, gently bumping his hip. "What are you making?"

"Omurice. That rice omelet they make in anime all

the time? I thought I'd give it a try. I'll warn you, it may suck, mostly because I don't know what I'm doing."

"Can I help?"

"Please do."

They made the omurice together, and it didn't suck. It was delicious. But to give Skylar the full anime experience, Xander wrote *daisuki da yo* in hiragana and kanji on the top of the omelet in ketchup, and when that proved far too ambitious to write with the nozzle, he got a brush, washed it thoroughly, and *painted* "I really like you" in Japanese onto their food. Skylar was impressed, but Xander couldn't help being his own critic.

"I'd rather have written *ai shiteru*, as it's a stronger statement of affection, but that kanji is tricky enough with a pencil. I'd have never managed with ketchup."

Skylar laughed and kissed him on the cheek.

After they finished, Skylar held Xander's hand and told him all the things he wanted to do, now that he saw himself properly. Now that he, as he put it, was finally free.

"First of all," he began, "I want you to use *Fudō Myōō Comes to Remove Benzaiten's Obstacles* in your show."

Xander blinked. "You…do? But it's so personal, and so obviously you."

"Yes. It's also your best work. I'm proud of it, and you, and of who I am in that painting, of who we were in that moment. I don't want to hide it. Please don't do so on my account. Unless it's too manga for your show."

Xander's heart swelled. It *was* too manga, but fuck if he cared about that. "Okay. I'll use it."

Skylar went on. "I *am* serious about teaching in Japan, but I feel the same way as you, that I don't want to do anything after graduation that doesn't involve you. We need to talk to Pamela about the programs we'd have to apply for, and you need to investigate what this would do to impact your grad school career. If I wait to go, then I wait. We make the decisions based on what's best for the two of us, and we make them together. All right?"

Xander rubbed Skylar's wrist with his thumb. "All right. What's next? I can tell you have a list."

"I do. The next part is complicated, because everything hinges on other parts, but…I'm going to leave Delta Eta Sigma."

"You're sure about this? I mean, I know you are, but it's such a big part of your life, or it was. I can still quote half of that speech about fraternities you gave me."

"That's just it. It *was* a big part of my life. It's changed. Unc is going to stay, but he's disappointed in it. If it doesn't get disbanded before the end of the year, it will be entirely due to his efforts. I don't want to stay and watch that. It's not where I want to spend my life." He lifted Xander's hand, laced their fingers, then took his other hand and did the same. "I want to be here with you."

"I want you here too."

"But here's where it gets complicated. Once I resign and move in here, I need to pay my part of rent and food and so on. Which is easy, until my family finds out what I've done. And as I've told you, soon enough he's going to figure that out anyway."

They had one more week until Skylar *didn't* get an email from the LSAT people. "What happens then? What do you want to do when he finds out?"

Skylar sat up straight, pale and nervous but also resolved. "I'm going to go to my father and tell him everything. That I didn't take the test. That I've left the fraternity, I'm dating a man, and by the way I'm moving to Japan."

"How do you think he'll respond?"

He sighed. "Poorly."

"Do you think he'll disown you or something?"

"I don't think so, but…I really have no idea." He looked almost green, he was so uneasy. "I think it'll be bad, that he'll find a way to make me feel awful, at the very least."

"Would it be easier to go to your mother?"

"Possibly, but she's in France for the next two months. I checked already."

Xander frowned, but before he could say anything more, Skylar captured his hands and squeezed them.

"It's all right. It's going to be rough, but I don't care. I'm going to get through this, tell them what I want to do, who I want to be, who I want to be with. But I do have one request of you, if that's okay."

Xander turned his palm over and squeezed back. "Anything."

"I planned to go to Manhattan to see my father next

weekend. I wanted to know if you would come with me."

"Of course I'll come."

"Thank you." Skylar kissed his hands. "And thank you for yesterday. That was...I don't have words for what that was. Magical. Surreal."

Xander smiled a self-satisfied smile and opened Skylar's hand to kiss the center of his palm. "I agree. I feel like we just leveled up so far past people who have conventional sex I'm going to pity sigh every time I see porn now."

"I'm going to need a moment alone every time you get out your brushes." He touched Xander's face, his own countenance full of love. "You're right. I'm so glad those assholes destroyed your mural."

"Sometimes we sacrifice things to the gods, our payment a surrender for bounty yet to come."

Skylar pressed his lips to Xander's forehead. "I don't know what I surrendered to get you. But I'd give it up a thousand times more, no questions asked."

That was the extent of Skylar's revelations for the moment, though there were a few more minor ripples—in the next two weeks he pulled back on some of his organizations, reorganizing some of his business focuses, and arranging to audit the Japanese course for the rest of the semester since it was too late to take it officially as a class. Ms. Mary was devastated he was leaving the fraternity but was mollified when he promised to visit her, though not on the house grounds. The fraternity itself didn't much care, was mostly annoyed with him.

Their reaction stung Skylar and enraged Unc. "They think they fucking own him," he growled to Xander as they worked in the *Lucky 7* office one afternoon. "That's why they're pissed. They lost their Silver Stone. Never mind that the man is still there. But they don't want *him*. They never did."

Xander had known this all along, but apparently Unc hadn't been prepared for this. Xander worried where else he'd be right. "How do you think this is going to go down with his father?"

"Terrible. Like the shit with the Greeks but on steroids."

Fuck. Xander ran a hand through his hair, debating whether he should even ask his next question, then decided, screw it. "What's Leighton Stone like? As a person, I mean."

Unc considered the question. "He's brusque. Doesn't take any shit. I think he came out of the womb a lawyer. He's always negotiating."

"It doesn't sound like he was much of a father to Skylar."

Unc's laugh was bitter. "Yeah, every time I think my old man is distant, I look at Sky and remind myself it could be worse. If it weren't for Stone's executive assistant deciding someone should parent Skylar, he'd probably be one of those horrible sociopaths with a trust fund."

That would be Ellen. Xander made a mental note to find out if the woman liked art and if so, he would paint her as much as she could put on her walls. "I can't get over how neither one of his parents pay any attention to him—and that they *never* have. I feel isolated from my family now, but I at least have memories of my mother's affection."

"Yeah, and what's weird is his dad's the one who gives him the most, and he's *nothing* like Leighton. Not in looks, habits, or behavior. I met his mother once, and she's pretty much like Skylar except she's a little cold-hearted and inconsistent. Skylar never has any time for her, though. He's always been after his father, and it's only his father that reached back. Except I think his dad only wants a Skylar doll to install in his firm."

The idea made Xander want to throw up. "Will Skylar's father disown him if he doesn't fall into line?"

"Nah. But he'll guilt him like fuck. Shout at him. Threaten to cut off his allowance. He might do that, for a bit. Sky won't care, though. And I'll fund him as much as I can if it comes to it. Pamela will let him live rent-free, she's already said."

"He's already looking for a part-time job. He's got his bases covered. And it's not like they can take back his tuition."

"Wouldn't do that. So it's all moot. But they can make him feel like shit."

Xander grimaced. "I don't know that I'm going to be much good at this meeting. This is my nightmare setup, facing down an asshole father. I'm going to do my best, but damn. It's not like I'm great with my own."

Unc rubbed his chin. "Well, what if we pulled another deal like when we went to Albany? What if the seven-god posse and Fudō Myōō all went together?"

"What, we all storm his office? God, that sounds like a cheesy 90s after-school special."

Unc shrugged. "I mean, why not?"

But Skylar nixed the idea when they brought it to him. "I appreciate the sentiment, but you all have other obligations. I feel bad enough I'm pulling Xander out of class."

"We don't mind, honestly," Jacob insisted, and everyone nodded in agreement.

Xander read the expression on his boyfriend's face, realized Skylar wanted the two of them to go *alone*, and interceded. "It's okay. We'll be all right, the two of us."

Pamela, not missing a beat, backed him up. "Very well. I expect you'll keep us informed?"

They promised they would, and so Friday, two weeks after Skylar should have received his scores, they got on the train and rode all the way into Manhattan to have a showdown at Leighton Stone's firm.

"Has he contacted you at all, since that last time?" Xander asked as they rode. He'd deliberately avoided talking about the matter too much before, trying to give Skylar space because it seemed to be what he wanted, but there wasn't any point putting off talking about the subject now.

Skylar shook his head. He was rigid with nerves, but his jaw was set with determination as well. "I talked to Ellen about it when I set up this appointment. She knows I didn't take the test." He blushed. "She knows about you as well. She says she's looking forward to meeting you."

Xander blushed too. "Oh. That's nice." He cleared his throat. "I'm glad your dad hasn't been pressuring you, though I'm surprised. I thought he'd want to know the score right away."

Skylar's hands closed into fists on his legs, and he stared at the seat ahead of him. "He probably assumes I did poorly and that I'm coming to explain why. I doubt he expects to hear I didn't take it at all. He won't be pleased."

Xander put his hand over Skylar's.

Skylar turned his palm over, lacing his fingers through Xander's.

They went to a tall, gleaming-gold office building just off Wall Street, where the doorman knew Skylar on sight and ushered him to an elevator and the thirty-seventh floor.

The entire floor was a law firm. Men and women rushed around in suits, speaking in hushed tones, carrying briefcases and armfuls of files, leaning in to speak to one another, holding cell phones, chuckling with colleagues as they sauntered past. Interns looked harried as they rushed past, toting trays of coffee.

This was the place Skylar had been meant to work. The thought filled Xander with horror. It was death. It was cold and unfeeling. It was devoid of color and life. It was power and drive and cunning and opportunity and money and everything Skylar, the true Skylar, was not. It was the suit Xander had painted, except it would never, ever wash off.

The receptionist had someone lead them into a deeper part of the office, down a maze of halls to another reception area, where a black woman in a sharp navy suit and sparkling gold jewelry rose to greet Skylar with a warm smile.

"Well, look what the cat dragged in." She hugged Skylar close, closing her eyes as the embrace lingered. When she drew back, she kept her hands on his shoulders and ran her gaze up and down him, clucking her tongue. "You're not eating enough, and you've been too stressed." When Skylar tried to give her a *ting* smile, she shook a finger at him. "Don't you try and fool me, child. I raised you. I know when you're treating yourself poorly."

"Yes, ma'am." Skylar's voice was meek, but warm. Xander's heart melted, watching the pair. He'd never seen Skylar light up like this. He looked like he'd love nothing more than to be lectured by Ellen all day long.

Ellen raised an eyebrow and nodded at Xander as she released Skylar. "Introduce me to your friend, now."

Skylar startled. "Oh, I'm so sorry. I'm forgetting my manners." He turned his body and gestured between Xander and Ellen, but Xander could see Skylar's hand shaking. "Xander, this is Ellen Mansfield, my father's executive assistant. Ellen, this is Xander Fairchild, my—boyfriend."

Xander smiled wide and extended his hand to Ellen. He'd worn his suit coat and a button-down shirt, but they weren't as fitted as Skylar's, and they limited his arm movement, so he had to lean in to extend his reach. "It's a pleasure to meet you, Ms. Mansfield."

She smiled warmly and accepted his handshake. "Please call me Ellen. And it's a pleasure to meet you too. I've heard so much about you."

"I've heard a great deal about you as well. It's an honor to make your acquaintance."

"Well, someone raised you right." Ellen gave him a tight nod of approval as she released his hand. "Did the two of you have a good trip down?"

They chatted briefly, about their train ride, about Xander's upcoming show, about the weather in Takake-to, about Ellen's family, everything except for the LSAT and Skylar's reason for coming into the city in the first place. Finally, however, Ellen curtailed the small talk and brought them around to the subject of Leighton Stone.

"He's finishing up a meeting, which I'm hoping won't take much longer. The two of you can have a seat over there in the waiting area and make yourselves at home. I'll send someone over to get you two something to drink while you wait."

Xander didn't take Skylar's hand, but he kept a hand behind his elbow as he ushered him to the chairs beside a bank of windows. When Skylar went to the glass instead of sitting, Xander stood beside him.

"Breathe," he said.

Skylar released the air in his lungs in a ragged huff and stared at the buildings below. "This is going to be a disaster. I barely managed to introduce you to Ellen, and she was a cakewalk. How am I going to survive *him*?"

Xander stepped enough behind Skylar that he could put a hand on the middle of his back and trace reassuring circles. "You're going to be great. Form your new straight line. Out of this building, out of his version of your life, and into your own."

Skylar sighed again, but this time Xander thought he heard some determination mixed in with the fear.

A male assistant came and asked if they wanted anything to drink. Skylar said no, but Xander asked for water, and when the man came back with it, Xander encouraged Skylar to sip it. They sat there for nearly half an hour, which Xander was sure was some kind of power play on Leighton Stone's part, but Xander did everything he could to keep his boyfriend calm.

Then, at last, Ellen told Skylar his father would see him now.

Xander gave Skylar's hand one last squeeze, and off they went.

The office she led them into was huge, almost the size of Xander's entire apartment, which was weird because there wasn't much in it. There was a seating area, a small conference table, bookshelves and filing cabinets, and of course Leighton's desk, but mostly there was cold, empty space, and windows. It had a great view of the city, and the furniture was incredibly comfortable, but all Xander saw was wealth, power, and emptiness.

He also saw Leighton Stone.

The man looked nothing like Skylar. Nothing at all. Xander had thought this when he'd seen the photo of Skylar's parents, but when he saw the man in person, the force of *how much* Skylar didn't look like his father was arresting. Leighton Stone was shorter than Skylar by at least four inches. His hair was dark too—mostly gray now, but the color remaining told Xander Leighton's natural color was more the color of Xander's than Skylar's. It was thick and wiry too, unlike Skylar's more wispy, fine hair.

The contrasts went on and on. Leighton's nose was flat and wide where Skylar's was long and narrow. Leighton's eyes were brown and shaped differently than Skylar's. His ears were a different shape. His fingers were stubbier, his hands smaller. He even stood differently. The only similarity Leighton had to Skylar was the suit he wore.

This was Skylar's father?

Leighton Stone had been standing at the window as they entered, but after glancing at them and waving them in with a flattening of the lips, he sat at his desk. "Come in. I assume, since you made a point of coming all the way here, what you have to tell me isn't good." He sighed, but he also cast a critical glance at Xander, assessing him and his cheap suit as if he were deciding which recycling bin to send him to.

Xander could feel Skylar tensing, but he knew he couldn't touch him, that drawing attention to their relationship in front of Skylar's father would only make matters worse. He leaned in close to Skylar instead, close enough so he could whisper without Leighton overhearing.

"New straight line," he said, then stepped to the side again and did everything he could to telegraph strength to his boyfriend.

Skylar squared his shoulders. "I wanted to meet with you personally to discuss the LSAT. I wanted also to talk to you about my future and to introduce you to Xander."

Leighton leaned back in his chair and steepled his fingers. He cut another glance at Xander, this one decidedly cutting, but he said nothing to him, keeping his focus on Skylar. "What were your results?"

For a moment Skylar's eyes fluttered closed, and when he opened them, they were almost glazed. "I…didn't take the LSAT."

Leighton lowered his hands, his cool expression evaporating as he leaned forward. "You *what*?"

"I didn't take the test." Skylar's resolve had melted, and he was floating on his fear now, like a child who knew the devil was coming for them. "I got to the center and I panicked, and I didn't take the test."

"For *Christ's sake*." Leighton pushed at the stack of papers in front of him and sat back in his chair.

Skylar began to shake. "I meant to take it, you see, but as I arrived I realized it wasn't what I wanted—"

Leighton regarded his son incredulously. "Wasn't *what you wanted*?"

If Xander went to hell, this would be his sentence, he decided, watching Leighton Stone strip pieces off his boyfriend, one by one. Skylar kept clenching and unclenching his fists, unable to find his footing in the conversation. “Please—let me explain. I want—I need to do something different with…I mean, I *am* someone different than—”

“What you *are*?” Leighton made a *tsk* noise and wiped his hand over his mouth as he shook his head. “I should have installed you somewhere closer, where I could have kept a better eye on you. If only you’d have gotten into Yale in the first place, we wouldn’t have had to go through all these hoops. This is my fault, for not taking enough responsibility, for leaving things to Ellen because she’s so capable. I’ll make some calls, see what I can do.”

Skylar was wrecked now, wringing his hands, unable to meet his father’s gaze. “Please, sir—I don’t want to go into law, I want—”

“What you *want*?” Leighton all but sneered at Skylar, his gaze far too cold for a father. He still hadn’t risen, but he seemed to tower over his son all the same. “This isn’t about what you want. You’re a Stone. You’re going to behave in accordance with the honor and dignity I’ve given the name. You’re going to take that test. You’re going to the best law school I can bribe you into. Then you’re going to smile that pretty smile and win us the clients we need. I haven’t put all this effort into you for nothing.”

“He’s not here for your use.”

The words were out of Xander’s mouth before he could stop them. Skylar didn’t move, still frozen in place, but Leighton's gaze shifted to Xander.

Xander went cold as the full force of that disdain turned on him. Leighton Stone's smile had no *ting* whatsoever, only the sharp edges of a thousand knives.

"Ah, yes. You must be the one from the telephone. And you are what to Skylar?"

Xander darted a glance to his right, but Skylar was still immobile. Xander took a leap. "I'm his boyfriend."

Skylar didn't wince, exactly—it was more of a flinch, and the reason why was evident as Leighton Stone's countenance turned stormy. "You're *what*?"

Skylar looked ready to pass out. Xander decided this was his show now. He did his best to forge ahead to face the dragon. "I'm his boyfriend. We've been dating since—" He faltered, unsure of when to count the actual onset of their courtship.

"*Dating.* You've been dating my son. Well, that explains quite a bit, doesn't it?" Leighton turned away from Xander, as if he couldn't so much as see him any longer. All his focus was for Skylar now. "You aren't dating anyone. You're taking the test and applying to Yale. End of discussion."

This, finally, unfroze Skylar. "*Please*, you need—"

"You've had your rebellion. I assume this was to get my attention? Now you have it. I'll speak to the house mother at the fraternity—"

"I left the fraternity. I'm living with Xander."

Leighton rose, looming over his desk. He looked so murderous Skylar stepped back, quaking again, but Xander stepped forward, arms spread out in defense, his blood pumping like fire through his veins as he faced his enemy down.

"Jesus, will you *stop*? He's trying to talk to you, can't you understand that? He wants to tell you about his future, what he wants to do with his life, and you won't even let him speak—"

Leighton jammed a stubby finger in Xander's face. "Stay out of this, boy. None of this is your business."

Xander didn't back down. In fact, he leaned in. "It's absolutely my business. Skylar's happiness is my business. Why isn't it yours? How can you be like this with your own son?" He shook his head, pulse thumping in his ears. "Christ, you're about as bad as my stepfath—"

Xander froze.

No.

No, that couldn't be.

But it was as if Leighton read the thought as it passed over his mind, and for a split second as their gazes met, the glint in the man's eye confirmed the terrible thought that had just run through Xander's mind.

It's almost as if you aren't his father at all.

Xander couldn't breathe.

"Step aside, boy," Leighton commanded him.

Too rocked by the revelation he'd had, Xander complied.

Leighton turned his focus to Skylar once more. His gaze was flinty, his voice as cold as a December wind. "You will return to your fraternity. You will take the

LSAT. You will enter Yale Law. And you will end your relationship with this man." He sat at his desk again and began shuffling paper. "Go back to school. I have work to do."

Xander stared at Skylar, waiting for a cue. His heartbeat rang in his ears, doubt and confusion tripping over one another in his mind. When Skylar meekly left the room, head bowed, Xander followed, thoughts swirling.

Was it true? Had Leighton actually confirmed in that glance that he wasn't Skylar's father? Had it been a trick to shut him up?

Oh, but it fits so well. Everything about it fits so well.

When Ellen saw them, she ushered them into a conference room. She got them tea and cookies, and after a few whispered words to her staff, she closed the door and sat with them, rubbing Skylar's shoulder as she tried to get the story out of him of what had happened. Eventually Skylar stammered out a rough rehash, his voice sounding slightly teary. All through it, however, Xander sat quietly, not drinking his tea, almost too shell-shocked to move. When Ellen touched his hand, he startled, nearly falling out of his chair.

She regarded him with concern. "Hon, are you all right?"

Xander didn't mean to do it. He never would have, normally, but he was staring at her, and she was so kind, and after the cold hollow that was Leighton, with the weight of his potential discovery, he didn't think. He simply tried to unload it. "Leighton—he can't be. He can't be Skylar's father."

Ellen went still, her expression one of shock—and sadness.

Xander wilted.

Skylar turned to the two of them, blinking. "What?"

"Never you mind, child." Ellen's hard gaze on Xander was a reprimand, an order to keep quiet.

Skylar wasn't having it. "No, what did you say, Xander? What did you mean, my father can't be my father?"

Xander shifted his focus from Ellen to his boyfriend. Skylar sat with the windows at his back, where the afternoon sun was setting, but with the tinted windows, it didn't get through. *Everything about this office is sterile.* Xander wanted to throw a chair through the glass and let real air, real sun inside. To gather Skylar in his arms and sail with him out of this nightmare back to Takaketo.

Where they belonged.

Despite the tinted windows, the sun rose on Xander's heart, showing him the way to his answer.

He took Skylar's hand, held it tightly. "The man in the other room has no hold over you."

Skylar looked ready to cry. "Xander, he's my *father.*"

Xander drew a breath, felt the fire of rightness burning inside him, saw the Palace of the Sun shining in the morning light inside his mind's eye. "No, Skylar. He isn't."

Skylar stared at him. "What?" He turned to Ellen. "What is he saying?"

Ellen took his hand. She looked older, sadder. At

first Xander thought she would deny it, but after what appeared to be some kind of internal struggle, she shook her head with a heavy sigh. "What your boyfriend says is the truth, though I don't know how he figured it out. Leighton Stone *is* your father. But he's your adoptive parent, not your biological one."

Skylar looked back and forth between the two of them. Panicking. "I don't understand."

Ellen never let go of his hand. "Your mother was pregnant when they met. Some French tutor of hers. He had dreams no grander than being a poet, and she had higher ideals. She didn't want an abortion, and she didn't want to give you up. Your father liked the idea of a pretty society wife, and they made an arrangement. But your mother tired of playing house and chased her own dreams, which is when I came into your life."

Skylar looked poleaxed. "So he's not my father."

Ellen shook her hand, clasping his hand with both of hers now. "He *is* your father. He adopted you. He's taken better care of you than your mother."

Xander wasn't having any of this. "No, Ellen. *You* have."

Skylar's tears ran down his cheeks. "Why didn't anyone tell me?"

Ellen looked so tired. "That was your father's choice. He wanted you to believe you were his son in every way possible. He does love you. No matter what else you believe, believe that."

The façade was starting to crack around Skylar now. When he spoke, his voice was lost, and sad. "Does he love me, or the Skylar he wants me to be?"

Ellen sighed, "Oh, honey."

Xander picked up his boyfriend's other hand, giving him a gentle kiss with his thumb. "I can't say how much he sees the real you, but I bet Ellen's right. He does love you, in his own way. You know I understand about parents who aren't there for you, who don't see you for who you are. What I can also tell you about is that sometimes you have to let go of your parents, even though it hurts. Both the ones who gave birth to you and the ones who stepped in for them. You can't keep chasing down their approval. *You* have to be the one who decides what your life is worth, and if they don't like what you're doing with your life, you have to let them go. Even if it hurts."

Skylar stared at Xander, tears still falling. Still lost, still trapped behind the same wall of glass he'd been in since he entered the law offices. A wall of fear—fear of failure, fear of rejection, fear of being left behind. Fear of being all alone.

Oh, how Xander understood that terror.

Lacing his fingers through Skylar's, Xander leaned in and pressed against the glass. "Just remember. No matter what happens with your father, you aren't alone. You have everyone at the Palace. You have Ellen and her family. And you have me—for as long as you want to have me."

Skylar's wall of glass shattered. With a sob, he let go of Ellen and pulled Xander into a tight embrace.

Shutting his eyes, Xander wrapped his arms around

his boyfriend and held him right back.

EVERYONE KEPT ASKING Skylar if he was all right.

Xander gave him space on the train ride back, only holding his hand, but when they got back to the Palace of the Sun, everyone came up to Skylar looking at him as if he'd come back from war. He escaped to the apartment, where he cocooned himself in bed with Hiromu and Hokusai, but when the loneliness was too much and he wandered down to find Xander, everyone looked at him with even sadder expressions, and Skylar knew they knew everything now.

Which was good, because he didn't want to have to tell them that his father wasn't his father. That his whole life had been a lie.

For days, he wandered like a zombie, replaying every scene from his life, trying to find clues that would have given away the secret if he'd been trying to look. He couldn't find anything. He still didn't understand how Xander had figured it out so easily, so eventually he asked.

Xander looked sad, and slightly embarrassed. "You don't look alike. At all."

Well that was a ridiculous reason. "All kinds of people don't look like their parents."

"No, that's not true. I'm a portrait artist. I look at the details of faces. I should have been able to see something similar, and I found nothing. But that wasn't the only thing, really. It was more…the way he behaved.

He reminded me of my stepfather. The way he regarded you wasn't like a father. I mean, it's not like my birth father is any good either. But there was something so familiar about it. And then I said it, and he looked at me, and I knew I was right. Then I said as much to Ellen, and I knew."

Skylar spent a lot of time on the phone with Ellen too—her home phone, not her line at the law office. She told him more about how his parents had come together, how he'd been adopted by his father, and why she'd taken such an interest in him.

"You were such a sweet little boy, and all you wanted was love. It broke my heart to see you left alone like you were."

This alarmed Skylar. "They left me alone?"

"Not literally, no. You had nannies and babysitters and *au pairs* and everything a rich little boy could want, except the thing you wanted most. Someone to hold you on their lap and read you stories and tell you how to be a good boy. So that's what I did, and what I taught my girls to do. You turned out all right, I like to think."

Skylar shut his eyes, basking in the praise. "Thank you, Ellen."

She told him about his birth father too, as much as she knew. His first name was Charlie, but she didn't know his last name. He'd graduated and moved on from his mother's college, but after that he'd practically disappeared. She said she'd do some hunting to help him find out more. She answered every question Skylar put to her, patiently, kindly. She even looked up his father—Leighton's—blood type when he asked to know what it was.

"He's type O," he told Xander one night as they lay in bed together. "If I'd have known that, I might have figured it out sooner. I can't have a type O parent, if I'm type AB."

"Well, technically you can—there's precedent, though it's rare." Xander sighed. "But yes. If you were looking for more evidence he's not your birth parent, which I suspect you were, you have it."

Skylar didn't know what he was looking for anymore. He *was* waiting for the other shoe to drop from Manhattan, because he hadn't gone back to the fraternity and he hadn't broken up with Xander, and at some point he assumed his father—Leighton—would have something to say about this. Ellen said she would speak to him about it, but Skylar knew there was only so much she could do, and at the end of the day she wanted to keep her job, that she *needed* to, with a daughter still in college and a wedding to plan.

He stumbled through the next week in a haze—he attended class, but he didn't take notes, and he actively avoided engaging with people in the halls. After his phone ID told him his father was calling, he panicked and started leaving it in the apartment so he didn't have to answer it.

The others did their best to help. They tried to get him to eat, to go on walks, to laugh. Skylar wasn't much company, though, even when he was with himself. He couldn't stop worrying. Wondering. Thinking.

He wondered where Charlie the French tutor was now. Had he married someone else? Did he know he had a son? Would *he* be excited to hear that Skylar had found someone he loved, that he knew, at last, what his dream for his life should be? Or would he never have stayed with his mother even if she had tried to make it work? Had his mother, in the end, truly chosen the best path for herself, but this path simply hadn't been the best one for her son? Of course, she had yet to so much as call him after his father's revelation. Did she know? Did she even care?

Had she ever cared about him?

What was his birth father's last name?

What should his last name have been, instead of Stone?

Where do I belong now?

With Xander—that he knew, that truth enfolded him every night, literally, as Xander wrapped his arms around him, teased him with his paintbrushes, bullied him into eating, nagged him forward through each day. Created with him. They still worked on *Hotay & Moo*, but they lay twined together and whispered of other stories they could make too. Sometimes Xander would lean over to reach for his sketchbook, roughing out ideas.

Sometimes Skylar invented wild story concepts just to see if he could get Xander to sketch them.

Skylar kept waiting for his father to make his next move, to try harder to bring him to heel. He didn't know yet what he'd do when that happened. Zelda was eager for it; they wanted Leighton to come for Skylar so they could eviscerate him. Unc devised amateur legal scenarios and promised to share his trust fund with him when it kicked in at twenty-five. Jacob and Cory huddled together envisioning business schemes, certain that they could come up with something the four of them—Jacob, Cory, Xander, and Skylar—could do to keep them all solvent enough that parents wouldn't matter.

Pamela didn't say much, but whenever Skylar got too nervous, she told him not to worry, that his father didn't scare her, and she'd take care of him as long as he needed a parent to help him through.

Skylar appreciated their help. In the end, though, he knew ultimately he had to walk through this moment alone, at least inside his heart. Walking was, largely, what he did. He went out a lot in the evening, in the state park. Sometimes he went in the morning instead, wandering the trails until he was too tired to move or his mind unclouded.

One morning in late October, three weeks before Xander's BFA show, he woke up before the sun rose, unable to go back to sleep, and he had the most powerful urge in the world to start walking. Normally he stuck to the main trails so he didn't get lost, but that morning the trails were full of fog, and as he came over the hill, the first rays of sun were creeping over the horizon, just a faint glow, and the woods he passed were full of soft, rolling mist that beckoned to him. Even though he was more likely to get lost today than ever, he couldn't turn away.

He started through the trees, heading toward the sun.

He didn't know where he walked, only that he felt he was walking somewhere, that something led him. *Toward the sun.* He kept going, moving faster and faster, his feet soaked from dew, caked with mud. He had to ford a stream, the same one, he thought, he'd waded through the day he'd cut his leg, and he shivered with cold and damp as he huffed up the ridge.

The ridge overlooking a valley with a great rock in the center of it.

Skylar cleared the crest just as the sun reached the horizon, streaming rays of gold across the valley, into his face, into the crack in the great, weathered rock that stood before him. This wasn't Xander's ridge—it was someplace new, somewhere Skylar had never been before. The rock was *huge*, something no human had put there, something which had stood there long, long before any white man had deigned to defile the state of New York. It was a rock which, when he looked around, stood sentry over what he knew from his history lessons were Native American burial mounds.

It was a rock which, sometime in the last hundred years or so, someone had quietly turned into a shrine.

He could see the sacred objects from where he stood. A jar, a mirror—there were a few other pieces of what should have been an altar tucked beneath the ledge, but time and the elements had taken them away. Even without them, though, Skylar thought he could have felt the presence of the god, the *kami* here. Certainly the indigenous residents of the area had—they'd buried their ancestors around it. And after all this time, tucked into the woods, the god carried on.

Skylar fell to his knees. Clapped his hands twice, bowed his head, shut his eyes, facing the god and the sun.

"I don't know what to do." His voice was soft, quiet, but it carried on the wind, lifted into the trees, nestled in the leaves. "I want to move forward. But I feel like no matter what I do, I keep getting tied down." He opened his eyes, lowered his hands, and stared at the *kami*. "I try to see myself as Xander sees me. I don't want to follow my parents' path. Especially since they, not together, aren't truly my parents. They raised me on false pretenses. They never saw me. They never let me see myself. How can I do that? How can I keep from letting their vision cloud mine? How do I replace what they took from me? I try, and every time I just get pulled back. I don't want to fail anymore. I want to stand before my father—the man who played that role—and show him who I am. But I don't think I have the strength."

The sun hit him, and he turned to it, opening his arms, tears on his face.

"Please help me," he whispered. "Please, please help."

He wasn't sure what god was listening at that point. But there in the glade, with the god and the ancestors of those who had lived in Takaketo before him, he knew one thing for certain.

Someone heard him.

Chapter Twenty-Two

XANDER'S SHOW WAS all set to go. And he felt fine about it.

Which was driving him crazy.

He didn't want to feel *fine* about it, which was ironic, because as little as seven months ago, he'd have settled for *fairly adequate.* His advisor was over the moon with his promotion, his theme, his prepared works. "You have some real promise in your oils. Have you given thought to where you'll be applying for your graduate work?"

No. No, Xander had not. And he hated all the oils he'd submitted. He'd done the last five landscapes with his teeth gritted, feeling like he was filling in the numbers. When those were his advisor's favorite, he wanted more than anything to cover them with primer and start over.

Why was he so put out by it, he wanted to know? He didn't give a fuck about the show. He just needed the damn grade. Get the check mark and move on. He didn't have to do another oil painting if he didn't want to. Didn't have to go to grad school at all. He literally had to stand in a room and breathe while people told him he'd done a good job, get graded, and go home. He didn't even have to dress up. Artists could be moody. It was almost assumed.

So what was up his butt, making him so crabby? He had no idea. All he knew was his work made him pissed off.

He wanted to talk to Skylar about it, but he didn't know how to phrase it, and anyway, poor Skylar was too far in his own head at the moment. Xander thought several times maybe sharing his shit would distract him, but every time he tried to bring it up, it felt wrong. So he stayed quiet and sulked in silence, waiting for November 15 to arrive so he could get this shit over with.

While he marked time, he took care of Skylar, and there was plenty of caretaking to do. Skylar was starting to engage a little more, but he was still fragile. Xander had gotten him to use the phone again, or rather, he was using Xander's old burner phone, the horrible flip one, which meant he swore a lot whenever he texted, but Skylar barely did that these days. He said he liked the break from social media, liked the quiet of knowing the only people who were going to text him would be the *Lucky 7* crew.

Xander, drowning in the weight of his preshow social media, tried not to be jealous.

They made dinner and breakfast together every day, and met for lunch on the hospital hill whenever they could. They almost had the second edition of *Hotay & Moo* ready to hand off to the rest of the staff to wrangle, and they'd started working on their own manga, Skylar's story about a god who fell from the sky into the wrong land and lost his memory, couldn't use his powers, didn't know he was a god, and had to find his way back to his people and his identity.

He was so sad, though. Whenever he caught Skylar alone, Xander could see the sadness coming off him in waves. He wanted to take it away. He *needed* to take it away. But it wasn't his to remove. He'd tried everything he knew how to do—he'd literally painted on the man—and there was nothing left. He could only stand beside him and be patient.

But God, it was killing him, this plodding along, not being able to give him anything more.

Then two weeks before Xander's BFA show, his mother called to tell him she wasn't going to be able to come.

"I want to come, I really do, and I'd planned to, but it turns out I can't get away. I'm sorry, honey."

Xander was in the kitchen, making Skylar a cup of tea when she called. Skylar was in the bedroom, taking a nap. The sun shone through the window, landing on Benzaiten's altar, giving a gloss to the surface of the cup of jasmine tea sitting beside the candle burning silently for the goddess. Xander stared at the flame, trying to wall himself off, to tell himself it didn't matter, he didn't care, he didn't need her, it didn't matter if she was there or not.

But there was a crack in his wall now. Several cracks, one of them huge and Skylar shaped, and six others of smaller size but no less damaging in moments like this. He couldn't shut the pain out, not this time.

It hurts, he whispered to Benzaiten. *It hurts when she chooses them over me.*

His mother spoke again, sounding strained. "I'm really sorry."

Xander shut his eyes. He'd spent months watching Skylar angst over his LSAT and his family, and now Skylar was reeling from realizing his whole life had been a lie. Xander acknowledged he wasn't much different. His lie was more subtle, but it was there all the same.

You don't ask me to be someone I'm not, but you look right at me and let me bleed alone. And it hurts.

It hurts when you look right at me and choose not to see me.

There was real pain in his mother's voice now, and he suspected she was crying too. "Honey, it's not that I don't care. I know your art is important to you."

He laughed, a bitter sound that caught on the edge of his tears. Oh, she knew, did she? *Maybe you care, but not as much as you do about them.* He drew another breath, a steadying one. He saw Skylar's keys on the counter, and he closed his hand over the *Shichifukujin* keychain for support.

"Yes, it is important to me. It's the only reason I can keep going, some days. It's the thing that got me through being bullied in high school. It's been my only companion through most of college, where I've been so socially isolated I didn't believe I had any friends, not until someone taught me how to see them. Which, I suppose I should tell you. I've gotten close to one of those friends, and because of him, I've made some important decisions about my future. In fact, I'm probably leaving the country."

There was a pause. "What?"

He wished it felt good to hear her shock. It didn't. "I'm hoping to teach English in Japan. My boyfriend and I are both going after graduation, if we're accepted."

Pamela had given them the application for an organization she had connections with, and they'd filled it out. They were both laying not only tea but sake for Benzaiten every night. And they'd started setting some out at the statue of Tenjin, the god of learning, where he sat in the *Lucky 7* offices too. Not that this made it a sure bet or anything, but Xander didn't figure it would hurt.

"But why? Why do you need to leave the country? I thought you were going to graduate school?"

"Because it's where my boyfriend wants to go, and he's my family." The words felt so right to say, and he smiled, an ease settling over him. He was still sad, he still hurt, but he could forgive her now. "It's fine that you don't come. I have friends and family here. They'll be there for me."

"*Xander—*"

"Bye, Mom. Love you."

He hung up the phone—and turned it off.

He couldn't leave it off for long, though, because he was deep in the throes of the damn promotion that had thrust him together with Skylar in the first place. They'd fixed it, with some help from the rest of the *Lucky 7* staff, making it more representative of Xander's true self, but he still had to be present, responding to at-replies, posting teasers of his images, reminding people of his upcoming show.

The show he felt was wrong, that he hated more with every hour of every day.

When his phone rang the next day and he saw the Pennsylvania area code, he braced himself and answered, sure it was his mother. He assumed she was going to explain again why she couldn't come, and he was ready to assure her once more it was fine.

It wasn't his mother, however. It was his stepfather.

"What the hell do you think you're doing?"

Xander blinked at the wall, not sure how to respond. "Nick?" was all he could say in the end.

Nick never called him. Had never called him, ever, not even to tell him he was going to be late picking him up from school, because he'd never done anything like that. Nick always delegated "dealing with Xander" to his wife.

Why in the world was he calling now?

"I'm done putting up with your crap." Nick's gruff voice rumbled through the phone, sandpaper against Xander's ear. "You hear me? I'm done. Kirsten may be willing to put up with your whining and carrying on, but I've had enough for ten lifetimes. You want to behave like a fucking sissy, you can do it on your dime."

Wait. "Um, what?" Xander shifted his grip on the phone. "Hold on, what are you—?"

"I'm cutting you off. Whatever money you have in the bank is what you're living on until you make your own wages. End of discussion."

Xander staggered into the kitchen counter, gripping the edge to stay upright. "What—you can't do that, it's *November—*"

"I can do whatever the hell I want with my damn money. Kirsten's been crying ever since she got off the phone with you. She's always crying over you. You're always in the damn way. So either fix whatever you just did, or I'm removing you from the fucking equation."

Xander couldn't believe this. "I didn't do anything. I told her it was fine that she couldn't come to my show."

"*Jesus.* Who the hell cares about your fucking show?"

I care about it. And I wanted to think she did too. But Xander cared a lot about being able to pay his rent too. He felt as if he were underwater. "I wanted her to come, but she said it wouldn't work out."

"Yeah, you know what's not going to work out? This whole bullshit art career you think you're going to have."

Xander caught the slur in his stepfather's words and realized Nick had been drinking. Now he *really* didn't know how to handle this. He decided to say nothing.

Nick filled the silence. "You're not going to get any kind of a job, and you're going to end up back here, and I'm going to have to pay for your ass. I never wanted to pay for this fucking art shit, and I sure as hell don't give a fuck about your show. So it's done. You figure out how to pay for the rest. Good luck."

Nick hung up.

Xander tossed the phone across the counter, afraid he was going to be sick.

Skylar was still in class, and no one else was home from class yet either, though Pamela's car was in the drive. Xander's first instinct was to bottle up, to hide from everyone. But the truth was he couldn't afford to. Literally.

He'd spent almost all his money on the body painting. He wasn't going to be able to pay his bills for December. For the rest of the *year*.

He paced his apartment until he drove his cats crazy, then went downstairs, ready to face the music, or at least Pamela. Except by the time he got down there, she'd left to run errands. So he paced her front porch instead, worrying himself into a pretzel, trying to figure out how to explain to her he was completely broke except for whatever jobs she gave him from now until he graduated.

God*damn* fucking Nick.

He was still pacing when the car came up the drive—he thought it was Pamela at first, or maybe Skylar, but as the car got closer he realized he didn't recognize it at all. It was some kind of sleek black number, a BMW, and when it parked near the top of the drive, two people got out that he didn't know. Two men, both white, clean-cut and clean-shaven.

Both of them wearing suits.

The taller one took off his sunglasses as he approached, smiling the fakest fucking smile Xander had ever seen. "Hello there. Would you happen to be Xander Fairchild?"

Xander went to the edge of the stairs but didn't descend. What the shit was this? He glared at them. "Who the hell are you?"

The tall one smiled wider as the other suit pulled out a tablet and began to tap unsmilingly into it. "So you *are* Mr. Fairchild?"

"Yes." Xander crossed his arms over his chest. "Who the hell are you?"

The tall suit came up enough stairs to stick out his hand. "Edward Preston. I'm with Carslie, Waters, and Stone, Attorneys at Law. Would it be all right if I came inside and asked you a few questions?"

Jesus fuck, these were Skylar's dad's suits. "No, we can talk right here."

The plastic smile strained a little, but mostly held in place. "Very well. I won't take up much of your valuable time. But on behalf of Mr. Stone—Mr. Leighton Stone, that is—I'd like to confirm…" The smile stretched back into full, grotesque glory. "What exactly is your relationship with Skylar Stone?"

Oh, if this fucker wasn't a lawyer, Xander would punch him in the mouth. But God knew he couldn't afford to get sued right now. "None of your goddamned business."

"I see. And if I were to express Leighton Stone's displeasure in your relationship with his son, you would—"

"Tell you both to go fuck yourselves." This was fun,

actually. *Bring it, asswipe. What else do you have?*

The shorter suit didn't look up, only continued tapping into his tablet.

Edward Preston's smile remained in place. "Am I correct, then, in surmising that if I hint he could make your life miserable, you would remain unmoved?"

"No, I'd be pretty moved. But good luck to him. My own asshole stepfather has done a fine enough job fucking shit up as it is. There's not much left for him to maim. Next shot?"

Short Suit leaned over to say something into Preston's ear, and Preston nodded. Still grinning. He was a creep show, this one. "Yes, your stepfather does have a long history of neglect, and of course your birth father has never been much of anything at all, has he?" He glanced at the tablet. "And…Kirsten. Your mother? How is your relationship with her?"

Fuck it, Xander was going to punch a lawyer anyway. "Get the hell out of here."

Preston held up a hand. "Only one more thing to say. Leighton Stone is nothing if not a man of business. While it's understandable that you feel something for his son, he's sure your feelings will change once you hear he's prepared to offer you—*Shit!*"

Whatever numerical figure Preston had been about to prattle off was lost as he and Short Suit dodged the tall piece of painted barn board folk art Xander picked up from beside the door and hefted at their heads. Before they could recover from that missile, Xander had another piece of art primed and aimed at them, which he didn't throw but instead used to chase them to their car.

"I don't *care* how much he's prepared to offer me, you stupid fuckheads." He lobbed the art anyway, deliberately missing them, then picked up a wire piece of yard statuary and waved it threateningly as they scrambled to unlock their doors. "I don't want that asshat's money. I want his son. Who, by the way, is a thousand times better at your job than you are. Which is probably why the asshole's so desperate to get him to come join his shit-tastic fucking firm. Except *too damn bad*, he doesn't get to have him. Nobody gets to have him, because he's not a fucking prize anybody wins. He's his own person. He's going to make up his own mind about what he does, and he's probably going to end up even poorer than me, God save him, but I'm going to follow him all the way to the welfare line if that's what it comes down to. I don't care who cuts me off or what anyone threatens me with. I want Skylar Stone. As he is, not what *you* want to turn him into." He chucked the statue at the hood of the car. "Tell that fucker that! *Tell him, and then never fucking come here again.*"

He threw more art at the car as it drove away, then threw more art around the yard just because he could.

Then he took a long walk up the hill, into the state park.

He wandered for a long time, not sure where he was going, his head splitting. His anger had been spent, but he still felt full of fire, as if something was about to burst out of him. Like he had a thought, an idea in his head, and he needed a hammer or a knife to pry it out.

He came to the clearing at sunset. The sun was a soft orange ball nestled in a line of clouds, the fingers of color etching across the evening sky. Alizarin crimson and cadmium red and yellow and orange. If he had his oils, he could paint it. Except he didn't want to paint it. He wanted to take a black marker, outline the edges, and turn it into a manga.

He stopped breathing.

The sun was low enough that it moved fast, and he watched the blazing ball roll lower and lower into the bluffs. Saw the hills and trees darken, their shadows lengthening and their colors taking on more blue and black.

He saw the sharpness of the lines. Where he would draw the outlines. Where he would make the edges of the manga-like painting, how he could turn it into the style that Skylar and Zelda and everyone loved. That he loved.

The vision that was his, not that of his department.

The vision that went so well with someone who had no money, whose mother had broken his heart, with someone who had just thrown art at a lawyer's expensive car and was probably going to get the clothes sued off his back.

The vision everyone but a handful of people would hate. The one that would not get him the grade Peterson wanted.

The one that wouldn't look wonderful on a grad

school application.

But I wonder what you would think of it, Japan?

Two weeks. Two dozen paintings. He had at best five he could use.

Paint, he'd need so much new paint. And he had no money to buy it. Well, he had a tiny bit of money, but he'd need to buy canvas. More than he could afford even if he ate nothing at all until his show.

Unless you painted over every canvas you have.

His heart clenched. Too big of a risk. What if he couldn't finish? He'd have no backup. Nothing. He could ask Skylar—

Except he couldn't. Skylar had no money. He had to save it.

Unc—

Pamela—

He could ask everyone for one canvas, and he could sell every single record he had, every article of clothing, every pot and dish and—

The clouds parted, the sun turned red, and exploded into his face.

Xander had been staring at it, just as you weren't supposed to, and he tried to shut his eyes, but he wasn't fast enough, and his vision streamed, the ball burning against his retina. Except something like wings burned there too, wings and a crown. Like a figure coming at him with a sword raised.

You need to sleep more, buddy.

Rubbing his eyes, he turned back toward home.

His eyes were blurry as he walked, and he stumbled,

clutching at trees, his mind still racing.

He couldn't ask any of them. It wasn't right. If he did this, he had to do it. He kept tripping, falling twice, but every time it only steeled his resolve. When he got back to the main road, the sun itself burned inside his chest, lighting him on fire. He felt as if he *were* fire.

He went to Art Building West, his heart beating like a drum inside his ears. His breath came fast. His chest hurt. As he stood in the middle of the studio, all alone, a voice whispered to him that he didn't have to do this. He could leave well enough alone. He could ask Pamela for help. He could call his mother and beg. Or Nick and beg. He could do so many other sane things. He didn't have to follow some crazy notion he got while hiking up a mountain.

The voice sounded a lot like his mother's.

As he stared at his oil paintings lined up for his show, the fire wings burned across his vision.

Taking a deep breath, then letting it out, blinking through his tears, Xander hefted the brush full of primer and swiped it across the canvas.

Chapter Twenty-Three

SKYLAR HAD NO idea what had possessed Xander, but something clearly had.

"I'm redoing my show," was the only answer he got. Skylar tried to press him for more details. He got none.

"What do you mean, 'redo'?"

No reply.

"How much are you changing?"

No response.

"Do you need any help?"

Here, at least, he could get Xander to shake his head. Imperceptibly.

This was when Skylar became nervous. "Did I do something to upset you?"

Xander unthawed slightly then. "No. You're fine. It's nothing to do with you. I want to change things, is all. And it's tense. But I need to do this on my own. It's nothing against you, but my process doesn't invite people in. In fact, if you're involved, even a little, it will fuck it up. Also, if you thought I was cranky before, you're in for a ride now. You've never seen me cram for a project before, and I've never crammed for something like I'm about to do. It's not even that it's best that I don't talk about it. I can't talk about it. I'm sorry. It's not personal. And I apologize for not being there for you right now. But...I need to do this. For just another ten days." He let out a breath. "Form new straight lines."

Skylar gave in to a temptation that had been eating him for some time now. "What does that mean, exactly? I know it's the *Lucky 7* slogan, but...why? What does it signify?"

"It's something to do with Shintoism. Straight lines are prized in Japanese culture."

"Yes, I know that, but...why form *new* ones?"

"I...don't know? I guess it's just always been the slogan." Xander was harried, running his hand through his hair. "Probably it has to do with Benten being neo-Japanese culture. God, I don't know. Maybe it's bunk. Maybe I've been repeating this fucking mantra this whole time and it's messed up. Maybe everything is messed up."

Skylar, watching his boyfriend deflate, did his best to prop him back up again. "No, no. I think you're right. I think it's something unique to Benten, and I think it's clever. It makes sense. Straight lines are pleasing and good, but sometimes we have to make new lines. Sometimes our lives are too full of familiar grooves. Sometimes the straight lines are our prisons, not our paths."

The fire had come back to Xander's eyes. "*Yes.* That's exactly it. *Thank you.* And now I have to get back to work."

It was tough, Skylar wasn't going to lie. Because Xander was *cranky*. He barely slept. He forgot to eat. He came home late and left early.

He wouldn't talk about what had happened with his stepfather, but Skylar knew Xander was out of money now, that as soon as his show was over he had to get another part-time job, maybe two.

When the next care package came from Mason City, Xander wouldn't so much as look at it. Skylar opened it, and inside, instead of the usual *I love you*, it also said, *I'm sorry*. There were also four times as many cookies, and Skylar noticed they were almost all oatmeal chocolate chip.

He put a large plateful in the kitchen without comment, along with the note. Both remained untouched, and Skylar noticed the junk mail had been shifted to cover them up.

Mostly though, Xander worked. If he painted in the apartment, which he rarely did, he kept his easel turned away from the main part of the room and admonished Skylar to *not ever* peek at it. But then, sometimes, whether or not it was convenient for him and with less and less grace in the request, Xander asked Skylar to sit for him. With and without clothes. In some strange positions too—standing, sitting, lying down, holding random objects around the apartment. The weirdest one was when he had to hold a colander.

"Is this some kind of cooking-themed picture?" Skylar asked, unable to contain himself. Because he wasn't wearing any clothes and was holding a colander, and that was odd as hell.

"The colander isn't important. I just need you to be holding something, so I can judge the hand position."

He wasn't abrupt *exactly*, but he was terse, and Skylar was almost out of patience with his cranky artist boyfriend. "It's a little late to ask, but am I myself in this portrait, in which I'm not holding a colander but am wearing nothing at all?"

Xander stopped painting. He turned to Skylar slowly. All the color had left his face. In fact, he seemed ready to pass out.

Skylar couldn't tell which was worse, breaking his pose to check on him or letting him fall onto his painting. "Are you all right?"

Xander was not all right. He was shaking. When he spoke, his voice cracked and trembled. "I—oh my God. I didn't…I didn't even…*oh my God.* I didn't think." He dropped his brush and covered his mouth. "I didn't ask you. I didn't ask you. Yes. Yes, you're in it. And you're naked."

Skylar wasn't sure he liked that, and he was annoyed, but something about Xander's freak-out told him he was about to be a lot more than annoyed. "What aren't you telling me?"

Xander sank to the floor. He looked like he was having trouble breathing. "Every painting. You're in every single painting."

Skylar's eyes widened. Now *he* was having trouble breathing. "I'm *what*?"

Xander shut his eyes, shaking his head. "I'm sorry.

I'm so sorry. I wasn't thinking. It's such a dick move—I don't know why I didn't…*I wasn't thinking.* Which is no excuse. I was panicked, though. And I was in the woods, and I had this stupid vision on the bluff, and then I went to the studio and painted over all my canvases—"

Holy fucking shit. "*You painted over all of your canvases?*"

Xander nodded, eyes still closed. "It was like a crazy dream. I just painted them all. Everything that wasn't in that manga/oil style. And then I stood there with no show. And then I started painting. You. Over and over. You. All I could paint was you. It was so right, it just burned in me like it was the most right thing in the world. I didn't question it. I didn't think." He put his hands in his hair. "*I didn't think.* Fucking hell, I used you the same way everyone else did! I turned into everyone else that fucked you over, and now I either have to go through with it or fail my entire senior project. I'm a fucking shithead. I'm the biggest asshole in the world, *I'm so fucking sorry—*"

Skylar went over to him, knelt on the floor beside him, pulled his hands from his head, held them in his own grip. "Look at me."

Xander did, reluctantly. He had tears running down his face.

Skylar wanted to kiss him, but he made himself wait. "You are not the biggest asshole in the world. And you are not the same as the others. You used me in a different way. Yes, you should have asked for my permission, and no, I'm not happy that you didn't. If anyone else had done it, I'd be angry, but I'm not, because it's you. I know you wouldn't use me for anything bad. And I'm the one who told you to use the Benzaiten painting in the first place, so you could argue it's my fault for giving you the idea. Whatever you're doing with the paintings, I trust you. You have my permission."

Xander looked poleaxed. "You don't understand. You're *the* exhibit. You're not only in every painting. You are the theme."

Now Skylar was curious. "What's the theme?"

"I don't want to say."

"But don't you have to? The forms, you have to have them filled out, and the social media—"

"The forms had to be turned in months ago. People change their themes all the time. For social media, all my old samples are still running, but three days before, I'm changing everything to black squares and saying the theme is TBD. I'm announcing it on site." He rubbed his thumb against Skylar's. "So you know, they're going to hate it. The committee. They'll call my theme insipid. The style—that's more complicated, but they won't like it."

"They might surprise you."

"No. This isn't a movie where there's a dramatic reveal and everything works out and the hero gets the big prize. I'm going to pass, but I won't get the grade and the marks and the reviews I was going to. It will affect my admissions to graduate school. But I don't care. Or rather, I care—and I'm happy. Because this is who I am. It was bothering me a lot, my old show. It was just what they wanted and nothing that I did." He laced his fingers through Skylar's. "I don't care if I go to graduate school or not. That was a dream I had when I thought I was going to marry my art."

Skylar's heart skipped a beat. "Is there…something else you want to marry now?"

"Yes. You."

Xander wasn't smiling, still too caught up in the seriousness of his decisions. But it was perfect, Skylar decided. A very Xander proposal.

If, in fact, that's what it was.

"Are you saying this generally, or are you asking me formally and wanting to set a date?"

"Formally." Xander considered a moment. "Does New Year's work for you?"

"New Year's sounds wonderful. I don't want anything fancy. I definitely don't want to wear a suit. I only have one request."

"Name it."

"I want to change my name to Fairchild."

For the first time in almost a week, Xander smiled, and it was a wonderful one. "I'm fine with those terms."

Skylar smiled back. "Good. Then it's settled. We'll get married on New Year's." He kissed his fiancé's nose. "Now I'll go back to my colander so you can finish your painting."

"*Don't look at it,*" Xander said as he stood, downshifting immediately back into cranky-artist mode.

Skylar didn't mind. Not even when, as the day of the show came closer, Xander became practically a bear. He simply reminded himself this was his bear, that he was marrying him for better or for worse for the rest of his life, and the grouchy beast in his living room became the dearest, most wonderful creature on earth.

Then it was the day of the show, and time for him to see what Xander had been working on all this time.

Unc had convinced Xander, once he saw the god-awful black squares and TBD notices, to run a more sleek *Coming Soon* banner with an actual graphic. Since he was, you know, a visual arts major. It was Zelda's idea for the graphic to be a red *tori*. And it was Sara who designed it.

Cory and Jacob beat the drums with a special edition of the *Lucky 7*, letting everyone know they should go see the show to find out what the creative team behind *Hotay & Moo* had in store for them today. They leaked the information that Xander, the artist, would be featuring a series of paintings based on his boyfriend and scriptwriter, Skylar, and that they would be done in a style the administration didn't care for. They didn't say it was the art administration, and they made it sound like porn, which was misleading as hell—but they ensured the instructors would have no choice but to mark that Xander had a sellout crowd for his show, if nothing else.

Family, they said, took care of family.

Speaking of, Skylar was surprised but pleased to see Xander's mother, against all expectations, had come up from Pennsylvania and was waiting at the Palace of the Sun to go over with the others. She hadn't seen Xander yet, having arrived too late, and privately Skylar was glad because he worried it would have upset Xander's mental balance.

He wondered if Kirsten had known this as well.

Xander's mother looked a great deal like him, except where he had a natural scowl, she was warm and sunny, smiling brightly as Pamela introduced her to Skylar.

"Are you Xander's boyfriend? My, aren't you handsome."

"Thank you very much." Skylar couldn't help but like the woman on sight. They chatted together as the two of them rode along with Pamela and Zelda to the show. "I must confess, I've been enjoying your cookies all summer and fall. The chocolate drop ones with frosting are my favorite."

She blushed, but she smiled too. "I enjoy baking for people. It's how I show them I love them. I try to give Xander enough extra so he can share with the people he loves too." Her smile faded a little. "But he tells me the two of you are leaving the country, going to Japan?"

"We hope to, yes. We got notices of our interview just the other day. It will be in January, on the second, in New York City. We'll probably do the wedding there at city hall, then stay and do the interview."

She blinked at him, twice, and he realized she didn't know, because Xander wasn't talking to her. "Wedding?"

"Ah." He rubbed at his cheek. "Yes. Xander and I plan to get married. A small ceremony at the justice of the peace."

She covered her mouth and shut her eyes. Tears ran down her cheeks. "I've missed so much. I let him get away, and I missed so much."

Skylar touched her arm. "It's not too late. You're here today. And you can be there for him tomorrow, and the day after that as well."

She squeezed his hand and nodded.

Skylar was eager to get inside the building and see the exhibit, to put family drama behind him. But as they pulled up, a black town car blocked the stairs to Art Building West. He had a bad feeling about that car. As he walked to the stairs, he found he had good reason for that feeling.

Leighton Stone stood beside the car, chatting with President Hardin.

Pamela took Skylar's arm. "It's going to be all right."

Zelda came up to flank his other side. "Do you want me to kick his ass?"

Skylar wished his first instinct upon seeing his father wasn't fear and flight even after all his work to feel otherwise, but there he was, right back in the soup.

Kirsten looked concerned. "What's going on? What's happening?"

"Skylar's father," Pamela explained, leaning in close to speak quietly, keeping her gaze on Leighton.

"Not actually his father," Zelda added, also not looking away from the enemy. "The guy's here to bully

Skylar into something, that's for sure. But we're not going to let him."

"Oh, my." Kirsten put a hand on Skylar's arm, and for a moment it was like looking at a feminine, gentler Xander. "Can I do anything?"

Skylar shook his head. "Thank you—all of you. But I'll deal with this. Alone."

Zelda regarded him dubiously. "I think that's a stupid idea."

"How about a compromise?" Pamela motioned to a shady area near the entrance. "We'll wait for you there. We can see you, but not be involved. If he tries to stuff you into the trunk of a car, I'll send Zelda over with a battle axe."

"I think if it comes to *that*, we should call the police," Kirsten said, alarmed.

Skylar smiled and nodded. "All right. It's a deal. Except I'm not going to end up in the trunk. And we won't need the police."

I hope. He took a breath, squared his shoulders, and went over to face Leighton Stone.

The president scuttled away as soon as he saw Pamela waving at him, but Leighton advanced at the sight of his son, and Skylar could see the man putting on every trick he'd ever taught Skylar to use. Squaring his shoulders, positioning Skylar into the afternoon sun. Avoiding eye contact until the last possible second. Adjusting his swagger—God, it went on and on.

It made Skylar so tired.

Skylar already knew this wasn't a battle he was going to win—it was going to come down to strategic withdrawal. He put his hands in his pockets and stopped walking, waiting for Leighton to approach him. When Leighton came close enough Skylar didn't have to raise his voice, he began speaking.

"I'm not sure why you're here, but this needs to be brief, because my fiancé has an important event about to start, one I will not miss, so choose your words carefully. And bear in mind there is absolutely nothing you have that I want."

It would have been such a great speech, if his voice hadn't quavered there at the end.

Leighton pursed his lips and adjusted the cuffs of his sleeves. "Yes, about this event. I heard rumors you are the center of the theme, and I have my doubts anything I'm about to discover inside is appropriate. Be advised if I don't care for what I see attached to the Stone family name—and I won't—I'll sue that boy until he bleeds."

The words were meant to fill Skylar with terror, and for a moment they almost did. Except Skylar was *so tired.* And so absolutely over this man. "On what grounds? It's not you in the theme, and I'm certainly not giving you permission for anything."

"I will cut you off, boy. Completely. You won't—"

"*Do it.*" Skylar took a step closer to Leighton Stone, standing up tall so he could tower over him. He still trembled, but he wasn't giving in. *I'm leaving you. I'm walking away. Watch me go, Father. Watch me turn away, just like Xander said I could.* "Please, sever all ties with me. In fact, let me do it for you. I don't want anything to do with you, or my mother, or anyone involved in what has been my life." He held out his arms. "There. Now you have no grounds to go after Xander. And with that, I'm going to go see Xander's show. I hear it's going to be incredible."

He spun on his heel and walked as fast as he could toward the stairs, trying to look cool and confident, not like he was about to crack into a heap because he was shaking so hard. Behind him he could hear his father stomping angrily after him.

"Don't you walk away from me. I'm not done with you—"

Skylar stopped and turned around, borne on fury this time.

"Oh, but you *are*. We're finished, you and I, *sir*. I don't want to be the man you raised me in a bottle to be. I'm not your ball of clay, not anymore. I'm my own person, and I get to be who I want to be. You don't have to support that person. You don't have to fund my choices, or stop them, or love me any longer if you don't like them. But you don't get to control them. Who I am is my choice. Though to an extent I don't get to make that call. Who I am is who I am."

Leighton curled his lip. "Are you going to quote that insipid pop singer at me?"

"Who, Lady Gaga? No, but I could. I could quote Shakespeare to you instead, if you like. *To thine own self be true.* Or Katherine Anne Porter: *I was right not to be afraid of any thief but myself, who will end by leaving me nothing.* Or how about: *If we keep un-perverted the human heart—which is like unto heaven and received from the earth—that is God.* That's a revelation to Mikado Seiwa, the fifty-sixth emperor of Japan."

"I'm not going to stand here on the street and listen to you spout a bunch of nonsense philosophy."

"That's fine. Because as I said, I have nothing to say to you, you have nothing for me, you seem incapable of seeing who I am, and I have somewhere else I need to be."

He turned and headed once more toward the stairs.

Leighton continued to follow him. The fury was gone from him—he was almost desperate now. "I see you fine. I see everything you can be. Everything you should be."

"What I can be and what I need to be, what I want to be, are not the same. And should is a dangerous word."

"This is that boy's doing. He clearly put nonsense into your head."

"It's absolutely Xander's doing. But he didn't put anything into my head. Quite the contrary—he helped me get the nonsense out."

He felt Leighton make a swipe for his arm behind him but managed to dodge it in time. "Goddamn it, boy, turn around and listen to me when I'm talking to you—"

Zelda, Pamela, and Kirsten stepped between them.

"The boy has somewhere to be." Pamela's voice was silky dangerous. "Oh, and for the record, if you sue *any* of these young men, don't think you can railroad over them because they're poor, defenseless college students. I'll pay for any legal fees you try to stick them with. And I'm happy to countersue as well, if you step the wrong way. Tread lightly, Mr. Stone."

Skylar heard Leighton grumbling, but he ignored him—*new straight lines*, he told himself, and went through the door, into the exhibition hall, to Xander and these paintings he'd been modeling so blindly for. He was at the top of the stairs now, but before Skylar could so much as reach for the doors, they burst open, and Sara, Cory, Unc, and Jacob came through them. Their eyes were wide, and they looked like they'd seen a ghost. They were all staring at Skylar.

Oh no. "What happened? What's wrong? Oh my God, are they shutting it down? Is he all right? Is he okay? I need to go to him—"

Sara put a hand on his arm. "He's fine. His show is fine."

Skylar frowned at them, totally lost now. "Then why are you all looking at me like that?"

They stopped looking at him and looked at one another.

Leighton fought his way through the crush and stepped between them, his cool reserve breaking down. "Skylar Stone, I am *not finished speaking with you.*"

Christ, Skylar couldn't wait to get married and change his goddamned name. "Funny, because I'm totally over this conversation."

He pushed past Leighton, his friends, and through

the doors.

And saw his fiancé, draped in fire, standing on a dais of cracked and glittering silver stone, surrounded by…Skylar.

Xander wore a crimson toga, clipped with a gold fastening at the shoulder and a gold belt at the waist, but the fabric was…iridescent. It really did look like fire. He wore a gold leaf circlet on his head, and he held a golden paintbrush in his hand—he'd dipped it in gold paint, rendering it useless as a brush, but it was gorgeous as a piece of art. The tip was red, though, to match his toga. He had a manga marker in his hand too, and it wasn't colored at all.

The paintings hung all around him, on the walls, stood on stands. And all of them were Skylar.

Fudō Myōō Comes to Remove Benzaiten's Obstacles was there, and it was gorgeous, but next to the ones Xander had done in his last-minute flurry, it was clearly an early work, the artist whetting his appetite. His manga/oil style had only strengthened, to the point that the other paintings looked almost like manga panels propped up around the room. He'd done a proper painting of the sketch he'd done of Skylar beneath the cherry tree, only he'd dialed it to eleven and made it nearly life-sized. Again, manga style in oil. There were ones of Skylar sitting, standing, lying—looking vulnerable, soft, sad, scared, angry—he was himself though, always himself. His true self, his *sakura* suit self.

But better than any other painting in the show, behind Xander's dais, was the masterwork. A huge, filling-the-wall piece stood there, Skylar larger than the painter below by twice the size. He was nude. Completely, utterly. Gray top to bottom—a dull, flat gray, like the color Xander had painted him that night, that wonderful night. The painted Skylar's eyes were closed, and he held out his hand—this was the colander business, Skylar realized.

He didn't hold a colander in the painting, though. He held the sun. All around him, up his body, his arms, the earth and sky, were cherry blossoms.

Snaking up him, blooming on him, falling like rain around him—the cherry blossoms were everywhere. They were, in fact, all over every painting, once he looked more closely. And in the main focal painting, smaller, hiding in the vines, were Sara and Pamela and Jacob and Unc and Cory and Zelda.

It was so perfect, so *incredibly perfect* that Skylar could barely breathe.

"What," Leighton growled from behind him, "the hell is this?"

Skylar met his lover's gaze. His lover standing in a pile of shattered, glittering silver stone, his expression serious and intense, ready to do battle. *For him.*

Do you see yet? Do you see what I see in you? What I'm trying to show the whole world?

Oh, Xander. Oh, his heart.

Both their hearts.

"*What the hell is this?*" Leighton demanded more loudly.

Skylar kept his smile on Xander as he nudged past

the velvet rope of the exhibit and the placard with the name *Pygmalion.*

"This is me," Skylar said, loud enough for his father, the room, the earth, the stars, and all the gods in heaven to hear.

Then he took a seat at the feet of his lover, who had shown him, and the world, who he was.

Chapter Twenty-Four

April, two years later
Tokyo, Japan

THE DRAWING WASN'T the most beautiful thing Xander had ever seen. But it had a lot of promise behind it, and what was more, he felt connected to this artist. She reminded him of himself when *he'd* been fourteen. Quiet. Withdrawn. No phone in her hand while she waited to be picked up from cram school. She stood off by herself or doodled in her notebook, not giggling with the other girls during breaks.

Yes, Xander saw *a lot* of his younger self in Sakura-san.

He looked over the top of the notebook at the girl before him, standing with her head bowed, ready to be disciplined. He supposed he must. She *had* been drawing instead of paying attention to her English lessons, which her parents were paying for. Yet he couldn't stop wracking his brain, trying to find a way to reprimand her for not following the rules while reaching out to the shy artist inside as well.

"As portraits go," he said in English, "it's not bad, but your proportions are off." He tapped the arms with his pencil. "It doesn't look like you started with proportional sketching, and that's why the arms are long and floppy like pieces of spaghetti. Also, you're clearly hiding the hands instead of drawing them, which is cheating."

She frowned at him, looking worried. "I don't understand," she said in Japanese.

Xander raised an eyebrow. "You would, perhaps," he said in the same language, "if you listened in class, instead of drawing." Ignoring her blush, he picked up his own pencil and began to sketch an angry Moo and cheerful Hotay on either side of her character, giving the lesson in Japanese this time as he went along. "You must map out your figure first. You see? Then, once you have that in place, you pencil in the lines you mean to keep, erase the ones you don't, and…there. A proper drawing." He passed her the paper. "If you hadn't been doodling in class, I would sit with you now and teach you more drawing. But since you weren't paying attention, I'm going to give you extra English to write out at home, and speak to your mother. Next time, however, if your English practice is good, I'll teach you more drawing."

Sakura's whole being lit up with wonder. "Yes, thank you, sensei!" She bowed, waited for him to write out her homework, then bowed again as she accepted it and hurried out of the room. She wasn't even upset as he had a quiet word with her mother, and she only nodded when her mother scolded her, casting a quiet look Xander's way.

It took everything in him not to smile and wink back.

Once Sakura and her mother were gone, Xander gathered his things and looked around the hallway, but his husband was nowhere to be found. After a few polite inquiries of other lingering staff and the janitor, Xander headed where he should have gone all along: the building's roof.

He found Skylar standing at the rail, looking over the city in twilight, wind rippling gently at his hair. He wore a suit, but it was a cheap one, ill fitting, the kind that was all a teacher could afford, especially one living in an expensive city with his part-time artist and cram school teacher husband and their two cats who had been incredibly expensive to move overseas.

Xander enjoyed this view for a moment, then pushed out of the doorway and went to stand beside Skylar. "*Konbanwa.*"

Skylar smiled without turning his head. "Sorry, I lost track of time."

"It's all right. I built fetching my roof-gazing husband into our travel itinerary."

Skylar had come to collect Xander with their suitcase in tow, and their neighbors were already set to feed Hokusai and Hiromu while they were gone. Skylar taught full time during the day at a private school in a suburb on the other side of town, whereas Xander usually worked at the cram school helping students study on evenings and weekends, and then as an artist whenever the *mangakas* called him in. This weekend however they had some rare time off. They were on to the bullet train that would take them to Kyoto, where they were set to meet Pamela and the others, who had come, at last, for their long-promised trip together through Japan.

Xander and Skylar's dinner that night was *ekiben*, the bento lunch served on the train, which according to Skylar was one of the greatest delicacies in the world.

"Did you hear anything from the others yet?" Xander asked as they dug into their food. "Have they arrived?"

"Confirmation text of landing, but that's about it. They're all on Wi-Fi only because of international rates, and remember only Pamela speaks Japanese. I suspect she's got her hands full keeping them from freaking out at the moment." Skylar wiped his mouth with his napkin. "Oh—and I forgot to tell you! My dad called me today. Charlie, I mean."

Xander dropped his chopsticks and turned full on to his husband. "Shut up. Really? How did it go? What did he say?"

Skylar shrugged, but he smiled too, a gentle blush staining his cheeks. "It was fine. A little awkward because it was the first time, but it was a good start. I didn't have much time since it was on my break and I was in the workroom with all the other teachers. He's going to call again next weekend when I'm at home. The time difference is rough."

"But it went okay? He was nice?"

Skylar's smile expanded like a slow sunrise. "Yeah.

He was…he was great. He said I sounded like an amazing young man and…" He stopped, taking a breath, reaching for Xander's hand. "He said he was proud of me."

"Oh, *Skylar*. I'm so happy for you."

Skylar nudged Xander with his knee. "And you? I heard you on the phone with your mom this morning. Tell me how that went. Is it still on?"

Xander nodded and let out a breath. "Yeah. She's got her ticket. She and my aunt are coming in September." He laughed. "God, if I actually get that job I'm hoping for working on that manga, I don't know how I'll have time off to see them."

"We'll work it out. Don't worry."

Xander laced their fingers together, and for a long time they didn't say anything at all.

The others were waiting for them as they arrived in Kyoto. Unc came up to them first and smothered them in hugs. "It's so good to see you. Missed you guys *so much.*"

Cory's eyes were huge. "I can't get over how fast we got here from Tokyo."

Jacob shook his head. "The US needs to seriously take notes on Japanese infrastructure."

Sara hugged them next. Xander noticed she had no arm braces on. "You're looking well."

"Feeling well," she said. "It's been a good run, lately. I'm hoping it lasts as long as possible."

Xander also noticed Unc had his arm around Sara, and that she leaned into the crook of his shoulder. He smiled, pleased to see his friends still together and happy.

Pamela looked radiant. She was in her element, leading her tribe. Zelda looked nervous, not in their element somewhere they didn't know the language, but they perked up as soon as Xander asked how the campaign was going.

"*Excellent.* I love working for Senator Schumaker. She's going to be president, I swear."

"Or maybe you will be."

"Or maybe I will."

Pamela clapped her hands. "All right, we need to check in to the hotel. Are you all ready? Does everyone have their things?"

They did, and everyone trailed after her as she led them to the traditional Japanese inn she had picked out. Skylar and Xander took up the rear, smiling as they watched everyone they loved argue and fuss and in general be present with them.

They had a meal together, where Xander and Skylar got to show off everything they knew not only about the language but the culture and the dining, helping their friends avoid things they wouldn't be adventurous enough yet to try and nudging them to attempt things they might. Afterward they all went to the onsen together—the men to the men's section, the women to the women's section, and…

"Binary bullshit," Zelda grumbled.

"Form new straight lines." Jacob tried to soothe them. "Just maybe not while you're on international soil."

"It's so wonderful to see everyone," Skylar said to Xander as they lay in bed together that night. "I wish they could stay forever."

"We should probably look into getting back state-side again soon," Xander admitted. "I didn't realize how much I missed them until they were all here."

They twined their fingers together to kiss good night, wrapped their arms around each other, and went to sleep.

Pamela met them at breakfast with a printed itinerary.

"We're going to hit all the temples on the list today. I have it mapped out. There are breaks planned, but if we need more—Sara, I'm looking at you—let me know. We'll stop for other things that catch our eye, but these are the temples I thought we should hit. I think you'll see why."

They stared at their sheets. Jacob frowned. "I don't get it." The others agreed.

Everyone, that is, except Unc and Skylar, who gasped and looked at each other, then Pamela. "Oh my God," Unc whispered.

Pamela's eyes danced. "I think you mean, *oh my gods.*"

Xander was curious now. "Why? What's going on?"

Skylar held up the sheet to him. "This tour is called the journey of the seven gods. She's taking us on a tour of ourselves."

"There's a stop for Fudō Myōō too," Pamela said,

beaming, "though there's a hike involved. I guess the guy likes heights. We'll get a wonderful view when we finish."

Everyone was excited to start out after that, and they rushed through breakfast and set out for the first stop, Fukurokuju, which was the masculine form of Kichijōten, Pamela's god. She insisted it was only because of the timing, but everyone teased her for being a blood type B, and they had a good laugh before they got serious and went up to ring the bell and call the god.

Xander had been to many temples and shrines since he'd moved to Japan, but he'd never been with his own personal tribe of *Shichifukujin*, and it was a sacred experience indeed. They laughed, they teased, they communed with one another—just like the old days back at the Palace of the Sun. Except now they were in the Land of the Rising Sun, in the city that housed the most sacred heart of Japan, the houses of the gods that had brought them all together.

As they hiked up the hill to Fudō Myōō's temple, ascending the two hundred fifty steps to the hall where the deity was housed with Skylar's hand clasped in his, Xander reflected how far he'd come from the day Skylar had burst into his studio and insisted his art was worth something. As his legs burned with the ache of the climb, his heart swelled with the realization that somehow, through this journey, he had truly become something more.

Become? Or acknowledged, at last, what you always were?

The thought felt too bold on the stairs, but as he entered the body of the hall, as the altar of the deity came into view, flanked by the panorama of the city below, the last of his self-doubt sloughed away. No, it wasn't too bold. He had always been something more.

He was Xander Fairchild. And he was just getting started.

The power of that conviction burned in him as they left Fudō's shrine and headed for Benzaiten's, where there was not a mountain of stairs. Instead they were greeted with a lovely bridge over a pond, and a riot of cherry trees in full bloom.

Skylar grinned and hurried toward the shrine. "Come on, Xander. Let's go."

Xander followed him over the bridge, but he held back, smiling as Skylar eagerly went to see his goddess. He had thrived in Japan the same way Xander had—Skylar was so happy here, always smiling, beaming wherever he went. As usual, everyone in Japan loved Skylar. But they loved *sempai* Skylar, the kind and clever teacher, and *kawaii* Skylar, who was always so excited to unwrap the carefully prepared bentos Xander made for him every morning. They loved good neighbor Skylar, who had learned to make mochi and shared it with everyone at New Year's. They loved the real Skylar, the same as Xander did, all the parts of him.

The real Skylar was here now, in full bloom the same as the cherry trees lining the bridge to Benzaiten's shrine. Xander watched his husband move, memorizing every detail, ready to sketch him the second they were finished here and on their break. But he needed to see his face…

"Skylar!"

Skylar turned to face him.

The wind picked up, whirling through the grove. It ruffled Skylar's hair, his polo and his khaki pants, his pink cardigan. It shook the branches of the cherry tree above them, and sent the blossoms raining down on the bridge, onto the man standing there beneath the boughs.

Skylar glanced up as the petals fell, then held out his hands, laughing as he caught the flowers.

Xander smiled and etched the image onto his heart.

ABOUT THE AUTHOR

Heidi Cullinan has always enjoyed a good love story, provided it has a happy ending. Proud to be from the first Midwestern state with full marriage equality, Heidi is a vocal advocate for LGBT rights. She writes positive-outcome romances for LGBT characters struggling against insurmountable odds because she believes there's no such thing as too much happy ever after. When Heidi isn't writing, she enjoys cooking, reading, playing with her cats, and watching anime, with or without her family. Find out more about Heidi at heidicullinan.com.

Did you enjoy this book?

If you did, please consider leaving a review online or recommending it to a friend. There's absolutely nothing that helps an author more than a reader's enthusiasm. Your word of mouth is greatly appreciated and helps me sell more books, which helps me write more books.

OTHER BOOKS BY HEIDI CULLINAN

There's a lot happening with my books right now! Sign up for my **release-announcement-only newsletter** on my website to be sure you don't miss a single release or re-release.

www.heidicullinan.com/newssignup

Want the inside scoop on upcoming releases, automatic delivery of all my titles in your preferred format, with option for signed paperbacks shipped worldwide? Consider joining my Patreon.

www.patreon.com/heidicullinan

THE ROOSEVELT SERIES

Carry the Ocean (also available in French)
Shelter the Sea
Unleash the Earth (coming soon)
Shatter the Sky (coming soon)

LOVE LESSONS SERIES

Love Lessons (also available in German, French coming soon)
Frozen Heart
Fever Pitch (also available in German)
Lonely Hearts (also available in German)
Short Stay
Rebel Heart (coming fall 2017)

THE DANCING SERIES

Dance With Me (also available in French, Italian coming soon)

Enjoy the Dance

Burn the Floor (coming soon)

MINNESOTA CHRISTMAS SERIES

Let It Snow

Sleigh Ride

Winter Wonderland

Santa Baby

More adventures in Logan, Minnesota, coming soon

THE SPECIAL DELIVERY SERIES

Special Delivery

Hooch and Cake

Double Blind

The Twelve Days of Randy

Tough Love

CLOCKWORK LOVE SERIES

Clockwork Heart

Clockwork Pirate (coming soon)

Clockwork Princess (coming soon)

TUCKER SPRINGS SERIES

Second Hand (written with Marie Sexton) (available in French)

Dirty Laundry (available in French)

(more titles in this series by other authors)

SINGLE TITLES

Nowhere Ranch (available in Italian)
Family Man (written with Marie Sexton)
A Private Gentleman
The Devil Will Do
Hero
Miles and the Magic Flute

NONFICTION

Your A Game: Winning Promo for Genre Fiction
(written with Damon Suede)

Many titles are also available in audio and more are in production. Check the listings wherever you purchase audiobooks to see which titles are available.

CPSIA information can be obtained
at www.ICGtesting.com
Printed in the USA
BVHW080724090621
609089BV00002B/42